RAMONA
IN THE REALMS

ANDREW EVANS

Black Rose Writing | Texas

ISBN: 978-1-68513-321-4
PUBLISHED BY BLACK ROSE WRITING
www.blackrosewriting.com

Printed in the United States of America
Suggested Retail Price (SRP) $25.95

Ramona in the Realms is printed in Andalus

*As a planet-friendly publisher, Black Rose Writing does its best to eliminate unnecessary waste to reduce paper usage and energy costs, while never compromising the reading experience. As a result, the final word count vs. page count may not meet common expectations.

My humble thanks, to my publisher, Black Rose Writing.
This book is for all of my friends and family.
Especially my Rose. From Dad.

RAMONA
IN THE REALMS

Prologue
The Holiday

It is easy to ask the questions now, after the event. Still, I have written them down anyway. For posterity. James liked to write things down, so I'll do it for him. For anyone, actually. So its here, in my diary. Oh, and never go to Oakhampton. Ever. They will take you. My name is Ruth. I am Ramona's mother.

So, what would it be like if there were parallel worlds and alternate realities, running in an ignorant tandem of each other? Could these two existences somehow meet in the middle? Perhaps there was a place that acted as a gateway, a law unto itself. Unsure which reality it belonged in, if any. Could such a place be an access point to both? A way in, or out.

We had so many questions. We just did not know it at the time. How would a family be affected if their universe was altered completely and thrown off course? Torn apart, changed forever. Can you imagine, if you or I had gotten off our train at the wrong station? What would we do? Sensibility would tell us to wait for the next train and go on to our destination as originally planned. Of course, we would think so. But what if we got off our train at the wrong station and could not get back, regardless of sensibility? Because there were no next trains here, and logic had been scattered to the four winds.

What if our destination was no longer there anyway, because our pathway had skewed into another one, from another reality.

Impossible? Something unseen had intervened perhaps? Something ethereal. Now we are stuck. In new and confusing surroundings.

What if we had family members that had also arrived here in this alternate reality, that back in our own timeline, we had never known about? Mind bending. Could we adapt? How would others react to us? Were the people friendly in our new surroundings? Why were we all here? Were they all just, people?

What if there were other beings? Not recognisable to us human folk. Other cultures and societies that would baffle us, as our ways would them. Imagine there was no way home. Too many questions. I could do with James help here. To explain. He saw more than I did, at the start.

What if there was a dark force at work, changing this new and shifting reality for its own gain and we had walked into the middle of a minefield? The mind would boggle. We would find out how strong we could be. Here in this strange place, were the ethereal of the realms. A sort of invisible watching force of goodness. Unseen but all seeing. That was the phrase their folk used. The ethereal domain. Looking for their chosen one. Looking for my daughter.

The spirit I came to know as Ualdin had begun his work the moment we arrived at Oakhampton. To find my Ramona.

We were a little family, you see. A young and happy couple, James and I. We lived in a quaint little house in a pleasant town named Gardelwyn. A place of markets, book emporiums, greengrocers, coffee houses and an archetypal country inn. All was rosy. Very olde worlde. James and I were lucky enough to be deeply in love and we had married after a fairy tale romance, the like of which we would all want to happen to ourselves but were sometimes unsure it ever would. I felt blessed.

After a few years of exclusive bliss together, working in steady, respectable jobs, with our small circle of good friends, we were content. Relaxed in life. Gardelwyn fulfilled our social and work needs. We soon felt ready to start a family. I had just given birth to our first baby. At least, the first baby that I knew of. That is another story.

She was a healthy, inquisitive and delightfully bonny girl. We named her Ramona. Both James and I, although happy at home, would enjoy our holidays away from the hustle bustle of work and town life. We liked to get to the coast, near to the sea, and yet away from the parts we may call touristy. Off the beaten track but close enough to find your way back onto it. Something about that bracing salty air washed out the soul. Fresh and sea-weedy. You wanted to bottle it. We would always return with healthy glowing faces. Our friends would say that it looked like the seaside air had airbrushed our cares away. 'We have no cares when we travel.' I used to say.

So, this particular year, with baby Mona on board, we had decided to head to a log cabin that we had discovered at a place just off the coast. It was called Oakhampton. It had met our needs beautifully. Situated in a small secluded woodland area with a lake and not far at all from the picture book horseshoe beach and the glassy blue sea and its abundant nature.

As we settled into life at Oakhampton, the days felt dreamily long and the nights calm and peaceful. Dappled sunlit days and moonshine walks at night. We always slept better than ever when we were away and it was as though any real life niggles evaporated. We enjoyed long and leisurely walks with Ramona, already very alert and wide-eyed. Our healthy little baby absorbed the sights of birds and trees, flowers and plants. Her little nose wriggled on smelling the organic food we cooked out in the open when there was a warm evening. The soothing sound of the waves lulled her at night and the whistling sound of piping curlews and oystercatchers going to roost, fascinated her as she was rocked to sleep by myself and James.

Picnics on the beach had been a daily staple of course. Ramona and I would throw sandwich crust and bits of cake for the grateful and noisy seagulls. There were two great black-backed gulls, whom were there waiting every day and became instant favourites to baby Ramona. Familiar. Her eyes lit up with joy as they nipped and bobbed at my feet for the tasty offerings. I thought they were very enamoured with our little one. They were so gentle around Ramona. Almost tame, protective and watchful of her.

'I'm daydreaming!' I thought, as the seabirds cocked their heads and looked quizzically at us when the supply line ran out. As Mona and I played, James liked to stroll to his rock pools and have a look to see what he could find. His inner boy was enjoying it very much. No one here to stop him being a kid again!

Crabs, shrimps and a small fish, called blenny, were plentiful in these pools and he sat on the sand with his flask of coffee. He looked out as terns and gannet dive bombed the still sea for fish. He loved to report back to us with his sightings. Guillemots patrolled up and down the bay like stunning little model boats with their pristine black and white features. Wild horses pranced and swished tails in a clifftop field, full of buttercups off the tor. It overlooked the emerald waters crashing over weedy, craggy rocks.

'I am a very lucky man. Its like a different world!' He said it every day that week. We would stroll back smiling wistfully. My husband, myself and our baby Ramona. Perfect. James liked wiggling his bare feet in the cooling sand as he ambled across the beach. As the sun went down, we deliberately slow walked back to the log cabin for dinner and set it out on the porch.

We would light candles and listen for the 'kee-wik' of the resident tawny owls, it was usually answered by a 'hoo-woo'. We rarely switched on the owners television or radio there. The entertainment was organic as well as the food. We had come to get away from gadgets and instant demanding updates and incessant access to everything. We had told our families and friends that we wanted total peace for baby and had left phones and laptops and games at home.

'Society coped before mother. You know that more than I do! Don't worry. Its just a week of peace and rest. I love you.' I had said in a phone call to my stricken mum, prior to us leaving.

'At least take one phone Ruthie. For emergencies. For your old mum?' She did protest, did my mum.

'Don't be silly mother. Its fine. No gadgets and that is that.' We would send postcards and see them all on our return. If, we returned.

At the holidays end, our little family was, despite the bliss, ready to go home. Having naturally exhausted our mine of ideas and walks, we were now happily tired and content. As I wrote of earlier though..

What if there was an alternate reality and you were thrown off course? What if a family's timeline had skewed into another one? Blended somehow. On the way home. This is what happened. This, is the story of my daughter, Ramona. The wizard who did not know she was a wizard.

Yet.

CHAPTER ONE
THE FIGURE

Ramona, did not even know the journey she was to embark on. For she was a newborn baby. A tiny bundle of bubbling life, with a happy and doting mother and father, returning from a hard earned jaunt away. Their first holiday all together. A fortnight away from their home commitments in the town of Gardelwyn. Magical it was too. In more ways than they could ever have expected. But magic was not always good.

Ruth and James had been married for ten years now and had found the most beautiful thing in life. The connection of true love. They had shared these holidays together since meeting and loved to find new and unexplored places. Hidden gems. They were always looking for nooks and crannies around the seaside and country areas, especially the coast.

How they loved to be near to the sound of the waves, the long, hilly walks, lunching on the beach, watching wildlife. The couple enjoyed the mystery of looking for places off the map with quirky names. Places where they could decide when and where to look around until whatever time they so wished.

They adored the quiet life and still looked into each others eyes now, the same way they had when they shared their first kiss on a hilltop during a country ramble. Ruth had liked that about James. He was smart and handsome but there was no bravado or manipulation.

He worked in wildlife preservation at home in Gardelwyn and enjoyed his books and films and walking.

No talk of money, fast cars, gold watches or bad pick-up lines. Just James. Though as she grew to know him, his jokes were sometimes so bad that it made her howl with laughter. He had a kind smile and mischief in his eyes. He had seen Ruth several times before in their hometown. They always seemed to smile at each other in passing, and they were always alone. Neither suspected the other liked them. They had both hoped separately, in the nicest possible way, that the other did not have a special someone.

Yet.

One day, James was coming out of the local bookshop and he had spotted Ruth, walking toward him down the high street. She was clutching a lot of shopping. They exchanged their usual pleasant smiles, but this time, a surge of adrenaline told James that it was time to take a chance.

"Would you like a hand with those at all, madam?" He blurted out.

She glanced at the awkward looking James, "My car is just over there, so I'll be alright, thanks for asking."

James stood blushing and replied, "Oh well, it was worth a try."

Ruth smiled genuinely and it showed in her eyes. James thought her smile was sweet and her face, full of life. Sometimes while on a night out, Ruth would get invited to pubs and bars, or the archaic wolf-whistle would ring in her ears as she walked past admiring males. It made her smile and gave her a boost, but she was not really looking for a special person. She was happy in herself and not in any sort of rush.

Ruth was quite content in her modest and tidy home. She always enjoyed having an evening out with her friends or lunch with mother. Cinema, books, sightseeing. These were the sort of things that interested her, but this dandy fellow, James, seemed to get her attention when they passed each other. Now she thought, 'He actually speaks!'

James pressed on regardless now. "You are parked so near. If your car was further away, I was going to ask you for a cup of coffee."

Ruth raised her eyebrows in mock surprise.

"Well..You don't mess about, do you!" She giggled." James smiled. He saw that Ruth was gently teasing him.

"Nope. Life is short. Just like that queue in the coffee shop."

Ruth had taken to him. There was something different about him. Fun. "Ha ha, well now that you say, I wouldn't mind a hot drink."

'She's beautiful, different, fun.' Thought James. 'Now stop mucking about and help carry her bags'. The angel on his shoulder was prodding him into action.

Ruth smiled at him. "Im shattered! I always get too many things and I'm decorating the house at the moment. Came out for more paint." She gestured at what was in the bags.

James laughed. "Well, if you need any help, I'm pretty handy with a brush" He blushed a bit. "Sorry. I shouldn't have said that. Inviting myself to your house!"

Ruth grinned. She already knew he hadn't meant it that way. "You know if you get me that coffee I'll tell you how I want it all done. Im not even kidding!" So, she let James grab some of the shopping and then grabbed his other hand with hers. It felt natural. They soon got to the car, sharing the load.

"So, whats your poison?" James passed her a bag as she opened the boot. "Cappuccino, brown sugar, very sweet." Ruth replied.

"Done." Smiled James.

"I certainly have been!" laughed Ruth.

James was enjoying playing the role of a clown, which Ruth had later grown so fond of. He was happy to do it, as long as he made her smile. He had gotten by on his sense of humour in many situations. He would do again. Despite his joking, James was smart, well dressed and quietly assured.

"Right. Shopping sorted. Lets get that Cappuccino!" Ruth locked the car and off they went together. With that, they chatted away at the coffee shop for a good couple of hours. The occasional silences were comfortable and not awkward. Ruth took James up on his offer of help with painting and he had meant it.

Together, they decorated her peaceful and quaint little home. It was easy going. When the decorating was done, they stayed in touch regularly. James would not take payment for his help. Ruth had felt he would not. They grew closer and closer. They met each others parents. Walking became a nice shared pastime for them both and they enjoyed each others company very much. There were no grand declarations of 'We are a couple.' or 'We are girlfriend and boyfriend.' Their friends thought them great together.

They just slipped into a warm and caring place with each other, that blossomed. And so, on one such wandering ramble, they had stopped at the top of a hill to admire the panoramic view. They had just turned to each other smiling contentedly. And that was finally it. Their eyes met, they both smiled and they kissed tenderly. It was worthy of its own fairytale ending. Cliched? They didn't care if it was. But there was a lot more to come. In the shape of the newborn cries of a bundle of love, named Ramona.

Ualdin and the ethereal counsel, stirred in the clouds some place else. A signal had attracted them.

This was the couple's first holiday with their bonny little child and they had found a lovely coastal town. A tiny advertisement in a magazine they never usually bought, from a newsagent run by a quirky, gnome-like man.

'Escape to Oakhampton. Quiet and close to a rare coastal path.' The article declared, reeling the couple in. It was just off the beaten track but near enough to towns to go for supplies to the bigger places. So, that was it. Decision made.

Oakhampton was wonderful, but it seemed sometimes to be a complex place to negotiate. On foot or by car. It appeared to be full of unexpected twists and turns. There was deciduous woodland, long walks and a fabulous, near deserted beach.

They had stayed in a wonderful log cabin with a boat and a small lake. Fallow deer roamed freely, grazing on dewy grass at dawn. There were then, long hazy days in the sun and cosy nights in with baby. Ramona, was already gurgling and giggling and waving her arms, kicking her legs. Finding wonder and curiosity in everything.

One such day on the ancient beach, Ruth was throwing sandwich crumbs and watching how close the gulls were coming.

"Bold as brass they are." Said James.

"Aren't they just?" Agreed Ruth.

"Its these two big, black-backed ones that are the bravest. They're stood right by my feet!".

"Or the greediest." Retorted James above the clucking and cawing of the seabirds.

Baby Ramona however, was impressed and her eyes were joyous watching these comical gulls pecking at ham sandwiches. Ruth was right though. A lot of birds would pinch a few titbits and fly off. But this couple stayed close by as though observing the family as much as nabbing a free meal.

"Aren't they lovely Mona." Ruth picked her up to show her the big friendly birds. She was beaming at them like a friend. The holiday was serene, for this young couple with child and would live long in the memory. For many reasons. But all good things, as they say, and soon the day for returning home to Gardelwyn and back to the faster pace of town life, was upon them. After a final cup of tea by the beach, they ruefully said goodbye to Oakhampton and Ruth sat in the backseat of the car with Ramona, now settling after warm milk for a nap.

The two black-backed gulls were there as usual and pecking at something unfortunate in a shallow rock pool. Ruth was sure it was the same two birds as before. Large and somehow comical, but wise.

Off James drove now, and they took in the peaceful scenery as they found their way onto shifting, winding lanes. They were going along nicely, but had decided tried to find a short cut shown on an old, tatty map. Somebody had scrawled in slanting ink, 'This map belongs to the Ivywyrld Inn.'

'Never noticed that before.' Ruth mused briefly.

But now, this was becoming a long winded diversion, this old supposed short cut. Twists and turns again. Grassy banked, narrow lanes. It began to confuse the couple. No bus stops, postal or telephone boxes or farmhouses to be seen. The sort of things you would expect in these quaint country areas. This was like drivng back in time. Oakhampton had been wonderful. But a strangely complex place to negotiate. James, slightly flummoxed, pulled the car into a gravelly roadside lay-by.

"Well, Ruthie, we do love a challenge. I'll try to find someone to point us in the right direction. I need a leg stretch anyway. I won't go far. Can you wait here with Mona for a minute? There's no point in all of us getting out."

Ruth nodded, but her smile was thin in mild concern. She observed the fading light. It was getting dusky. James words, 'I won't go far', began to resonate in her mind. Forbodingly so.

Ramona's father had now disappeared from the roadside looking for a garage, a passer by, the local elderley font of all knowledge. Anyone. For some reason, the way home had become unclear. Despite the detailed map, this part of Oakhampton and the surrounding areas seemed out of place. They liked to be off the beaten track, but this felt different. Like a new place had just.. appeared. Mysterious.

Had they perhaps gone off course on these dark country lanes? Why were they not on the map? Ruth could not pinpoint where they were, despite pawing over it. Then, James was suddenly back. He got in his seat.

"Its strange. I know Oakhampton was quiet, but I cant even see a building, let alone another person, Ruthie. What does the map have to say?"

"The map is no good, James. It says to install satellite navigation, my dear!" Ruth put her hand on her husband's shoulder. James laughed.

"Funny woman!" He kissed her cheek fondly.

"Come on. Lets follow the lane a bit further. Surely it should take us on to a main road. We can find someone there. I think we are all ready to go home now." A Quiet tension had crept into his voice. Barely detectable, save for Ruth.

He looked lovingly over his seat, back at his tiny daughter, Ramona. She looked so content, sleeping away. He wondered if she was dreaming about the big pair of seagulls. James pulled the car out of the small lay-by and off they went again.

"Right, my love. Seconds out. Round two!"

"Home, James!" Said Ruth, trying to flash a smile.

Then, the swerve came. As James drove, the car began to spin. It suddenly felt like driving on an ice rink. It was a slippy, oily sensation. Very hard to control. As he battled to steady the car and remain calm, he looked ahead onto the road. His mouth fell open in disbelief.

A huge, dark shape stood at a distance in the middle of the lane. From the car it was hard to make out what it was. Bad vibes instantly hit James nervous system. The sky was now a midnight blue. Drizzle and mist had come from seemingly nowhere. Then, two flashing red eyes suddenly manifested and hung alone in the road as a dark, hooded cloak formed around the now glowering and malevolent looking eyes. Just.. staring. It beggared rational belief.

A huge man? No. A bloody awful looking.. thing! Tall, bulky, dark and cloaked. The eyes flickered and flame lived in them. They flashed menacingly towards the car. The cloaked dark thing held a skeletal looking hand up and a hissing voice whispered in James mind, "Go away.. or you will die. I know of you. Man of two places."

"What the hell? My god!" Shrieked James.

Then, it had gone. The eyes hung alone though, for a split second as the rest of the dark thing dissipated and then there was nothing. That was it. James was distracted. Too shaken by what he had seen, he lost control of the steering wheel.

"I can't.." He never finished his sentence.

The car skidded and veered off the road into a hedgerow in a greasy, dewy field. Then, all lay still. The car had rolled down an embankment and turned slightly on its side. Ruth was badly shaken up, but conscious. She cried out for James. She felt wobbly from this sudden terrifying event, but she retained the motherly instinct enough, to check on baby Mona.

She thanked god. Ramona was still strapped tightly into the infant seat and although woken from her sleep, it seemed she had not been hurt. It was hard to tell in the dark. The little girl looked confused as much as anything and cried out only a little. Ruth stroked her face and whispered sweetly to her. Small mercies. Ruth did not question any further what might have happened. She could not bare to imagine.

James stirred in the drivers seat, dizzy. He felt sheer disbelief at what he had seen to make him veer off the road. That awful entity. It was remarkable for the little family that this was all that had happened to them. James tried to focus now. The car was turned awkwardly on one side. He unlocked the door and just about scrambled out and rolled onto the wet grass.

He breathed deeply and went around to help his wife and baby out of the back. Ruth was beginning to feel trapped inside, but was trying to keep calm for Ramona. She too was now feeling faint, and scared, nauseous. Ramona rarely cried. Now though, she finally wailed. Babies pick up on so much. Especially the chosen ones of the ethereal.

The couple began to work on instinct. James took Ramona gently through the door from his wife, so that she could push herself out too, onto the grass. Then he had opened the car boot. Grabbing for clothes, coats, warmth. The flask, water, food, baby's bottle. He stuffed what he could into a travel bag he had emptied. Wrapping a hooded top around Ruth's head like a scarf, he hugged her and kissed Ramona's cheek.

"Take these Ruthie. Stay here. Look after Mona. I'm alright. I'll get help. We can't stick around here."

"What? Don't you leave us again, James." Both were still too shaken to converse for long, but still, Ruth went to protest again.

"I have to Ruthie. Stay exactly here." Exclaimed James sensing his wife's concern.

James had already gone off into the dusky blue once before this evening, but she knew they were in dire need of help now, so she stayed silent. James ran, but in the dark and with his mind racing, he slipped and fell, and then, he knew no more.

Something was watching him now though and absorbing his presence, something familiar. Observing and feeling. Time itself was doing something. James had drifted away from consciousness, his head had thumped on the road.

"My girls." He had thought, before his eyes rolled white and shut. Then, James true journey began. That was when the figure stirred.

'Has my other one died then?' Thought the figure. 'Accidents happen, they say. Whoever they are.'

Ruth had sat in the cold on a moss covered tree stump, next to the travel bag, with baby Ramona pulled tight to her chest. It was happening too fast. Her mind was in a whirl. Why had James gone off again? She tried to piece it all together. Frantic. They were in the car. What happened? She remembered.

"Oh lord no!"

Lost and shaking now, and with her husband off seeking help, Ruth stood up, grabbed the bag and walked briskly in the direction James had gone. She had to do something. She kept Ramona wrapped up as snug as she could. But the little wide-eyed baby was awake now with all the jigging about. Ruth slowed down as common sense kicked in. She didn't want poor Ramona to be sick or to set her off crying.

"Its okay Mona. We are going for help, my darling." Still, she glanced left and right. Looking for sanctuary and for help. 'Where was James now?'

"Hello, is anybody here? I need help. Please, I have a baby we are lost!" She cried in the increasingly chilly night.

He was not far away, sensing something. Hearing Ruth in his blood like synaesthesia, and seeing her in his heart. A man promptly stood up. The figure of the Ivywyrld Inn. He had been sitting at his oak table. His hot drink, his study book. It was a book of maps, fault lines, geographical oddities. Candles lit. His evening ritual, at the hub of this Ivywyrld Inn.

The other one had fallen. Now he was here, sleeping within. It was nearly time. He saw the particles around his aura. Millions in neon blue, crystalline white. He had felt something. Sensed fright in something. Someone. His face was now studious, his eyes narrowed, as though in deep thought. The figure put down his mug and closed the book. His face was kind and not old as the candlelight revealed his handsome features.

He pulled his hood up and walked out. Out of the old inn and onto the winding lanes. They always looked and felt different. More so at night. Especially around the Ivywyrld. His head bowed as he walked. He knew already that it was the chosen one's calling. There were ethereal observers within the night mist. Ramona was the child that the realms must have selected. His baby, the one whom had fallen. After all, the Takers were on the move now and things were changing quickly in these lands. The peace had been disturbed by the red eyes.

"I will help them start the changes." Whispered the figure to the ether and then walked on more purposefully.

Ruth had continued to shout for help. Nobody came. She found a large oak tree and sat underneath it with Ramona, still swaddled.

She gulped in some deep breaths and tried to become calm.

"Its okay Mona. We are just going to find your daddy. Let mummy get you some milk."

Surprisingly, the tiny little girl seemed very sedate. She had not cried or screamed as you may expect. Instead, her eyes looked playful. She was trying to look over her mother's shoulder at something. Wriggling. Ruth, holding Ramona with one arm, scrabbled through the bag for her feeding bottle. Looking up, ahead of her, she drew breath sharply in surprise as she saw the figure walking toward her.

Not the red eyed one though.

She sensed it was not dangerous. Adrenaline warmed her blood. A familiar sensation ran through her. A feeling of déjà vu. So fleeting, and then gone. Ruth unknowingly posessed magic herself. That of empathy and instinct. She felt a sense of a parallel and a shiver ran through her. She put Ramona's milk back into the bag and stood again.

Clutching her inquisitive looking baby to her chest. Running again now, approaching him for help, she shouted..

"Help! Hey, you, please can you help us?"

The approaching man carried a tranquil aura with him. A familiarity that she could not pinpoint.

"My husband. Please, help us. The car. James, he went for assistance. Have you seen a man looking around here? Is he with you?" She sucked in oxygen.

"My baby is cold, please... we were going home. The car has gone off the road. He went away, he went away.." Ruth began to sob.

"Where is everyone?" She had got a lot out very quickly. She stopped for breath again. Aware that she was babbling and becoming frantic. 'Don't frighten Ramona.'

The figure drew closer. Head bowed and silent, listening. Feeling no need to interrupt the woman. As Ruth quietened, the figure motioned to her with one hand.

"Come with me to safety. The Takers are on the move. He has arrived. Normality has gone."

'What is he talking about?' Mused Ruth, puzzled. The figure remained silent and set off back the way he had come from.

"Come. You will be alright with me."

Ruth, feeling she had no other sensible options, followed on at pace with Ramona bundled up. Strangely, she was feeling a lot heavier to her. Probably tiredness. Shortly, the figure held up a hand.

"We are here."

Ruth looked about. It was a large and slightly dilapidated old inn. A public house. But there were no other houses, no vehicles, no people. Nothing. Save for a sign.

'The Ivywyrld Inn.'

'It said that on the map in the car.' Ruth shivered again at the thought of what James was going through. What with that demon thing appearing.

Why would an old pub be stood here in the middle of nowhere? Ivy grew all around and up the walls. The roof was thatched. The door was huge solid oak. Then, the figure bowed, gestured to the door and showed Ruth and baby into the shambly, yet homely looking inn.

"Come inside, I will do what I can. Help you to find him. They send out scouts, the Takers. You saw the red eyed one then?" His voice was a deep whisper. Almost inaudible and sounding like it was an everyday question.

'Who is this man? He feels so safe and familiar to me.' Ruth thought, feeling something akin to memory recall.

"This is a home, of many different times. Please, come through." Whispered the figure.

After this, she and Ramona were welcomed without further speech into the hooded, yet strangely warming figure's meagre home. The old abandonded Ivywyrld Inn. 'A home of different times', he had said. But she wanted help fast. For now, she had a cryptic, softly spoken figure. Yet to give a name or show a face, but something told her heart to trust him.

Warm light flickered from the candles and the smell of home cooking and hot cocoa drifted sleepily around the place. She would normally say how cosy it all was. The map book lay on the table. The crinkled pages lay open at a page headed 'Oakhampton as it is now.'

The figure stood quietly, as though to ask Ruth if she could explain. Why she and baby Ramona were running around? It was cold, wet.

'Unusual to see people around here. Ethereal intervention.' He thought.

"My husband and I. The holiday, the car. There was nobody. Nobody to help us. We got lost going home. Where is everybody? Help us. Please! Do you have a phone? Listen to me.. Say something, anything!"

The figure, still for some reason hooded, seemed unmoved, serene. Almost annoyingly so now. Steadfast, ghostly, still. As though pondering. His features still not revealed.

"Will you and your baby take some warm drinks? They calm the mind. They will soothe your baby also. Believe me Ruth, Ramona will save her father. She will save us all."

Ruth shed a tear and gave a shrill cry of despair.

"We don't want drinks, I want my husband. Ramona's daddy. How do you know our names? I want the police. I want help. where is your face?"

"Please sit." The figure motioned Ruth to one of the chairs near the old bar area.

She sat. Anything to speed this peculiar man up. Baby Ramona slept in her shawl after she had cried herself out. The figure had let Ruth tell him more. She had eventually sat and taken the drinks. They were indeed calming. For that, she was grateful. Ruth, even though tired, cold, and exhausted, felt something good about this person. Perhaps that he would help.

"Nobody wants to be lost in the middle of nowhere Ruth. But we all get lost in the middle of somewhere." He said in his whispered tones.

"Cryptic. You seem nice. Enough mystery now please. Where is my husband?"

"I will help. I promise." He replied, barely audible.

'This could be difficult. We will need others.'

A hot meal was made. Nourishment was needed. He busied himself. Food shortly appeared and was gratefully and blindly ingested by Ruth. She caved to the inviting aroma, still perplexed at his incessant calmness.

'Who is this person? Why would anybody live in a disused inn? It looks.. ageless. It does not fit in my time. What is it doing here in this.. nothingness?'

Her mind was becoming frantic again. On eating the hot dinner though, a calmness began to wash through her and ease her woes once more.

'She will need her father back, the little baby Ramona.' Thought the figure.

After Ruth had eaten and gotten warm, she and Ramona were taken upstairs and shown to a good bed. It looked so inviting.

'I trust him. I know he can help us.'

After much protest about immediate action and guilty feelings about her missing husband, while she had eaten and drank, she became overpowered, tired and sleepy. Ruth accepted the kindness. Ramona could not be out in the night. Ruth took to the bed with her baby. In this abandoned, unnoticed inn. Abandoned, save for the figure. Tears were welled in Ruth's eyes as she prayed James would appear. She somehow knew though, that she and Ramona were safe.

'We shall have to find Ramona's father.' Thought the figure.

'I have promised. He has merged with me fully now. I will tell Ruth in the morning.'

He smiled warmly at his wife and growing baby, closed the bedroom door and trudged back down the stairs with thousands of blue and white particles following and attaching themselves to him. To complete the merging of the two James from two worlds.

In this town, there were no police. No ambulances. No wise locals to give directions. Because this town, was not a town. It was Oakhampton. Strangely unearthly. It was a gateway.

After the figure had checked to see that mother and baby slept, he went back to his table and map book and drank his cocoa. His merging was complete.

'I am him. We, are now one. This is not a town. It is the way in. She, is Ramona and now we shall see what the realms have planned for her.'

Presently, the giggling sound of a dreaming baby, came from the other room and then, the figure smiled to himself. 'We will find him, the bad one.'

Ruth too, smiled in her sleep and the figure.. the husband, rested. His merging of two into one was complete.

His name was James.

CHAPTER TWO
THE KIND ELF

It was much needed a deep sleep, from shock, exhaustion and full from the relaxing food and drink, Ruth had allowed herself to be lulled by the soft, downy quilt. Now she awoke. Baby Ramona though, slept on. She looked like a tiny doll on this huge, warm and comfortable bed. Ruth reached into the travel bag she had fled from the car with. Where was Ramona's milk? Ruth was acting on motherly instinct. Looking after her baby's needs first. She found the bottle and got it ready for Ramona. She would wake her soon but she was happy to see her resting peacefully.

Then, as the fragments of sleep dissipated, she had a sobering flashback. Ruth suddenly remembered where she was, or thought she was. She still needed help. At least she had rested. Of that she was glad as she had feared she had been becoming hysterical. She would try to rationalise this now. In the light of day.

How could this be, after such a wonderful holiday? Oakhampton, they had both said the same thing. Lovely, but difficult to negotiate. Every day of their time there had been fabulous, but somehow it always looked like it had changed slightly during the night in the subtlest of ways. A shifted hilltop here, a different cluster of rocks or trees there. The lanes, winding and deserted. But they had laughed off any of these minor observations and gone about their relaxing beach walks and wooded rambles. Now, Ruth carried Ramona quietly down the stairs. She almost tiptoed. The sleepy baby was slowly waking in her arms. Where was the figure?

'I have to find him. Ask him where we are. Where did he go after last night?' She had suddenly felt bad for resting. But she had not been able to fight the much needed sleep. 'Where is my James?' Her thoughts raced again.

Downstairs in the living area of this big old place, there on a wooden table, lay a bundle of new and neatly folded clothes. The sizes for woman and baby. They looked fresh and clean. Warm. Who could have put these here? Who could have known? The figure perhaps? Was this a guesthouse?

'No. Its too shabby. Too run down.' Ruth quickly felt ungrateful for thinking that. Then a brief moment of dread. 'My god, did he kidnap us? No, no never.' Ruth felt strongly that this man would not do that. She chastened herself for her panic.

She had a look at the clothes. They were very basic. Nothing faddy or modern. They were more like robes. There were pullover type garments, trousers, vests. All handmade it seemed. She imagined it was something the people of old times would wear. The baby clothes were very welcome and Ramona would feel better washed and changed. Oakhampton. The alive and changing town. This, was not part of the holiday.

There was a kind, sensitive elf nearby. He came from a woodland dwelling not too far from the inn. By a lake named Whitsomin, where he liked to fish and watch the birds. He had a good connection with the land, its nature and keen, sharp senses. He had felt compelled to come here alone, with the clothing and a parcel of food. Something told him he was needed.

He knew of the Ivywyrld Inn. It was near the gateway. When things shifted, he sensed it. So he came. An aura of kindness surrounded him. A busy and helpful soul with a good heart had been at work. This elf was a protector. The protector had waited long days. He knew the Takers were on the move. He felt that the realms would find help in their inimitable way. Having done his job, the elf crept out the back door of the kitchen and retired back into the woodland.

He would need to keep an eye on them. The mother and baby. The figure, the elf sensed, was going through its own process. Arriving into its full self. He felt a merging. Helping those who needed it came naturally to elves. All three folk at the inn definitely needed a caring and watchful eye. For now, he left. Back to Whitsomin lake.

The figure from the night before, had known of the elfs presence. He had not sought to speak with him. Nor question him. For he sensed the kindness in the air and so, let him do what he wanted to do. He himself had merged with his other self from the gateway. He had to accept it. He had remained hooded and quiet. He had not wanted to frighten the mother or baby during his merging. He was confused enough and needed time to grow into what the realms had decided for him.

Ruth, carrying Ramona, moved through the hallway. Now there was the smell of fresh coffee. Sunshine was glinting through the opened windows. The strange dusty inn, from last night, had a new lightness and airy feel about it. Yellow, welcoming and warm. But even so. James had not shown up.

'All I can remember is, I was in the backseat of the car, watching Mona.' Thought Ruth.

'The car.' It came back to her. 'James! He went to ask for directons and then, a swerve. Now, we are here. Where?' She began to panic again.

The realms felt timelines shifting. Alternate realities coming together. The ethereal were at work. Unseen but all seeing. Ruth continued to look for the figure. He may know more. He must. She carried Ramona, looking around, past the old empty bar of this deserted yet somehow homely place. There was the chair she had sat on. The table with the map book, like the one from the family car. She could hear a quiet voice in the kitchen. A hum, soft whistling. Cooking aromas permeated through the vicinity. A flutter of light danced about this deserted place.

"Are you there?" And he was.

"Yes, I am here. Good morning Ruth, come through. I didn't like to wake you or Ramona too early."

The ethereal spirits felt the changes happening now.

This was enough mystery now for Ruth. She stirred herself, breathed deeply and made her way into the kitchen. She drew a sharp intake of breath, when she saw him. The figure. She tried to remember. Brief flashes of a past. A previous life. A parallel? Don't be silly. Déjà vu perhaps. Ramona wriggled about in her arms.

'She feels bigger.'

The figure continued to mutter and whistled cheerfully with his back turned to Ruth, tending to food.

"Any breakfast Ruthie?" He called.

'He called me Ruthie! It can't be..'

"Please turn around! Listen, I don't know what you are up to. You must help. Thank you, really, for what you did. But please.. show me your face." Ruth's voice was shrill now, pleading. She felt an impending sense of dread mixed with these moments of familiarity. She held Ramona still.

"Show me your face!"

The ethereal tuned their senses.

Ruth looked down at her baby, gurgling away. A little yawn. She felt longer, bigger. Heavier somehow. She squeezed Ramona.

"Have you grown overnight, sweetie?"

Ruth had never been more correct. Then, the figure turned around. It was James. She screamed. Ruth had already known somehow. In her subconscious. Her husband. From the road. But somehow different. He was dressed still in the hooded robe. Not cold or in shock like she remembered. Racing into the night for help, as she had sat at the tree praying.

"I need to explain. There is no point in keeping anything from you. There has been a crossover. A merging. You have to believe me Ruthie." He said. "I'm only just getting to grips with it myself."

Ruth's legs almost buckled at seeing her husband, the figure, and she grabbed at the kitchen top with her one free hand.

"I.. James.. What?.."

It was no good. No logic was here and the right words would not form. There were no right words. Ruth pulled up a chair with her one free arm, baby in the other. She needed to sit before she fell. James took a deep breath. They talked. Ruth really tried to digest it, whilst still looking after Ramona. She still needed her feed whatever else was going on. She felt bigger yet again. This was too much. Here was her husband as good as new, after disappearing into the night looking for aid, after the accident. Now claiming he had found his alternate self from another reality, and merged into one person. And it seemed that he lived here. Ramona was here for a purpose, he explained. She had magical powers. All wizards did. And she would need them. For Alatar had conquered the tower.

"Magical powers? James, What are you on about? Its like it is you, but different. You live here? There are two of you? Mona is a wizard! I think its your explanation that needs to be magic. Maybe its the effects of concussion. Alatar. What is Alatar? What is the Takers tower? We were driving home James. The car went off the road. Good god you must remember?"

But James had a head start. He had met his alternate self. The figure. And here he was. Blended into one. He had been through all the turmoil in his mind and he now hoped his wife could accept it, as he had to. James was part of the realms. Sent to be with Ruth and the unborn Ramona, in their timeline. In Gardelwyn. He had no knowledge of any of it prior. Only after his merging. Now he was back. Become one with his realms self and although he understood more now, he did not expect the same from Ruth.

Ramona felt even heavier now. Ruth only registered this subliminally. She had been trying to take all this in. She was looking at James still. Wanting to believe what he was telling her. She needed time to absorb it. And then, for all the previous gurgling and giggling, Ramona spoke her first words.

"Don't worry mummy. Daddy knows what to do. We found him. We found daddy!"

Ruth gasped in disbelief. She looked down at her baby. She had grown alright. In her arms she had grown. Bigger and taller. No wonder she had felt heavier. Most startling of all. She was no longer a baby. Her hair was longer and darker and she had the features of a growing young child. Ruth was stunned.

"Mona? But I...Your..!"

No more words would come. Now, the figure was there. He took the child in his own arms as Ramona beamed and said "Silly daddy! Why were you hiding?"

It had been James, all along. Hiding himself during his merging. Time had to catch up and make him one again. Not that either part of this now complete man could rationalise it. It was a rare occurrence for two timelines to meet like this. There had to be a reason. The realms did not like to meddle with precious lives unless there was a need.

James felt so sorry for his wife having to take all of this in. He was changing. He had not wanted to frighten her. When he had gone for help he had slipped and banged his head. He had disappeared. He came round at the Ivywyrld Inn, found the figure. It had stepped into him. There was bluish light and a calm sensation. Then the figure was gone. James was the figure.

He was struggling himself. But he understood more now. The James of the realms was now him. Now, a whole again, healed. He made sure all was as well as he could make it for his mystified wife and growing daughter. He put a warm blanket around Ruth and squeezed her shoulder. Ruth did not react as she usually would. She shuddered at the touch and pulled away. She was taking in deep, gulping breaths.

She felt confused and disloyal. Disbelieving as she now looked at a young girl where a baby had been. In her fathers arms. The figure. James. For now, he began explaining more in depth. Trying to reassure her. Hoping to take away some of the shock. She shuddered and gave in to it all. Then, he held her close and let her cry. She had just wanted to go home after their holiday. Why all of this?

But still. The Takers were on the move.

CHAPTER THREE
TWO GULLS AND MEETING A WIZARD

Having talked much, James passionately tried to help Ruth unravel the accident and of the events that had happened while they were separated following it.

"I think I have lived here before." He said.

"I know its hard, but when this figure became me, or me him. I felt something. A belonging, for all of us. As though the holiday was preordained, to bring us here. Time or dimensions sort of caught up with us. We were needed Ruth."

"You mean a parallel universe?" Ruth looked skyward.

"I don't even understand myself. Our holiday was meant to be a little celebration. For Mona, as well as us. Now she is talking. Full, intelligent sentences. Why has Ramona suddenly started doing this? Who are these wizards?" He blew out his cheeks in despair.

"What do you mean, 'she is here for a purpose', James? Magical powers, all this intelligence and wisdom. Who are these others? Who is on the move? You are being so mysterious. You obviously know more than I do. Why did we get lost? What is this village? A dream? The fifth dimension? Why did you go, and how come we are now all here? What has happened?"

James sat quietly as Ruth, understandably reeled off questions.

"I don't understand James. Red eyed.. demons, making us crash. Then you, joining with another you. Time shifts, good lord James, this is.. crazy. There is our baby, looking like a five year old girl. Sat chattering away. I'm not stupid James, we survived a freak accident. Off you went, and now, I'm sat here with a ghost and our baby who looks bigger and older every minute. Explain that."

Ruth was annoyed at herself for being annoyed at James. She drew in deep breaths having understandably vented. She felt a pang of guilt. Poor James, he too was in shock and he had ran for help on two occasions. She looked at him and Ramona, who had just been sat listening and looking at one of the many old maps lying about, and smiling as though listening to some well acted bedtime story by mum and dad. She looked quizzically at her mother. And Ruth looked back at Ramona.

"Were on holiday mummy."

Ruth welled up, melted inside and then she hugged them both tightly.

"I love you both so much. Please, lets find out what is going on."

"Im a magic person mummy!" Giggled Ramona. The unexplained onset of childhood was upon her now.

Outside, two great black-backed gulls landed on the roof of the Ivywyrld Inn. In gull-speak they were known as Biggle and Baggle. The same two bold and friendly birds from the beach at Oakhampton. Ruth had said they came every day for scraps. They had also been observing. They knew this family were special.

"We shall help. We shall help." They cawed, bobbing about.

And they laughed and created a happy noise on the rooftop. As seagulls do. Inside, Ramona pointed at the old map, looked up and said to James and Ruth..

"Alatar's tower. Bad magic."

Chapter Four
A Brother Searching.

Jude awoke. He was a good, brave soul. Funny, witty and selfless. Looking for his family, for he had lost them in time and parallels. He somehow knew of Oakhampton. For some reason he felt something. A calling. He was stuck on the borders of lands who knew not where they belonged. He was also homeless.

There was a family though. A car. Something he could not yet pin down. His parents?

He vaguely remembered belonging somewhere, once. So his search began for home. He knew he wanted to help. For he too had been born into a strange dimension. Yet, there had been something. Jude was sleeping wherever he lay at the days end. He was strong and kind of heart. He asked for nothing. He had been separated by time from those he loved. How, he knew not. He heard the name Ramona, over and over and knew this was his destiny. In his dreams. Inseperable, yet separated.

He left his cardboard shelter and headed for the Ivywyrld Inn. The inn he had never been to. And yet, he felt he knew where he was going. To James and Ruth, his mum and dad? The strange magic continued. Jude knew all about time-shifts now. He needed to find his parents, his sister, the young wizard. Jude was meant for another purpose.

But why was time rolling around like this? Even the ethereal could not answer that question. 'I will find this out, somehow, I will.' Thought Jude. With that, he upped and walked away from the empty streets.

CHAPTER FIVE
THE TAKERS

The Takers. Also known to many realms folk as drones. They were now an impressive dark and shadowy unit. Always building, taking folk from towns and villages, back to the tower. To become them. With Alatar using any means to grow his army and draw up his plans. The family. James, Ruth and Ramona, this little wizard? Well, the Takers did not like wizards, because wizards could outdo them.

Now there was this traveller, Jude. Somehow, the family knew they would have to bring down these apparitional creatures, sooner or later. Alatar himself felt they would try to meddle. Damn the ethereal. It would take them time to adapt though, the family, and Takers will take.

Biggle and Baggle, the scouting gulls flew over the old Ivywyrld Inn again. Making sure that for now, the Takers could not take from the wizards. They were keen protectors.

A cocktail of swirling forces were mixing and working in the ether as this stunned little family tried to regroup. Jude was on his way now. Quietly working things out in his confused mind. Where did he belong?

The car lay abandoned back in the lanes of what was meant to be Oakhampton. Sat like a relic or a permanent reminder of the start of something strange. The road ahead was as singular and as clear as

Judes mind. Like it had been placed there for him. A new, if unexpected beginning.

'I will find my mum and dad. I will look after my baby sister. I will do whatever I can to help.' Jude steadied himself and walked down a new path.

CHAPTER SIX
JUDES ARRIVAL

Now that Ruth and James had rested and talked of all the strange events. The accident, their separating. These bizarre changes. Ramona and her unfathomable growth. Their holiday had begun to fade from memory like an old, forgotten family photograph.

Ruth, asking the figure to help her find James. The figure then turning out to 'be' James. Their heads were spinning. They discussed the accident, but James said he remembered checking on them before running to look for help. Asking them to sit tight. He had come across the inn and spoke to a figure who said he had been waiting for him. He had said he 'was' him. James told Ruth he had felt a rush of adrenaline surge through him, as though he was becoming one with this figure. This other him.

He said he had awoken in the bed with visions of eyes. Red eyes in the road. They had caused the accident. Then, he had melded into this James. He had gone back out, which was where he found Ruth holding Ramona. It was hard to explain, when he could barely fathom it himself. Except that when the figure had become one with him, he said that it felt like another dimension had been waiting to catch him up.

He felt as though he had lived here before. Or just 'did' live here. What that now meant about home, work, friends, the rest of their family, Ruth's doting mother. He did not yet know. He just wanted them all safe. All the while they talked, James had an incomplete feeling and a vision in his mind. A boy. A young man. Left behind. But it was hazy.

It was becoming clear to Ruth now that they were in some sort of other dimension. They had both said from the outset that Oakhampton seemed to have a life of its own. After all. Driving home from a family holiday. A break from work, routine. Normal. Feeding the birds with baby. Playing on the beach. Long sleeps in the warm cabin on the coast.

It had been initially hard to get to grips with this spiral into something surreal. Now all this magic talk. But at least they were all together, at the inn. Well fed and warm. Very confusing, but now they were unravelling things a little. Ramona had sat across the table, chattering away about magic and finding a tower and 'Has the elf been again while we were asleep?' Ruth thought this mind boggling to begin with.

Days earlier she had been bottle feeding and changing nappies and singing lullabies to her, as the sound of the sea outside lulled them to sleep. But it seemed, every time they slept now, and awoke again, Ramona had grown. In years, not just height. It was frightening. Ramona though, was seemingly unaffected and just.. being Ramona. Nothing surprised Ruth after the whirlwind since the car had overturned. They would just simply have to be. Or go mad.

Out on the winding, changing lanes, was the young Jude. Cardboard beds on the streets of strange places, miles behind him now. Perhaps, dimensions behind him, was the home he had been thrown out of. The home where nobody knew him. He sensed where he was going now though. To his family. To help. An arrival. Weary after constant trekking. Always going forward. Following his instinct. Jude needed water, rest. Then on turning a corner, he spotted the Ivywyrld Inn. He knew his family would be there. Felt it. His was the magic of foresight. He walked faster. Got to the huge door at the inn. He took a breath. Knocked politely. The door opened. It was Ruth.

"Mum?" It was all Jude could say. And suddenly, Ruth knew.

"Jude! My Jude." She sobbed.

"They took you from our minds. They left you.. how could we.. how could we know? Oh Jude. Im sorry, my sweet boy."

Ruth's mind was a complete jumble of homes, houses, babies, children, figures, wizards, hoods, cars. But all she knew now, was here was her beloved son.

And they embraced.

CHAPTER SEVEN
AND THEN THERE WERE FOUR

Ruth had shown Jude through to the living room of the old Ivywyrld Inn, where the family, by circumstance, now resided. Somehow, it felt like they always had.

The two gulls patrolled the roof, padding their feet and bathing their wings in the yellow sunlight, contemplating a quick fishing trip. Food was plentiful with the flight to sea, estuaries, rivers and lakes all within a good wing-stretch of these handsome birds.

Ruth was glad of them. They were on the beach during the family's holiday from their home back in Gardelwyn. She was certain it was the same two birds.

'What was our old home like?' To Ruth, it was fading. As was the holiday.

She now felt guilty. 'I can't remember how Jude came to be. But I know he is my son.'

As though reading his mother's mind, Jude then spoke. "Our home is empty mum. I woke up and you had all gone. Its empty and its not in this world, I can tell you that much. Nobody knows us back there now at Gardelwyn. I couldn't remember you or dad or my baby sister at first. Its like you said mum, they stole our memories. By the way, erm.. did Mona grow or something? I don't know what's going on mum. It freaked me out at first. I dreamt a lot. And something has happened with the timelines."

They had fairly normal lives, good jobs and enjoyed their spare time together. Unwinding, driving, cooking together. Long walks. All with their wonderful new baby, Ramona. It was perfect. But all the while, both parents had nagging feelings that something, or someone, was missing from their family. Preordained time-shifts did strange things that did not always know who or what they hurt.

Now, sat next to James on the comfortable sofa, was the ever growing Ramona. It was not like a magic trick where she just shot up and changed. It was subtle. If you had looked away and looked back, she would be taller, older. A few facial features subtly changing. Hair, slightly longer and darker.

Dad, James looked healthy and well to Jude. Mum, looked beautiful to him. Seeing his mother up close after all this haze was a godsend to him. But she was visibly upset and confused and quite sad at this sort of amnesia state, crossed with a huge dash of disbelief. Ruth had spent so long sleepless and baffled. She had eventually given in and slept for days. Undisturbed until Jude arrived. James had spent this time with Ramona, talking about anything and everything.

She now finished his sentences. Seemed to see and know things before they happened. She had asked about the red eyes too and said she too dreamed a lot. Of a blue magic and saving the poor people. A prison. She needed to free them.

Ruth had come to a conclusion of sorts now. You can only analyse so much. It is what it is. Now, she was learning acceptance. James smiled and motioned to Jude to take a seat in a welcoming armchair. Ruth brought him hot sweet tea. Jude gratefully drank it down.

"Aw thank you mum. I've not had a proper hot drink in a long while." He winked. Trying to make his mum feel better. It definitely helped her as she smiled broadly. James did not question. Nor did Ramona. Ruth's eyes told them all they needed to know. Here was a son, a brother. A brave young man. Unbroken. Jude exuded warmth despite his experiences at the mercy of the street. He looked up. Smiling at all three. He spoke with quiet dignity.

"I had to find you. I knew I would. I don't know how. But I knew your faces and I knew you were my family. I knew we had gotten separated."

Ruth gave Jude an empathetic look, tinged with sorrow at her boy's plight, from which she had not been there to shield him from. Ruth was a selfless mother.

"Its alright mum. Time does funny things around here. Like its all jumbled up, back to front, sideways. Just weird!" He found a grin for her.

"I had to come here."

James leaned in to ask, "Jude. You know of these others? The Takers?"

"Yes dad. I know of them. I have seen them as I travelled. More, felt them, actually. A bad presence, shadowy. They move subtly in the background. Most people don't notice. Especially in the busy towns. If the towns are still there. But I do. I notice. I know Ramona does too. I had to find my sister. I knew she would be growing up fast. I just knew."

Ramona looked up. In recognition at the sound of her name being called by the familiar voice of her older brother from who knew when.

"Jude, where have you been? What is time doing? Look at me, I'm meant to be a baby. Why do I know so much? I've had no teachers. I just grow and seem to know more and more. I had seen these others, through the eyes of a newborn. I couldn't tell mum and dad. I couldn't bloody talk!" Ramona too, now grinned. It showed how alike the siblings looked. Tears were now forming in Ruth's adoring eyes.

"He caused us to crash. The red eyed thing. That demon. Its not a man. He made the car swerve. I tried to say something, but how could I? Now, I see you for the first time. At least, I think it is. But somehow, I already knew you, in my heart. I'm struggling here now, Jude. I woke up today and I feel like am sixteen years old. I get pains in my bones."

Jude pulled down his hood. Put down his cup. "Ramona, lovely little sis. We grow for a reason. It does hurt, its growing pains, worse for you because of the speed of your growth. That is why I am here.

For you, mum and for dad. You know why you are growing so fast don't you? Because like you say. You saw him in the road. Red eyes, bad, strange. Even then, instinct told you, but you couldn't warn mum and dad.

That is why you grow fast. Now, you can stop them. Ours is the power of foresight, of visions. These Takers, the red eyed ones. They must be stopped. I'm like you, sis. I've seen stuff. I know stuff. There will be many more lost souls than us, living in this confusing world. Do you see sis? I think dad is right. You, were brought here for a reason, by those who control time. To help stop them. That too is why I believe I found you. I see things. I was sent to help."

The young wizard looked at her brother and nodded, thinking deeply.

"Yes. I see Jude."

CHAPTER EIGHT
THE TAKERS

There was a counsel gathered. Equilibrium had been disturbed. This is why he had sent the Takers out into Oakhampton. The place on the borders of two timelines. In search of the cause of the perturbation. The Takers had been met by an unseen force of ugly goodness. They could not get close enough yet. They needed to know what they were dealing with first. This was unfortunate and unexpected.

No one had meddled in their affairs before. No one had disrupted their carefully laid plans. They had lain low long enough. Hidden away in the shadows, just enough to not be seen. Their work was not to be spoiled, by this out-of-time family. These meddlers, bought in by the self-important, ethereal ghosts. Control was what the Takers were looking for. Total power. Then, they would show themselves. Then, the realms would be theirs, to do with as they saw fit.

He stood. Banged a gnarly fist on the table. The drones, startled, jumped to attention. "I want them found. I want them brought before me. I want them neutralised."

The Takers murmured. The leader had spoken. "Do you all understand? I do not tolerate.." He spat the last word..

"Wizards."

The leader sat, sipping some steamy liquid from a pewter goblet.

"We have come too far. The accident did not finish them. And now they grow. We must eradicate this before it gets started."

More hissing and swaying.

"We must go back to the shadows and seize them. They will not halt us. These realms are ours. We shall not be stopped by a wizard who does not even know she is a wizard."

"Ten of you, the strongest, shall move at dawn. Locate and bring them here. To the tower."

A Taker named Waredd, mottled and slimy looking, stood to face the leader. "There may be others, my reverance." He then shrank back into his seat.

"It does not matter Waredd. Any others, will also be dealt with accordingly. First, we stop the family. You concentrate on doing as I say. Or this lavish lifestyle I have given you can just as easily be taken away." Waredd bowed and said no more. The leader sat again. Pensive, in deep thought. He drank from his goblet. Without looking up and uttered to his followers.

"Dismissed."

They left quickly.

CHAPTER NINE
THE ELF HAD HEARD EVERY WORD

The counsel had dissolved, for now. The Takers had slunk off in different directions. Going about their business of manipulation and subtle narcissistic control. Following strict orders. The leader had given his instructions in no uncertain terms and then retired to his quarters alone. Two cloaked Takers guarded the thick, heavyset door. He was not to be disturbed.

Ten of his finest newly assembled guard had been dispatched to find the out-of-time family. He would have no outside interference in achieving his vision. They had lain in the background. Slowly manipulating the realms for their own ends, for many years now.

Growing in size and stature and reputation. Seizing villages and settlements. Playing off friend versus friend. Rich promises, glittering manifestos to sway susceptible minds.

Causing accidents. Such as the one which ran Ruth, James and Ramona off the road. Causing distress to good folk by planting subliminal messages of confusion and self-doubt. Signs. The good folk unknowingly absorbed the Takers drip fed messages.

Do not bother trying, it will not work. Do not be happy. Do not love. Do not be creative. Do not travel. Stay within your boundaries. It is safer. This campaign had been administered from the tower for so long now. Weaken them subliminally. Affect their neural pathways. Soften them up.

It was that or reveal themselves and start the killing straight away. The centre of Oakhampton was deserted. Gone, was the hub of the coastal town. Some had seemingly just ceased to be. Save now for this wretched family. This concerned the new leader. For it seemed time bent and shifted around them. And an unknown force had somehow galvanised them.

Bought this James back. The leader continued to muse. Outside the tower, behind a cluster of large rocks, the elf had been observing. Since he had helped at the Ivywyrld Inn. The clothes and food and suchlike, he felt a sense of care, duty even. More importantly, he liked this family.

He felt they could help bring back the light. In particular, the girl. For the elves too, had suffered oppression from the Takers. Their resources drained and happy spirits dampened. Seized as prisoners by his Takers. The elven numbers were now few.

They too had waited in the background. In hope of help. So, the elf had gone to the tower on a whim. A feeling. He had concealed himself. Listened to the courtyard counsel. The elf was very earthed and in tune with the lands. This wise fellow had heard every word. Now, scurrying away from the tower, he must return to the inn and do something he had never done. The two gulls flew overhead, keeping watch. The elf looked up in thanks. They cawed and swooped alongside. It reassured him.

He would show himself now, to the family and tell of what he had learned. These realms were for all, not for oppressors. He knew the family could help.

Especially Ramona.

CHAPTER TEN
JAMES MEETS CORMAC

It had been a long, cross-country journey for the kind elf. He now returned from the Takers tower. At last, exhausted, he approached the Ivywyrld Inn. Ruth was in the back garden area hanging up washing. Ramona and Jude sat on old, timeless deckchairs. This mysterious place on the cusp of two realities, it seemed, of provided everything they needed. Sheds, outhouses and a cellar that contained earthy food, drink and tools. There was even a little allotment with fruit and vegetables showing.

"Fancy having a huge place like this all to ourselves Jude."

"I know, sis." replied her brother. "Pretty weird really isn't it?" Jude crunched down on a carrot and gazed about the sunlit grounds of this old establishment, wondering where all the people had gone to.

"Jude, how did you find us? What I mean is, how did you even know about us? Dad says he never knew he had a son. He feels really sad about it. Guilty too, he says, but they messed with all of us. Its not dad's fault. Mum says you were never there to give up for adoption, and she'd never do that anyway. They loved you. But how did we lose you? Somehow Jude, when you arrived, we all felt you were part of our family. When you turned up, it didn't shock us. Why?"

Jude sipped his tea stroking his chin. There was maturity about him that belied his years.

"Do you know Ramona, I've stopped questioning. I lived on the street, but I imagine its gone now. Been taken I expect. Shifted into these realms. Those are not our streets anyway now. I got up one morning and I had dreamt of your faces and this place and I set off. That's really all I know. This place? Well, I knew it wasn't a normal town.

Its a way in. To these.. realms. So, what with your growth acceleration, sis. This place that we feel we have lived in before? Dad in two places at once? Feels like you are going mad, right?"

Ramona nodded in strong agreement and looked skyward. Jude went on.

"None of us are going mad. What we are doing, is learning to accept the way of things. Without question. Then, do what we can from that point. So here I am and all I can say is I love you all." He smiled. Ramona returned it warmly.

Ruth watched them chattering away. Despite the bizarre circumstances, she felt content for the first time in a long time. The sunrays lit up the gardens. Ruth hugged her children.

"Aw, mum!" said Ramona, girlishly grinning. Jude was so happy to have found them. Inside, James was cooking dinner. Chopping and peeling. Whistling away. It smelled wonderful, even if he thought so himself. It all seemed quite normal.

Now, the little elf turned the corner. He needed food, rest, water. His trek had been worth it, but draining. He made for the front door and gave a polite knock. The door opened. There, open mouthed, stood James. Slightly perplexed on seeing a real little elf.

"James. May I speak with you. It is a matter of urgency."

James, though perplexed, sensed a familiarity about this bonny little fellow.

"I think you had better come inside. You look hungry, and thirsty."

"Oh, I am to be sure, sir. I surely am." replied the weary looking elf. He was shown to the kitchen table, where he gulped back much water.

"Thank you sir. I surely needed that." He relaxed a little.

"You are welcome my friend and please, call me James. There are no sirs here."

The little elf smiled.

"I do know of your name James, and of Ruth, Ramona and now Jude. I am always close by. Though I do not like to presume. I find politeness is.. well, polite."

James returned the smile.

"Then it was you who brought the clothes, the extra food. Tidied, let in the light?"

"It was to be sure, sir, sorry, James. I reside by Whitsomin lake. There are not many of us now. When you all arrived, crossed the gateway, as it seems, I sensed good wizadry. I wanted to help, in my small way." The elf looked at the floor.

'So humble and kind.' Thought James.

"Well, I would say you have helped in a big way and that we are truly grateful to you." James dished some stew into a bowl and passed it to the elf.

"It isn't michelin star, but it should fill a gap."

The elf looked grateful but confused. "What is michelin star James? Some astrological term I do not know of? I do pride myself on the star charts.."

James laughed out loud.

"It does not matter. Just eat up, you look like you need it."

And the elf did just that, relishing a hot dinner, and had a second bowl for good measure. James shortly asked "Now, will you tell me friend, why you came today? You have never shown yourself before. Do you have a name? That would be a start."

At that moment, Ruth, Ramona and Jude breezed into the kitchen, hungry, and there was the little elf. Glances were exchanged to say the least. The elf clasped his hands together in a friendly gesture and bowed slightly. Sensing this as a greeting, the family returned the bow.

"My name, is Cormac of the elven woods. I bring news. The Takers are coming."

CHAPTER ELEVEN
A SIEGE

The ten Takers moved swiftly. The leader had dispatched them with a simple briefing. 'Find that damned family. Bring them to me.'

They were hard to describe. You would think you had seen something out of the corner of your eye. Feel, or sense a presence. It would drain your energy. Make you feel gloomy, listless. You may feel a dark, shadowy residue. They seemed to glide, not walk or ride. Slithery and faceless.

From the tower, they followed their senses. They needed only a few provisions. A little food and water was all they took. There was a mixture of human and more feral, orc-like creatures. Pure Taker, these were known as. They found their chief sustenance in the draining of good folk. Almost like a battery charge for them. Feeding off energy. Through the woodland they went, past Whitsomin lake. The remaining elves shrank expertly into the greenery. They had lost enough of their own.

The Takers paused. Sensing the elven presence. They were hanging like dark spectres in the air. They had strict orders. They moved on. The elves breathed again. They were too few and too sapped to fight. Merely existing. Cormac had not yet returned. The Takers rarely spoke. Merely exchanging glances, nods and grunts. Almost like extra sensory perception. Onto the lanes they came now. Deserted. If there were any people, they were in hiding. These realms had become a netherworld.

Now, they could smell the goodness. Warm hearts. They latched onto this goodness as though it was a tracking device. They continued to glide. Barely visible to the human eye.

Cormac back at the Ivywyrld Inn, stood bolt upright. "James. They are close. Lock all the windows and doors."

James nodded automatically and motioned to his family. They all dispersed. Locking all the windows and doors to the Ivywyrld Inn.

Ramona spoke. "Now what Cormac?".

"We need to be a collective. All sit together. Think the word 'resist'. They cannot enter. You have the magic Ramona. They are as scared as we." Cormac beckoned them to the living room. Jude shook his head in frustration.

"Cormac. My sister has magic, I know. But she doesnt know how to use it. None of us do. We are only just working this out. Its too soon."

"Jude it is not too soon. It is now or we are taken, like the others, to become like them. It is now, or our eyes glow by tonight. Ramona's instinct will prevail. Believe me. Now join hands. Resist."

The Takers now circled the Ivywyrld Inn. Covering all angles. Hovering apparitions. "Let us enter. Let us enter. No harm shall come to you. We wish only to talk to the girl. Only to talk." All ten of the Takers chanted this in perfect, whispery synchronicity as they circled.

"They are getting in my head. Like termites burrowing, I can't stop them.." Cried Ruth. The elf ran from window to window. There was no escape route. "Keep your hands joined. Think resist. We resist."

The shadows went on though. Relentlessly hammering into the brains of the family. "Let us enter. Let us enter. You must come to Alatar. You must.." It was incessant. It made their heads hurt. The family fought back with the mantras Cormac had instructed them to use.

"We resist. We resist. Leave us. Leave us."

The Takers were too strong. They fell back, but only a little. They soon came forward again. Chanting, whispering, circling. Ruth's eyes rolled and suddenly, she fell forward and hit her head on the floor. Jude sprang up. "Mum.. No!"

James knelt and held his wife's head in his lap. She had fainted. Suddenly Ramona got up. She strode briskly past Cormac and went for the door. Cormac cried out. "Ramona, what in the realms are you doing? No."

Ramona had zoned out, she opened the door. The instinct Cormac had spoke of was taking over. She stepped into the grassy yard of the old Ivywyrld Inn.

"I see you. Takers. Where is your big leader? Where is he? Cowards. I am called Ramona. You want me? Stop creeping in the shadows. You will not take my family."

The Takers became unusually uneasy. Their perfect circle became disjointed. The chanting subsided. Ramona stood in the centre of the yard. They closed in on her. All ten of them. She clenched her fists into balls by her side.

"Go back to your leader. Orcs and wraiths. Tell him he needs to do better. Tell him he faces more than he bargained for. Tell him, today, he will take no one." She raised her arms above her head and clasped her hands together in a praying motion.

"Now.." She spoke with a new venom. "You Takers." They began to withdraw. Uncertain now, doubt crept in. "You will leave. Or I will be forced to destroy you."

They still persisted. "We do not leave. You will follow us. Follow. Only to talk.."

She brought her arms down. Spun around striking out with her arms and screamed.. "Then you give me no choice.." Suddenly, swathes of electric magic poured forth at the Takers. Like a spinning catherine wheel of cobalt blue. "Leave my family alone. Tell him to come himself, the red eyed one."

Ramona's defensive magic struck all but one of the Takers. They fell and dissipated into black, hissing particles. Cacodem, was the name of the survivor. A dark spore-like powder scattered all about the yard, was all that was left of his fellow takers. Dark rags dropped to the floor. Whispers now, on the wind from the disappeared Takers. Dead and gone in an instant. "The power of good. We never knew. We never knew.." Their shock and surprise faded into the air. And then. Nothing. Silence prevailed again. Ramona's legs gave way and she dropped to her knees. Jude raced out into the yard.

"Mona. Say you are alright, please!" She looked up. Smiled through a grimace "I'm alright Jude. I'm OK. Where are mum and dad and Cormac?"

Jude held onto his sister. "They're inside. They're alright. I can't believe what you just did, its unbelievable sis! They've gone. All gone! How did you do that? You did magic!" Jude looked gobsmacked.

"I don't know Jude. Cormac said instinct would prevail. Not bad for a wizard who doesen't know she's a wizard, eh brother." Ramona looked at the mass of rags and the dark scattered spores over the yard. A rush of guilt and sadness came over her.

'I have killed.' Ramona thought, privately. It was a numb, empty hurt. She finally put on a grin for Judes benefit and hugged her stunned sibling.

"Jude?"

"Yes sis?"

"Can I have a cup of tea now?"

They went inside.

CHAPTER TWELVE
BIGGLE AND BAGGLE THE GUARDIAN GULLS

What of Biggle and Baggle? Husband and wife, so to speak. These two great black-backed gulls had lived in and around Oakhampton since birth. They found now that Whitsomin lake had a plentiful supply of fish. Though sometimes they still enjoyed a jaunt to the beach in search of their favourite, sea bass. A rare treat. However, wherever they chose to eat, they would tease each other about who had the biggest cut of fish, and how unfair it was, or how the other was selfish and greedy! They both did it. Truth be told, they always shared equally but had a sense of mischief and fun.

Biggle and Baggle and many of the gulls were looked upon as clownish or bumbling. The fact was, they saw a lot from the air. It was they whom explained to the elves that something was happening at the old tower. Something or someone now resided there and it made them uneasy. None of the gulls would go there now. They had met Cormac at Whitsomin lake, by the elven woodland. They told of what they had observed. Actually, it was more of a sense, a feeling. They told, in their chattery, clucky language, of hooded shadows. Faceless, cloaked drones, unlike any others. They spoke of a strange drifting menace.

A large table in the old royal courtyard. Figures gathered in counsel. Pewter goblets and steaming liquids. They said they projected a heavy, draining feeling and no black-backed gull nor kittiwake would fly there, while this presence resided. Biggle and Baggle, post meal, liked to perch on the rooftop of the old deserted inn and let their food digest. They chattered away, sometimes had a pleasant siesta as the dappled sunlight, danced through the trees and warmed their wings on the roof.

They told Cormac that a family had appeared and were now living there. At first, a single being named James. He had lost his loved ones in the lanes. Then, two more. A mother, Ruth. Carrying her young one, Ramona. They had gone there for help, and stayed. Lastly, a tall and handsome young man had arrived. He had come from the centre of Oakhampton. The people had gone, he had said. He had crossed the ley line to find them. Biggle and Baggle liked this family, and so, would perch atop the inn more often. In a lookout capacity. For they knew of the others. The Takers.

Cormac had taken a lot in. He told the gulls that his people too, had sensed a shift in balance and feelings of lethargy and despondency. They did not know why, but it had something to do with the tower. This is when Cormac had taken food, clothing and made the Inn sparkle with light. Changed from the dusty deserted shell it had been before. This is when the elves and the gulls decided that this family was to be nurtured and protected, as they felt wizadry. They felt the family could restore equilibrium to their lands.

The gulls bobbed and bowed and flew away.

CHAPTER THIRTEEN
THE BANSHEE

A dark, ragged shape drifted towards the tower. It was the one Taker whom had survived after Ramona had defended the Ivywyrld Inn. His glide was no longer smooth. It was stuttery, slow. Nine had simply disappeared into the ether, vanquished, following Ramona's defensive blue magic. Screaming spores on the wind. His circle of Takers had been broken by the force of a family's strong will and togetherness. So he had fled and saved himself. Just. Approaching the wrought-iron gates, he grunted something that must have been a command or a password.

The gates creaked open and the Taker, feeling a sense of impending dread, nodded at the two guards and surveyed the courtyard. It was just as he had expected and feared. There at the counsel table, pewter goblet of steaming liquid, his life-force drink in hand, sat the leader. Head bowed.

"Cacodem, you have failed me. Why?" He did not look up. Cacodem could feel scorn and a simmering rage projecting from the imposing, mysterious creature.

"Alatar, my leader. We have underestimated this out-of-time family. The others.. they are dust. Dark powder, dissolved. We encroached as you ordered. Circled their temporary abode. They resisted. They joined as one. We were too strong at first. The woman fell. The circle was broken and so we seized the advan.."

"Silence. Insect."

Cacodem instantly hung his shrouded head.

"I know what happened, Cacodem. You, and nine. Nine others. Could not suppress a weak mother, an injured man, a wizened little pixie and two children? Cacodem, you are a withering insipid excuse for a Captain. Shame on myself for trusting you."

Further derision for the fearful Cacodem.

"Alatar, I can only give you my word that next time I will be more prepared. This girl.. Ramona. She is the one you foresaw. She possesses powers I have never witnessed. They all do, but not to her level. She acts on instinct, powerful magic yes, but she does not yet have the understanding or control to be a threat. If we act now.."

Alatar sipped his life-force liquid. Slammed the goblet down on the table and stared at Cacodem. His eyes were like dancing fire.

"Captain Cacodem. If I leave anything else to you. We shall all be shredded to this spore-like dust you speak of. This you have proved to me. You are risible, small minded and incompetent. I shall see to this matter myself. No, I lie. I will enlist.. The banshee. She will come. She will drain them. She has become a twisted recluse since I banished her. She is broken. She will give me what I require."

"Alatar, the banshee is not dangerous to the good folk. She cares for them. She would drain us, seek vengence, given chance. We cannot trust her."

"I am to trust you then, Cacodem? A failed village peasant? Do not worry about the banshee. She is no threat to me. She will help. Or I will send her back to her watery domain. She knows of my power. I tolerated her existence for such occasions as this. I kept her alive for future use."

Cacodem fell silent again. Wondering of his fate. Sensing this, Alatar glowered at the deflated Cacodem.

"You, Captain? You will now spend some time in the jail. With the little humans. The good faithful, dull loyal folk. I shall give you time amongst those urchins, to remind yourself of our ambition. I will not let this little group of pilgrims stop me. Believers in dead Kings, and royalty whom cares nothing for them. I will rid this realm of the light. You shall see Cacodem. It is inevitable."

"Alatar. Please. I have learned. I will not fail again. Let me be part of this. I shall avenge the others. I implore you." Cacodem's glowing eyes pleaded to his master.

"Avenge? You performed an act of cowardice!" On occasion, Alatar did have a better nature. But not today.

"Fool. You make me feel so very weary. Take him away." Two guards bound Cacodem's gnarled hands together with a living, lashing electrical red rope. It gripped him, vice like, burning. The captain was ditched into the grim jail cell.

Humans, elves, many innocents, lay on straw. Crying, crawling. Scooping dirty water from wooden buckets to extinguish perishing thirst. Chewing on grain or a tepid gruel-like substance. Reduced to feral, animalistic behaviours. Cacodem would now live like this. He made a sound that almost could have been a sob. Alatar's punishments could last hours or weeks or worse. Depending on his mood.

Cacodem floated into a dark corner and prayed it was the former.

Chapter Fourteen
Leaving the Ivywyrld Inn

It was the day after the Takers had attempted to breach the Ivywyrld Inn and capture Ramona and her family. They had not prepared for that fight. Expecting it to be easy, straight forward kidnap. Alatar had forewarned them there was magic within this family. Especially this girl wizard on his radar. Though even he, it seemed, was paying lip service. There was no real threat to his plans. It was meant to be a useful training excercise for captain Cacodem and the guard.

If they captured them now, any threat would be extinguished before it began. Alatar saw things before they happened. He could feel magic. Good or bad. He could sense it when used close by. He had worked hard to capture the Oakhampton coastal fault line and the towns and villages beyond as settlements fell within the realms. As he did this, he drew new maps. He rearranged the realms and beyond, to his vision.

He wanted to rid the lanes and streets of those crawling humans, scurrying woodland elves and faerie followers, who would not accept his magnificent new cause. To him, they were litter in the lands that he wished to rule. Sheep. These were to be his realms. A totalitarian leader was needed. One set of rules. One way of living. His way.

The initial foray had paled into farce though and there was nothing to show for it but scattered rags, the dark spore-like powder and a captain whom had fled like a coward and not gone down fighting, with his men. Cacodem, was now whimpering in the jail with the other captors. The ones that had been spared. If you could call this feral way of living, spared.

They observed him and Cacodem studied them. Cacodem's eyes were no longer red. There were tears. He pulled down his veil. Here was a human face. The others in this cell reeled backwards. Staring in disbelief. "What have I done?" Whispered the imprisoned Captain.

"My name.." He seemed to be recalling something. Pewter goblets of steaming liquid. The changing process. The drink was changing them. Alatar's new life-force liquid was numbing these poor folk. Making them all the same. Docile, easy to manipulate. Mind control. The Takers were recruiting human drones.

"I am Domacec. I am human."

He was awakening.

"Alatar has done this. I was not always Cacodem. My wife. I had a wife, my Bisera. Was she taken too? Please Bisera, no. We must all escape."

At the Ivywyrld Inn, Cormac held court in the living room. Ruth, James, Jude and Ramona sat listening. Drinking tea and gathering their thoughts. It had been extremely difficult to sleep. They had taken turns in watching for any more Takers through the night.

"It appears we have to depart." Cormac paced back and forth.

"Sitting ducks here, to be sure. Yes, sitting ducks. Easy targets. Oh dear me.."

Jude interjected "Cormac?"

"Yes Jude?"

"How is this helping dude?"

Ramona sniggered, grinning. Cormac shrugged, puzzled at the young siblings shared mirth.

"Dude? I wàs of the understanding your name was Jude?"

Ramona creased up laughing despite the tension. "You are too funny Cormac!"

But, oblivious, the elf had entered a phase of panic and was not listening. Elves were good at worry.

"Dude? Curious word.. Ah, I understand. A term of endearment. Thank you then Jude, dude."

Ramona giggled into the palm of her hand. Jude shot her an admonishing look, but then sniggered himself. The affable elf was vacant to the apparent joke.

Cormac continued. "Well, I saw enough yesterday to know Ramona is the one to bring back the light. That is to be sure. But I still propose, we evacuate this place."

Sighs from the family.

"Oh no!" Mumbled James.

"We're only just getting used this inn in the middle of nowhere, Cormac, we have just found a son we didn't even know of. Like you said, you thought he lay in our subconscious and our hearts.. I did feel that."

Jude looked at his dad with a mixture of sadness and empathy. James continued..

"My wife carries our baby here in distress, looking for me. I had left the car to find help. There was none. In these.. Insane realms. I get back in the car, drive us off again and see a dark, red eyed ghost in the road. Crash the car, roll down an embankment. The car is upside down, we somehow survive.. I go for help.. again! My wife is alone, sat there freezing with our poor baby, then finds a kind hooded figure whom brings them here to the inn. He seems to know all about us. Why, Cormac? Well because he happens to be me. Oh it all makes perfect sense! What am I? A flaming shapeshifter?" James looked exasperated.

"No, James. Shapeshifters are evil, malevolent and cruel. But please continue.." Interjected Cormac.

"Cormac, our lost son appears. Whom apparently, we did not know of. Ramona turns from baby to six, ten. Now perhaps sixteen years of age, with blue lightning shooting from her fingertips. All completely normal.."

Cormac piped up again. "Sarcasm, James. Understable to be sure. Normal behaviours, given the circumstances."

James continued again. "How old will my Ramona be tomorrow, Cormac? Twenty or three hundred? Two and a half? Why not throw her back in reverse, she's only a living soul with feelings. Why don't the rest of us age? We are attacked by Takers. Clothed by an elf, find out we are 'special', and our daughter is 'the chosen one.' Its ludicrous." James paced up and down, oblivious now.

"I just want to go home, to our real home. To sleep. Go back to my job at the nature reserve. Put food on our table. Take my family out at weekend. Have a fishtank. Lie in bed on a Sunday morning. Take my wife to dinner. To go back to where we were Cormac. Get proper rest without all these weird dreams."

For a moment, James eyes glazed over, as though pondering his startling merging. Then, he snapped back to himself..

"Apart from that Cormac, everything is absolutely fine. Tickety boo in fact! More tea anyone?" James sighed and breathed deeply. Feeling bad for venting all this frustration to Cormac. James was truly grateful for the elfs help.

"Tea would be tickety boo, dude, yes." Muttered Cormac innocently.

James stopped, gulping for breath, post rant, then burst into fits of laughter.

"Oh Cormac, I am so sorry. Listen to me babbling like a madman. You are one in a million. Come here my friend."

The elf toddled over, unfazed, to receive a warm hug from a relieved James. His tension gone. Ruth squeezed her husband's hand.

"James. Its so hard I know, but Cormac is helping us to understand. Sarcasm isn't your thing my love. And projecting your frustration onto Cormac isn't fair."

"Its sortèd dude Ruth. I promise, to be sure." Smiled the elf.

Ruth clasped Cormac's hand tightly and smiled at their new friend. James felt more tension lift and reminded himself how lucky he was to have such a loving wife. Ramona and Jude, gazed at their dad. He had bottled such a lot up. Cormac had listened intently and without objection.

"Now, James.. all of you. These questions you ask are very valid. I do have some answers for you. But no time to discuss them fully at this moment, to be sure. You shall return to your home. This I make an elven promise. But for now, gather all you can. Blankets, food, clothing. Some weapons are in the outhouse. Crude but.. Alatar will not delay now he has found us. We make for the lake. Today."

Cormac may have been gentle but on this matter, he was very firm. The meeting dispersed.

CHAPTER FIFTEEN
THE LAKE

With bags stuffed with clothing, blankets, food and whatever utensils they could find, Cormac and the family departed the Ivywyrld Inn. Biggle and Baggle perched as usual, atop the roof, preening their feathers and babbling in gull-speak about what was for lunch. Cormac had turned and looked up at the seabirds "Will you fly for us, my fine friends?" He bowed.

The gulls both returned the bow, cawed their agreement. Stamped their feet and shook their bodies in preparation. It looked comedic, but it was very necessary preparation to the gulls. Ramona and Jude looked at each other and giggled playfully, which turned into laughter. But they were thankful and had become very fond of their new friends. The gulls were not upset. Quite the opposite. If they raised a smile in these circumstances, then they considered it a small victory. They cocked their heads to one side and chattered back at the two youngsters.

"What are they saying Cormac?" Asked Ramona.

"To my limited knowledge of gull-speak, young lady, they are saying you are both.. very cheeky, or words to that effect.." Cormac flushed and chuckled at the gulls.

"They will let your mischief pass, as they are fond of you."

Jude looked suitably embarassed. "Uh-oh. We didnt mean to upset them Cormac, will you tell them we are grateful for all they are doing."

"They already know that Jude. Where would we all be without a sense of humour? After all, laughter releases feel good endorphins, which leads to energy and alertness. Which we need in abundance to be sure. Let us move."

"To be sure Cormac." Giggled Ramona.

The gulls cackled their approval. Jude hid his face in his hands. Cormac rolled his eyes skyward in mock despair. He felt real warmth in this rag-tag outfit and allowed himself a smile at the fun and games.

Ruth and James had decided to sit on the lawn eating apples from the tree, while the youngsters talked with Cormac and learnt a bit of gull-speak. James threw his apple core onto the garden. Sensing a retort from his wife he said "Its not litter. A fox or a badger or even a blackbird will think its.."

"Its birthday?" Ruth intervened, smiling.

"You say that every time James. I'll let it slide. Real rubbish goes in the bin please. I don't care what the situation is. Values are important."

"Oh blimey kids. She's lecturing me. That means she's feeling better."

Ruth laughed "Shut up you silly little man." and she playfully pushed James over. She creased up laughing at her husband rolling round on the grass.

"Don't give up the day job dad. You can't act!" Shouted Jude.

"To be sure, dude James. A poor actor would you make. Very poor Indeed." added Cormac, trying to keep a serious face.

"See kids, see what I put up with? Your mother is a tyrant, and you Cormac, a friend.. I expected better from you!" James clowned for the group.

"I thought we were the kids, dad? Laughed Jude.

"Well I'm a sixteen year old, from being a baby, apparently." Chirped Ramona. "I'm handling this really well dont you think father dearest?"

"Oh Ramona. My wonderful daughter. Is there no end to your talents?" James chuckled away, but he hid sadness inside at the growth acceleration his beloved daughter was going through. He had hidden his inner heartbreak at this rapid transition that his 'Mona was just dealing with. Ramona still smiled though and jumped up. Then she ran, sprang into the air, did a triple somersault and landed perfectly.

"Don't worry. Lets go dad."

"At last, some common sense." Said the elf pensively.

"Wow though Cormac.." Said Ruth. "My daughter the gymnast!"

"Nah, just a wizard, mother." Ramona had a glint in her eye. "I'm still learning my trade though, so we'll do this together. Right gulls?" She glanced up as the feathery couple took off. The black-backed gulls swooped low over their heads and then soared high into the sky.

"They'll be our eyes and ears while we make for the lake. Stay out of the lanes. Walk in the scrub, stay alert." Cormac had become businesslike. Someone had to!

"No shouting. If any Takers should appear, let each other know immediately, and quietly. Now, come on."

With the fun and games over for now, the group gathered their belongings and set off briskly. The Takers tower had been left heavily guarded. The prisoners given basic rations. Alatar swigged his life-force liquid from the pewter goblet. His eyes glowed red underneath his hood. He would need another batch making up soon. Best to summon the druid from his quarters. But that could wait for now. He enlisted five of his highest trained Takers. He would normally have Cacodem with him. But his captain had failed and so, must learn.

Domacec, formerly Cacodem, now slept. He had revealed himself to the other prisoners for what he was, and had become. Initially, they had stayed away. Shrank back. Some were still very angry. He was a Taker. But as the mist of the liquid cleared. He shed tears. Spoke of a life. A wife named Bisera. A thriving town and of towns and hamlets beyond. His memory still cloudy. He spoke of masses of people, being rounded up and herded like cattle. The strong ones were given the liquid and not seen again. The weaker were slung into these catacombs. Others were slain in a cruel example. Alatar must have come from somewhere. Some other realm. He must have family? Domacec slept on. Tossing and turning. Whimpering.

Alatar cared not. Domacec deserved to suffer for his failings. His five wraiths readied themselves, as goblets of the steaming juice were passed down the counsel table. The drink was drained and more eyes glowed red. Alatar rose. Nodded at his group and stood. Hovering.

"To the banshee then. We do not return without her."

The wrought-iron gates clanked open and the Takers floated off soundlessly into the misty forest.

CHAPTER SIXTEEN
MAHREUBEN

It was a simple dwelling. Tucked away into the cliffside, off the coastal path. A good trek from the tower. Tranquil, you might have said, in better days. A darkened, crescent shaped cove. Well hidden. A small arched entrance and a flickering orange glow were all that betrayed its existence. A dank cave life for anyone. Let alone a stricken Princess. Seals kept their distance from the rocks around here. Terns and guillemots would fish elsewhere. Embittered, she now was. Reclusiveness and forced isolation had made her begin to wonder if she was indeed a banshee, as Alatar had told the populace.

Sea spray whooshed off the sheer cliff face. Waves crashed as the tide came in ferociously on this bleak night. A disused lighthouse stood offshore. Frozen in its own era. Exuding residual energy from another timeline. Some things did not seem to know where they belonged in these parts. Mahreuben ate in silence. Sat propped up against the wall. Fiery shadows danced. It had been so long since she had entered isolation and withdrawn from any contact with the outside world. A year or two? A decade?

Mahreuben did not know. She had stopped caring. No, she just did not know she cared, buried as it was under a defensive shell due to the cruelty she had been subjected to. Her wailing could be heard for miles around on a dark night. Folk would not want to be out alone hearing her blood-curdling screams of heartbreak. Since Uzaleus had disappeared from her life, her heart had grown cold, angry and vengeful. She finished her tepid seafood broth and walked to the cave mouth. Drizzle, salty spray and the howling of nearby hungry creatures. Sirens perhaps.

"Uzaleus, my love. Where did you really go?"

A tear rolled down her cheek. Her long, lank whitened hair, hid away a very beautiful face. Now muddied and weathered. Battle scarred. The worst of it was, she had been driven from the towns as a witch. Accused of taking her Prince's life. At one time Uzaleus and Mahreuben were the golden couple of these realms. She a Princess. He, the Prince and protector of the good realms folk.

When the dark times came and the people sought out Uzaleus for counsel, he had gone. Or had he been taken in a ruse? Doubt crept in, because of Alatar's web of lies. Mahreuben, it was said, had blood on her hands. She was judged. Her choice was to flee or she would be burnt. She pleaded. Spoke of shapes. Red, glowing orbs, hissing orc-like things, kidnap. Drifting faceless cloaks. A powerful new force that they had to stop early. Mahreuben was deemed mad and run out of town. She was not mad. Only villified wrongly. But now, hidden in this rock home, lank and haggard, she felt she had become the thing they believed she was. Time and unwanted solitude can make you believe. Had she killed Uzaleus?

"No. I am certain." She said this aloud as though to reaffirm her innocence. She would do anything to bring Uzaleus back to her poor cold heart.

Alatar breezed to a halt on the tops. Turning to his entourage. "We are close. I smell the banshee. The witch, Mahreuben."

Murmuring amongst the Takers. "The cave in the inlet. See the fire? That is where she dwells."

One of Alatar's guard, Tanwyn, spoke. "What will you tell the banshee, my leader?"

The leader's eyes glowed. He emitted a low, gravelly laugh.

"I will tell her, Tanwyn, that this interfering wizard, Ramona, took her precious Prince away, just as I was planning to release her. This new, dangerous sorceress that I was trying to protect them all from, has imprisoned him. I will tell her that only I can prove her innocence, only I can safely return her to the realms with a guarantee of safety and that only I can give her back Uzaleus.. And only if she rids us of this experiment named Ramona."

"Perfect, my leader. If the banshee succeeds?"

"Tanwyn, when, she succeeds, she may rejoin her precious Uzaleus and be reunited with him.. In the cells, feeding on gruel. A belated honeymoon gift." Alatar made a sickly grin, amused at his own vision.

"Enough. We move."

The Takers glided across the gorse laden paths in dewy mist until halting at the clifftop. An orange glow from the small fire within acted as a homing beacon to Alatar's keen eyes. They hovered close to the cave entrance.

"Mahreuben! Banshee. Come forward. It is I, Alatar. Come now, no tricks. Help me and I will give you Uzaleus." At the mention of Uzaleus, from the cave came a scream borne from the bottom of her gut, not the whimper of a petite little Princess. It was complete heartbreak. It would turn any mortal to stone.

CHAPTER SEVENTEEN
FREEDOM HOUR

At the old royal tower, the atmosphere was for once, relaxed, for the Takers at least. Heavily guarded and left in the hands of Alatar's high counsellor, Elphinias. He had his strict instructions. Elphinias had seen how dispensable Alatar's devotees could be. Very little in fact, was known of the odd, skulking Elphinias.

No reprieval had been passed for the captain, Cacodem. Who still was to be kept in the jails with the prisoners until Alatar's return. The minions, knowing no better, went about their tasks like robots. The higher ranked guard issued orders. The lower, carried them out. Although the tower was run thoroughly and methodically, Alatar's temporary absence had boosted the spirits of his followers. The Takers still did what they needed to do. Still heeded Alatar's manifesto. Still believed in their share in the pot of gold at the end of his rainbow.

But they felt lighter. If they had known what happiness was, then you could almost say they felt it. Alatar was no fool. He knew they would be glad of respite. He did not care, as long as those drug addled servants did his bidding. All expendable. All punishable, later. Now, Elphinias and a throng of Takers approached the jail. A brief murmured conversation took place with the lead guards.

"Any deaths, fevers, rebels? No? Good."

The cells were unlocked one by one. The prisoners led out slowly in two's. Heads bowed. Eyes blinking at the sudden exposure to daylight. Their hands were bound and legs shackled. Though they had enough give to allow them to walk and stretch. A loud siren pierced the silence. Followed by a shrill voice coming through a loud hailer.

"Freedom hour!"

Hundreds of prisoners were led into the courtyard. Guards on all sides. The siren blared again, piercing. White noise now though, to a seasoned captive.

"Walk!"

So, they were shunted and poked and prodded by the guards into the centre of the barracks and there they began to walk as briskly as they could around the circumference of the grounds. Any stragglers were subjected to the red whip. More burning, electrical stinging punishment. So even the weary pushed themselves. A handsome, regal looking man, grimaced as his group were stopped and ordered to do push ups, stretches and rock lifting. The regal looking man spoke.

"For pity's sake. We need food, water, rest. You ask too much. Alatar will pay for his treatment of these folk. You are poisoned. All of you. Can you not see?"

A hooded figure, sinister looking eyes glowing under a shroud, produced the red whip and lashed the protester to the floor with a sizzling blow, sparks emitting from the electrified rope. "Hold your tongue Uzaleus. Your title holds no sway here. Be silent. And be thankful for the daylight. Food will be dispersed after excercise." The Taker, twirled the whip menacingly.

"Food? Food you say, Elphinias? What you give us would not sustain a youngling elf for half a day. The water? Diseased I would think. But we must drink it, or die anyway. You won't rule the realms this way, Taker. Do you think you can seize and imprison and hold every town? You are as deluded as your leader, Elphinias. No souls of your own. Bowing and scraping to a maniac so as to preserve your own grim existence for one more day."

Elphinias snarled.

"Silence Uzaleus. Enough blabbering. You will be quiet." The huge, mysterious chief aide shrieked and raised the whip. Again lashing Uzaleus to the floor. The Prince writhed in pain. Bloodied but unbowed.

"Any more Uzaleus, and your punishment shall be more severe. You are only alive because Alatar wishes for you to be reunited with your pathetic banshee." A grin spread across the hidden features of Elphinias.

"Mahreuben? You leave her alone. You let her be. She has suffered enough."

"Uzaleus. You fool. She is entering a deal with our leader as we speak. Your Princess is going to be of great service to our cause. First, she will help us eradicate this Ramona creature and her little family. Then we have promised her a grand reunion with her Prince. You, Uzaleus".

Elphinias was taking great delight in this role of tormentor.

"She thinks me dead, Elphinias. Do not hurt her. She has become a recluse because of your lunatic leader. Let her be."

"Pleading now, Uzaleus? Too late. She will come. Here. To see that you live. And then she will carry out her orders. Bitterness and isolation have given her powers. Heartbreak has made her strong. With this power harnessed and nourished by Alatar, she will help destroy this Ramona creature, her family and any chance of the realms overthrowing us will be extinguished.

Then you can be reunited together. Rotting in the catacombs. Now get up. Prince."

Someone had been watching this unfold. Staying quiet. Walking behind. Listening as best he could. Perhaps the Prince Uzaleus could help. Awoken from the mist of the steaming liquid. Thrown into a cell with humans. Laughed at as a failure. Now almost coherent again. He would continue to play the role of Cacodem for his own plan.

'If I can get into the same cell as Uzaleus, perhaps we may talk. Perhaps we can find an opportunity.' Domacec. Cacodem, to the Takers, carried on walking. Lest he feel the red whip too.

CHAPTER EIGHTEEN
ARRIVAL

At the top of a lush green hill overlooking Whitsomin lake, the group rested for a short time.

"Well my friends. Will you look at that view? Magnificent to be sure." Cormac glowed with pride and exuded happiness upon the sighting of his home. The little elf checked himself though.

"Ramona, all of you, I am sorry we had to leave your home. I just do not think it safe to stay there. If the Takers were to send another wave.." He tailed off.

Ruth nodded "We understand Cormac. It was hardly home to us. It was just familiar. Like it was from a previous life. A bit of stability in all of this chaos."

"Nothing shocks me about this life anymore. Maybe we did live a parallel one." Added James.

The elf was empathetic with the family. "Upheaval to be sure. Unfair upheaval."

Ramona, sat on a sun-baked, red rock and sipped some water.

"You know, Cormac, Its been so crazy. Really, I'm not sure what is happening. Mum and dad took me on holiday as a baby. Now I am a young wizard-to-be. When I stop, its just hard to get my head around. When I wake up, I worry how old I'm going to be. You know?"

The elf smiled soberly.

"This I understand, Ramona. I told you I would try and explain. Firstly, we had to leave the Ivywyrld Inn. Shortly, we will descend to the woodland beside the lake of Whitsomin. There, you will meet more of my folk. James, you spoke of parallels. I myself, believe the universe selects certain people for certain situations. You were returning from holiday. Lost at night. I believe that when you had your accident, that the 'you' of this realm, felt it. It stung you into action. To leave the inn and search for your wife and child. As any doting husband and father would.

Ruth, as any loving wife and mother would, ran for help. Finding you James. Hooded and mysterious. I believe this was the beginning of a transition. As for living here before? I believe on becoming lost, that you somehow stumbled upon an alternative timeline. I believe that you could have inhabited the old inn and moved here. New beginnings. Away from your old town life. Seeking tranquility. We are faced with decisions and when we go one way, I believe our souls can still skew off in another. I think your timelines became jumbled."

James stood up, trying to ingest Cormacs synopsis.

"Well, Cormac. I would be inclined to say unbelievable, but given what has happened.. But what about Ramona's.."

"Growth acceleration?" Cormac interjected before James could finish.

"Yes, preordained by whom we call the ethereal, guardians I believe. She needed her parents as young, strong guides. This is why I believe you have not aged. And also, Ramona, to allay your fears.. This is why I believe that from now on, you will grow at a more normal, natural and.. well.. human rate."

Ramona exhaled. Relief spread across her face. Ruth made to say something. Again, Cormac, sensing the next question and interjected.

"Jude. Living on the streets. Watching the towns and realms become quiet, erased. Jude, I believe you were simply existing. Waiting in this limbo state, for your family to join you. All so surreal and eerie for you. It is commendable you came through. To, catch the rest of you up, as it were. When you upped and set off for the inn, I believe you had this in your subconscious. A knowledge of when to move.. where to go."

Jude listened intently. As did all of the family.

"And so, Cormac?" motioned Jude.

"And so. Right now, you are united as a family. All how you were meant to be. Close knit. Young. Intelligent and strong. With a dash of magic."

"We need to know more Cormac. This is helping us to understand." Said Ruth.

"I understand Ruth. These are just my theories. Though I will say I am well read and have seen many things in my time. So much to explain and to work out. And work this out we will. But we must move now." Cormac stood, picking up bags.

"Some food, herbal tea and sleep I think." He set off walking.

The family exchanged glances, absorbing more of this puzzling back story, and followed. The gulls, perched in a large tree, finished their titbits and soared into the pink evening sky.

Chapter Nineteen
The Deal

"Come forward banshee. Step out of the shadows woman. Hear my offer." Alatar drifted ominously to the mouth of the cave, his guard circling behind him. Mahreuben stood at the entrance now. Light was fading.

"Here he is then, the brave Alatar. The liar. Offer? What can you offer me, Taker? More lies, deception?" She strode into the open moonlight and faced the new leader of the tower, not afraid. Staring him down.

"Alatar, the faceless wraith. Red eyed coward. Conqueror of the weak of mind, drinker of souls. You have drip fed your poison among the people of the realms. Driven me here. Lest I be burned as a witch by those drones you create, whom were once my people. My Prince has disappeared. Gone, without an explanation. I find this strange that it coincided with the manifestation of you, and your insects."

Mahreuben became angry. More urgent.

"Where is my Uzaleus? You are vermin. You are a plague." Mahreuben spewed her words at the Takers.

A sudden flash of red light, struck the banished Princess in the midriff, knocking her to her knees.

"Hold your tongue, witch. You are in no position to dictate."

A misty smoke, emanated from Alatar's spindly fingertips.

"You will do well to shut your screeching mouth. Or not only will you not see Uzaleus again, you will also be tried and convicted for his murder, as outlined when we allowed you to live. Your little Prince and his rabble are safe enough. Only no longer a hindrance to the new order of things. But, alive.. In a fashion."

Mahreuben got to her feet. Brittle. Tired. Alatar gave her a cursory glance of mock pity.

"You were once so beautiful, Princess Mahreuben. How would it be, if I were to clear your name? To restore the faith of the realms in your wholesome goodness?" An unnatural smile curled about the barely visible features of the leader.

"Well, lady?"

Mahreuben faced Alatar, now emerged fully from her cave dwelling.

"There are no realms anymore. And you know why, Alatar. Because you and your virus have swept over them as surely as molten lava. Eradicating us. Spreading lies. Building these unthinking armies. Taking what you desire and disposing of the rest as you see fit. Why should I trust you? What is it I can do for you that you cannot do for yourself?"

She fixed him with a quizzical glare. He had pricked her interest as much as she despised the creature.

"You, Mahreuben, have visionary abilities. You see things. You can prophecize. You can foresee. You can help me stop whom I need to stop."

"The girl wizard?" Spoke Mahreuben.

"Yes, I have seen her. I know of her capability. Brave. I had hoped she would come. Afraid of a girl and her out of time family. Poor Alatar."

Alatar whirled and raised his hands again. Red sparks crackled threateningly.

"Do not mock me woman, or I will blow you into the sea. There, you can 'hope', all you like. I want you to come back with me to the tower. I want you to tell me where this girl is. Where she came from.

How to combat her instinctive magic. She has already dissolved nine of my guard and outwitted my captain."

"Yes. I saw Alatar. A strong young wizard. Though she knows not the full extent of her power. The chosen one. The ethereal have selected wisely. Chosen her, to rid the realms of parasites. Of you, Alatar".

Alatar let Mahreuben have her moment. After all, he had kidnapped Uzaleus and fabricated a lie about his death being at the hands of his beloved Princess. All to create more panic within the realms. To make it easier to manipulate and imprison the people. They turned on the Princess and she fled.

Mahreuben continued.

"You see Ramona as a threat perhaps, Alatar? An unknown quantity. And this is why you have need of me. Yet I have no quarrel with this girl and her family, Taker."

Alatar was seething now.

"Then you will have quarrel with me, Princess!" Another volley of red flame splayed Mahreuben against the cave wall. Beaten. She slid down to a heap on the floor. Alatar roared, a defiant cry of anger that resonated around the cave mouth like a sonic boom.

"You have had your chance. Death by the sea it shall be then, Princess." Alatar began to chant unfathomable incantations.

Clouds broiled, there was thunder. Humidity, static electricity. Red lightening bolts shot at the cave mouth, bringing an avalanche of rocks from the clifftop. The cave collapsed and was buried in flame and stone. Mahreuben gasped, dived and rolled. Landing at the feet of the leader.

"I will come."

"I know you will. No more games then, wretch. Come. When the girl is gone, you can have back your beloved Prince and your reputation. I will give a treaty. You and Uzaleus and your good folk shall be free. In a fashion. Refuse and you all die."

Mahreuben stood up, ragged and weak. Tears rolled down her face. "Please. No more cruelty. You must feel something in that bleak heart of yours, somewhere? Yes Alatar, yes I will obey." Her prettiness was hidden under layers of mud and grime.

"There will be no more harm to my Prince and his folk? You will reunite us and let us leave? I have waited so long. Been broken, made so hardened, bitter." She looked beaten. Ready to make this deal. Alatar, intended to harness her yearning for Uzaleus, to his own ends.

"As long as your folk interfere no further with my project. You will live, Mahreuben. And yes, also your precious Uzaleus."

"Then I shall come, Alatar. I shall lead you to the girl. And reveal her weaknesses."

Alatars eyes glowed red fire.

"You will indeed banshee. For you have no choice."

The Takers circled Mahreuben. Her arms and legs were bound by the red shackles.

"Enough of this." The leader turned from the clifftop. Waves crashing in the twilight.

"Back to the tower."

Mahreuben dragged along. Wracked in pain and torment. Thinking blindly of the Prince. Her agony, partially numbed by this flicker of hope, at any price. She would perhaps give Alatar this Ramona in exchange for her freedom, and that of Uzaleus and his folk.

But she would hold a little back. For as she had said, she had no quarrel with this girl and her family.

CHAPTER TWENTY
RESTED AND READY

The family slept. It was the most fitful of sleeps that any of them had had in quite some time. Much needed and with no disagreements, they had simply followed Cormac's lead. Jude in particular. Their lost son. Living in the towns, snatching damp, cold moments of slumber wherever he could, before being moved on as a beggar. Now he slept blissfully, gratefully. For his life had already seen hardship as he waited, homeless, for time to catch up. Praying for his family to appear.

A huddle of elves had greeted the small party and led them into the woodland, nicely off the beaten track. On arrival at the elven scrubland, by Whitsomin lake, where grebes and moorhens chugged up and down. Cormac had had his folk make up food and a hot, herbal sleep beverage for his four weary companions. He had asked Finola, his lifelong friend, to make the hot drink a little more potent than she usually would. The food was gratefully eaten and the drink savoured for its relaxing qualities. Too tired now for the usual good natured chatter, Ramona said very little, save to thank Finola and the other elves for the welcome hospitality.

Cormac had showed her, James, Ruth and Jude to a shelter, made from branches, bracken and twine. Inside, they clambered under warm, woven blankets, thanking the elves after only the briefest of introductions from Cormac. He was happy to be back among his people, albeit a smaller band, after many elves had been taken while out in the realms on their wanderings.

A bittersweet homecoming. But home all the same. Sensing Finola had wanted to ask questions, Cormac sat with her and a few of the elves in a small circle by a roaring and welcoming fire.

"Better to let them sleep Finola. You see how exhausted they are. Constantly running. Like our folk. Hiding and moving, moving and hiding. No way to live, to be sure." he exclaimed.

Cormac went on to describe to Finola and the elves, all he knew and had seen since he had come across first James and then Ruth and the baby at the Ivywyrld Inn. He spoke of what he described as disrupted timelines and of transitions, Ramona's changing, and of her instinctive magical defence of the inn. The shredding into dust of nine of the Takers.

"This is why I brought them here Finola. The Ivywyrld Inn is no longer a safe place. They are drained, in mind if not body. Now hunted by them, I would wager it, to be sure. Despite Ramona's abilities. She has not yet honed her many skills. They will keep coming. Here, even, where we are well hidden. They will search."

Cormac felt a sudden twinge of sadness at the thought.

"Your news is not unexpected Cormac my friend." replied Finola, sipping at her herbal drink.

"Since you left to find the poor girl and her family, we have seen many Takers skirting our woods. We lie low and keep quiet. So far, none have come into our hides. But moving and hiding we too, have been, to be sure." Finola sighed.

"We must let them sleep as you say. Help each other. We also must sleep Cormac, for tomorrow.."

Cormac was musing.

"Tomorrow, my dear, I think we must get a closer look at what is happening at the tower. I have seen on my earlier travels what is happening. I heard their counsel. Saw the liquid they drank. Liquid of souls. Building they are, Finola." Cormac was animated, eyes far away as though reliving his journey.

"They are harvesting, and I do not mean crops. People. To be sure."
Finola and the other elves around the camp looked stricken.

"They take people. Humans and elves. I do not think they care
whom. The weak are thrown into jails. The stronger.. Potions and
concoctions they are given. They lose their minds and personalities.
Their eyes turn red, like Alatar's himself. They become these Takers. A
manufactured army is being built. Multiplying. Seizing our towns and
hamlets. For a purpose I dare not imagine. A regime he wants.
Totalitarian. With himself as leader. Tomorrow, I go there again. I will
not ask of you to follow. But if some of you feel you wish to come, to
help us find some way in, some way of stopping or even slowing this
madness, then glad of you, I will be. No elf, nor this family, nor human,
should be forever running. I for one, seek our freedom restored."

Cormac raised his goblet. "To the return of peace, my friends."

The elves stood and charged their own tankards. "The return of
peace."

The fire crackled and as night watchers sat on guard, the others
made for bed. The two gulls huddled for warmth after gratefully
sharing a fried fish given by an inquisitive youngling elf. Their
scouting skills would be needed again.

Ramona dreamed. She saw her birth home at Gardelwyn. A cot,
softly sung lullabies. A doting mother and father. Feeling snug and
warm and cared for. Then, the sun and the waves of the sea. A sweet
and happy gurgling baby. Then, a distant voice. A figure, hooded. A
sadness in his kind, whispery warm tone.

"I bring you here with a heavy heart Ramona. I had not wanted
this acceleration. We need you. You will stop Alatar. You are chosen.
We love you as though our own. We know you are the only one. With
the realms help, you will end him. Then, you can go home."

Ualdin of the ethereal had visited her dream.

CHAPTER TWENTY ONE
A STRANGE DUO UNITE

After what was known as freedom hour, the prisoners were marched back towards the gloomy cells. Deemed sufficiently exercised, albeit bound and chained. The routine was to fling them back into the cold gloom of the jail. Domacec had remained a keen observer during today's hour away from confinement. He was under no suspicion from the guards as they were frog-marched back to their dreary dens. He was prodded and poked with staffs and swords and largely mocked by the Takers for his new-found shame as a failure. Now, he was just another prisoner.

"Let me be. I am your captain. Alatar shall hear of this."

Domacec forced his recovering eyes to flare angrily, playing up the role of Cacodem. Staring the guards down menacingly. Despite the orders to keep him under lock and key while Alatar was out seeking the banshee. Captain Cacodem was still Alatar's trusted aide to the guard until it was confirmed otherwise.

The taunting died down. Alatar may yet reinstate Cacodem after his incarceration. No Taker wanted to inflict injury or render Cacodem useless, for fear of taking his place in a cell.. Or worse. Some Takers had been electrocuted by his misused magic in recent times. An example of Alatar and his counsel's disregard for other lives. Even of their own followers.

Up ahead, Prince Uzaleus was being pushed back into confinement with a cluster of other prisoners. Domacec walked faster. Pulled up his hood and melted into the groups, still being prodded and shoved, but just another figure now amongst the throng. His eye was constantly trained on Uzaleus. As Domacec caught up, he managed to slip his group and tuck in between a few stragglers ahead.

"Get inside, speed up, inside now. All of you. No stopping."

Guards barked and grunted orders, herding the human and elf groups into the jails. These orc-like guards were known as the pure Takers. Not forced to join, they were firm followers of Alatar's new realm order from the outset and had little or no need for the mind control drug, other than morbid escapism. They were a different breed to the drugged or kidnapped Takers, cruel and sly.

One human prisoner, Ailbe, gasped as Domacec, Cacodem to everybody else, looked directly at him. Domacec's eyes switched from the Takers fiery red, to a humane green. Ailbe was wide-eyed. Domacec whispered to Ailbe.

"Say nothing. Trust in the process. I can help."

A look of astonishment crossed Ailbe's face as they were dumped into the cell. The same one as Uzaleus. Domacec had made it. Some had not. Some were just too weak and had not managed to keep up with the exercise. They were loaded unceremoniously onto crude wooden carts and taken up to the ramparts, led by the shady Elphinias, who was in temporary command and keen to impress his prowess upon Alatar. The guards began to bolt and lock cells. Then, the doom heralding loud hailer sounded from above.

"Prisoners of Alatar!.."

It was the voice of Elphinias, loud and harsh. Bellowing from the tower ramparts.

"Witness this. Those of you who do not meet life-force requirements, are of no use to this regime, and so shall be dispensed with accordingly. Raise your efforts. Be grateful. Or, this.."

Elphinias nodded at a long row of guards. The guards bowed as though receiving some silently communicated instruction. The prisoners below, raced to the front of their cells, clinging to the bars. Squinting to see what was happening above.

There on the ramparts, the weakened prisoners were taken off the carts and brutally manhandled onto huge, grim looking catapults. They pleaded, screamed, kicked and cried, but could not fight. They had heart, but no strength. Malnourished and starved of sleep. Six or eight at a time, were dumped into these primed, massive slings.

A few had managed to clamber out, pleading to their captors. They were pushed over the side to their deaths for their brave efforts by the heartless Takers guard. Below, from ground level, Prince Uzaleus, among others watched in horror. A hooded figure pushed through to stand next to him. The shrill voice of Elphinias barked again.

"Witness this evenings finest macabre entertainment, you sloths down below. This is where the dispensable go." Elphinias nodded to the guards whom lined up next to the catapults.

"Get them primed." Elphinias raised his right arm to the sky then brought it down quickly in a chopping swish.

"Release."

The guards pressed release levers and a hundred bodies, still clinging to life by a thread, were launched high into the grey skies, to rain into the sea way out over the plains. Such was the power of these huge mechanical tools. There would be no heroes here today.

"Good. Good." muttered Elphinias.

"You waifs below.." His voice again echoing round the grounds.

"Eat, drink, wash and sleep. Do not cross me. Let us hope not to have to do this again tomorrow." The imposing outline of Elphinias, stepped down, gesturing, and hissed something to the guards.

He could be seen from the ground by the prisoners, stunned at this cruel show, with no mercy given whatsoever. People in the jails wailed and cried for their families. Red whips were whirled about in mock threat by Takers and cracked at the bars, causing the survivors to shrink back. The new figure in the cell spoke quietly, but with purpose. "Do as Elphinias says." said Domacec to the small group around him.

"They will bring food and water soon. We must eat and drink. Keep silent. Conserve strength. Obey them. We will have a chance at escape. I know them and how they work."

Noticing the hooded newcomer whom had been stood by him during the macabre display, Uzaleus approached him.

"You are new to our group brother. What do you know of the Takers? And how do you think we may escape against these odds?"

Domacec pulled his hood down and looked at the Prince. "Greetings Uzaleus. I know, because I was one of them."

The whole cell fell silent, open mouthed. Uzaleus could only stare in disbelief at the newcomer. Eventually, a look of complete shock on his face, he managed to blurt out..

"Captain Cacodem. You?"

CHAPTER TWENTY TWO
MAHREUBEN IS BETRAYED

The tower was silent at nightfall, save for the howlings of mysterious nocturnal creatures. Following on from the shocking display of barbarism by Elphinias, whom was revelling in his role as Alatar's deputy leader. The cull of those weak captives had been a cruel motivation for the remaining prisoners to follow orders and not to question the regime of those with the glowing eyes.

Huddled in their dilapidated cell, warmed by only straw and torn shawls, bunched up close for any extra heat, were Uzaleus and now Cacodem. Domacec, in fact, as he had been named at birth. Along with Ailbe and a few of the other prisoners, Uzaleus had been dumbstruck to find his new cellmate was in fact Alatar's former Captain. Punished for failing to aprehend Ramona and her family at the Ivywyrld Inn, he had been flung into the over populated jail, like so many nameless others. 'The factory', as some would call it now.

Prisoners were either dispensed with, or you would never see their faces again once selected. More new recruits and obeyers to swell the growing ranks. Cacodem had been judged to be inept, unable to carry out a simple task with a party ten strong. Now, he had been left under charge of the guard while Alatar had taken matters on himself and rode to coastal pathways in search of Mahreuben, the so called murderous banshee.

During his withering spell in the jail however, Cacodem, stripped of duty, had been given none of the drink that the Takers called life-force liquid. Nobody had been briefed to redose him. He had been given water, grain and some kind of tepid porridge. No special treatment had been administered. During his time in these cells, Cacodem had dreamt. His burning stomach in knots. Foggy memories came to the forefront of his mind. 'I am Domacec.'

Could it be that the absence of this liquid was allowing him to remember who he was. A strange, scary detoxification? It was a slow process, but he was certain his full identity would become clear as the time passed. He felt the brain fog slowly clearing. He wanted his wife back, Bisera. He thought that this potion was given to subdue prisoners, to change them. To make them obedient and to take any name or order that was given to them. Henceforth the conveyor belt of prisoners and the emptying of towns, villages and hamlets within the realms with barely a whimper from the inhabitants. When the prison within the tower became full, they had now seen first hand how room was made for more. The weaker were gathered and dispensed of into the sea. It was questionable whether any survived. The Takers wanted only the strong.

Domacec had at least now weaved himself into the same cell as Uzaleus, the fallen Prince. Now, after much explaining and understandable initial rage from the Prince about why Domacec should be trusted. He had now seemingly done enough to convince Uzaleus that he wished to aid an escape. It would be a waiting game. Now, they slept as best they could. At the gate of the tower, the night guard stirred. They heard an approaching rumble outside the walls.

"Elphinias, awaken! We are returned with the witch of the caves. Hurry, you idle swine!"

It was Alatar and his entourage. Tanwyn to his immediate right. The other mysterious Takers, seemingly hovered above the ground. The air was humid with their now familiar murmuring and hissing. In tow and given no comfort during the journey back to the tower, was Mahreuben. Formerly Princess of these realms. Now dubbed the banshee and outcast, thanks to the mean stories concocted and drip-fed to the towns by Alatar's Takers.

She cut a forlorn, beaten looking figure. Out on her feet now with exhaustion. Her long and once shimmering and beautiful hair now lank and matted. Her white dress torn. Her head hung in defeat. Hiding her beautiful face, now mottled and palid with the ravages of an isolated cave existence. Her mania was welcomed by the Takers. This would prove to any doubters that she was in fact, quite mad. A wailing banshee indeed. Trouble.

"Elphinias I say!" Alatar bellowed.

The peculiar deputy shuddered by the gate and nodded to the guards.

"Let them in."

Elphinias then turned and walked briskly to the table in the courtyard. Candles had been lit. The moon was full and the sky, midnight blue. He lifted a pewter goblet of the steaming liquid to his thinned lips and drank. He wanted the fortifying shield of the potion to face his leader this night. Something hateful yet dutiful, fostered in Elphinias. But now was not the time. He would watch Alatar carefully.

And so, on re-entering his stolen empire, Alatar drifted towards the table. Mahreuben shoved along by the dulled minions. Sore and still bound by red, electrified shackles.

"Welcome back leader. I See you have her with you. I knew you would find her my young friend." Elphinias passed a goblet of the drink to Alatar. He gulped it down.

"You do not need to feign pleasantries with me Elphinias. All I need to know is that all is as it should be."

"All is well leader. The prisoners sleep. Some of the weak had to be.. removed. We have news from our scouts that a new batch of strong men, women and some useful elves have been captured to the west. They will be good additions.. When converted."

Elphinias seemed quite smug with his recent efforts. Alatar simply nodded.

"No escapees?"

"None, master."

"Good, and of Cacodem?"

Elphinias half-smile disappeared.

"I assume he sleeps, Alatar. He was of no trouble during your absence. He is weak. He is paying for his inept work."

"Assume, Elphinias?" Alatar's eyes narrowed, fixing Elphinias with a scrutinizing, silent gaze. Elphinias was disconcerted, uncomfortable.

"He is in the jail, my leader. Licking his wounds."

"Good. I will deal with him soon enough."

Alatar turned his attention and grabbed at Mahreuben.

"Now my lady. You will sit. For refreshment."

The Princess eyes widened as Tanwyn, under instruction, poured liquid into a pewter goblet and pushed it towards her lips.

"No. NO! Alatar. I will not drink. You have cast me out to a cave, you have blackened my name. Labelled me a banshee. You have taken away my love. You have dampened my soul. Enough. I will not drink." She struggled and wriggled. Kicking out at Tanwyn.

"You will find us this.. Ramona as you said?" The leader quizzed Mahreuben.

"Yes. Yes. I will find her, as I promised. Now make good on your promise to me. Bring me my love. Bring me Uzaleus."

Mahreuben's eyes pleaded with her captor.

"You shall join Uzaleus. When you locate the girl wizard. Use your powers of foresight, banshee, find her."

Alatar motioned to Tanwyn to use force to administer the drink. Mahreuben struggled, spluttering, and eventually swallowing the life-force liquid. She had no choice, she had no resistance. The drink settled in her stomach. It felt fiery, it felt ugly. It burned. She looked up at Alatar.

"Wretch. What have you done? I gave you my word. What have you done?" Her eyes began to change, to a faint red.

"You are evil itself. I will resist."

Alatar's lips curled into a smile.

"Insurance, witch, and now.. You will find Ramona."

CHAPTER TWENTY THREE
MAHREUBEN APPEARS AND JUDE IS GONE

Since the elven sleep drink and the warmth of the homely shelters, Ramona and her family had slept soundly for hours untroubled, thanks to Finola's elixir. Dreamless and snug. Worries suspended by deep rest. Save for one, Jude. The lost son. Since the apparent timeshift had affected him greatly, he had felt happy and accepted. He had been ecstatic to find his family. But he had always had trouble accepting this time lag. This dimensional meddling. He mistily recalled the family home.

Waking alone in an empty shell of a house. Abandoned, thrown out as a squatter. Unrecognised by neighbours. Ramona, mum, dad. All vanished. Then, homelessness. He had awoken early. Silently angry, rare for him. He wanted to find this bringer of carnage. The leader of these Takers. He wanted to confront this Alatar. To ask him, why his family? Why had he done this? Why, if so powerful, did this Alatar, need to build armies of servants from innocent people?

He had slipped out of the shelter in silence. Putting in his backpack some water, a small amount of food, his blanket and an elven dagger. He was fleet footed and the elven night watchmen were nodding to sleep by the glowing embers of a dwindling fire. He knew the Ivywyrld Inn was the key. He headed there. There was unfinished magic at that place, he felt. Where his sister had first used her raw power in reaction to the Takers attempts to kidnap them. He remembered the way. He had found them before.

Hours and hours passed, but this was nothing to this well travelled young man. He found the Ivywyrld Inn. Once Jude had this mindset, there was no point reasoning with him. They were all asleep anyway. Once again the dilapidated Ivywyrld Inn lay abandoned, where until recently, the family had a brief happy spell there with Cormac the elf. Another home taken from him. Taken by Takers. He carried on up the lanes. Something else was on his mind. The car. His father had spoken of the accident. Veering off the oily road. A hulking, red eyed spectre stood in the lane. Then the swerve. There it was now, around the corner the family car. Baby clothes, maps, flasks and all manner of things, strewn over the seats. Signs of a quick departure.

Jude used every ounce of his strength to push the car back onto all four wheels, it having lain slanted on its side. Panting, he got in the drivers seat. The keys were still in the ignition. The engine revved.

'She's still good.'

Jude felt a surge of adrenaline go through his body. It enhanced his anger towards this manic sorcerer. The plans for retribution were too slow. They were insipid. Alatar needed taking down now. Not 'At some point'. Not after meetings and careful consideration. It had to be now.

In the early moonlight of dawn, Jude stood on top of the car roof and roared at the sky.

"I'm coming for you. You messed with our timeline. You messed with me. You hurt my family. I'm coming for you Alatar!" Jude leapt down and got in the car.

In the elven woods, near Whitsomin lake, a wispy shape materialised above the sleeping shelter. "Ramona.. Ramona.." A gentle, quiet and kind voice came from above the little hut. As though carried on a faint breeze. Meant only for the young wizard. She stirred. Not yet noticing Jude's absence. It was still quite dark and the relaxed breathing of her parents told her they were still asleep.

"Ramona, come outside. Do not be afraid when you see me. The dark one is trying to change me."

Ramona crept outside and on top of the shelter was a bedraggled, careworn outline of a woman. Beauty buried under pain. Ramona put her hands over her mouth to stop a scream escaping, such was her initial shock. For the woman was not in physical form, but in visitation.

"I am Mahreuben, Ramona. You will hear tales of me, concocted stories, a banshee they called me. Alatar has me now, but mine is the power of foresight. So I come before his potion takes hold. He tries to change me with the liquid. He asks me to find you, to take you to him. I would not willingly aid him."

Mahreuben hovered, transparent, as the young wizard looked on.

"I was Princess of these realms, Ramona. My Uzaleus is also captive here, in their tower. The evil one tries to bargain with me. You, Ramona, and your family, in exchange for the reunification of my Prince and I. I do not believe him. I believe he will throw me to rot like the others, in these jails. He thinks me without sound mind. I was cast out to a cave existence by his followers. Called a witch. He declared me mad. Now he says he will restore my good name. In exchange for you. He sees you as his only threat. And with the strength and support of your family, he is scared you may stop him."

Ramona, open mouthed, rubbed her sleepy eyes and stared up at this hovering woman, thin, wearing old cloth, opaque.

"I want to stop him, Princess Mahreuben. I know I can. I am sure, but not sure how. I am very frightened inside. I grow so fast, yet my family do not change. Why?"

"Yours is the power of instict Ramona. This is why he fears you. For your magic is strong, unpredictable. This is why he wants you now. You age because the ethereal guardians of these realms chose you. Knew you were the one to defend and save us all. You will age no more rapidly now than any other. You are strong enough now. The spirits know this."

Mahreuben seemed so gentle and kind. It brought a sadness to Ramona to see her ghostly appearance. So beautiful, yet tired.

"How do you know all of this, Mahreuben?"

"Mine is the power of foresight my young one. This is why Alatar uses me as a conduit to find you. I will fight this mind bending liquid, but if you meet me, and I am changed, please, do not hate me. I only want my people returned to happiness. But he drip-feeds me this liquid to loosen my tongue. Please, wake the others. You must leave. I fear you will be discovered. You must flee. I have to go Ramona. He sends guards for me. Fight for us young wizard. Fight for us. We will meet soon enough. I know it."

Mahreuben began to fade from view, but as she did, Ramona heard one last whispering sentence..

"Then.. I can help them to send you home.."

For a full minute Ramona stood. Trying to take in this visitation. This magical place was becoming more and more real. She ducked back into the shelter to awaken her family.

"Jude, you won't belie.. Jude?"

He was gone.

Chapter Twenty Four
Alatar's Wrath

Alatar looked out of the huge, beautifully crafted bay window from his heavily guarded quarters at the top of the tower. Out to the open sea. The surface was calmer today. Alatar did not like calm. Today he had plans for the banshee, for the Prince, for Cacodem. For all of them. They were unpleasant plans. The repressive atmosphere that always seemed to prevail over and around the tower was bittersweet to him. For Alatar had not built this place.

He had, in his own untrue words, inherited it. It was what you would once have called elegant. Picturesque, pretty and scenic. It was now a grey stone fortress with a deep moat, a huge courtyard and jails had been built where workers living quarters once were. This is where the weak were put. The protesters, pugilists, royalists, the malnourished and those waiting against their will to be administered with the mind control drink. The queued.

Alatar had, on the face of it, just appeared. A sideshow to begin. Wandering with a small, yet growing following, around the townships.

Had he left his own home for other crimes committed? Did he just come into being via osmosis? Since then he had been making noise. Making himself seen and his name known. He declared the realms a fools paradise, run by dreamers and faerie folk, and had sewn seeds of doubt in some and feelings of unease and uncertainty and dislike in others.

He had split opinion. Some wondered if he was indeed a better choice to rule. Strong and not a dreamer. He was pleased. He did not care though, who thought what. Alatar was an ambitious creature with his own solid vision and was not to be stopped. Of this he was certain. He took in willing followers, promising riches. Such as the strange Elphinias. Another who seemed to just turn up in the inner realms. Previously unheard of. A power seeker himself, he revelled in his role as confidant and consultant. Elphinias, basked in his crumbs of clout.

He was a distant second to Alatar. Some of the Takers were not originally, willing followers. They were.. persuaded. Alatar pitched his grave concerns and fresh ideas wherever he and his guard roamed. A strong, cogent, yet caring leader was needed he said. Visions of a new organised realm. Tough, strong and totalitarian. His. What if other forces invaded? He would tell villagers. Outsiders with huge, strapping armies, looking for new lands to conquer and inhabit.

"What if you good, benevolent folk were driven from your homes by such an event? Such a real and very possible threat?"

Alatar did not bother to mention that he 'was' the threat. A minor detail.

"I have come from a place where there are such forces. And they will find these realms in time and they will want them for themselves. They will want the land and sadly, not you. To them, you are petty and unnecesssary. I have seen entire cities perish by such invasions. I offer you a real protection. A strong central tower with a uniformed and regimented guard. I offer you food, warmth, shelter. Safe in the knowledge that should any threat arise, that it will be extinguished. Like so.."

Alatar had raised both his arms skyward, looked his growing audience over, and bought his hands slashing down. Red bolts of fiery, electric-like lightning, shot over the heads of the crowd. Scything down an entire copse of tall trees, setting them burning. Destruction.

A proud hillside was crumbled into cinders, pebble and soil. Some ran. Some stood in mute shock at this sudden, violent display from the creature in black.

"There.. is your invasion.."

The trees burned and withered, birds scattered, and the crowd backed away. Panicked, scared. Yet transfixed. The hillside was razed level to a flattened heap of muck and grit. Alatar raised his arms above his head once again. The crowd were now frozen in fear and stood in a morbid fascination.

"Here.. is your protection.."

Down came his hands again in that slashing motion and in the sky above, the heavens opened. Torrential rain sluiced down. Extinguishing the fires almost immediately. Alatar pointed skyward.

"Stop!" He bellowed.

Unbelievably, to the folk of the realms, the rain ceased instantly. The fires were out. Steam rose now from the whole area. Warm steam. Suddenly, the sun came out.

"Now, you must observe." hissed Alatar. His eyes flared his now familiar red. The jittery people looked on. Green shoots were springing up from the ground. Saplings.

"The trees!" Cried an onlooker named Domacec. "They are regrown." Domacec paused, intrigued. He looked at Alatar, stood tall, dark and with his leering face, menacing. Despite his so-called offer of protection, onlookers were shaken.

"Why did you destroy them though, Alatar? Why should we join a man who tries to win us over with demonstrations like this? Why do you burn our ancient trees? You are a scaremonger."

As Domacec bravely spoke, stone and soil and gravel swirled and meshed together like a retracting hurricane. A reversal of time. The hillside was reforming as well now. Shaping and rising again like growth sped up.

"Powerful indeed. I can barely believe it." said Domacec pushing his way to the front of the stunned crowd of his folk.

"Alatar, I venture that it is you whom is the biggest threat to our realms and that you should pass peacefully and take your impressive sorcery and strange plans to other lands. We have no fight here. We are peaceful and no such invasion has ever come to pass in our land."

Alatar stared at this insolent villager, Domacec.

"It has now. Take him."

Alatar's guard wrestled Domacec away from the throngs of his people. A few villagers made to go to his aid. Alatar raised his arms aloft again, shaking his head in a disapproving, forboding manner at the restless crowd.

"I would not advise your encroachment."

The crowd backed off again. Domacec had been bound by glowing red cuffs and was held by several of this burly new guard.

Alatar gestured at the growing saplings and the reforming hillside.

"See how they grow again. Your idiot spokesman jumped in too soon. They are now stronger, larger, fresher. I offer you all this. Will elven bows and arrows fend off the threats? Faerie daggers then, to tackle monsters? Join me. It is time for change. The reality of this new dawn has not registered with your Prince and Princess and folk of pretty magic. The days of sunlit banquets and bluebell carpets are finished. Just as are you all, if you do not wake up and heed me. Your forest will be regrown by the morning. I will then return for you."

With that, Alatar and his growing guard drifted away, new followers among them, disappearing into a hazy mist. That was the day everything changed.

Domacec had been given the mind control drink and became captain. Alatar was pleased at his strength and aggression. At his change of heart, albeit enforced. The life-force liquid had been forced upon him and so, Cacodem, was born. Cacodem however, had now failed to kidnap Ramona and her family at the Ivywyrld Inn. Despite leading a guard of ten Takers. Now, he had been stripped of his captaincy and left to fend for dirty water and gruel in the cells like all the other weak links and deluded fools. Now Cacodem was dwelling in the same cell as Uzaleus. With the liquid wearing off during his prison time, he had become the man he was before. Domacec.

He would keep up the facade of Cacodem though, for it may prove useful if he could get back into the good books of Alatar. He hoped Elphinias was not sneaking around with his threats of catapulting more prisoners into the sea. After Uzaleus had berated Domacec for his part in the Takers destruction of the peaceful realms, he had seen that the former captain had been under the control of dark magic. The liquid. Now, Uzaleus believed him. He even pitied him. Though Domacec had asked him not to. Asking instead, to let him help plan an escape.

The two, along with Ailbe, another good realms man in the cells, had lain low. Been obedient and participated daily in freedom hour. They exercised and ate with no protest and acted with no suspicion. Uzaleus acted outwardly hostile to Domacec in front of the guard, even taking painful lashes, in the hope that this would keep up appearances for the sake of the watching Takers. Presently, Alatar and Elphinias appeared at the top of the tower. The guards hushed the prisoners. Wielding and cracking their whips until all fell silent.

"Prince Uzaleus! Prisoner of my rule. The anguished warrior. I bring you today, a special gift.."

Alatar's bellowing, resonated around the courtyard. Uzaleus gripped iron bars, straining to look upward. Alatar was motioning to Elphinias who went inside again, reappearing shortly after with a slender, weeping woman at his side.

"Here is your Princess. Look, Uzaleus, heartbroken man. Worry no more, she still lives, for now. Your pathetic banshee has returned."

Elphinias pushed Mahreuben to the edge of the turret, dangling her body over the side for all to see.

"Mahreuben. Oh Princess.."

Uzaleus thrashed against the bars, kicking out and punching at the guards through the gaps.

"You waste your energy Prince. Be still, or she goes in the catapult."

Uzaleus was whipped again and fell backwards. Domacec wanted desperately to help but could not blow his cover.

"Mahreuben, is the key to my divine power. All of you. Know this, she is locating a young wizard as we speak. A foolish girl, who wishes to rescue you all. A pitiful and fanciful fairytale I am afraid. Know this, Prince Uzaleus and any of you whom try to oppose. I hear the mutterings of your escape plans, fools. This banshee, your treacherous former Princess, is about to betray you all again, and bring to me the wizard who was to save you. Take a good look at your haggard Princess now, Uzaleus, oh mighty warrior!"

Elphinias yanked Mahreuben's head up for them to see and scraped the hair from her face. Her eyes now fully red, soulless. Uzaleus shrank back and slid down the wall to the floor. Head in hands. "No. My love, fight them. Fight the liquid.."

Then the strength went out of him and he passed out of exhaustion from the beatings. At the top of the tower, Alatar sneered.

"The show is over. Take her back inside. Put her to work."

CHAPTER TWENTY FIVE
CORMAC'S PLAN

"This is a worry, yes, a worry to be sure, Ramona. Your brother means to fight Alatar, of that I am positive. He has left in the night with no warning. I believe he carries more on his shoulders than he cares to let us know."

Cormac was pacing up and down while Ramona, Ruth and James sat on an old, fallen oak tree, listening intently, now the initial shock of Jude's disappearance was wearing off. Ramona got to her feet. "What do you mean Cormac? Carries more than he lets us know?"

The elf sat, sipping from a woodland tea, brought to him by the friendly, but concerened Finola. She passed them all hot drinks.

"Your brother was disconnected from you around the time of your inaugural holiday, Ramona. As the baby you were, and technically, still should be. For some reason, the muddled timelines meant that when you departed for Oakhampton with your parents, Jude was, there is no easy way to say this.. abandoned, or left feeling like he had been."

Tears welled up in Ruth's eyes and she buried her head into James shoulder. James held his wife close.

"Cormac, you are a good man. A good elf and you have helped us. Saved us even, but do you think that Jude really believes that we, as a family, would up and leave on a jolly old jaunt and leave him at home? As you say, abandoned? We were with our baby, at a log cabin, on a beach, walking, cooking, resting, sleeping. Being normal. Doing what happy little families do. It is as though to us, we were not aware we had a son. We feel tampered with. Intruded upon. Our memories feel altered, erased."

Cormac kept his own counsel and let James go on..

"When Jude arrived at the Ivywyrld Inn, we knew he was our son. Ramona's older brother. Returned to us. But do you know, Cormac? We were not conscious he had been taken. Its too much to take in my friend. I work on a nature reserve near Gardelwyn, with lakes and birds and fish, just like yours here. I am just a man. Look what this has done to my wife. Look at my fully grown child. She is meant to be a baby, Cormac. Now she is a wizard. Says who? She's my little girl!"

James had slipped back into ranting. Once again, Cormac let him vent.

"All this trying to save the realms from a ghoul, a maniac who wants to kill us all. A ghostly Princess appearing in visitation in the night. We should never have gone on that bloody holiday, Cormac, enough is enough. I give up this time."

James gently slipped from his wife's arms, stood up abruptly, kicked out at a rotting branch and walked a good few paces before resting his head on the side of the shelter in sheer frustration. Ramona made to go after her father but Cormac shook his head gently and motioned at her to stay.

"Let him be for a few moments, young one. Your father is a strong man. He wants to protect you all. He has taken a lot on board. You all have. Your mother especially, when she cradled you on the night of the accident. Her sheer will found the inn and James again. You were a baby, growing at a rapid rate. Ramona. You are resilient and aware now. You really are strong. You have coped admirably. I do not say this lightly, but you are allowed to vent. To lash out, to shout."

Ramona understood, but it still hurt to see her father upset. Cormac put a comforting arm around Ramona's shoulder. She was grateful for warm and friendly contact.

"It can and will pass. This is why Alatar fears you as an individual and all of you as a family. Borne of love. Love is something that Alatar cannot understand. Therefore he fears its power. He fears you. This is why he has captured the Princess. She is no banshee. She is the fair Mahreuben loved by all. I assure you that he has not fooled me."

Ramona listened to her wise and insightful friend. It made her mind feel quietened. The elf could see that they all needed to have a break. He continued to analyse with his rationale.

"I could join your father and Jude and go racing off in vengeful bloodlust, and justifiably so, to be sure, but we would all die. It is Alatar whom blackened the name of Mahreuben and banished her to a cave existence. We of the woods love our Princess and Uzaleus, our Prince. No matter what this manufactured army say or do. He wants to create a totalitarian regime. Look at his Takers, Ramona. Cloaked and faceless. Obeying and unthinking. Dead behind the eyes. Drifting under blackness. This is how he would like it to be everywhere. Why he pillages towns and villages. It is why others like Elphinias and Tanwyn willingly herald him. They found a leader whom held similar beliefs. Remember, Ramona, I went to the tower and saw first hand what goes on around that counsel table."

Cormac accepted some water from Ramona and finished his summary.

"We now know many of the Takers were unwilling and innocent. Forced to take this liquid. We know it exudes some sort of mind control. The longer this goes on, the more drones he creates and the stronger his tower guard becomes. I vote we make for the tower and find your brother. I hope we can intercept him before he gets there. His intentions are valiant and courageous, but I fear they are futile. James.. Will you come?"

Cormac looked over at James who was still listening, but gazing vacantly into space.

"I will come Cormac. I will not let my son down. Not again." James eyes cleared and a more positive look, a man ready to fight, spread across his face.

"I will come too." This was Ruth.

"Finola, you are very kind. She asks me to stay here and rest, but I cannot rest until my son is back with us, safe. I won't abandon him. I won't lose him again." Ruth smiled at Finola, whom returned the smile. The understanding of woman, communicated silently.

"Then that leaves just me." Ramona felt now, something must be done immediately.

"My brother found us, came through time. Homeless and underfed. He found us and stood with us. He defends us and loves us. Thank you Cormac, for everything you have done for my family. Thank you for standing with us." Ramona bowed to the elf. Cormac bowed in return.

"I stand for you Ramona and your family, for being dragged into this with no preparation or knowledge. I stand with you as you hone your skills of wizadry and learn your craft. I believe you were chosen by the ethereal of the realms, to be sure. I stand for your stolen childhood. I stand for Princess Mahreuben, Prince Uzaleus and all good men and elves. Now, Ramona wizard. Let us go and find your brother."

The little elf drew his dagger and pointed it skyward. A small band of elves cried out in support and readied themselves for another journey.

"Now. To the tower." The whole family and Cormac and Finola all embraced.

Across the plains, a young man was behind the wheel of a car. A beautiful, kind young soul. But an angry one. He sped across the valleys, barely staying upright. Driving too fast and full of intent. Jude now approached the tower. He slowed to a halt to observe. The gates were wide open as Takers came and went, carrying weapons, food, water. Doing Alatar's bidding. Building his stocks and supplies. Jude revved the engine and a grim look crossed his puzzled looking features. He put his foot down hard and drove.

The car sped uneasily onward, across the drawbridge. Knocking startled guards flying into the moat like skittles. He was through the gate, but his mind was out of control. Jude ploughed the car headlong into the huge counsel table in the courtyard. No thought for his safety. Just anger at this place. The car groaned to a stop and the young man threw open the door and scrambled out. For once, the Takers were stunned and they hovered, gazing quizzically at this delirious boy, stood glaring back at them.

"Cowards. Where is he? Alatar.. the little mouse. Where are you? Vermin. Come on out and face me. You won't take my sister. I'll kill you. I'll bloody kill you."

Then, as Jude turned, looking manically in all directions, a huge shrouded figure with glowing red eyes, stood before him.

"Interesting. Very interesting. You must be Jude, the proud and strong brother. You will make a useful addition to my guard. Such raw, unharnessed aggression."

The guards made to go to capture Jude.

"No!" Gestured Alatar, swishing dismissively at the guards.

"Let us see what this puppy dog, has to offer.."

Jude faced the tall, dark creature with no flinch, no fear. Or he hid it well. He drew the elven dagger from his pocket. He charged fifty feet across the courtyard at the leader of the Takers.

"Coward. I'll bury you.."

He slammed into Alatar. Briefly stunning and knocking the dark leader backwards. That is when Jude plunged the dagger into his target.

CHAPTER TWENTY SIX
CHAOS REIGNS

Ramona and her family, minus Jude, strode with grim purpose behind Cormac and his small band of elves. There were with them, approximately half of the already small woodland unit. Cormac had been sure to leave half of his strongest kinfolk behind. There were of course young elvlings, children, to be looked after. Taking them charging on a crusade would be tantamount to lunacy. Only willing volunteers were with them, and there were many. So Cormac had asked half of the many to stay. In the woodland shelters.

For all anyone knew, Takers could yet be on the way now to their shelters and they would need a defence. It was too late and too long winded a plan to suggest a whole encampment upped and looked elsewhere to settle. They would be found wherever they went. The Takers guard had grown large and ruthless. Any independent, empathetic feelings of compassion or conflict, within Alatar's guard was unceremoniously and routinely numbed by regular doses of his life-force liquid. The steaming pewter goblets of unknown, mind bending content.

Ramona jogged up alongside Cormac, her hood slipped away, revealing the face of the young and fiercely determined girl. She was forgetting how she had become this way. All she could remember of being a baby, was a foggy image of a beach and two smiling adult faces, being fed, watered and carried. She also recalled the two gulls, who now flew overhead. Flying off for short periods and returning to the group shortly after. Circling and cawing from above. Cormac looked up at them and bowed. They had been scouting the coastal path and it was currently clear of danger. Save for a small group of scouting Takers, gathering wood and fruit, presumably for their camp supplies. Manageable they were, if need be, thought Cormac.

To Biggle and Baggle. The elves had named the seabirds, simply after the cackling noises they made. The great black-backed gulls, comical although they had been, they were now proving of true value to Ramona, her family and the elves. More than this, they were proving to be friends. As they swooped down, Cormac produced some bits of fish from a small bag he wore, tossing it to the grateful birds. They too, had to eat and drink and sleep.

"Cormac please, just slow down a minute. I need to ask you something."

Ramona herself slowed to a halt, bowed her head and put her hands on her knees. Looking up again only to take a long drink of water. Cormac and his folk may have been slightly smaller in stature than their human counterparts, but they were fleeter of foot and very durable, as Ramona and her mother and father were now discovering.

"Ah, cool water, Ramona. A good idea to be sure." He puffed his cheeks out, taking a deep breath and sipped. Then, he smiled affably at the young wizard. "I forget myself sometimes, to be sure, young one." He chuckled. "I get no younger!" Then he barked a loud shrill order. An order but a necessary one. "Elves! Take a drink and rest a while. Eat something from your sacks."

The throng of elves, male and female, gratefully sat. Having some much needed fluids, sharing some food and chattering amongst themselves about what was to be done. The sea was approaching and the coastal path. This would lead to the Takers tower and ultimately, Alatar. Cormac now sat down himself.

"I apologise Ramona. I was all business just now, to be sure. I do tend to get my head down and charge on. What would you like to ask me?"

The young wizard looked up. Feeling better for a short break. She was fit and strong and borne of magic, but keeping pace with a determined elf was a whole new thing for her. Not to mention Ruth and James. Ramona's father gratefully sat now.

"Good job you are grown up now Mona. Imagine mum having to carry you all this way!" James winked at his wife and daughter. Cormac stifled a snigger despite the circumstances. James winked again, this time at his elven friend. Ruth rolled her eyes and feigned a gasp. Pretending to be offended.

"You my friend, are so close to trouble."

Ruth made a sign with her fingers that suggested James was an inch away from a stern talking to, but she was laughing. They all were. For the first time in a good while. It lightened the mood. The other elves relaxed a little. Not too much of course. They needed to be vigilant. But James attempt at wit had worked and he looked quite pleased with himself as Ruth playfully pushed him on the shoulder.

"Of course, I would carry you Mona. Once your mother got tired. I like to do my bit."

James was enjoying his comedy cameo and his chortling elven audience. Ruth let her husband have his moment. Their love was strong.

"Oh dear. How archaic father." said Ramona, she giggled and replied. "Children will be children. You two need to grow up! Look at me. Nought to eighteen in a few weeks!"

"Aye, 'tis astounding to be sure." Cormac chimed in. "I think your rapid growth spurt shall slow to a halt now young one. Other than the natural order of things. I hope this will at least ease your worries and end your troublesome dreams. And I am warmed that there is no bitterness in any of you. Acceptance is a hard but yet ultimately rewarding and necessary part of our lives. It can be frustrating. As well you all know, and still so many questions to be answered."

The family nodded in unison.

"With my limited knowledge, I will keep trying to answer as many as I can to ease your concerns. But Ramona, yes, I feel it was preordained in some way, that you were put at this stage of life rapidly, by the realms. You all know now, a little of the timelines, the shifting and blending. It cannot be controlled. It never could be. I am still saddened by the way in which you were bought here. But, I believe it was so that you and your family, myself and the elves. The Princess. The Prince. All these good folk, can get back to where they need to be. You hold the key, Ramona. So mote it be, to be sure. Now young wizard, your question?"

Ramona smiled at the elf.

"Cormac, you just answered it, thank you. I feel something also though. Something not so nice." She looked a little puzzled. Cormac rolled his hands in a motion that told her to elaborate. She obliged.

"I see Jude. In here." Ramona tapped the temple of her forehead.

"Not running, or walking. I see him in a car. Dad's car. I think he went off track. I think he returned to the lanes where we crashed. I think he is.. or was, in the car. Heading for the tower like all of us. I think he thinks he can kill Alatar.

Cormac, I think he is in trouble. Big trouble."

CHAPTER TWENTY SEVEN
ESCAPE

All the prisoners in the jail cell knew, was that something was happening in the courtyard. You could see only so far from behind wrought-iron bars. But the commotion and rushing around of the guards told Uzaleus and Domacec, that all was not running as normal in the grounds of the tower. An angry cry of a young man. A voice unknown to Uzaleus, but not to Domacec. The former captain of the guard, Cacodem, as he had been, was straining his eyes as though trying to remember something. And it came to him.

"The boy, Jude."

Uzaleus and Ailbe looked puzzled. Domacec elaborated.

"It is the brother of the girl wizard, out there in the courtyard. I last heard his voice, when I led the guard of takers to the Ivywyrld Inn at which they were residing, with the elf in attendance guiding them. I led nine others to the inn. Nine other Takers. We were to capture the family, but chiefly and most importantly, Ramona. We failed. We underestimated the power of not only her wizardry, not yet honed, but strong and so powerful, but also we.."

Domacec paused, hung his head as though ashamed and feeling remorse. Uzaleus interjected.. "Continue brother. We know the liquid had you. Do not feel shame. Look at you now. Returned under your own determination. As can Mahreuben, our beautiful Princess, do the same. You give me hope she too can hold against the potion. Continue brother."

Seeing the hurt Uzaleus was going through and had been exposed to. Seeing it through his eyes now. How he had watched his beloved Mahreuben being dangled from the tower by a sneering and mocking Elphinias. What strength it had sapped from the Prince, seeing poor Mahreuben dragged about in torn clothing, matted hair. Her skin mottled, run out of the realms as a banshee.

What bravery these two royal guardians of the realms had showed, and continued to show even now. Looking at Uzaleus now and thinking of the Princess, up in that tower, drugged and red eyed. This not only saddened Domacec but also enraged him. Domacec wiped a tear from his eye.

"We.. Alatar.. he underestimated the power of a family's love for each other. They united as one and kept our circle at bay. We tried to exert a sort of mind control over them. To entice them. It is a technique that comes naturally to some of the pure Takers, but is learned by others. We spread around the inn. We told them there was no choice. They faltered yes. They wavered. The mother broke their circle. She had fainted, but they remained unified. We did not expect what happened next." Again, Domacec hung his head.

"Good, bad or drugged, Uzaleus, I led nine to their doom. Seeing this unfold before me, this blue magic from Ramona. I had never witnessed such raw power, unharnessed, borne of love and of answering a knee-jerk reaction. Of emotional response. I have seen bad magic as powerful, in Alatar's. But not good magic, defensive, protective magic like this. Necessary magic. The girl, Ramona. She raced into the outside yard. I had never seen a young face so enraged, Uzaleus, so focused"

The now emotional Domacec, went on to tell Uzaleus, Ailbe and the others in his cell, how Ramona alone, had called upon swathes of blue flame and turned the Takers to dust. Save for himself.

"I fled Uzaleus. I ran. It does not matter what side I was on and whether I now do the right thing. I abandoned nine. Some of whom, like me, were unwilling followers."

Uzaleus put a hand on the shoulder of Domacec.

"Brother, listen to me when I say. You are a good man. Those actions were not your own. You were under a spell. Now, I say to you. Do you now, as the clear thinking Domacec.." Uzaleus emphasised his words.

"Do you now, as you are, here, think that you would willingly lead a powerful guard of ten to kidnap an unwitting girl? A whole family, utterly confused as to what is happening to them? Dragged through time and separated, Completely oblivious to this dimension. I ask you Domacec. Not Cacodem. Would you have done this?"

Domacec looked at the Prince directly.

"No, no Prince. I would not."

"Then unburden yourself from any feeling of guilt or shame. Not a soul in this cell thinks that any of this is your doing. The young man, Jude. He has gone silent. They all have. Look, all of you. What do you see?"

Uzaleus, motioned to the outside of their iron cell. The rest of the group gazed outside. Then at each other. Blank looks. Uzaleus repeated his question.

"What do you see?"

Domacec now saw, and he drew a deep breath, but it was Ailbe, Uzaleus friend and aide whom spoke.

"Uzaleus, it is what I do not see. I see no guard."

Ailbe was correct and a half-smile flickered across the face of the Prince. There was no guard outside any of the cells. They had abandoned sensibility and raced into the courtyard en masse. Any threat to Alatar, however miniscule was the only thing they would abandon their robotic duties for.

"Brothers. We cannot be hurt with the red whip. We cannot be driven back. Let us break these bars."

Uzaleus raced forward at pace and shoulder charged into the cell bars. He bounced away. With seven more men seeing what he was attempting though, there was seven times as much strength. Together, as a force, and with the unseen guidance of the ethereal by their side, the eight prisoners pushed and barged and pressed. With this, the lock gave way. The locks were not that strong. Rusty and weathered. They needn't have been. The guard were previously always outside to lash any rebels.

Some of the Takers guard turned and saw what was unfolding. They had been too busy witnessing their leader fall to the floor, with a boy stood over him, wielding a dagger. They had momentarily frozen in disbelief. It was too late however. Uzaleus, Domacec and the small group had broken free. They were hurriedly prising the locks of the other cells open using anything they could get their hands on. Metal, strong wood, brute force. Grim determination was winning. Anger, vengeance, desire. The will to live.

They went along a row of cells, managing to free many. Using a combination of the barging and pushing from those inside, to the pulling and prising from the band of eight outside. Iron gates fell to the ground. Prisoners scattered. The Takers quickly regrouped. The guard was huge now. All resources deployed to the scene at the jails. The electrical red whips lashed out catching some escapees, sadly, half of the freed, fell to the floor. Some were swarmed upon by the drones in hooded dark uniform.

They were bullied and ushered back to the remaining secure cells. Some died of shock. Thrown back in. Causing overcrowding and silencing the incarcerated, but previously cheering prisoners. But half of the freed ran and kept running. Uzaleus shouted aloud. Motivating the throng of men.

"For the realms, for the Princess. For our new family!"

They charged past rushing Takers and made for the top tower. Uzaleus wanted to free Mahreuben. Now, as they clambered up the ramparts, trying to avoid the lashings of the whip and onrushing Takers, they drew all their strength and courage.

"Will you join me brothers?"

Uzaleus was breathing heavily. There was no doubt that the good folk would follow the Prince. They had been given a head start thanks to the unexpected and welcomed chaos, brought by Jude. They continued to scramble upward.

"Let us free our Princess." Uzaleus called.

The prisoners, weakened but not broken, continued on. Domacec, more determined than any, to atone in any way he could.

At the top tower, Mahreuben was under lock and key. She had been given the liquid. Her eyes had turned red now. She was inside Alatar's personal quarters. Only Elphinias could gain access as Alatar's aide and confidante. Elphinias, the snake had his own agenda.

He had watched the entire scene from the top tower. He had seen the car come across the drawbridge. He had seen it crash into the counsel table and had seen the boy charge into Alatar with a dagger. He had seen his leader fall. At no point had Elphinias raised the alarm. He had simply watched from on high with a curious smile curling from his sneering, contemptuous face. He was not a nice creature. He had craved power, way before Alatar appeared. A long time ago.

Alatar was a very powerful leader but not a mind reader. He could not see of Elphinias plan to overthrow him. Alatar had captured Mahreuben. For she could see things that he could not. She could locate Ramona. She already had located Ramona. But to warn her. And now as Elphinias entered Alatar's quarters, she could also see of his intent.

"Ah, banshee. I see you are still with us. Do you know of the interesting developments below?"

The Princess had been bound to a stone pillar. Her head bowed, her once shimmering hair hung over her pretty face.

"I am still here snake. I see what has happened." She looked up, her eyes switching from her natural blue to the potion induced red. She was still fighting it.

"Charming as always. Withered Princess, broken little banshee. Siren of the seas. Now that you are calmer, I bring you more refreshment."

He motioned to one of the two personal guard, always deployed at the heavy oak and iron door to Alatar's domain. The guard brought forth the pewter goblet. The life-force liquid. The mind control drink. It was passed to Elphinias. He held forth the goblet as though cherishing a personal trophy.

"You must have developed a thirst Princess. I can now help you to slake it."

With this, Mahreuben was once again forced to swallow another dose of the mind corrupting liquid. She spluttered. She did not even attempt to spit it out this time. It was futile. She would be whipped. It was of no help.

"Good, good.. and while the drink settles, here is your meal. The guard will feed you. I cannot have you weak." Elphinias slid a bowl of what looked like soup and bread across a wooden table. The other guard nodded and came forward.

"Now eat, my witch. After that, you will tell me where this girl is, where she is headed, and what her intentions are. Any lies, or anything that turns out to be misleading or attempts at delay.. and I will kill you myself. Slowly".

The guard pushed a spoonful of soup to Mahreuben's mouth. She ate. It was under duress. It tasted of vegetables and was not unpleasant. She was hungry. She chewed and swallowed the bread and soup. It was nourishment, but she resented the source from which it came. She knew it was not tampered with. What would be the point?

She had already drank the liquid. She was forced to eat quickly. Elphinias had been sat. He had drank more liquid himself and ate at the table. His gaze fixed on Mahreuben all the while.

"What of your leader, your Alatar? See how he has fallen to a boy. What do you say to that, Elphinias the snake?" Mahreuben returned the gaze of the traitor.

"Alatar has paid the penalty for his lack of foresight. He was not invincible. He trusted me far too easily. Bequeathed me with his secrets. Now, he lies in the courtyard, at the feet of a child. The boy will be dealt with. The prisoners on their way to free you, banshee? Do not raise your hopes. They are also being dealt with. Now it is time to tell me the location of Ramona. This, girl wizard."

He spat the last words.

Mahreuben's hands had been wriggling behind the pillar, wriggling free of her shackles. She too had powers, of foresight and of will. She had willed the shackles loose. But still she answered the sneering Elphinias.

"Ramona is on her way here. She wishes only to save her brother and to free the prisoners. She will use her powers when necessary. I would not want to be on the end of her magic, in her current mood."

Mahreuben slid her wrists free of the restraints but did not move. Elphinias smiled that unpleasant, curled grin.

"Strong girl, true, very strong. Do not worry though banshee. I have no intention of facing her. You will, and your Prince and his men and the entire guard of the Takers. You will disarm her magic. You will lie to her. You will tell her of Alatar's death firstly and you will misinform her that the tower is captured by your useless Prince. You will put her at ease, or of course.. Die."

Mahreuben was free now but still maintained her position.

"Yes Elphinias. I will tell her." She allowed her eyes to redden, appeasing the twisted Elphinias. She went on.

"I shall tell her that you are all fools. I shall tell her that you are the biggest fool of all. I shall tell her not to underestimate Alatar as you have. I shall tell her that love acts as an antidote against this awful liquid. This drug you all use." She looked up and smiled sweetly at Elphinias.

"What do you have to smile about, banshee?" He walked up and pressed his contorting face against hers.

"Do not meddle with me. Do not push me. You will tell Ramona what I told you to tell her." Elphinias was now angry. "Alatar is dead. Get to work and tell her."

Mahreuben's heart raced, adrenaline coursed through her.

"I will tell Ramona that Alatar.. Your leader.. Is stood right behind you."

Elphinias puzzled face crumpled and turned ashen as he looked around. There indeed, was his leader. Bigger and taller than ever. Huge. Under his hood, those eyes now seemed demonic to Elphinias. The leader strode towards his shrinking counsellor.

"Elphinias. You have lots to say. Shall we talk perhaps?" With that, the leader fired skewering, red electric from his pointed fingertips, sending the wretched Elphinias screaming into the hard stone wall.

"You go first Elphinias."

The scheming aide now faced his leader..

"Alatar, I only meant to serve. To scare this witch into serving you. Please, leader, I used a plan, I only.." The voice of Elphinias trailed off. He would never finish his sentence.

"Save your babbling, you pathetic flailing Idiot. I am amused how you thought me the fool. Amused, but not impressed. Goodbye Elphinias. Your purpose here is now at an end."

Elphinias mouth hung open. Alatar paced back and forth.

"Traitors always die."

With this, another bolt of red lightning blasted clean through Elphinias. Sending him through the window and off the top tower. To his certain death.

Mahreuben, with her now free hands, rushed for the window herself with Alatar preoccupied. She gave no thought and flung herself off the top tower. She did this through choice. Elphinias had not. He now floated, motionless in the moat. Looking quite dead.

Jude was stood looking down at an empty space where Alatar had lain. Jude had initially thought him vanquished. But the leader had disappeared. There was no blood on the elven dagger he had stabbed at him with, and now, Takers were approaching him.

Jude saw them coming and ran for his life.

CHAPTER TWENTY EIGHT
THE SAVIOUR OF STONE

The realms were currently in confusion. Lost in a heady mixture of factions and battles. Of morals and of those who had none, but the realms as a vast land, were still very beautiful. They always had been. Save for this new, permanent mood, hanging over the tower like a perennial damp morning fog. The atmosphere it projected was a draining one. Hence you now very rarely saw its wonderful birds or wildlife within its vicinity. Before, it was resplendent with hawks and falcons nesting, with all manner of coastal birds passing through. The wild horses also seemed to have gone. Nature had become suspicious of Alatar.

The tower, previously housed many other eras before it fell to the Takers. Including many old royals. Inland, there was the elven woodlands, Whitsomin lake, vast green meadows and untouched scrub. Green and vibrant. Wild gorse and trees of many varieties. The realms were hilly, and huge open spaces lay unoccupied before you came to the next dwelling or settlement. Strange nocturnal creatures, hooting and howling in the night. Daytime life respected the night and vice versa.

Beyond the tower in the other direction, was the open sea. When still and when the sun bounced off the glassy surface, it was the most transparent pastel blue. Beneath the rippling waves there were schools of mackerel, conger eel and sea bass, the favourite of Biggle and Baggle the scouting gulls. Guillemot, razorbill, and gannet, plundered the waters for easy, plentiful food. The fish were many. Not that they appreciated the bombardments. Kittiwake and cormorant bobbed up and down on the surface. When going inland, the birds would veer well away from the tower now, to look for wetlands, lakes or rivers. Never the tower anymore, despite the presence of water and food.

Mahreuben, in spite of her cave dwelling being small, and the isolation breaking her heart and mind, had survived here. She sang laments, recited poems, cooked what she found washed up. Sometimes, the gulls would drop fish at the mouth of the cave. People could, and did survive this way. Some had begun to thrive. Because of the saviour of stone.

King Theonyra, had lain dormant for many years now, deep beneath the waves. Away from the shoreline. He had been known as the stone King to a generation long since vanished. A race of people, or elves or gnomes. Nobody knew. It was never spoken of in the realms as they were today. A thriving cove was once here. A bustling township. Good people. No bad had destroyed it. It had simply ceased to be. Expired and ran its course, such as ancient places do. Azmarine had receded into the ocean. The people had fled. There were battles fought here before the sea took all. The township and its buildings, monuments and homes were washed away or eventually crumbled under constant erosion.

To the people of the realms it had become a myth buried under a myth, but old Theonyra was no myth. The stone King had stood firm, as a mighty oak tree might stand in a storm, and not be blown away like one of its leaves. Theonyra was waiting. Waiting silently year after year, decade after decade. His had been the role of guardian and watcher.

Even a stone King though, could not hold back the forays of the ocean. So he carried the suffering people of Azmarine. Took them to shore and saw them safely inland. Hundreds had clung about the arms and legs and shoulders of this kind monolithic giant. He scooped up the trusting people from the beaches, the way you or I would collect pebbles and shells.

Theonyra had seen that the sea would claim Azmarine and acted in advance. The Azmarinian's accepted without question and dissipated inland. They began to form new settlements and over time, Azmarine became a name of fantasy. Theonyra, when the town was quiet and emptied, then resumed his position of lookout. He stood strong as he too, vanished beneath the waves. The surface then became still and Theonyra, the stone King, became a myth himself.

Some inland Azmarinian's told of him to neighbouring hamlets and villages. The people would smile, be enthralled and captivated. But always in a way as though being told an entertaining fable. Yet they were happily fascinated by the idea of a stone saviour. They intermingled with neighbouring camps and down the years, began to forget. The name of the settlement of Azmarine, evaporated like the seawater from rock pools on a hot day. Theonyra, dormant but conscious, had become aware of the alarming regularity of humans, elves, other folk landing in the sea, like raindrops. It was the ejected prisoners. Flailing about in dread and treading water as best they could. Sucking in oxygen after the trauma of the catapult.

Kicking and flapping to stay afloat. Fish out of water, in water. Wide-eyed and so scared, they remembered to breathe, only when their lungs screamed. They were all assumed drowned by Alatar and the Takers. Even if a few had swum ashore, they were no threat to the Takers tower. At the time, it was a source of amusing anecdote to the now vanished Elphinias, who used the catapult like a toy when the mood took him. How he had loved to recall those moments. The launching of terrified captives out to deep water. Flinging those lives to sea when the people had become too weak to be of use.

Or as a warning to the other prisoners. A macabre display of barbarism. Sadly, as and when the bodies dropped into the deeper waters, some had already passed of shock. Some disappeared beneath the waves, drowned, but some, many in fact, were saved. This kind leviathan, stirred from his wait of several lifetimes and strode through crashing emerald waters.

The spluttering and gasping prisoners clung like limpets to the stone King. The saviour from the sea was real. There was blood pumping beneath a folly of rock. Blood and magic. Theonyra was granite and the colour of slate. But he was alive. He could not erode. He was born of the realms and now this was his time again. Theonyra scooped up many at a time. Depositing them in quiet coves around unknown, hidden beaches of shingle and shale. Huge caves there were. Habitable. After their unwanted death flight, the prisoners were not going to question a miracle.

A miracle of salvation. They thought it divine intervention. Theonyra never spoke. He simply carried them and gently dispersed scores of grateful throngs among these caves. Then he would withdraw backwards into his watery home. Thousands of beads of glassy droplets rolling down his body of stone, like tiny marbles. Then it was as though he had never been. Azmarine. It still existed to Theonyra. Now, it would again. The survivors made fires, made tools from wood and stone. Found warmth in the caves with bedding of dried seaweeds, grasses and straw.

As Theonyra saved more of the catapulted prisoners and they too went through the process of the miracle, the cove population grew. They ate well. They stayed hidden and quiet and did not attempt to go back, as much as they were enraged at Alatar and his cruel tower. The stone King rose every now and then. A colossus in the water. He would turn to look back inland. In the direction of the tower. Then turn to the New Azmarinian's and hold up the palm of one of his gigantic hands. It was well interpreted by the cove people.

It was a silent yet strong 'No'. It said 'Do not go back. Not yet.'

The cove people accepted this subliminal communication from Theonyra and carried on making their quiet and safe new home. Presently, Theonyra noticed that no more bodies were falling. No more raindrops. The stone King was happy at this. It meant the realms were still with the good folk. Still strong, so Theonyra anchored himself again to the ocean floor. Content to wait again. Sad at the losses as he had been when Azmarine fell. But his rock body warmed at its rebirth.

Two seals playfully swam through and around his giant legs and pushed for the surface, barking and smiling. All manner of sea life felt safe in the presence of the stone King as did New Azmarine itself. As Theonyra rested, his final thought before allowing himself respite, was this..

'I will help the girl wizard. She is their chosen one.'

And then, the stone King was dormant again.

CHAPTER TWENTY NINE
OF MAHREUBEN'S FATE

On their ascent to the top tower, Uzaleus, Domacec, Ailbe and the escapees, were stopped in their tracks in jaw dropping style. Firstly, they had witnessed a plummeting Elphinias, wrapped in red electrical magic, meeting his fate with a crackling hiss as his body hit the moat. Barely able to perceive this, they then saw their own Princess, Mahreuben, launch herself from the high window and such was the power of her jump, it looked as though she had headed out to sea. It was like a skywalk. For a moment only, it seemed she flew. There were no anguished screams.

At the top, Alatar paced. Looking out on the chaos unfolding in his kingdom. He was enraged at the ineptitude of his guard.

"Tanwyn.. get down there, sort this mess out. If these idiot bandits will not submit, then execute them. I am entrusting you to replace that dead fool in the moat."

Tanwyn bowed to his master. He did not crave power. He just did not want to die.

"Leader, what is happening to Elphinias?"

Alatar looked down at the moat and saw the body of his former aide being tugged at, shaken and then dragged below the surface by something with fins and humps.

"Better you do not know, my friend."

Uzaleus and the brave group had been driven back down by Tanwyn and his reinforcements. It was no good. They must run to fight another day. As they fled down a hillside, an onrushing Jude was approaching.

"The drawbridge, we have to hurry, they're raising the drawbridge.."

The Prince looked ahead with wide eyes and turned to his men.

"Straight across no stopping, its our only chance."

Red whips lashed at their tail ends as they called on all their reserves for the effort. Whilst running, Jude, almost breathlessly grinned, "Its good to meet you Prince."

Uzaleus despite himself, smiled "You are a brave young man. Jude, son of the realms."

Heads down, they rushed the bridge as the guard were winching it up. Sadly, a few men were caught and tossed into the moat. But they hadn't got back to full strength at the drawbridge and the majority of Uzaleus escape team made it across, despite aerial bombardment and showering arrows. Once outside the grounds of the tower, Jude took the lead.

"My sister is coming. I know where she will be headed. She has a small elven force with her."

Domacec spoke "I know of your sister's power, Jude."

For a second, recognising Domacec as Cacodem, Jude looked as though he might draw his dagger, but then Uzaleus intervened.

"Do not fear young warrior. This is Domacec. Healed of the liquid. A good man."

Jude tilted his head to one side, dubious.

"You're the boss, Prince."

They took some water and pressed on. Something had entered the sea with tern-like agility, from a height. Barely causing a ripple. The Princess had many powers of her own. Many guises. One of them being that she could manifest as a mermaid. As she entered the water, the transition was flawless.

A tail fin of azure blue replaced the legs built for land. The red eyes had gone. Mahreuben's faith and love had kept her safe in the end. Here were the deep emerald eyes of an empath. Cool marine water had washed away the muddied, matted hair and now, here was the most shimmering blonde that glinted like crystal. Her face, hidden for so long was now showing features of such fragile and porcelain beauty, that men could make fools of themselves. She swam in the waters of New Azmarine. Out towards the coves. Presently, she surfaced to survey.

On the beaches of shingle and shale, she could see a gathering of people. Men, women and children that Alatar either knew nothing of, or did not care. She watched. Campfires burned, fish, shrimp and seaweeds were being cooked. Children played. Huts were being constructed. A group sat cross legged in meditation by stones, arranged so perplexingly into perfectly balanced piles. Mahreuben smiled and dived down again. A little further along and there stood the silent guardian. Anchored through will, to the sea floor. Theonyra stirred and opened his eyes.

"Ah, a refreshing sleep Princess. Most refreshing." He smiled, and the Princess, tiny in comparison, returned it.

"Theonyra. It warms my heart to see your guardianship has remained steadfast. You are a kind giant." Theonyra gazed warmly down at Mahreuben.

"Princess, it warms mine to see you returned safe and well. Yours is the power that deep belief in the good and true shall prevail, and here you are."

"And here I am, Theonyra."

Mahreuben shed a tear, of happiness. A giant stone fingertip, reached down and wiped it away so gently.

"Is it time then, Princess?"

"It is time, Theonyra. Ramona is headed to the tower. It is chaos there. Mayhem."

"Then let us go and pay this circus act, Alatar, a visit. See if we can get back our tower. I will show him that trust wins over his scaremongering and displays of bad magic."

Theonyra winked.

"Let us return the realms to your people Princess."

Mahreuben giggled in excitement.

"Our people, King."

It had been so long. Her smile was like dappled sunlight in the New Azmarine water.

CHAPTER THIRTY
THE REALMS REVEALED

Ramona, Ruth, James, Cormac and the elves pressed on. Knowing nothing of the chaotic events at the tower and beyond. It was hard terrain. Steep inclines and tough underfoot. Cormac had suggested a rest period several times but had been met with a firm 'No' by Ramona. Now though, the young wizard turned to the stoic little elf.

"Cormac. I've been stubborn and a bit selfish. I think we should take that break. Everyone is tired. I've just been charging on thinking of Jude. Why would he run off like that? What was he thinking?"

"A break is welcomed to be sure Ramona. None of us will be of use, nor ornament, if we plough on until we are floundering at the feet of Alatar. Though I understand your desire to find your brother. I do not think that to be selfish. Remember, those of us that are here, chose to be. Let us sit though, for a while."

Ruth had found a spot under an old looking willow tree. "Come on Mona. Curl up for a bit here. We're doing all we can to find Jude. He's got a good head on his shoulders. He's lived alone on the streets, he will find a way."

Ruth looked over at James who tried to appear reassuring. Ruth knew she was trying to convince herself as much as Ramona.

Cormac had produced a vessel with more of Finola's tea in it and poured some for Ramona and she gratefully drank it down. It had the same effect as before, calming her swirling thoughts and aching temples, loaded up with scenarios and ideas, plans. Overload. The young wizard curled up beside her mother and rested her head on Ruth's lap. Soon she was asleep. Ruth smiled and eventually dozed herself.

Some elves did the same, some took watch. James sat, in a silent union with Cormac. Pondering. The sky was rose red and a few silhouettes of cormorants, decorated the scene, flying to roost. It would have been a peaceful camp but for the worry. James too, nodded now and Cormac pulled his blanket about him.

"An hour or two should boost us to be sure James, my friend." and his eyes closed.

As Ramona slept, she again began to dream. It was such a melting pot. As though her brain was trying to make some sense of all that was happening.

"Who are you? What are you?" She was on the beach calling out at the sky.

"We are the ethereal watchers of the realms, Ramona. The spirits and ancestors. We are the unseen. We are sorry we had to intervene. We knew you were the one. We want to send you home. We look after these lands. This time, circumstances fell beyond our control and we had to find you. You came here for a reason. You were selected. It was.. Preordained."

The soft gentle voice came more into Ramona's mind, clear to her now.

"Why me?" She shot, upset at the unlived years taken from her.

"Why not?" Came the answer.

"We saw of your potential when the two gulls came close to you. They sense magic. They were not afraid and neither were you. Your senses were already keen and full of intrigue. Magic was there."

"But the accident then? You could have stopped it. Stopped the car going over. Stopped that.. that freak from making my dad lose control of the wheel?"

Ramona was tossing and turning, mumbling. Cormac came over to Ruth and motioned to leave her be.

"It is the process. It will help her, Ruth, she is safe with us."

The gentle voice came again.

"No Ramona, no. We could not foresee of Alatar. He is a dark one, shadowy. He too sensed you. Even as a baby he sensed you could be the one to upset his master plan. So he manipulated timelines, mingled dimensions. As your father drove you home, it was Alatar who stood in the road and flashed not only his eyes, but a glimpse into your father's mind, of the parallels that were happening. This confused him briefly enough for the accident. It is sad. We are sorry, so very sorry. He overpowered even our will to intervene. It was then we knew, we needed you. Alatar being there meant we had to work faster."

Ramona, still in her dream state, sat on the sand, cross legged, meditative, looking at the emerald green waves, gently rolling in. White sand and a sky of pastel blue. Shooting stars journeying to who knew where or when.

"And this is why I aged and nobody else in my family? Because you wanted me to get up to speed? To be able to carry myself better, physically?"

"Yes young one. Correct. To have the speed and strength of young adulthood. The alertness, the keen eye. The will of instinct. Your magic cannot be trained into you, studied nor harnessed. It is raw and this is why we know you can banish Alatar. Look at your display at the Ivywyrld Inn."

"Where I killed nine people you mean?" She answered sadly and with a touch of resentment.

"These were not people Ramona. These were willing followers of the dark one. The pure bred Taker. Save for Domacec, then Cacodem. He had taken the liquid. The rest? They were only too happy to try to obliterate you and your family. Do not be sad. Their end was swift. Returned to dust to no longer do harm."

"When I confront Alatar? What do I do then? Aim magic at him? Get angry, wave my arms around again and hope something happens?"

The voice began to fade now, Ramona was coming out of the dream.

"Yours is the power of instinct. It will come. Remember, you cannot be trained. The rawness of your magic is what will win the day. Also, the magic in your heart. Your brother.. He is safe.. He is looking for you.

Please Ramona. Trust the realms. Trust the ethereal.. Then you can all go home. Ualdin will be ready."

Ramona sat bolt upright.

"Jude's alright mum. He's coming back. Ualdin, he will send us home"

Ruth hugged her daughter as Cormac strolled over.

"Feeling a little more knowledgeable young one?" He smiled.

Ramona raised her eyebrows in recognition of her dreams.

"You knew Cormac. You knew to let me sleep. That I would find more out than shouting questions at people."

The elf smiled wryly.

"Sleep not only has restorative powers as we all need. It gives our brains uninterrupted time and space, to work things out, Ramona. It seems you are well on the way to doing that. Here, eat this and drink this tea."

He handed her cheese, nuts and berries on a wooden plate. Ramona ate with verve, keen to move on.

"We can all leave soon. I have a feeling more help is coming. In many forms. I felt ethereal murmurings also."

Alatar paced the courtyard. He aimed a burst of red flame at an ancient royal statue and it was enveloped until it could not be seen and then blown into the sky, causing a spectacle that resonated for miles.

Jude, Uzaleus and the others saw it.

"He is angry." Whispered the Prince quietly.

Alatar scowled at the Takers now.

"Let this wrecked heritage serve as a lesson to any more of you who doubt my power. This bundle of misfits have run away. They have no answer. They escape only by good fortune and by your own idiotic blundering."

Alatar walked up and down in front of the guard, lined up before him. Jail cells had been reinforced. Would-be escapees, denied food and water for the day as punishment. The bridge was raised again and the Takers worked liked drones to tidy the scene and make all pristine again for their leader.

"Now, they may attempt to come back or we may have to hunt them down. But know this. I do not want any more prisoners. I now want them killed. All of them."

He turned, bowed his head and simply vanished.

CHAPTER THIRTY ONE
A GATHERING

Jude's group arrived at a wooded copse. It was off the coastal path and away from the bracing winds. It seemed reasonably well out of the way and a decent enough place to stop. He turned to Uzaleus.

"I think we should stop here Prince. It seems safe. Well covered. The Takers seemed disorganised. I don't think they will come chasing just yet. I believe my sister will find us here. Its like she is calling to me to wait. I hope you trust me. I trust her. I think she is not far off and will find us. She has great instinct."

"Then here is where we stay Jude. I feel I must thank you, not just for myself, but for every man and elf in this brave group. You showed tremendous courage to break in to a place that most spend their lives trying to break out of. To delay Alatar as you did, to surprise him and stall the guard. It allowed us to be here now. Damn him. You did so well young one. We are way from those grim cells. I thank you. I would like to avenge those who remain there. Now, I have that chance. Thanks to you, Jude the courageous brother."

Jude bowed, in both respect and in modesty.

"I only wish we could have done something for Mahreuben. I feel a sadness after all she went through for everyone else, bearing their pain. I wish we could have got to the top tower before.."

Jude tailed off. He did not want to refresh Uzaleus memory of the events, but the Prince smiled.

"Do you know Jude, I do not believe she has passed. I and every brave man and elf here, saw her jump from that tower, shortly after Elphinias was destroyed. I think she saw an opportunity while Alatar was busy. I saw with my own eyes, she did not fall. She seemed to.. stride, across the sky, out to sea and then out of view."

Jude hoped Uzaleus was correct. The Prince seemed convinced.

My Princess has many guises. Many powers. Much magic of her own. She is often underestimated as she is at her happiest when she does not have to use it. Meaning the realms are at peace. I like to think she is with us, somewhere. She knows the ocean and its creatures. Despite her banishment, those skills kept her alive then. I believe they have now too, Jude."

The Prince drew from his water bottle and sat on a large rock, stretching.

"It is a good day to be free. Thank you brave Jude."

Jude smiled.

"If you say Mahreuben is still with us Prince, that's good enough for me. I know how much you love her and that she is empathetic with these lands and the people she sees as her own. It was the thought of these Takers. If they did anything. Took my sister or any of my family away. Then I would be distraught. So, I stand with you as much as you do me. Together. As one."

Jude offered his hand to Uzaleus. He took it and shook firmly.

"Together. As one."

Ramona and her mother and father had all slept, as had most of the elves now. Feeling more refreshed and with food and water, hot tea in their bellies. They were fortified and encouraged to set off again across the gorse filled moors and scrubs. A fairly barren part of the realms. Barren to people but a huge benefit for the now more secretive hare, grouse, rabbits and badgers.

"Cormac, I feel my brother is close. That dream. It was too vivid to be just fanciful. I know he is alright. I feel he is with others. Come on, lets get going again!"

Cormac smiled at Ramona's new enthusiasm.

"A welcome prophecy to be sure young wizard and as I believe in you, I am sure you are right. But do not abandon your vigilance in spite of your well founded excitement. Alatar will have regrouped by now. It would not be unlike him to send parties out and stronger than before, given what he now knows you are capable of."

Ramona nodded.

"Yes Cormac, I agree. I am keeping my eyes peeled. Don't worry. I just think Jude and I have a good connection. I know he is close by, waiting. I had tried to transmit that to him with my thoughts. I just kept saying 'Stay there. We are coming.' Over and over. I don't know if it worked. But it was worth a try."

Cormac had a glint in his eye "Ramona, if you called him, I have no doubt he heard you. If there are others, then we are strong indeed. Mum and dad, are you ready for more?"

Cormac winked at Ramona's parents. James smiled and with his dry wit, replied..

"We are ready Cormac, but after this, we want a holiday, right Ruthie?" Ruth nodded in strong agreement.

"Two holidays together. One after the other. Just not in Oakhampton!"

Cormac laughed.

"A fair deal then and well deserved I would say. Men and elves.. let us now find Jude. He is near."

So they set off at pace on the brisk morning mist.

Chapter Thirty Two
A Liquid Shortage

The lead Takers were busy working feverishly in Alatar's private quarters. The large open window, which had seen the end of the treasonous Elphinias and the last ditch dive for freedom by Princess Mahreuben, was now fully restored. All evidence of the previous second in command, swept away. Dark powder and that spore-like dust, all gone. The room was now pristine and the leader sat at his central table. Pondering with his pewter goblet of the steaming liquid named life-force. Alatar knew very well that this potion was not life giving at all. He sipped away though. Enjoying the sense of calm it brought him after the manic events. It was a suppressant. He called for Tanwyn, who appeared presently at the door.

"Come in Tanwyn. Do not stand on ceremony."

"Yes leader. Thank you." Came the somewhat meek and predictable response from Tanwyn.

Cacodem, Alatar's treasonous captain, now returned to sanity as Domacec and escaped. Elphinias, a traitor in the midst. Planning to overthrow him. A foolish idea, but yet more evidence that something was not working within. Mahreuben, freed from her restraints and leapt out to sea. Presumably preferring suicide to imprisonment under his rule.

Tanwyn drifted up next to his leader at the work table and Alatar looked up for the first time.

"Tell me friend Tanwyn, do you see these?"

Alatar unravelled several parchment scrolls out on the table. Intricate drawings and writings. All it would seem, by his own hand.

"Yes my leader, I do see."

"What do you see Tanwyn?"

The aide was slightly flustered but mustered a response.

"I see plans my leader. Plans for construction across the realms, very intricate indeed Alatar. Skilled artwork, this is by your own hand then, master?"

"Yes Tanwyn. My own work and I thank you. You are a transparent individual Tanwyn and I wish you no harm. These are plans of the realms to be. Not of the realms that are. You see, when I came across these lands and pitched my campaign to its people, many laughed. Poured scorn on everything I offered. The newness I was bringing."

'Fear.' Thought Tanwyn, privately.

"They were insufferably set in their ways and bound to the sickly sweet Prince and Princess. They knew nothing of the threats beyond their own flowery circumference. I did. Life to these insular dimwits was all pretty banquets, decorated tables, grandiose speeches, celebratory dances. Gambolling in the forests. They are naive, Tanwyn.

I offered them a glimpse of these threats and of what I could do to help nullify them. They wanted no part of my offer. But what these fools had not known of, they could not foresee.

'It has never happened to us before.' They said. I could hear the cogs turning in their limited, stunted brains. Stubborn little men and elves. Fishermen and downtrodden wives looking after brattish children. Village gatherings. Prasing their ethereal.

So automatic Tanwyn. So predictable. So insipid. What I proposed was exciting. Fresh. I would not have had to banish Mahreuben into banshee status. Nor capture the Prince or turn plush living quarters into jail cells, if only they had just listened. All I wanted to do was to give them work in exchange for safe homes and guardianship, Tanwyn."

The aide remained silent, studious. Not wanting to interrupt his master or incur his short temper. All the while Alatar looked him in the eye. Tanwyn did not falter though, as Alatar recalled his rise to power.

"I offered safety, Tanwyn. From the threats I had seen. Not too far away, in dark lands my ancestors know of. But they refused. They laughed me away as a shaman, a travelling circus act. This angered me, Tanwyn. So, I destroyed their hillsides and forests, in front of them, to show them. All reversible of course. Such is my power. Then they began to listen. Some villagers challenged me. Minor scuffles. This is why I had to have the life-force liquid invented. To help them adjust and yes, sadly, force was used to capture those whom would not come of their own accord. Hence the cells."

Tanwyn listened intently. He had never heard his leader discuss anything in such detail, with such emotion in his voice. Tanwyn even empathised with Alatar.

"I understand my leader. I indeed, came of my own free will. I had grown tired of this 'out to pasture', way of living. I did not need to be sold your idea. I believed."

Alatar almost smiled.

"Tanwyn, do you know, I believe you. I do not think you say this to impress me. This is why I would like to involve you further. As you know, the guard we have has grown large. But, it was still not enough to stop that impetuous boy from smashing his motorised chariot through our bridge.

He may well be of magic, but he is just one, a little thug. Why was he able to wreak such havoc Tanwyn? The little idiot could never kill me. But why was he able to do what he did? It took more than courage. It took stupidity on our part. On my part. I have been too free and easy and have underestimated many. But having a guard act so slowly, without a clue as to what to do. To abandon the cells in large numbers as they did. To allow a full scale breakout? It will not do Tanwyn."

Tanwyn ventured a question..

"And so.. my leader?"

"And so, aide Tanwyn. I have new proposals. Take note and get started as soon as this meeting is over. The guard is to be given a smaller dose of the liquid. I do not want them drugged. I want them tame and alert. The prisoners in the cells are to be given a standard dose of the liquid. Take away the gruel. I want them fed on fish, meat, vegetables. Hot drinks, fresh water.

I want them clean, bathed. Grateful, obedient. I want them strong. I want them tested and converted and I want those cells strengthened and emptied. Yesterday will do, Tanwyn. Do you understand me?"

"I understand Alatar. I shall make haste."

Alatar glanced up again.

"Tanwyn. Before you go. I need for you to meet somebody.. Selanius!" He barked.

Out of the shadows from the back of the room, stepped a tall, thin sneaky looking man. Dressed in white robes with a red sash.

"Alatar.. Tanwyn." Selanius bowed. Hands clasped. Alatar continued.

"Selanius is of druid origin. He has been with me from my beginning. He is too important to be out in the open. He and only two of his aides, know how to mix the liquid we need. Eventually, when the new order is established, I hope we have no need of it. For now, I trust no one. Tanwyn, your last duty on the list, is to have a strong guard of twenty, escort Selanius and his aides into the barrens to gather what they need. The cauldrons run low."

Tanwyn bowed.

"It shall be, leader."

Alatar drew the last from his own goblet.

"You have done well Tanwyn. Now you leave with two of my best guard. Put all these orders in motion. I know you will not let me down."

The last words were spoken with menace as Tanwyn bowed and tried not to look as though he was scurrying away.

"Druid.."

Selanius stepped forward.

"Yes, leader?"

"Mix up what is left and then prepare to leave for the Paaniz barrens. The guard will administer it. Have your aides ready."

"Yes leader."

Selanius bowed again and receded back into the shadows.

Chapter Thirty Three
A Coming Together

Mahreuben had been given a tour of what was now affectionately known as New Azmarine, by several of the small, but growing populace. A handsome looking man, Luca, and a younger, feisty looking woman, Elysse, seemed to be representatives, or spokespeople, for this old, and now new land reborn.

Another woman joined them later, it was Luca's wife, Giula. Home from her day of work, teaching the young and also helping to rebuild the cove, she made tea and they all sat. Luca kissed his wife fondly. He told of going to a place called Oakhampton with Giula, but that as quaint and quiet as it was, its emerald sea and glittering sands, he felt that it seemed strange. Even eerie, at times.

He even said to Mahreuben..

"Please, do not laugh Princess, but my wife Giula and I, both felt that some days we had lost time. Other days we had gained it. We would wake and see a cottage that had not been there before, or a tree without leaves was now green and fresh. The same with flowers, poking through the soil one day, the next, in full bloom.

The landscape also seemed to change. Hillsides one day. Flat as far as the eye could see the next. Why? Some days, I would awaken with longer hair, the beginnings of a beard. Giula said she felt younger though. She was beginning to look it. In the end, now scared, we left, or tried to.."

Luca looked sad and wistful and he looked down, kicking a pile of sand forlornly. When Mahreuben asked why they could not leave, Luca replied simply..

"The red eyed one."

It seemed Luca and Giula, were early prisoners of the new jails Alatar had built to harbour many unwitting, potential members of his guard. They had been separated until Theonyra's intervention. They had feared each other dead. The last he had known of his wife, was flailing arms and her being taken away screaming with other women. Luca and Giula had been victims of Elphinias cruel demonstrations and had been catapulted into the sea.

There, they had, like many grateful others, been found by the saviour of stone, Theonyra. Mahreuben placed a hand on Giula's and with an understanding smile, told her..

"Thank you both, for telling me of your coming to be here. I know we will find a way, Giula."

Giula managed a thin, hopeful smile.

Mahreuben found Elysse, the young flame haired woman, quite fiery but very humorous. Her story was similar. She had been in a small group from Emeralfre village, just out of the woodlands. Looking for fruit, mushrooms, nuts and firewood. When a tall, gnarly, hooded figure in a black robe, had intercepted them. Alatar and his guard. He had told of dangers approaching the realms and spoke of his desire to protect all. But the undertones in his voice spoke volumes to the intuitive Elysse.

"I think he is what you would call a manic despot with delusions of grandeur. Horrid looking thing, and that voice.. Made me shiver, Princess. That and the glowing eyes. I did not like, nor trust him. I was happy with you and Prince Uzaleus at the helm, thank you very much." Explained Elysse, adding a curtsy.

Mahreuben had put a hand over her face, she had grinned at Elysse's description of Alatar. But only allowed herself to giggle because Elysse was doing the same! Elysse too, had been pitched out to the waves and scooped up by Theonyra. Her smile hid her heartbreak though. Her children had been kidnapped, and she had yet to be reunited with them. They regained composure, remembering all that had transpired. Sometimes Elysse was not always ready for laughter when she felt such loss. Mahreuben smiled and hugged Elysse.

"Thank you Elysse. Please, no need to treat me as special. We shall find your young ones, I promise. I am grateful for all you have shown and told me. I am just one of the realms folk like you, eager to help."

The tour went on. Theonyra had chosen to remain out of sight behind a large cliff, though he was no longer beneath the waves. Huts had been built. It seemed food, water and firewood was plentiful and children played on the beach in the cove.

"No one must know of New Azmarine." said Mahreuben. She had not aimed this comment at anyone. Simply looking up at the blue sky.

"It belongs to them. They deserve it."

Afterwards, a meal and hot drink was prepared over a cooking fire which Mahreuben thoroughly enjoyed. She spent time talking to the rescued children, whom were giddy with excitement at meeting a Princess. She told of happy times in the dells and woodlands, and of freedom. Times that she and the stone King were going to make sure would return. Later in the day, Mahreuben manifested as a mermaid again and swam the short distance out to Theonyra. Stood firm and anchored as always, watching, guarding.

"It would seem we should make our move shortly, Princess." The stone King said, glancing left and right. Always surveying.

"I agree King Theonyra. The New Azmarine folk are thriving, though not without much torment. They are at least well fed and most of all, hidden. How does first light sound to you?"

The stone King looked down at the beautiful Princess in her mermaid form. Hope and determination shining in her eyes where before there was resignation and despair. He felt something familiar. Could, she be one of his own? A surviving great grandchild? He wracked that intelligent brain, beneath its stone casing and felt it to be so. For now he would stay quiet. The Princess had been through enough emotional turmoil. Instead, he went on as normal. As normal could be, for a stone King.

"At first light Princess, we shall leave. I know a path that will not draw attention to the cove. Though once on land my dear, I will be as conspicuous as the tower. I can only hope that before we are noticed, we may be nearer our destination."

After all, Theonyra was indeed a giant. He had not moved for lifetimes. Save for saving Azmarine.

"I know of this, Theonyra. Sadly, I posess some magic, but am no wizard, or else I would turn you small. Like a mouse and carry you, well hidden."

Theonyra shuddered in mock fright. It made waves.

"And then be picked off by falcon or kestrel? No thank you my lady. I would rather face the Takers than become a peregrine's breakfast."

Theonyra chuckled at the scenario. It was the first time Mahreuben had heard him laugh. It was infectious.

"Oh Theonyra. Not so serious after all!" The Princess was looking up, giggling at him.

"No, Princess. Not so serious all of the time. Nobody is made of stone." Theonyra winked. Then they both laughed. Mahreuben bobbed up and down on the waves. Such was the force of a chortling giant. Then, they made off to sleep. The King was certain now. He wanted his great grandaughter to know she had loving family left. He would tell her, soon.

Jude and Uzaleus and the escapees, including Domacec and Ailbe, were sat resting under the willow trees. Having had a much needed break. Waiting. Elves were making their fortifying tea in a pot over a small blaze. Scattering dried leaves and herbs into boiling water. Jude was gazing across the flat land over at a slight hill in the distance. He looked suddenly very alert. Jude stood, squinting now, trying to see better and then he drew a sharp intake of breath. Another group were coming more into focus, walking very briskly down this hill and towards the temporary camp of Jude and Uzaleus men.

"Prince, look!.."

Uzaleus and Domacec stood up, snapping out of sleepiness.

"Its Mona! Look, she's here."

"Your sister, the wizard. Ah, this is good news Jude. You were right my friend, you were right. I shall meet our brave young woman."

Uzaleus slapped the young man on the back. Domacec, Ailbe and the rest looked eagerly at the approaching figures. Jude was beaming. He dropped his tea and ran towards the new group. Sure enough, as they drew closer to each other, Jude could make out his sister's flowing raven locks and his mother and father, together, hands entwined. Led by the diminutive, fleet footed elf, Cormac.

"Mona, mum, dad!" Shouted Jude. Beside himself at a happy reunion. The two black-backed gulls circled overhead. Biggle and Baggle. Another scouting job well done.

"Extra fish for you my friends, to be sure." Called Cormac, slowing to a halt. They cawed in appreciation. Finally, they all met on this huge landscape of land. Brother and sister embraced. Ruth cried into James shoulder. Happy tears this time, from this strong young mother.

"My sister, the wizard. I knew you'd come." Jude waved over at his parents, glowing. He had found his family, whatever the circumstances.

"My brother, the impetuous one! Wow Jude. You had us in pieces, but I knew you would make it." Ramona hugged her brother again.

"Hey, I lost you once. I can't be letting that happen again sis."

"Ha. I won't let you. I'll magic up some shackles on you when you go to sleep!"

Jude was open mouthed. "You can do that now?"

Ramona giggled playfully. "No, but I had you going. No more disappearing acts. Look at mum, shattered! And our poor dad's gone grey with worry!"

They shrieked with laughter. At this, Uzaleus smiled, looked towards his men, he told them to relax for a while. James, pulled a mock sad face, but his eyes glinted with mischief and happiness.

"Hey! You two. Less of that. I am not grey, I'm.. dignified. Isn't that right Cormac?"

The elf winked at Ramona and Jude and shifted from foot to foot. He couldn't resist it..

"If you say so James, if you say so.." Ramona and Jude rolled around laughing. Cormac went on with his comedic onslaught.

"A little grey now James, but only noticeable at close quarters, to be sure. Ageing must be embraced, not feared, my old friend. Perhaps leave be this 'hair dye' you spoke of. It does you no favours, to be sure."

The elf grinned towads Ramona and Jude who were unable to stop themselves howling with laughter at the display of comedy between Cormac and their fun-loving dad.

"Hair dye? Of all the cheek! Cormac, I am in shock. My loyal elven friend. Saying I look old! This hair is its natural colour my friend. Oh, I am so upset now, so very upset.. I only mentioned that I might try hair dye, in the distant future.." James went on, muttering hilariously. They all had a good bond, and both knew it was humour. It was nice to laugh amongst it all. Jude broke away briefly.

"Now, you lot. Come and meet the Prince, and there is with us, a new man. Returned to the good side." He glanced at Domacec, whom bowed his head in thanks. Although a sadness at yet again recalling events at the Ivywyrld Inn. It seemed a lifetime ago. He had been Cacodem. Captain of the Takers, and Domacec was still processing this.

Ramona was filled in on everything very quickly, before she could become angry with Domacec. She gave Jude time to help her understand. She shook Domacec firmly by the hand.

"I am sorry Domacec. That I had to use magic on your men. Even if they were pure Takers. They may not all have been willing. Like you. It makes me sad. Life is life, after all."

Domacec shook his head at the futility of it all.

"I am sorry too Ramona. Truly sorry that I.. that.. Alatar put us in that horrible position. I am, and will remain, at the service of yourself, of Jude and of the Prince.

"Thank you Domacec. We shall put this behind us now. We move on, my friend." Ramona bowed. Domacec looked grateful. As though a weight had lifted from his heart. The two parties became one larger one. They combined the food and drink they had into a good meal.

"I suggest we rest here until tomorrow."

It was Uzaleus.

"We have a good force now. We can set up a watch and move when light is better. Are we in agreement?" It was a general question.

But instant shouts of 'Agreed.' showed the thoughts of the large group. Rest and warmth were needed.

"Good, then sleep well, all of you. I will take first watch with any volunteers."

There were many volunteers. Now, Ramona got back to her feet. She stood on top of a large, rust-red rock. She felt compelled to address the small army.

"I just want to say thank you, to all of you. We are all here for different reasons. We all want to get back to where we would like to be. Yes, let us sleep well friends. Tomorrow, I am going to find Alatar. To end it. Are you with me?"

The noise was rousing given the size of the party, unbelievable. Fists punched the air. Swords were raised in salute. A roar went up.

"We are with you! Ramona of the realms."

The fire flickered and Cormac tossed some bread and fish for the gulls. They swooped gratefully down. Cormac whispered to himself in a more menacing tone than was his usual. "We're coming for you, red eyed one. To be sure.. We're coming for you."

The feisty elf, jabbed his dagger aggressively into the ground, grunted, put another log on the fire and grimaced, away with thoughts of Alatar. Brilliant sparks crackled up into the evening sky, as pipistrel bats danced in the moonlight.

CHAPTER THIRTY FOUR
SELANIUS STRIDES OUT

Tanwyn had been busy. Very busy indeed. He felt as though he needed more time. Alatar had shown faith in him by enlisting him as the replacement for Elphinias, last seen lifeless and dragged under the murky waters of the moat, by a creature Tanwyn never wished to lay eyes on again.

It seemed Alatar had put in many measures of his own, in relation to his own security, but only the realms knew what that awful creature was. Now, the newly appointed chief aide had so many tasks to see to, as his leader remained in his quarters. Probably working on his plans and his parchments. Tanwyn did not feel he had been honoured by his new role. He had not sought the position out as had the scheming Elphinias. Nor had he any wish to try and overthrow his leader.

Tanwyn had lied about being a conscious follower. He had lied about agreeing with Alatar and of not having to be sold his leader's ideas. He was really just another meek man of the realms, held in obedience by the liquid and he had developed the nous to see what was coming when the Takers had showed up.

Tanwyn, had seen of Domacec's attempts to fight and to stand up to Alatar, and then, he had seen the episodes that followed. Things that led to Domacec being transformed into the docile and obedient captain Cacodem. Tanwyn saw the futility of attempted heroics, and so adopted the approach of conscious follower, loyal member of the guard. His memories were hazy, as though under a layer of fog. But they were there.

He had been given a reduced measure of the life-force liquid, that insiders now knew to be a control drug. Alatar trusted no one enough to exempt them from some sort of dose. This was not a medicine. Tanwyn knew the difference between a medicine and a drug. So he had kept his enemies close as it were.

But with the liquid given, he also found it hard not to obey the rule of Alatar and the Takers. It was a limbo state and in his moments of clarity, he dreamt of a way out. An escape.

Perhaps some other army would take on the guard and win and set him free. To flee alone would be tantamount to suicide, Tanwyn knew this much. He would soon have been recaptured and flung out to sea as an example of treason. That would be his best-case scenario. If, he avoided a straight execution. No. There was nothing for it. He would, for now, obey and try to remain in the background as a staunch member of the guard. Now, this had become impossible having been bestowed the dubious award of chief aide.

Alatar sat up in his top tower quarters, heavily guarded while he pondered liquids and parchments. Irritation festered in him due to this Ramona. 'They follow an inexperienced outlander. Escaping. Amassing small armies.' Alatar suddenly let out a blood-curdling roar. The guard of twenty, assembled in the courtyard as promised, heard the leader's frustrations at ground level. Glancing upward, they saw fire playing on the ramparts. Rather the Paaniz barrens than here, when he is in this mood. The chief aide shuddered and hoped no one had noticed.

'I am no leader. How in the realms am I going to come out of this?' Tanwyn mused grimly as he approached the Takers. Lined up in four banks of five. Black shrouds. Glowering eyes under those drooping dark hoods. Faceless and nameless to Tanwyn. Who knew what sort of man, woman or elf lay under those menacing uniforms. Standing in front of the guard, finally Tanwyn addressed them.

"Guard of the tower and the new regime. Your job today, is to escort a druid and his men into the barrens. To see that no harm comes to the druid, myself, or his two men. Your job is to remain alert. To warn immediately of any danger and to ask no questions. By way of Alatar's gratitude, when the job is successfully completed, you will be given extra food and spare time will be awarded to you for rest. There is no option of asking any questions. We go where the druid tells us. We guard while he gathers what he needs. We return. Understood?"

A murmer of 'Understood.' from the guard. Obedient and toneless.

"Raise the drawbridge. We leave now. If you have no food and water with you.. It is too late, you will have to share or hope to come across it organically. Come Selanius!"

Tanwyn called the druid. He had hoped his speech had exuded some kind of authority. The Takers looked so drone-like, he guessed they had been dosed up. From the bottom door of the tower and down the small flight of steps, came the druid Selanius. Spindly, yet he had an aura of smug self-assurance. In his white robe and red sash and belt. He was flanked by two men in simalar dress but with green sash and belt.

'An authority thing.' Thought Tanwyn. Selanius sidled alongside Tanwyn, his men a few feet back.

"We are ready, aide Tanwyn. All we need is protection. Eyes and ears We know what we need and where it is. Alatar wishes we make haste."

Tanwyn nodded.

"Agreed druid. I do not want to be languishing in the Paaniz barrens any longer than necessary. Guard! Proceed forward.."

The banks of five separated and fanned out. A group behind Tanwyn, Selanius and his two men. A group in front. And one to each side.

"Set a brisk pace. Stay alert and vigilant. I do not want to loiter in the scrub too long."

A brief murmur and the bleak looking ensemble drifted across the bridge and away.

CHAPTER THIRTY FIVE
A CONSPICUOUS JOURNEY

The small population of what was becoming known as New Azmarine, stirred and yawned and stretched. Theonyra and Mahreuben were almost ready to leave the cove and make for the tower. Luca and Elysse, the spokespeople, along with Luca's wife Giula, had now been briefed of the plan. The cove people were told of the intentions of the stone King, that he would be assisting Princess Mahreuben in bringing down Alatar.

The New Azmarinian's were upset at first when Mahreuben told them that she and Theonyra were not to be escorted or followed. She was not fond of being strict or firm but when it was, for a greater good, she hoped they would understand. Mahreuben had then also explained that she had seen enough harm come to these people. The trauma of being pitched out to drown. The healing would take time. Strength would take time also, to return to bodies and minds.

She thanked the New Azmarinian's for welcoming her and for letting her stay in warmth and safety. She spoke of her love for them and their children and how that by doing this now that they could all live in safety. Even return inland, eventually, if they ever felt the calling. Everything she had said was transparently genuine and so, accepted by the people. Such was the reverence she was held in. Her aura did most of the work. Then she blessed the land in both human and elven tongue. Most now looked as though they were quite happy to stay where they were. They had seen enough of Takers drifting around and kidnapping and imprisoning. Murmuring.

Luca, Giula and Elysse understood Mahreuben's compassion. It was just that they wanted to help and see Alatar fall with their own eyes. Realistically, they would all be of more use to each other, continuing to build and gather supplies and stay within the cove. Unseen and prospering. The Princess, now looking more familiar to herself, stood on foot at a hilltop about half a mile away from the cove. It seemed a poignant meeting place. Just far away enough to be discreet. Picturesque and beautifully quiet. It had been named Azma Point. Dewy, thick green grass grew and a smattering of large stones stood like knowledgeable monoliths.

'Watchers.' Thought the Princess. Nothing in the realms was guaranteed to be as it seemed at first glance. The sea was still and she watched gannets arrowing in to catch fish. Soon however, waves formed and parted. The various gulls, merganser and tern, squawked their displeasure at the interruption of breakfast and flapped away.

A huge granite head began to poke above the waves, then, a broad torso, thick arms. Muscular looking thighs and strong, sturdy feet. The stone King, Theonyra, was a sight to behold. Very rarely had he ventured out of water in recent years.

"A good morning to you Princess. I thought I would give those poor mackerel and bass a break. I know we all have to eat, but those birds are getting as wide as they are long. Using their wings a little might help them feel fitter. Bobbing expectantly up and down on the waves like well cared for children. Go on, shoo, for now. There is food inland!"

Theonyra smiled. Then his thoughts turned. Would Mahreuben accept him, a stone man, as her great grandfather? He pulled himself back to the matter at hand and chuckled as the gulls cawed their displeasure at breakfast ending early. He liked the birds and they liked him. Though they remained the charming chancers of the sea and would only leave as though at great pains.

Mahreuben found the King familiar, enchanting. He could be family almost, she thought. He seemed to have many layers. No longer just a wise old sage of ocean and myth. He had character. A soul lived in. Now she had gotten to know him a little better since her unforeseen pilgrimage to him for help, she saw new facets to him every day.

"A good morning to you King Theonyra. How nice it is that before we go getting into more trouble, we may start the day with a smile and a view such as this. No wonder you have never seen the need to leave."

"Here is home to me Princess. Anywhere else I would look like a statue lost on his travels. Perhaps if it was old times.." Theonyra seemed to be recalling a memory. He thoughts drifted again..

"Theonyra?" Ventured Mahreuben, to see if her giant companion wished to elaborate. She wondered what was coming.

"Ah, nothing Princess. I was just going to say.." He trailed off, misty eyed.

"Go on, King.." The Princess, gently encouraging the giant, she so badly wanted to be right about her gut instinct.

He went on "If it was old times. Then I may have returned to land. Before I was turned to stone. Then I could have.."

"Its alright King. Please.."

"I could have found my only great grandchild and.. and told her, that I love her.."

Mahreuben's jaw dropped open. She became conscious that she was now staring at Theonyra in a different light. She had been right. She had a living relative. Not just that, but one she loved dearly. She had just wanted to hear it from her great grandfather, confirmed.

"You were not always of stone great grandfather. I somehow knew this. I have been confused. I thought it rude though, to ask you of your life prior. To pry. I am sorry if I have upset you or brought up unwanted memories. I hope in time, that I may bury my memories of caves and never hear the name banshee again. But I somehow felt it. That we were connected, related. I loved you always. Even from that.. that cave.."

Mahreuben shuddered, nearly drifting off herself into an unwanted recollection.

"How I feel for you, my grandfather. There are similarities with us King Theonyra. Different, but the same. Perhaps that is why the realms conspired that we meet? I just.. did not know."

Theonyra smiled warmly at his empathetic companion. He moved into shallow water and came to the Princess on a shingle stretch of beach, below the hilltop.

"How would you know anyway, dear Princess? I was afraid of more hurt for you. I could not hold in my love anymore. We are too few now, our bloodline. All this was lifetimes ago. Not prying at all, my granddaughter. Polite and endearing are you. My stone existence has now given me decade after decade of life that as a man, I may not have had. Generations indeed, have I spent happily existing in these waters. Certainly by now I would be dust had I prevailed against our foes in my human body."

Mahreuben could hear the cogs turning for Theonyra. She could almost visualise the battles he had fought for his land. His people. Selfless. Her swelling respect for him grew more in this one instant, and his for her. He shook his head as though making a conscious attempt to come out of a dream.

"No, I have adapted, and enjoyed what I am. Though I sometimes idly wish to be among mankind again. I then recite my gratitude for my extra years and the knowledge it has bestowed upon me. Though, through these centuries as a man of stone, I have learnt not to meddle, when possible. Lest they come back to finish the job and then I really would be a statue."

Another rumbling chuckle.

"Though I do not think the people behind my changing got their magic completely right."

A smile of irony flickered across his chiselled features.

"I think turning me to stone worked for them, to a point, but being left as a live giant was not in their plans. Half-wits. How I enjoyed playing dead while they celebrated. How I nearly broke character and swatted them into nothing."

His face was steely, fiery now. But only briefly. Then, the warm smile returned.

"Perhaps Alatar is descended from them, another half-wit, ha!" Theonyra enjoyed his own joke but Mahreuben felt a sadness on hearing more of his backstory.

"Now to the off my young Princess, feels good to stretch these old legs again. Let us stride out, as a family. The realms would not let true magic be held in the hands of a mad man. Despite what the red eyed one thinks."

Mahreuben watched in admiration as her King and now, great grandfather strode over the shale beach. He began to walk across the wet sand up to drier land, turned and beckoned to Mahreuben. She smiled broadly and followed. They walked westerly and gradually the path came away from the coastline. More grassy now and the sound of the waves and squawking gulls faded. They came to a huge and dense forest.

"Conspicuous I may be, Princess. But so far, so good."

Mahreuben nodded, although slightly less relaxed now than she had been at the cove.

"So far so good grandfather." She was glancing left and right. They rarely stopped, merely slowing every now and then to scout the land for possible dangers. The forest was quiet, save for a roe deer which happened across their path. The deer stood, anchored still. As still as Theonya himself would, in the sea.

Mahreuben and the King also stopped. A silent mutual admiration and respect, passed unspoken between animal, Princess and King. The deer cocked its head quizzically to one side and then suddenly receded from view back into the trees. Mahreuben took a long drink of water and they talked of the beauty of nature when left to its own design. They were not tired but it was nice to take a break from racing thoughts, to find out a bit more about each other away from the fighting.

They pushed on and the forest became less dense and shortly they came to flat and open land again. Passing boulders and large stones that had no real reason to be there, they were back among grass, gorse and all manner of vegetation. Presently, Theonyra stopped abrubtly. So much so that Mahreuben bumped into the back of his huge left calf.

She began to say 'Ouch.' In jest, but the stone King held a granite finger to his mouth in a gesture to remain silent. Mahreuben furrowed her brow and gave him a questioning look. Theonyra got down to his knees as best he could without causing the ground to rumble. He motioned her to come behind a set of boulders. His body still poked above and around the rocks but it was the best he could do.

Whispering, Mahreuben said simply "What is it?" Theonyra looked down at the Princess, still dwarfing her despite halving his size by kneeling. He looked across the land, motioning her to do the same. She gazed in silence but then she saw what he had seen.

A large group of Takers and some smaller ceremonial looking men, dressed in white. Mahreuben raised her eyebrows, shocked.

"Theonyra?"

Now, the King looked concerned.

"The Druid. I had thought him long dead."

CHAPTER THIRTY SIX
SELANIUS

Theonyra had been right with his observation. Out on the plains came a throng of Takers, forming a protective perimeter around the tall thin druid, Selanius. He had men of his own, one either side of him.

The druid was gesturing to his aides. They began to forage. They all held wooden baskets and were pulling up vegetation. Most of it was tossed back to the ground.

"No! Fools." Barked Selanius.

"The roots.. We must find the granyaak roots.. I do not want stew ingredients.."

The two aides continued to nose the ground, scraping and chattering to each other about Selanius demanding ways. Tanwyn paced back and forth, bemused. The new second in command had no real briefing for himself, or to give the twenty strong guard. They were just under strict orders from Alatar to ask no questions and to protect the druid at all costs while he got on with his gathering of ingredients.

"They are searching for the sources that make the liquid. I just know it." Mahreuben was whispering to Theonyra, but through gritted teeth. "He, has sent them. That filthy coward."

Her face was sheer aggression. Her pretty features wrinkled into a pained expression. She imagined the potion sliding down her throat, burning. It made her wretch just to think of it and of all the people and elves controlled by it. And here was the source. This arrogant little weasel. Spindly little puppet of the tower, hidden for so long by Alatar.

"He has been bought, I would say." Mused Theonyra, still watching and trying to squat even lower behind the rocks. "Probably offered impunity by supplying the liquid to the red eyed one."

Mahreuben boiled.

"We must kill him grandfather. Now! Let us see if he is given impunity by my dagger! They are all cowards. I am sick of holding back Theonyra. Sick of sparing cretins, hive insects whom would drown us without a care."

Mahreuben was already beginning to stand, fists closed into balls by her side as though she intended to beat Selanius to a pulp. Theonyra put a large finger on her shoulder, calmly restraining her. She harrumphed, but relaxed her stance. He had only just found her, he was not about to let her go storming off alone, he was looking across the barren land, but beyond Selanius and the Takers.

"No, Princess. Wait. I feel movement, in the ground." The right palm of the stone King was pressed flat against the grass. Mahreuben grudgingly crouched again beside her giant ancestor.

"Here, see.." Theonyra guided the hand of Mahreuben, tiny, delicate porcelain in comparison to his own. "Now Princess, push flatly against the ground." She felt it now. Very feint at first, but as her own magic broiled within her like a separate entity and her senses fine tuned, it became stronger. Her eyes widened.

"Forces.. The red eyed one sends more forces!" She had almost shouted, but Theonyra hushed her again with only a look.

"No, Princess. Not forces of Alatar. We would not feel the vibrations so strongly. They drift, these Takers, I see that. I feel feet. In a hurry, runners.. I think it is Ramona, the girl wizard, and she is not alone!" Mahreuben looked at Theonyra in bewilderment and recalled her visitation to Ramona at the elven shelters.

"Ramona!" A sharp intake of breath and the Princess held her hands to her face.

"I have been to her in dream form. When I was imprisoned. I have promised to help her. Her family too.."

"Perhaps now is the time to begin then, my young lady." Theonyra motioned her again to look beyond Selanius.

"Because here she comes!"

They had covered so much ground. The joined forces of good. Ramona and her family and Cormac and his brave elves. Her returned brother Jude and Prince Uzaleus, Domacec and the escaped throng of men and elves. The now large group slowed to a brisk trot.

'Together as one.' They had said.

"The Paaniz barrens." Observed Cormac.

"Not a place I am fond of to be sure." He held up a hand to slow the group to a stop. Ramona screwed her eyes up as though it would enhance her vision.

"There!" She pointed eastward.

Uzaleus was beside her.

"What do you see young one?"

"Takers, Uzaleus." She paused and her face went blank for a second. Still narrowing her eyes to see.

"Ramona?"

"Three others, dressed in white are among them. I do not know of these types."

At this, Domacec joined the two at the front and gazed out at the activity unfolding not far away.

"It is Tanwyn. I can see that much. The taller man and the two with him.. They are of druid origin. But it is the thing of fable in these realms!"

"Fable?" Ramona looked at Domacec now.

"What do you mean, Domacec?"

"I mean, young lady, that the druids were all supposed to be extinct. Cast out as sorcerers, demons. Burned or stoned. In a time not of ours. Until they became.. Just.."

"Fables?"

"Well.. Yes, Ramona."

Cormac now intervened. He was after all, something of a historian. Knowledgeable of eras gone by.

"And yet.." He observed Selanius and the Takers over in the distance.

"That, is a druid. To be sure."

Domacec flared a little in recollection of his own experience as a Taker.

"I know this much Cormac. Druids, fable or not, make potions. And they are surrounded by a guard of Alatar's drones. They are not picking daisies. What sort of potion do you think they are gathering vegetation for?"

Domacec looked angrily at the dark group, still foraging. Having been transformed into a Taker himself by the liquid.

"I'll rip Alatar to pieces myself when we get to that damned tower."

Cormac put a calming arm on the shoulder of Domacec.

"We all feel the same my friend. To have you with us, like this.. Well, It is proof that a strong mind with a strong heart, can beat the effects of this wretched drink. We cannot kill any of these poor souls, Domacec. How do we know if there are not good people trapped under those sagging hoods?"

Domacec nodded in agreement. Ramona stepped in again.

"We give them fair warning, Domacec. We tell them to leave. If they stand in our way, we then use force. I know how to get rid of Takers. And then we will see what this bought druid has to say for himself."

Ruth and James stood looking at their daughter. A mixture of pride, awe and sadness. This was not the end to their holiday they had planned. But to see her there, not just holding her own, but being counted upon.

Battle ready. The fierceness of youth. It made them so very proud.

CHAPTER THIRTY SEVEN
CAPTURE

'Ramona, young wizard. I need you to hear me again. Focus on my voice, as you did at the elven shelters..' A soft whisper came through the ether.

"Princess!" Ramona shrieked. She had heard Mahreuben. This time, she was not asleep though. 'I thought she was gone. How does she do this?' Very little shocked Ramona now in these lands, but even so. Her brother had heard her shout and approached.

"Sis, are you alright?" Jude whispered. The assembly of elves and men waited on some sort of instruction.

"Jude, it is Mahreuben. She is calling me, talking to me. She is near. Please Jude, ask the others, to get ready and be alert. I have to answer her right away."

"But how is she talking to you?"

Jude had been absent when Mahreuben had presented to Ramona previously.

"No time Jude. I'm sorry to rush you bro, but please, do not tell Uzaleus anything yet. You will see, shortly. I promise."

"Hmm, alright then, but whats the big secret Mona?"

"No secret Jude, short on time is all. The Princess is safe, but Prince Uzaleus would go tearing across the land for her, and I would not blame him, but this is our chance to get at Alatar. Let me focus Jude, stay hidden. Look after mum and dad. Please, be ready!"

Jude understood. His sister was in business mode.

"Don't worry sis. I'll do it." He squeezed her hand and scampered back to the waiting pack. They were keen to do something. To get some direction. Ailbe spoke.

"Jude. We follow without question. You saved us all from the jail cells, but what is going on?"

Jude, said nothing of the Princess, but explained that his sister was ready to advance, and simply passed on her instructions. 'Be ready to move.'

Ailbe nodded, satisfied, remembering where he had been not long ago. They had gotten this far after all. Ramona had moved away from the others, not far, but enough to have personal space, thinking time. She propped herself against a cedar tree and sat cross legged, eyes closed, almost as though meditating. The men and elves looked on. Some eating, drinking water. Taking off boots to give their hardened feet a small breather.

"Meditation, now?" Said a tall, handsome looking elf named Dayn, to Cormac. But the keen Cormac had sensed something and asked the others to let her be alone. When Dayn questioned his friend further, he simply replied..

"Wizards eh brother, mystical creatures to be sure! She knows what she is doing. We let her be for now, I think. We will observe from a distance for her safety. Come Dayn. Have some cool water."

"I'll slay my thirst and then some druid, to be sure, Cormac." Smiled Dayn, taking a large swig from Cormac's bottle and appreciating the reassurance of his friend.

"I will say this Dayn lad, water is all fine and dandy. It is in our beings. But it is not the same as a good hot woodland tea made by our Finola." Cormac missed the elven woods and his beloved friend Finola,left behind to help look after the younglings.

"Lets do this brother, and then we can go home to Whitsomin."
Dayn agreed heartily.

Under the cedar, where spots of rain were now pattering on the leaves, Ramona tried to channel her thoughts and answer Mahreuben.

Though she was working on hope rather than anything else. Only just beginning to harness her powers, she now had to believe in herself enough to communicate in this new way.

'Princess, I can hear you now. I can feel you close by. I heard your voice. Where are you? I am so happy you got away! I am on open land, gorse and scrub, now with many others.'

'These are the Paaniz barrens Ramona. I for one do not like it here. I feel bad magic.' Mahreuben answered.

Theonyra watched silently and kept a loving eye on her. The Takers and the druid seemed to be immersed in whatever it was that they were doing. Gathering something stumpy with roots into wooden baskets. He became Mahreuben's eyes and ears, while the Princess, her own eyes closed, began a silent exchange with Ramona.

'Ramona, my dear, brave girl. How I want to thank you. We can see you. I am with Theonyra. The stone King. I find that he is my great grandfather. See how good magic brings love and light. We have found each other, generations apart. So now I want to help you get home. More than ever. There is so much to explain, but not like this. Please, try not to feel any bitterness towards the realms. They just knew you were the one. Do you see the druid and the guard?'

'I see them yes. Pulling up plants by the roots. I have to tell you Princess. Uzaleus is with us. He is safe and ready to strike, as are we all here. There is no bitterness in my family or I myself Princess. Your news is so beautiful. I feel it is not a surprise, I am so glad to see you with our gentle giant, more so as he is your grandfather. Do not worry. We have much to tell also. We were heading back to the tower, to Alatar. Yet now we see those damned Takers, and men in white robes. The cause of all of this.'

Mahreuben answered.

'The druid. We think he feared for his life Ramona. We think a deal was made with Alatar. He sold his soul in order to live half a life in shadows. We think they are looking for granyaak root. It is a dangerous plant. Poison, if not prepared correctly. A hallucinogen. It no doubt is a key ingredient of the life-force liquid.'

Mahreuben had sensed that Uzaleus was alive, just as she had felt Theonyra to be her grandparent. Faith ran high. The Prince had stated his firm belief that Mahreuben had survived her own leap of faith from the top tower during the day of escape. Love had magic of its own. True telepathy. She had shivered slightly at the mention of his name. Uzaleus. She would see him again!

After living in caves. After starting to believe herself that she was the banshee that she had been labelled by Alatar. The red eyed one had basked in poisoning the minds of realms folk against her. Some scared, some willing, some gullible, most brainwashed.

Whatever the reason, she was run out of the realms and thrown into that dank cave off the coastal path. Her only company was the gulls. They took her fish and crab, whelks and suchlike. Two of them, large black-backed ones, even hunkered down in the cave for warmth on occasion. She drifted in thought, recalling how she was forced away from the inner realms and left to live in self-torment.

She had survived that. She had taken help from nature. Now she was ready to give it back, selfless soul that she was. She had survived the impact of the liquid. She had survived everything that had been thrown at her. Near starvation, dehydration and weak in body and heart. She held to her love and belief that the ethereal spirits would not let this mad charlatan win. She came back from her thoughts, aware she was daydreaming.

'Princess?' Ramona had noticed her silence.

'I am sorry. I had forgotten myself for a moment. Yes, I sense my Prince, Ramona. Thank you. We must not let our emotions interfere. Do not tell him just yet.'

Mahreuben felt her pulse quicken. It was hard not to race out into the open and scream for Uzaleus, but she did not. Ramona had her hands pressed lightly to her temples as though it helped her to concentrate.

'No, Mahreuben. I have not spoken of you. My brother knows you are near. He waits with our group, but wait.. Now I see you, little specks across these barrens. I see your grandfather, the King. What do you think we should do?'

The Princess looked up lovingly at her companion, Theonyra. Giving him a silent signal to be ready.

'We must charge them Ramona. You from your side. The King and I from ours.'

'Lets do it Mahreuben. I know what to do now.'

'Good, because you are the chosen one young wizard. There is no way they can harm us. Though, we must afford them the same courtesy. They are not of their own minds and we are not killers.'

'I am.' Thought Ramona sadly thinking of the Ivywyrld Inn. A lifetime ago it seemed. At some point she knew she had to talk with Domacec. As a former Taker, now recovering. The old captain Cacodem. A cheap lazy pseudonym, concocted by Alatar. It was a mockery. Domacec also felt similar sadness and shame, a desire for closure. Perhaps they could help each other.

Bizarrely now, Ramona heard a giggle in her head. Mahreuben had not heard Ramona's sadness, distracted by the stone King. Ramona was glad.

'You are laughing Princess?'

'Yes, I am sorry Ramona. I seem to have rediscovered my sense of fun. It is my travel companion. Grandfather Theonyra. He wishes to give the Takers a gentle warning. I have told him I can only imagine one of his gentle warnings. He will act only if I ask him. Royalty or not! Just wait until you see him in full!'

Despite the situation, Ramona laughed out loud.

'If you mean the huge rock man, I already have seen him. His toes stick out from your hiding place! I am more surprised that they have not spotted you. My mother would say, typical man!"

More joint chuckling.

'Theonyra says you are a scamp young wizard! He is telling me enough Tomfoolery. He is eager to make haste.'

'Tomfoolery, ha! I like that. I'll use it on my dad.' Ramona was getting quite adept at this silent communication.

James ears pricked up. He could see Ramona was busy, so he did not interfere. He squeezed Ruth's hand.

"Bang goes our hot bath and early night, my love. Much more fun to stop a nasty old druid on his poison run, eh!"

Ruth smiled wryly. She always felt safe when James gave his jovial reassurances. She knew he was not making light of things but she felt that they would come out of everything alright. Now, Ramona heard the sound of faster breathing and then the Princess' fading voice.

'You can tell Theonyra those things yourself Ramona, he has charged off ahead.'

There on the huge Paaniz barrens stretch of the realms, was a huge granite form, advancing. Causing the ground to rumble. Tanwyn, the new chief aide of the Takers, stood aghast. He watched this ghostly giant covering the vast stretch of ground with just short strides. Selanius the druid, got to his feet, granyaak roots fell from his hands, mouth hanging open agog.

"But.. Azmarine is dead, flooded. We turned this old man to stone. Surely, of all that I believed.. a haunting then, this is. It is King Theonyra!"

Selanius stood frozen, terror crawled over his previously smug features. These two had crossed paths in another time and it was unpleasant. Behind the stone King came the Princess, trying her hardest to catch up. Fins and a tail were no use to her on hard terrain. The druid violently shook one of his men to look. He muttered something and then shouted to Tanwyn.

"In the name of the realms, Tanwyn. It is Theonyra. Oh ethereal lords of the sky! We are all finished."

Tanwyn was looking the other way. At an onrushing small army led by a striking looking, raven haired young woman. The chosen one of the ethereal was coming. Tanwyn turned to his guard. He knew the odds were a waste of time. They possessed force, but not magic.

"Hold your ground. Surround the druid." They fanned out and made a circle around Selanius and his two men. To attack was futile.

"What are you doing Taker! Do your job. Kill them." Shouted the panicking druid.

"My job is to protect you. Glorified cellar hand. Not to sacrifice the lives of my men and I. You will be silent!" Tanwyn had finally found his own voice and courage.

'I may die of course.' He thought ironically. 'But I will not be spoken down to anymore. Not by a sneak, a manipulative lizard who makes that filthy poison. I will liaise with these folk. They are not killers.'

The druid had been startled at Tanwyn's fiery tongue.

"A bit late for bravery, drone. Be thankful if you die quickly here. Servant boy, another slave to my liquid. For if we survive, Alatar shall be informed of your negligible incompetence."

"Alatar is not here, stew maker. He sits idling in his tower, guarded by fools such as I and these wizened orcs and drugged men. They will not kill us."

"How do you know this, you, a mere follower, how?" Spat the druid.

"Because they are not of Alatar." Came the reply.

"And they are not cowards like you and I.."

Almost wistful, Tanwyn thought of what might have been had he been part of the escape.

The scene was quite spectacular. Here was a druid, thought long gone. Surrounded by a synthetic guard, borne of life-force liquid, a mind control drink. On one side of them was Ramona, Jude, Prince Uzaleus, Cormac and throng. Slowed now to a halt at the hand gesture of the girl wizard. Maturing all the time. She had earned the trust and respect of the people of the realms. Just as she in turn had respected them.

On the other side of the Takers, now looking like a shrunken force, were Princess Mahreuben and Theonyra, The stone King of Azmarine. A short stand off ensued. Then Ramona stepped away from her companions, walking towards the guard.

"So.. here is the driving force. Alatar's heartbeat. A man of myth. Responsible for so much death. For bringing my family here. For my own ageing. For trying to destroy a peaceful land. The banishment of a Princess.

The imprisonment of the Prince of the realms and innocent elves and men. You. A little sewer rat. You, poor deluded others, more drugged men in cloaks. Is this really the best your leader of the new realms could do?"

On the other side now, were Theonyra, casting a massive shadow over the druid, and Princess Mahreuben. Ramona went on with her verbal onslaught.

"A soup maker, his mindless assistants and yet more slurring fools of Alatar. Where is your hero? Where is the man, that thing that you so readily serve? Where is he, our revered leader?"

Tanwyn stuttered. In sheer desparation, he blurted out "Please lady, do not kill us!"

Ramona frowned. "We are not going to kill you, guardsman. Look behind me. Who do you see?"

Tanwyn gazed at the pack of elves and men. A thrown together but strong hearted outfit. Courageous and cohesive.

"Cacodem. It is you. You escaped the jail then I see!"

Domacec stepped forward.

"Yes Tanwyn. It is me, Domacec is my name. Not the Taker I was before. Even though I was assisted in escape, I would still rather have died in that cell, than served another day at the behest of these zealots."

"But.." Tanwyn got no further. Domacec silenced him with a wave.

"In the jail, I came back to myself. I was given no more liquid. I saw horrible things in my mind as it coarsed out of me. Addled I was, as you are now. But I saw whom I had been before, and am again now. Domacec, of the realms."

"And what is to happen next?" whispered Tanwyn, meekly.

Ramona stood beside Domacec. A bond was forming between them. A mutual understanding. She nodded towards Theonyra.

"I think Tanwyn.. I will let the real leader of the realms decide your fate."

Theonyra made two thundering paces forward. He reached down with a finger and thumb and scooped up Selanius the druid, as Tanwyn and the guard looked on in mute horror.

"Well then, druid Selanius, after all these years. I see your taste in company remains poor."

The druid was tiny in the grasp of Theonyra.

"Theonyra! I watched you turned to stone. Frozen solid." Squealed the now pitiful looking Selanius.

"Tut tut. Bad druid. The magic of the darkness you served was not complete. You are correct, potion maker. I was turned completely to stone. They took from me my human form. But not my life."

The snivelling Selanius wriggled and stared hatred into the King's eyes. Despite knowing he could be crushed by his huge hand at any moment.

"Very good Theonyra. Very good indeed. Tell me though, how does it feel to be entrapped in stone for eternity? To watch your own offspring die as mere mortals. No father should watch their young perish through ageing before themselves. You are a cheat via a mistake and you say you are lucky, ha! Your own mother and father, long since gone. Your own son and daughter are brittle skeletons."

Princess Mahreuben shivered to think of all of her passed away family, now being insulted by this bitter druid. She felt so sad for her great grandfather, what he must have seen, been through in the old battles. She put her hand on her dagger and stepped towards her grandfather, the old King. Still he silently clasped the druid as he continued to vent his spite.

"Your own offsprings children, dead, old King. Oh mighty warrior of stone. Do you see now, Theonyra? Do you not grieve? Why, even your granddaughter and her Prince. Yet another of the Theonyra generation, gone. All that is left.. Is you. Destined to live for eternity, or slowly erode. Go on, crush me. I do not care. My time is near an end anyway stone man. Alatar can do his own dirty work now. I would die happy knowing that you will have no one left. No lineage. No bloodline. Just you. A granite faerie tale."

Selanius glanced down to see Mahreuben glaring into him, approaching with dagger drawn.

"What are you staring at banshee? You will all be dead soon. What do I care?" Then, reading the exchange of glances between Princess and King, he understood.

"Oh, now I see. There are two of you left after all. Two survivors of the old royal bloodline. A pitiful freakshow, banshee and courtyard statue, together at last. Go on then, enjoy your brief and bizarre reunion, it will end in searing pain at the hands of Alatar, and good."

Selanius sneered and awaited some sort of brutal punishment. Death at the hands of a gentle giant would be swifter than the twisted, slow poisonous ways of the red eyed one. Theonyra did not get angry however. Nor did he crush the druid as would have been so easy. He simply put him back down on the ground. Then he flicked Selanius over into the grass with one finger, as a limp afterthought. A sad look was now etched across his kind, slate coloured face. All of that family was gone. His grandchild, Mahreuben, had missed out. He sagged and turned away from the floored druid.

Ramona was not so gentle with the druid or the group of Takers, shrunk together like a bait ball of fish, hoping their predators would leave them alone.

"You plague, shoud now leave this place. Go, far away! All of you. You are vile, twisted creatures, the bloody lot of you. You cannot hide your eyes from me. Shame on all of you. You, corrupted druid. I should cut out your poisonous tongue myself. You are dead, finished. Alatar will soon dispose of you. I am looking forward to telling him of your abject failure to even pick his flowers, before I end his life. Or should I start with ending yours? For practice?"

Ramona instinctively raised her hands above her head, clasping them together in her adopted praying motion. Everybody looked on in silence. She brought her hands down in a quick swish. Blue neon magic crackled at her fingertips. She sent the Takers flying to grim destiny. Scattered like leaves in the wind. Seeing what was going on, Selanius made to flee.

"I think not, little weasel." Cried Ramona and with another swish of her hand, she entrapped Selanius in a fizzing, blue circle. It moved around the druid. As though it were a live gigantic snake. She sent Selanius whooshing high into the sky with her instinctive and powerful will. Imprisoned. Floating in white eyed terror, despite his earlier bravado.

"This is no parlour trick little man. Be thankful. Remember this day. All of you must leave these realms or die at my hand. Final chance. Go, now."

With a final gesture of her hands, the blue circle disappeared. Selanius plummeted to the ground screaming. Ramona bowed her head and shut her eyes. Held out a hand towards the falling druid and made a closed fist. At the last second, he gently floated back onto the ground. His eyes were wide like saucers and black with fright.

"I do not want bad blood on my hands, little potion maker. Karma will see to you. Go away. You disgust me."

Selanius wobbled and shook. He ran off crazed into the barrens, as Tanwyn, the guard and the druid aides followed suit.

Ramona, breathing heavily now, slumped onto cold stone.

"Water! Get her water." Called Cormac. Dayn raced to her with a pouch of fresh water. Ramona drank gratefully and focused on her breathing.

"That one.. drained.. me!" She managed a feeble grin for her family. Her eyes began to roll back.

"Sis..sis!" Jude, frantic, had raced to her side.

"I'm.. alright.. Jude. Don't wo.." Ramona trailed off. Then, her eyes rolled back again and she was deathly still.

CHAPTER THIRTY EIGHT
LOST IN THOUGHT

Alatar was in his quarters. The top tower. It had been silent, even peaceful. Red eyes simmered under his hood. The hood that was always up. Nobody had fully seen his face. Only glimpses. If it was a face. The eyes were now faint though. The life-force liquid had all but run out. Of course, Alatar did not need it for himself. It was needed to control the others. The guard and his recently dithering entourage. Alatar simply liked to sip at the drink. He found it stabilised his raging moods. Even a leader of a new era could get nothing done if he suffered constant bleak thoughts.

He cursed himself silently for underestimating this girl and her family. He berated himself for the flimsiness of his grand plan. He walked from his table to the huge bay window and flung it wide open. He was for the first time, questioning himself. The view was stunning, panoramic. Yet Alatar's eyes saw only a land he had yet to conquer. To command. He saw the pastel blue sky. An osprey dropped from the cloud to seize a small sea bass from the ebbing tide. He saw the backdrop of the coastal path. The abundance of trees of all kinds. Monolithic stones in circles from mysterious eras of another time. Another dimension. It barely registered. All he saw was a vast land that he had yet to seize as his own. The land of the Takers. How he wished it so.

'All I have done is steal a small stronghold. Kidnap mindless, fidgeting elves and blundering humans. Fishermen and washerwomen. Foolish, ale swilling swordsmen. I should never have appeared in the road to that damned family.'

His startling admonishment of himself continued. At the time of sensing Ruth, James and the baby, Ramona, he had felt in his marrow that the timelines were shifting. They did so without warning in the realms. There was never a pattern to it, so that you may at least be ready for whatever the shifting brought. The mingling of dimensions. Parallels. They added confusion and uncertainty, anxiety. Not just to himself, but to all the folk when such shifts happened. Nobody knew why. Nobody questioned the silent will of the realms.

Alatar was angry at the appearance of this out of time family. Travellers. He did not need any intervention just as he was drawing his manifesto together. He sensed something about the baby. She had magic. Could she be a chosen one of the ethereal? He could not risk any threat so he had presented himself in the road as an apparition. His aim, to terrify the family. To see them off. He had not intended to kill. Not at first. Like his estranged father had in the dark land battles.

But their car had skidded off the road. The family survived. Alatar's magic was faded, spent. So he had disappeared back to the tower. Now Alatar was at the window. Talking aloud to himself. He felt he was losing control of his own mind.

"Curse the ethereal of the realms, curse that damned husband. Melding his parallel lives at that lord forsaken inn. Interfering with the growth acceleration of that wizard baby. Elves and lost brothers wandering about freely. It has opened up a gateway of trouble. Damn them all." Alatar paced the marbled floor. Seething. Picking apart in his mind, everything that had come to pass.

"Cacodem. That useless clown. If I had chosen somebody more ruthless as my captain. All of this would be over. Done. I have been a poor leader father."

Yet the self-styled figurehead of the new realms was being overly hard on himself. His own kin had been brutal perfectionists. Though he remembered very little of them. He did recall seeing fighting, killing. Himself crying. Visions of long ago battles. Blurry stories. Another warrior turned to stone. Others slain or banished. Outwardly, the red eyed one showed no emotion to his tower guard or his aides. But these recollections still flashed, unwanted, into his overloaded mind. He remembered a conflict within himself as a young child.

He had watched people die. Many good folk, perished at the hands of the old totalitarian army who once ruled the realms. Alatar was just a boy then. Young and very impressionable. He had cried for the slain. Prayed for forgiveness for his own father.

"No. Father! Please leave them alone. They do us no harm.."

Alatar, the crying little waif. He had gradually had the goodness driven from him. Poisoned by tales of power, riches and entire lands to be gloriously ruled. His sorrow and hurt for the vanquished, was replaced by a thirst for power. A desire to learn how to control dark magic. To replace his father. It was flooding back, now that he was alone at the window.

"Enough!" He shouted aloud, as though it would take all of this away.

The folk of the realms, even his more open followers knew nothing of where he had come from. He had just manifested. His displays of fierce and strong destructive magic, had convinced many to join his so-called quest for a united realms. His followers became the guard. The Takers. They were happy at first with his proposals of new homes, security, safety from threat. They had gone along blindly. Openly heralding Alatar in neighbouring villages and hamlets. The word had spread. His recruitment drive had begun, by fair means or foul.

Others were simply frightened and kept quiet. They had lived quietly in their own way for generations. Many, like Domacec, had opposed. Fought even, but were overwhelmed, overpowered and bought under control by the liquid. The liquid which was now being drip-fed in micro doses to the guard. Alatar wheeled away from the window. He looked at the table. Covered in his parchment, intricate maps and drawings. Designs of places not yet built. New names. His whole vision of a stone empire.

Flora and fauna did not feature on the drawings. Alatar pointed a long, sharp and spindly finger at his precious work table. The finger crackled an angry red fire. The table rose and flew into the wall and smashed into splintered burnt pieces. Parchment and papers were strewn all over the marbled floor. Still smoking, burning out of existence. But Alatar's dream would not be burned so easily.

"Guards!" He called out. Two of his strongest guard, always posted outside the door to his quarters, stood alert.

"Enter!" They pushed the huge, heavy solid oak door open. The two guards stood before Alatar, waiting for his command. These two were willing followers. Pure Taker. Alatar took the last of his liquid from the familiar pewter goblet.

"Clean up this mess. Then, get this entire tower and its grounds secured. Get the weapons ready. I am going out. You will answer to Vaangrad for now. He is awaiting you in the courtyard. This guard is going to earn its keep or you all be sent to the sea. Enough is enough."

Alatar folded his arms and bowed his head.

"So mote it be." He hissed. Then, he vanished slowly, until only those two red eyes hung menacingly in the air for a split second. The whole tower shook and groaned. The leader had spoken.

Chapter Thirty Nine
Vaangrad

Alatar had drifted anonymously away at the onset of dawn. Over the drawbridge and out onto the vast plains. He had grown sick and tired of placing his trust in incompetent idiots. He had not even called the now very dopey night guard to lower the bridge.

'Sleeping. Useless fools.' He thought. 'I should roll them into the moat for the creature'.

But he did not. He simply snorted in disgust at these dozing Takers. It was not their fault, really. He had made them all drone-like, save for his inner circle and a few of the feral, pure bred Takers. The bridge creaked into action as drizzle pattered on the surface of the moat. He did it so casually with a flick of the wrist and with his will. Power of will and chanelled thought.

It lowered silently and he crossed. Out through the impenetrable, ancient gates. Instructions had been left with his two senior guards and the temporary command, Vaangrad. Alatar turned and stared back at the bridge and turned his hooded face up to the midnight blue sky. The bridge recoiled back up again and the gates clanked shut, rousing the two night watchmen. They scrabbled about, straightening their cloaks and brushing off wet grass. Trying to look alert. It would not matter this time. Alatar had gone.

Vaangrad, was a law unto himself. He had joined the Takers very early on when Alatar and an assortment of omionous looking breeds of men, had taken his idea to a small, spiritual village named Skyfawr. It was a self-sufficient, busy and industrious outpost, known for tradespeople and good fish. It had a beautiful chapel in which folk could go to feel safe and pray for their loved ones.

Skyfawr was not exciting enough to Vaangrad. He had himself, ran a stall with his wife, Oona. You might have called it an ironmongers shop, with other general goods for the people of Skyfawr. It was an honest living. Honesty bored Vaangrad. He had no desire for children of his own. Oona had been upset at that. Now, later on, she was secretly glad. After several years of bartering for small change, Vaangrad had grown irritable,weary and left the village.

Left Oona without a word of explanation. To call him a rogue was a kindness. Oona shed no tears. She felt lighter. Vaangrad only offered protection in the way of violence. She was well liked and did not want or need his kind of protection anymore. Realms life was not enough for him. He wanted more. Vaangrad had a mean streak and was often found fighting after too much ale at local events. He would openly mock the Prince Uzaleus and the Princess Mahreuben for their peaceful outlook. Calling it laziness. He cut a frustrated figure among this inland settlement.

"Real leaders get involved. Stimulate their people. Find new things, new places, form armies." He would tell villagers.

He was definitely cut from the right cloth as far as Alatar was concerned. Alatar quickly recruited him. So Vaangrad joined the guard, the Takers. He never looked back or returned to Skyfawr. Oona was glad of that and she learned not to care. Skyfawr though, lived under the dark cloud of the Takers. Fearful.

Those who were strong and useful, were taken for the guard. The rest were deemed insignificant, controllable and left in the village with a cloaked shadow hanging over them. Vaangrad now strode into the tower courtyard. Hundreds of the guard awaited the instructions of this grisly looking nomad.

"We start today. This is a fortress. We start again and we start today. This is Alatar's tower. He gives us a home. Start to treat it as such and contribute. Or get out."

He mumbled a few words to the lead guards at his side and turned back to the huge ensemble. Bleak, shrouded, rows and rows of Takers. The familiar murmuring and swaying. It would drive a normal man mad.

"Be embarrassed. Be angry. Be thirsty. Be vengeful. Most of all.. You are going to have to be alive. There is no more life-force liquid. Rebel like those others, and you die. There are no more jails here. You are Takers. You will fight for your leader! He has given you all. He will return. When he does, you will be grateful. For now, you have me. I am Vaangrad and I cannot wait for one of you to try my patience."

CHAPTER FORTY
TO THE CHAPEL OF SKYFAWR

Even wizards are not invincible. In these realms, most wizard folk or folk of that origin would not use magic. There were two main reasons why. The first one being that a display of wizardry, or magic of any kind, would be felt. It would bring you to the attention of the red eyed one or anyone else of magic, good or bad. The second reason, was that use of magic, the really powerful, instinctive magic, that both Mahreuben, and now Ramona possessed, could be very draining. If it was used extensively or often, then there could be consequences. And there had been.

Princess Mahreuben rarely practised her magic anymore for both of these reasons. She had used hers only to aid her leap of faith from the top tower to escape Alatar. That had seemed a generation ago. Perhaps it had been. This was the realms after all. She had used her wilful power in jumping from the high window of Alatar's quarters. Only in a desperate and last-ditch attempt at freedom. This, while Alatar was otherwise engaged in the execution of Elphinias, chief of his counsel. The exposed traitor. Those back at the courtyard that had seen Mahreuben jump, assumed that she had chosen suicide, rather than die at the feet of a Taker.

She had also once used her ability to shapeshift, turning into a sleek, lithe mermaid, to swim out to the stone King at New Azmarine and speak with him. She felt it herself if she used magic regularly.

Even though it was for good. Contrary to modern belief, magic was not all fairy tale. It could take a physical toll on the user. They could become fatigued, suffer short term memory loss, disorientation and other such unpleasant things. Mahreuben had lived her life among magic though and had learned much on harnessing it.

Ramona had not. Ramona's power came from the rawness of instinct. Before her dramatic escape, Mahreuben began to believe that she was destined to eke out her existence in the caves as a creature. An outcast banshee. She had forgotten much and had become feral. Travellers rarely went near this section of the coastal caves. Riders, hunter-gatherers and such. They had heard tales that they did not wish to investigate.

The heartbroken and guttural screams for her Prince at night, would terrify anybody passing through. Some would describe a sad sensation as though having an out-of-body experience. Empathy coursed through them and they knew not why. Others simply fled in horror, not knowing that it was their very own Princess making the painful sounds. The tales went around and so people would not go that way. The area became even more wild and cut off. This damp dwelling became Mahreuben's existence until she was dragged back to the tower by the guard to be used as a seer by Alatar, to locate Ramona. Mahreuben had suffered enough. Skin and bone underneath torn rags. Malnourished, even though the gulls had tried to help with offerings from the sea.

Stood sturdy now, here was a woman who understood the true meaning of gratitude. Still beautiful, more so. Still fighting for her people. Her stoicism and belief in good and trust in the judgement of the realms, saw her through the most harrowing traumas. Now reunited with the man she had fallen in love with. Here with Uzaleus by her side once more. The Prince.

Himself escaped from prison. Thanks, in part, to the daring intervention of the brave but headstrong Jude. Both of them believing, praying that all of this could be stopped. All of these evil factions. Leaders and Takers and ancient bartering druids, heads turned by

Alatar. They had to trust that it could all be stopped. They had to think that they could beat the red eyed one and his army of Takers. Mahreuben herself, had to call on her magic to use her power of foresight and project a message to the young wizard.

She had gone to a dreaming Ramona and forewarned her of what was to come. She had done this knowing that she would be forced to drink the mind altering life-force liquid and wanted to act before its effects took hold. As a result and one way or another, they had finally all met. All sorts of folk. Men, women, elves, even birds and animals it seemed, had bonded through a united cause. To reclaim the realms for good. To go back to their rightful homes. To send this family back to their own timeline. So here at the grey and vast stretch of land, named the Paaniz barrens, these forces of good had joined. The bond was now struck.

Overhead now, circling and cawing in their familiar way, were the two great black-backed gulls. Biggle and Baggle. They had been with the family since watching over the baby at the beach at Oakhampton. They now swooped and searched the land with keen eyes, as always, scouting for any possible threat. Cormac had taken to them and would see them well fed and watered. They had become a constant on this journey. From the old, disused Ivywyrld Inn to the Paaniz barrens and all in between.

"Not what I had planned, to be sure!" Mused the elf. For their part, the gulls had been with Ramona from the start. They would not simply fly away now. That bond was now strong too. Mahreuben and Uzaleus had never considered themselves as rulers of the realms. To them, they were merely trying to look after their own. Hoping in their hearts that a King and Queen would return one day. There were grainy recollections by many, stories of battles. Lifetimes ago, that had taken the lives of Kings and Queens and their people.

Over by a circular gathering of stones, Uzaleus had briefly left the side of his love to stand with his men. He wished for now, only to be with her, but now to duty. There were brave folk waiting on him. Counting on his guidance.

"For our future. All our futures." He whispered to Mahreuben. She kissed his cheek.

"Your men need you, Prince."

He seemed to be saying something softly to himself. His eyes momentarily glazed over.

"Princes and Princesses may rule principalities. The realms are a kingdom. There is no King here. So we rule no one, the Princess and I. This is your kingdom, and we are deeply honoured and happy to serve all of you. In any way we can."

Uzaleus was recalling a spring banquet in the forest near the elven woods. A happy time. He was reciting back the very words he had spoken that day.

'Serve you, in any way we can.'

Now was the Prince's time to serve. He knew something was happening.

"Rest now, men. Eat, drink. Try to sleep in turns if you can. We must help our adopted and brave girl, Ramona. She needs us. Help the elves with their guard, but use the time to recover strength, where you can. We will need plenty of it."

Ramona was lain with her head in her mother's lap. She was unconscious, but breathing, albeit shallow and quick. Her eyes were closed but her brow was furrowed and gave her a confused expression. She whimpered and babbled incoherently about funny seagulls. Daddy's sandwiches, the seaside, sandcastles and wanting to drink her milk. She was regressing in her unconscious state, but using grown up language through the eyes of a baby. Recalling memories of the holiday.

Ruth stroked her daughter's forehead and kept her well covered up. Frightened to move her. James, and son Jude, were frantically pacing. Both worried. Theonyra, the giant stone King, was also standing guard around this makeshift camp. He could see for miles across the landscape and could see no iminent danger. Cormac, Ailbe,

Dayn and most of the other elves, spread out, watching for anymore of the Takers. Though they had now fled, they may return. It looked as though for now at least, the land was once again as barren as its name suggested.

"What are we going to do, dad? We can't just sit around." Judes frustration was boiling over and his eyes were welling up.

"Ramona is unconscious. She's mumbling like a baby. Can't you hear her? She's saved us all, again! Now look. She doesn't know what she is, baby or woman. How has she stayed so strong? She's had her whole childhood taken from her. Because, what? Some invisible force decided she is a chosen one? If these bloody realms are so magic, why do they need her? Or any of us. This is breaking my heart dad. For pity's sake, we shouldn't be here! All this, bloody magic. Where are these damned interfering spirits?"

Jude looked up at the sky for an answer.

"Do you hear me? I thought you were good? Why have you turned my baby sister into a woman! Where is the rest of her life? You can't fast forward a human life. Not where we come from. Why did you leave me alone in another world? Is this a game to you? Help her. Why are you putting her through this?

We've given our best to you. Let us go, just.. let us go." His voice was almost an inaudible whisper now. Jude slumped to the floor by his father.

"I'm not doing this running around anymore dad. We have to get away from here. I'm done."

James held his son close to him. Ramona's big brother.

"Shes going to be alright son. You've seen how strong she is. We have to be strong now too. Look how you took on Alatar by yourself and freed the prisoners. Its reunited the Prince and Princess. Be proud of yourself. You have magic too. We all do Jude. We have to accept where we are. Its hard, very hard. I feel sad and useless every day around you son. Because you were alone. Because we did not know of you. Yet when you came to the inn.."

James blinked away tears now.

"Our boy had come home.. It was a shift of the timelines, like Cormac described. But I still feel sad, I can't recall our past with you Jude. It really hurts your mother too. I just don't think running away will get us home. We have to be there beside our Mona when she wakes up, and she will wake up, Jude. Whether Mona is a baby, a young woman or.. an old relic like me, she will wake up."

Jude tried to smile but it registered as a thin expression of acceptance. Though he was feeling a little calmer now, frustration still burned within. Ruth, who would normally see the humour in her husband's words, could only glance at James and whisper..

"Be with our son, James."

So James let Jude go on.

"Please, don't try to be funny now dad. Its time things were explained to us. Its just.. I care about everybody here. I really do. But we don't belong to this place. Aren't you mad too? These realms, whatever they are, have turned our lives into a nightmare. Who are they? Where are they?"

A vision of being thrown out of an empty house by a greedy, red faced estate agent, flashed into his mind. Of waking in a huge, empty house. No mum or dad or baby sister. No car on the drive. He had not been on the holiday. Why had he stayed and been erased from the memories of his family? An alternate timeline in which nobody recognised him or knew of his family. He became a homeless wanderer. Slung out and suddenly unrecognised by his own friends and neighbours. Looking always for something that at the time, was beyond his line of vision. Special people somewhere. A whole family's memories had been altered.

'Am I just an alternate male version of my sister? What if I was lost because I was never meant to find them? What if I was unwanted? He perished the thought of all these dimensions, universes and parallel worlds.

'If we do get back home.. Will we all wake up at the house, or will we be split up once more? With me alone again.'

How he had searched. Not knowing what for, but knowing he would know when he found them. And find them he did. At the Ivywyrld Inn. A brother, seemingly forgotten. Maybe he had found the wrong versions of mum and dad? It was all very scary and speculative. He tried to slow his whirring brain.

"I'm sorry dad. I'm sorry, shouting at you. I just need to understand. I'm like.. Mona's little, big brother. I'm confused. I love you dad."

Father and son embraced.

"I love you too Jude. My son. My brave boy."

Ruth wept silently. Cradling her grown up, baby girl. The two parties of elves, men and folk from other lands, gazed across the barrens at each other. There was an empty space now where the druid, Tanwyn and the Takers had been. Something striped black and orange with fangs slithered away over a sand dune. It was not a place to be at night.

"Come on Jude, lets go and sit with your mum and sister. We're going to sort all of this out."

James hugged his son again and they went to Ruth and Ramona's side. There was not enough time for the benefit of hindsight. They were a family. They were together now. That was all that mattered. Mahreuben looked across the land. There in the distance was her Prince. She looked towards Theonyra. Her great grandfather of stone.

"Go to your Prince now. You should never be separated again. Even in duty. Go to him Mahreuben. I will see to Ramona and the family. She will be alright. Trust me. My great grandaughter."

The huge stone King knelt before the Princess.

"I love you. Thank you for finding me and for letting me be a part of your life, my Mahreuben."

Mahreuben too, cried a little. Holding on tightly to a granite arm.

"Theonyra. Grandfather. Can you be turned back to human form.. ever?"

Theonyra's eyes blinked rapidly. As though holding back tears. He did not answer the question.

"We must take Ramona to Skyfawr chapel. There, she will get the help she needs."

CHAPTER FORTY ONE
SCATTERED SOULS

Alatar had put some distance between himself and the tower as he drifted alone across the open plains. He was not scared or fearful. He had decided that if something needed doing properly, that he would do it himself. Vaangrad would do a good job in his absence. Alatar regarded the sullen and burly human as dumb. A brute with big fists, a loud voice and the ability to give orders. That would do for now.

All he wanted was for the guard to be better trained. To be ready and aggressive. To repel intruders. The life-force liquid had gone. The guard as a result of this, were now experiencing similar feelings to the ones that Domacec and Mahreuben had experienced. It was a gradual sensation. The liquid had been found to be a successful tool to nullify independent thought. Domacec had been the same when he was thrown into imprisonment after failing to capture Ramona and her family at the Ivywyrld Inn.

Of course, then he was known as Cacodem, captain of the Takers guard. He had experienced the power of the liquid. He had gone from a contented, hard working villager to an unwitting, sedated member of Alatar's guard. Glowering, confused and angry under his hooded black uniform. After Alatar had punished him by throwing him in the cells, Domacec had felt quite ill. Weak and tired with bouts of nausea. He had shrunk into the corner, frightened of retribution from inmates and was initially ignored, due to his status as a Taker.

But gradually, he blended in with the other prisoners and was given no more of the liquid, he was forgotten and left to forage with the others for gruel and water. As time passed in the cramped cell though, Domacec began to feel a clarity in his body and mind. He had spoken with Prince Uzaleus, also imprisoned at that time. The Prince could see that Domacec spoke the truth, or at least as he saw it, and that he was deeply upset and disoriented. The Prince could tell that Domacec had not been a willing recruit. He knew that the drink was effectively a drug and it became apparent that there never was a Cacodem.

Just a dosed up and obedient anagram. Then as Domacec's reddened eyes faded to his natural green, he remembered his real name. 'I am Domacec.' He knew he had opposed Alatar and faced him down and was Taken. He knew he had a wife, Bisera, who he missed. Wave after wave of recall was hitting him now there was no fog of liquid to suppress and twist his memories and feelings.

Much of Alatar's guard had been formed of willing followers of his cause. They were mostly nomads, troublemakers, lost souls and those who simply believed that this unknown magician would be a better ruler than the Prince and Princess with their gentle ways. Some strange creatures in the guard, indistinguishable from the others due to the hooded uniform, hissed and slithered, unlike their human counterparts. They were known as pure Takers. They could carry out any order without question, they would also happily kill for sport.

As well as these obedient, orc-like mysterious ones, Alatar targeted the easily swayed, or used force to recruit, and the others could rot. The self-proclaimed leader had deliberately created paranoia and scepticism among the people of the towns, villages and hamlets that he and his entourage had visited.

He spoke of approaching dark forces that men and elves with daggers and swords would not be able to repel. He would speak of how Uzaleus and Mahreuben were ignoring the inevitable outside threats and that they were playing up that the ethereal spirits would intervene if any such threat should arise. He would play up himself that he himself had never seen or met any such magical force from the realms and that for these lands to be protected and governed fairly and properly, that a new kingdom should be formed. He proclaimed that this would send a stark warning to any such approaching dark force.

Quoting his own words all the time to reaffirm and build on the discomfort now bubbling under the surface in many good folk. Those of the Takers whom had been originally opposed to Alatar, like Domacec, had also been drugged with large doses of the liquid. Pacified into becoming drones. They too, now experienced feelings of their own. The sick, nauseous, pulsing sensation in the head and gut. Tiredness, confusion.

Memories of who they were before being given the liquid returned. They were becoming themselves again. This was not without some emotional torment. None of those experiencing this within the ranks dared to break character though. They had seen Elphinias version of punishment.

The huge catapults at the towers ramparts had flung many such upstarts to watery doom.

As Vaangrad strolled around the courtyard with Alatar's head guards and aides around him, he barked out the words..

"Freedom hour!" The guard knew what this meant. Exercise and daylight for the prisoners. Security had been doubled up and there would be no repeat of an escape. The prisoners lived for this time, even though they were watched by the Takers and cajoled and pushed and shoved. Threatened with painful sores from the red whip if they deviated from instruction or took a breather. They had to be strong though now, these prisoners. As ordained by Alatar, they had been fed better and given proper water, hot blended herbal teas and a good variety of meals.

The prisoners were exercised fully. Men, women and elves were frog-marched around the vast grounds of the Takers tower. The children were kept separately and put to work or schooled in the ways of the Takers.

The prisoners would do short sprints, lift rocks and learn battle techniques in a new program designed to fashion them into a more cohesive unit. The stronger were selected for sword or dagger training or catapult duty in this new program devised by Alatar and his counsel.

The children whom had been captured were no longer just fed and watered in separate cells. They were put into classrooms to learn many subjects and survival skills so they would be ready to go out foraging for food and wood and such. False history was implemented by Alatar, history that put previous kingdoms and rulers in a very bad light. Made them look foolish and whimsical. He wanted the younger ones to learn early. To be regimented and clone-like. Full of the zest and speed of youth but with no loyalty to the Prince or Princess.

They were drip-fed tales of a new evil sorceress named Ramona whom wanted to destroy the realms and take them for herself. She must be obliterated when she comes. This was drummed into the impressionable children. They would be rewarded with playtime, fishing expeditions, extra fruit.

Following the exercise of the throngs, Vaangrad announced in his booming tones..

"Freedom hour ends!"

Red whips cracked at the heels of prisoners as they slowed to a halt and assembled in the courtyard. Vaangrad walked up and down the lined up men, women and elves.

"Good. Promising. Some of you are ready for the transition. Be grateful. We will come for you in time. For now, back to your cells."

He turned to the two head guard at his side.

"Get them properly washed and fed. Lockdown the tower. Brief the night watch."

They nodded and drifted to their own chores. Vaangrad spoke to himself now..

"Oh Oona, my love.." He was smirking..

"You foolish woman. How I am glad to be free of you and your relentless desire for squawking children. Your penny counting. How

I am glad to be free of Skyfawr and its insular, miniscule folk. You and your praying. Only the chapel keeps you safe."

Vaangrad strode across the courtyard in the midnight blue of dusk, heading for his bottle of mead and sleep.

"Skyfawr shall fall Oona. You will become like all these others. What a pity."

CHAPTER FORTY TWO
EMOTIONS OF THE BRAVE

The leader of the Takers drifted alone through the realms. He was still quietly seething. It was quite simple really, his plan, and it had worked very efficiently to a point, had now completely faltered. Alatar had captured the Prince Uzaleus and thrown him unceremoniously into the cells with his daydreaming, beloved folk. He had convinced the townships that his good lady, Princess Mahreuben, was nothing but a masquerading witch and a crazed banshee. She had been run out of the lands as an outcast and had grown scrawny and heartbroken in a damp, cold cave.

He had achieved so much and assembled a great new force in a very short space of time and claimed the tower by the sea for himself. An old relic, once resplendent and built by kings and queens of eras long since departed. The folk there when he arrived, were using it merely as a giant home for storage of goods. Food, drink, materials to be distributed to people of the realms as directed by Uzaleus and Mahreuben. Since the old battles, where many royals were lost, there had been no full time occupancy.

'What a waste of such a majestic building. A glorified grain store, run by scurrying village peasants.'

Alatar had marched in with the Takers and decided it was now his. The choice was to leave, or live in the workers quarters as conforming Takers. He would be transforming this area into a prison facility. So, he had incarcerated the more feisty inhabitants and banished others. Those who actually fought this bullish new foe, were slung to sea by the shady Elphinias and his catapult punishment. A few were made examples of by Alatar himself and shredded to bloody pieces by his red magic.

Nobody was going to test him again upon witnessing such individual power. Imagine what this unknown madman was capable of if backed by a compliant army. The old guard were no more. They had never been fighters, or true warriors. Those folk were capable of defending themselves and their families, but they were not ready for Alatar. The realms had been at peace for a long time. This was now the tower of the Takers. The new central point, as declared by its leader, Alatar. Perhaps Mahreuben and Uzaleus would make use of the tower someday. Before their separation, they had been happy to live among their people as equals.

Alatar had enlisted the druid Selanius and his two finest potion blenders to create the mind control liquid he called life-force. Selanius and his men worked in shadows, behind the scenes with ingredients known only to them, collected from the grey and arid land called Paaniz, in the dangerous barrens. Nobody was ever keen on staying there long, given its reputation for strange creatures. Disappearances and the like. Skeletal remains were often uncovered after sandstorms.

The mind control drink had curtailed opposing factions and gained many converts. 'By any means necessary.' Alatar would tell his guard when sending them out to gather more recruits. If not taken willingly, the liquid was forced down the throats of terrified villagers. It had served its purpose, to bolster the new guard and to scare the men and elves of the surrounding areas into believing in the new leader. They had little choice if they did not, it seemed.

It was a clever way to entrap non-believers into doing as he said. Better to have them in his ranks than waste time killing them all. After all, he was offering a fair way of life, was he not? With all this in mind as he wandered, he thought of the things he must now do to avoid more catastrophes.

So, it was to be a face off with this upstart girl. This baby turned woman. This accursed Ramona. He had already come up against her headstrong brother who assisted the escape of Cacodem and the Prince. Alatar had sensed something, way back when the family had blundered into this timeline. It had not felt right. The realms shifted regularly. He knew that very well, but it was rare for an alternate reality to cross over.

It was the place, Oakhampton, that did it. He was sure. Something about its position on the land. Ley lines and such. Whenever these things happened, shifting or transformation, it always seemed to be around Oakhampton. He knew that the ethereal had intervened and it was this that had made Alatar wary. Concerned enough to appear in the road and flash a warning to James.

Hoping the family would find their way out of Oakhampton and go back to whatever stone they had crawled out from underneath. Alatar's visitation had gone awry when James had lost control of his vehicle and it rolled down the embankment. So it was that this family had fully crossed over, making it a worry for the leader. The realms must have had a reason for keeping them here. In his bleak heart, Alatar knew that the unseen overseers of the realms would be most unhappy with his takeover plans. But what did this family have that they would send them skewing into his domain? He now cursed the answer to that question.

"Ramona! Look what you have cost me. It is time to send you away. Permanently."

Cormac was pacing again.

"I had not thought our young wizard would be asleep this long. Not this long at all." Cormac was fretting, such was his nature. Protector. It was Cormac whom had gone to their aid when the family first found refuge at the Ivywyrld Inn, where everything changed.

Cormac's relationship with the earth around him was a good one, subliminal. Sometimes he would pick up on things. He had a good intuition and it was this that had sent him from the woods to the old inn. There he had silently slipped inside and felt Ramona's magic, warming the empty looking building. He had not disturbed the family. He had left clothes and other useful goods on the table in the living area. He quietly had snook out again and back to the woods, but he would return and eventually stay with the family during the upheaval.

James had gone through his own transformation. When the car came off the road, he had ran to the Ivywyrld Inn for help and had ended up merging with the figure. His realms self. He became the one, true James. His wife nearly had a breakdown when she had come across her husband, not recognising him at first, hooded and still changing inside. He had stayed quiet and given Ruth a sleeping potion, food and a warm bed for her and Ramona. They were all all in shock.

He had wanted her to be rested when he told her of what he knew. To be fair to himself, he had not really expected to merge with another James. He was just driving home with his wife and baby from their holiday. Now, here was Ramona. Lay on a makeshift stretcher being carried by her anxious brother Jude and father James. Ruth walked briskly alongside with Cormac.

Theonyra had suggested that a healing could be done at Skyfawr chapel and it was there that they throng were now headed. It was a completely unexpected chain of events that had led to this day. Nobody would have believed it had this been a fireside tale. Ramona's parents certainly did not understand it. Jude, their young son, still had many questions but they would have to wait.

So, crossing the plains to Skyfawr were a band of brothers and sisters thrown together by fate. There was no time for sleeping or campfires. It was a long stretch to Skyfawr, Theonyra had said. Short food and water breaks were taken at secluded and convenient areas. They only stopped for brief rest periods before resuming their march.

Ruth bathed Ramona's head in water and talked away to her about where they were headed and that she was going to be alright. Ramona had stopped babbling and her breathing was now steadier. She was simply asleep. She had spent far too much energy and magic defending them once again against Tanwyn and the guard.

It was quite a force that gratefully took a short rest now, with the stone King, Uzaleus and Mahreuben in their midst. With the Prince's escapees and Cormac's brave elves, they were ready to face the Takers. Emotions were running extremely high among all of them. Uzaleus and Mahreuben, reunited after terrible ordeals. Theonyra revealing he was the great grandfather of the Princess and was not always a man of stone.

Domacec fighting his own internal turmoil having served as Cacodem, the original captain of the Takers army, now returned to sanity and his true self, but full of remorse and a desire to atone. Cormac the stoic and brave elf, feeling pangs for a return to his little woodland village. To his best friend Finola and her fireside tea. Fishing at the lake with the young ones.

Cormac knew he was doing the right thing. He had grown to love and care for Ramona and her family. The thought of losing any of them on his watch would be crushing to him. He put his yearnings to one side. He imagined how Ruth must feel. He felt that she had suffered greatly and although he admired her strength as a mother and a wife, he felt great empathy towards what she had gone through and taken on board since the family car had swerved off the road and their lives had changed forever.

'We would all do well to remember their journey.' He told himself silently.

Cormac offered up a prayer that Ramona and her family, be returned to their own reality and that their son of the realms, Jude, be with them in a life of peace. Dusk was approaching as they trudged across the coarse ground. Biggle and Baggle, the two great black–backed gulls, still soared overhead. Cormac, it seemed, had become their favourite person. If there was imminent danger, they would make a real clamour. This he knew from the caterwauling they were capable of making when hungry.

"Ah, come down here, the two of you. You only love old Cormac for his dried fish scraps and bits of fruit!" The elf laughed out loud for the first time in a while, as Biggle and Baggle swooped down very gracefully and tucked in to the food. Ruth, watched on and managed half a smile as the gulls bobbed their heads up and down and chattered away as they ate their well earned meals. She was remembering their holiday where they had first met the two gulls and how baby Mona had gurgled and giggled excitedly and how curious and respectful that Biggle and Baggle were.

Presently, Uzaleus stood before the gathering and called out..

"Good folk of these beautiful realms. It is a duty I do not care for, but we have no more time for rest. Let us finish our water and have one final push for Skyfawr. We can get there before nightfall is on us, and there, I hope we may find a place to sleep. It is my personal duty to get us all there and in particular, our young wizard. She and her family have saved our lives. Let us press on so that we may get her to the chapel and a healing be performed. Mahreuben and I are proud of each and every one of you. To the chapel!"

Watching from behind a cluster of standing stones, a short distance away, two bitter red eyes glowed underneath a dark shawl.

"To the chapel.." Hissed Alatar.

CHAPTER FORTY THREE
A HEALING

After much travelling across the realms, the assembly came to the outskirts of the working town of Skyfawr, interpreted as 'The big sky'. It was an industrious little hub, filled with markets and stalls, to attract custom from neighbouring areas. Colourful huts and stores, a large stream wound through the centre of Skyfawr that eventually fed into a huge river named the Ryygier. While parents toiled, the youngsters marvelled at fish, stoats and water birds.

It was also the home of Oona, the wife of the departed Vaangrad, who had turned to Alatar and left her. Abandoning their marriage, leaving Oona to manage the popular stall alone. She knew in the end that she had a lucky escape. She thanked the spirits that she had no children by him. The ambitious, but cold-hearted Vaangrad had been left in charge of the Takers tower while Alatar had set out to dispense with Ramona once and for all. It was Theonyra, the stone King who called out as the throng marched on, in need of decent food and rest.

"There! There is Skyfawr. Do you see the outline of the beautiful chapel?"

Princess Mahreuben, hand in hand with Uzaleus, her beloved Prince, beamed.

"Great grandfather, well seen. Now let us get Ramona there, for the help she needs."

Mahreuben gestured to James, "We are nearly there James. Try not to worry. She will be well cared for as Theonyra says."

"I really hope so Princess, she is still feverish. Come on Jude son, one last big effort." With that, father and son lifted the makeshift stretcher and strode forward towards Skyfawr under the pink sky of the early evening. The two would not accept a rest or have anyone else carry the young wizard.

They knew the men and elves would do so with great care, but as Ramona's father and brother, they had come all the way with her, with mother Ruth constantly at their side and cooing softly to her during the food and drink stops. Holding her close. Being her mother.

Ramona now mostly slept silently, but had previously mumbled a lot. She had been a baby, tottering happily with her parents and then fast-tracked by the ethereal spirits into a young woman. A growth acceleration, it was called here. She was chosen to face this new menace. Though her babbling during this sleepy fever had distressed those who loved her. All manner of voices. A baby laughing or crying, a toddler calling joyously, 'Again, again!'. A young studious child.. 'I'll make you proud mum.'

A teenager sobbing.. 'I want to see my friends. I want to go to school. I don't understand.' She had rambled her way through her rapid changing, to the heartbreak of her mother. She was talking in her sleep about her life that might have been.

"Alatar. He has taken my daughter's life. Look at her, our baby." James and Jude bowed their heads solemnly. To look at Ramona now, lay on a stretcher in the elven clothing, originally intended for Ruth, you would see a beautiful young woman, just sleeping. But in her drained and stricken torment, she babbled her way through the eighteen or twenty years or so, that she had not had chance to live.

"Its alright Mona, mum is here. We are going to get you home my baby." Ruth kissed Ramona's forehead and buried her head in the shoulders of Princess Mahreuben. Here were two of the strongest women. The ethereal of the realms sometimes had to make tough and clinical decisions. For a greater outcome, but these two, in womanhood, both wronged by the Takers, were proving a solid foundation for this small army, determined to break this rule of Alatar.

"She will awaken soon Ruth. I promise you, sister." Mahreuben held Ruth tight to her chest. Ruth had needed that for an age. The understanding of another woman. To everybody else they were stoic, strong, admirable. Here, together, was the warmth of mutual empathy. Strength was expected of these types of women. It was far from as easy as they made it look. Their selflessness pushed to its limit without complaint.

Skyfawr was well known for its diversity and culture and the chapel was not only a place of peace, but a symbol of it. Even raiders and petty thieves would not take from the chapel. Vaangrad knew Skyfawr all too well. Alatar could glean much information from the thug.

Vaangrad had said "If you mean to execute the girl wizard my lord, do not attempt to do it in the chapel. The realms will not let you."

To which Alatar had lashed Vaangrad to the floor with a swish of red magic.

"Idiot. You and your realms and your sacred ground. Do not lecture me, bonehead. I am from a powerful domain. Be glad you are here, in this elevated position. Do not let me down Vaangrad, or you will be doing more than tasting dirt. Get up, village drunk and go to your work."

Vaangrad had bowed and scurried off to Alatar's silent chief aides. Now however, Alatar waited and skulked a good distance back. Surveying. He was primed to finish his task and finally face the girl wizard. He knew Ramona was weak. He wanted to see what they were planning. He knew there was a bond between the spirits and the chapel. He was not going to risk all he had worked for, including his very existence, to attack her at the chapel until it was quieter. He would wait and observe.

Biggle and Baggle the scouting gulls from Oakhampton, flying above, cawed a cry of acknowledgement to Cormac, as though to announce they were close to their destination. As usual, and now, automatically, the elf dug into his pouch for some food scraps for the two friendly birds. Once again they came down to his feet and gobbled up the offerings and bowed in gratitude to Cormac.

The elf smiled. "You two have been true friends to old Cormac, to all of us. We are safe here for a while at Skyfawr, to be sure. Rest now my friends. Perhaps, after sleep, you may check on King Theonyra's people at New Azmarine. See how their little settlement is coming along. They will want to know that Theonyra is safe and will return."

Cormac had scribbled a tiny note onto a bit of parchment from his pouch, using a thin charcoal stick.

It simply said "New Azmarinine, all is well. Your King Theonyra will return. Harmony will prevail. Stay hidden for now. Live well, your friends are close." He then called to Baggle, the bonny female gull and she hopped up to the elf.

"My dear Baggle, take this note to our friends off the coast. They will welcome you. Rest there. The food and hospitality is good I hear. Other gulls and seabirds to mix with. Good fishing to be sure!"

Baggle bowed again and clucked in agreement. Biggle, her partner, finished his grain and dried mackerel and haw-hawed. He would do as Cormac or any of the party wished. 'But please, not when I am eating.' A gull and his food! So, shrugging, he turned his beak to more pressing matters, his fish and crab scraps.

After their food and water, the gulls had flown off to the coast to take word to the little cove village of New Azmarine. An assortment of survivors and escapees from the Takers tower, rescued and taken to shore in the hands of Theonyra.

Cormac's mind had settled a little, knowing how important this would be to Theonyra and his doting people. The rescued, beginning anew. The stone King's time would come to tell his own tale to Princess Mahreuben. His only surviving great grandchild. Skyfawr though, was now upon them. A small pine forest surrounded the town. At the entrance was an open winding pathway. The gathering walked on. There were little colourful huts and homes. Stalls and shops. Wild horses were here, grazing on hay and wafting their tails gracefully.

Horses were very rare for the realms nowadays. Almost mythical to the young. Many had been pillaged. Put to work and flogged for personal gain in the old battles, old times. Theonyra remembered this.

Before he had been turned into a stone giant, he had fought the old foe and despised that such magnificent animals were not cared for and used in a slave like fashion. Skyfawr was a sanctuary for these beautiful horses and work they did, but they ate, played, slept and rested together.

A mill was there now, and a huge wheel for grinding flour. The tantalising smell of freshly baked bread, enough to draw anyone in. The throng salivated. They were hungry, the men, women and elves, for proper food. The realms had provided the basics, but how they all yearned for hot dinner. Fruits, vegetables, bread and stews. A bed not made from leaves.

Uzaleus would talk to the people of Skyfawr. He would not take free hospitality though. He, the Princess and all of Ramona's group, would work for that, should it be offerered. The Prince would not use his title for an easy ride.

The local folk barely noticed the new approaching throng at first. Their heads down industriously. This was a day of trade. For coins, exchanges or what have you. They had no recognised leader as such, but there was a curator of sorts. A woman of the chapel. She held sermons there. Also she was a healer. The chapel was a multifunctional and very sacred place. It soothed the terminally ill, offered comfort to families and as belief would have it, was protected by the great spirits of the realms.

It was also a place where healings could be performed. To help the sleeping to wake, to restore the feverish. The curator of Skyfawr chapel was named Yesenia. A graceful woman of peaceful origin. A wanderer of the realms, until she found her home at Skyfawr. It had felt right to her. She worked hard and asked for nothing. Such was her positive influence that the people of Skyfawr had given her the nickname 'The teacher'. A moniker she had not asked for, nor revered in, but she cared about. Very much.

Yesenia had been tending to the beautiful gardens at the chapel, when her senses pricked up.

"We have visitors! Amato, prepare the chapel for a healing, summon the others."

Amato, was a young man of Skyfawr, humble and well liked. Yesenia had taken him under her wing and the boy would help her, and when told to rest, he would plead to help anyway.

'I can see I have a new student then. That is good.' Yesenia had said to the delighted young man. Work hard he had too. Tending to the gardens, looking after the cleanliness of inside the chapel and helping Yesenia to prepare any healing, be it spiritual or physical. Nothing was under lock and key here. Such was the trust within the village and within the people of the chapel. You could walk in to pray, or to just.. be.

There were others of course from within the village whom helped at the chapel, such was its importance to the Skyfawr people. As the stretcher bearing throng approached through the village, workers stopped, playing children gazed wide-eyed. Seniors looked in disbelief.

Here was their returning Prince and Princess, the stone giant of bedtime tales, some had thought a myth. Elves, men and who was this carrying a stretcher with a stricken, flaxen-haired girl? Could it be the child of the ethereal prophecy? Either way, to the villagers, they looked about to drop to their knees.

Here now, came Yesenia, calling gently, but with authority.. "People of Skyfawr, see that our guests are given food, water, rest. Immediately. These are the ones who will defeat the red eyed one."

The men and women of the village began to guide these visitors, soon noticing the Prince and Princess, albeit underneath grit and mud. They still exuded grace. Theonyra looked amused despite everything that had happened, at the looks he was getting from them, especially the youngsters. Hardly inconspicuous!

'Without our humour, where are we?' He thought, and offered a huge granite smile.

Uzaleus stepped forward to Yesenia now, "My good lady, we are in dire need of help. We have a stricken young wizard with us. We think she was chosen by the spirits to rid us of this red eyed one and his guard. Her strain has been immense. Her magic has seen off enemies, but at great cost. She is drained, delirious. Will you and your good people assist us in her healing?"

The lady of the chapel smiled at Uzaleus and Mahreuben. Then at the feverish Ramona.

"It is already being prepared Prince Uzaleus. She will be safe, as will you all. I see your good lady is returned, that is welcome news. The caves are unforgiving on the coastal path. Especially among scouting Takers and foul weather. Ah, King Theonyra.. You have grown taller!"

Theonyra instantly took to the humour of Yesenia. Her seer like qualities also became evident. But serious she was, about all she said. The group were surprised at her knowledge, and Theonyra, again amused at the reference to his giant outline.

"Not only a teacher, but also a seer. You are Yesenia. This is then, quite an honour."

The curator warmly nodded.

"The honour is mine and that of our small but peaceful village. Ramona needs a waking ceremony. Then, water, food. She will then naturally sleep again, in the chapel, watched by the ethereal only. She cannot come to harm in the chapel. The rest of you all here, the same. Drinks, good food, rest. Then we speak of the red eyed one and how our feisty wizard will tackle him, with all of our help. Now, we make haste. Inside the chapel Amato and Oona are preparing comfort for the healing. Let us go. Come Ruth, James.. and you Jude, adopted son of the realms."

With that, Yesenia turned and led the way. Ramona's family looked at each other in astonishment! A seer Yesenia truly was.

'How could she know of us all?' Mused Ruth. But then, little surprised her anymore. Not in this alternate world to their own. They quickly carried the drowsy Ramona to the chapel.

Nearby, a glowering, gnarly figure smirked in mock disgust.

"Healings, discussions, nice hot drinks, sleeping, ha! Led by a pathetic little fishwife, church gardeners and Vaangrad's downtrodden spouse. I am going in to end this charade once and for all."

Alatar's eyes flashed angry and fiery as he emerged from his hiding place. He had heard enough and he slithered through the trees toward the chapel.

The spirits were listening to it all.

Chapter Forty Four
Luca and Giula of New Azmarine

As requested by Cormac, Biggle and Baggle the two great black-backed gulls, winged their way back towards the coast and the reborn settlement of New Azmarine. Ramona was in good hands at the chapel of Skyfawr as her family and companions waited patiently but tensely, for her healing to be performed by Yesenia and her keen student Amato.

The gulls soared seaward with Baggle, deemed the more sensible bird, in the nicest possible way. She was carrying the parchment note that Cormac had written, to let the New Azmarinian's know that King Theonyra was well and would return. The community at New Azmarine was mostly built from escapees from the Takers tower. Also survivors of the brutal punishment administered to the prisoners there by the menacing Elphinias, Alatar's then second in command. The warped Elphinias had revered in demonstrating his power and cruelty, by catapulting what he saw as the weakest prisoners out to drown at sea. Slung by the giant misused weapons for his own pleasure.

A punishment which the also cruel Alatar, allowed him to mete out, while he worked in his private quarters in the top tower on his plans to turn the realms into a totalitarian land of his own rule, with his mighty and faceless guard, the Takers, ready to extinguish any opposition. He had offered them all a fair deal, had he not?

Elphinias had thought himself intelligent and secretive enough to overthrow his master. Now it seemed as a result, he had been blown to his doom from the highest point of the tower by Alatar's red electric bolts, his end completed as he landed in the moat and any hope of survival was surely extinguished as he was dragged under the murk by a grim worm-like creature, barely even known to the red eyed one.

So it was that the two gulls arrived at the clandestine horse-shoe cove of the rebuilding settlement named New Azmarine. A budding phoenix from the ashes of its long ago demise.

Biggle clucked at his loving but tolerant partner Baggle, that his mind was on fish or perhaps a tasty crab, for refuelling purposes of course! She stamped a foot and cawed a firm 'No!' at Biggle whom bowed his head in mock shame. They were to find Luca and Elysse first, the guides of the new cove people and deliver the note. So they fluttered from rock to rock, then began flying around to scout for them, or anyone whom looked approachable.

Luca, a handsome man had been selected to be one of the guides of New Azmarine and was married to Giula, a beautiful olive skinned woman with eyes of jade green. It had turned out, that just like Ruth and James, this husband and wife, were also not born of the realms. Just like Ruth and James, Luca and Giula were holidaymakers from their own timeline. Just like Ruth and James, they had chosen Oakhampton for their relaxing break.

In a tale that mirrored that of Ramona and family, Luca and Giula had been snatched away during another of the realms shiftings. The wrong place at the wrong moment. The secret mystery of the ley line. They too had found their own hysteria. They too had survived.

Elysse, New Azmarine's other chosen guide, was of the realms. Born and raised there and a hardworking woman who had been separated from her two children when she had been imprisoned by the Takers for objecting to Alatar. She was later catapulted out to sea for her belief in Mahreuben and Uzaleus. Elysse had since applied a controlled passion for revenge. Although that sometimes spilled into hatred, something that was not naturally within her. To be parted from her children turned her into a woman of fire and strength. These people had all been dumped here, assumed drowned by the Takers. Only to be rescued by the watchful giant of Old Azmarine, who they had since referred to as the saviour of stone.

King Theonyra. He had silently waited for his time to come again. Almost dormant. Having been turned to stone in a raging and bitter battle between darkness and light many moons ago. He was struck by a dark wizard, frozen it seemed, and left as a monolithic statue to be a figure of fun for the dark armies to laugh about in times to come. But the dark ones magic had been incompetent, although cruel. Theonyra had indeed been turned to stone, but within his huge granite frame, ran the warm blood of a man of the realms.

So, now he had left New Azmarine, for duty. He was with his beloved and newly found great granddaughter, Princess Mahreuben and the ensemble of realms folk gathered at Skyfawr. Aiding Ramona by getting her to Yesenia at the chapel, in the hope of a healing as the poor unwitting wizard lay in delirium.

During the building of the coves of New Azmarine, the folk had thought Luca and Elysse to be good selections as spokespeople, guides. Giula, like Ruth, yearned to go home with her husband Luca, but had also been extremely grateful to be plucked from the sea by the kind hands of Theonyra.

Giula enjoyed her own roles now she was here, saved. Organising play for the younger, helping them to be constructive in building rafts, fishing equipment and also teaching. As Giula was from the same timeline as Ruth, James and Ramona, she could teach them counting and social skills from her frame of reference. She did not enforce it however. Peace was imperative. Learning of realms culture had become a passion for her.

Luca loved his wife dearly and was only too glad they had survived the catapult together. Sometimes at night, the 'alternate folk' as they had been endearingly named, told tales of cars, computers, music videos and aeroplanes to wide eyed younglings. By day Luca would work as hard as any realms man for their universal cause. He and

Elysse grew into their new lives. It would seem to be just as ragtag a group at New Azmarine as it was in the ensemble of Ramona's quest. Men, women, elves, young and old. From different places and times. Now the settlement was coming together. More importantly so far, a haven from Alatar.

Taking a stroll along the shale beach that King Theonyra had left with Mahreuben in what had seemed an age ago, Luca and Elysse walked and talked about things to be done. Improvements they could make and most importantly, about the health and safe futures of the cove people. It was just then as they came to a small area of rock-pools that Luca said, "Ellie, look! Two giant gulls."

The feisty and pretty looking Elysse answered her colleague, "I see them Luca, but what is so special? We see all the seabirds here."

"They are not scared off Elysse, they hop towards us with intent, look again.."

She looked again, half tempted to shoo them away, but they did indeed look so intense, and warm hearted. There they were, Biggle and Baggle, making a clamour to be noticed and hopping towards Luca and Elysse.

"Come here then pretty ones." Called Elysse. The two gulls did just that.

"What do you have around your leg my lovely friend?" Biggle and Baggle clucked and cawed. Luca bent toward them and saw. He gently untied the scroll from the unperturbed Baggle's strong leg.

"Elysse, it is a tiny parchment. A message.. they have come from inland."

Cormac's flying friends had bravely done their job. The elf would be immensely proud of the birds he had grown to love. Biggle cocked his head to one side and looked lovingly at his female friend.

Baggle cackled at him as though to say, "Go on then, leave me in peace, now you can go and find food!".

CHAPTER FORTY FIVE
A WIZARD AWAKENS

The whole of the village of Skyfawr had fallen silent, tense and solemn. The healing was being prepared at the chapel by Yesenia and Amato, her student. It had been a few hours now since Ramona had arrived on the makeshift stretcher, borne by her brother and father. Ruth, constantly by her daughter's side. Forgoing her own exhaustion to mop her brow, moisten her mouth with water and most importantly, talk to Ramona, just like mum always had. Baby, girl or young woman. The travelling force had been made very welcome. They were fed well and given plenty of water and tea to drink.

Yesenia, the curator of the chapel and sometime seer, had gently ordered it, but she knew the people of Skyfawr to be very welcoming, regardless. After all, she herself had been wandering, looking for her own place in life. A spiritual woman on a quest for what at the time, she did not know. Some towns dismissed her as a babbling fanatic, a shaman, when she spoke of connecting to the earth or embracing surroundings or nurturing the self.

Not Skyfawr. They saw within Yesenia, just what they needed. A calming force of nature and a positive influence and so she gratefully accepted the honour of the chapel's keeper. The chapel, Yesenia had decided, should never be locked. No appointment should be needed to find some peace, to celebrate good news. Say, a birth, a returned loved one or simply to seek solitude, a safe space to grieve even.

"If I am to take this honour, which I would very much like to. Then I wish the chapel doors to be left open, always. I may not always be within its walls, but the realms will be. I cannot ask people to suspend their emotions until opening time."

With that, the chapel's majestic oak doors remained open. The villagers, already friendly, found that it fostered a healthy trust and as such, would offer their own services to its maintenance or to garden or help with occasional repairs.

Although this working village liked to keep to itself, they had heard of the intent of Alatar, the red eyed one, from tales of very early on in his campaign. When he had gone from place to place, at first laughed off as a travelling circus. Then, he began to raze villages to the ground with a swish of his gnarly hands.

They stayed out of it. The people of Skyfawr. Worked, kept their heads down. Spoke little of leaders. Perhaps they were even glad to keep the denial going as to this unforeseen menace. What if a villager were to become an informant to the Takers?

A quiet paranoia began to fester underneath the normally jovial working hamlet. Oona, a well-liked woman, who herself had run a stall with her rogue husband Vaangrad until he left Skyfawr, now also helped at the chapel. It was a 'sanctuary for tired minds and bones.' She had said. Not surprising, given her tyrannical husband. Even people from neighbouring towns revered the chapel as a place thought to be watched over by the very essence of the realms. The ethereal. The unseen that saw all.

Vaangrad, tired of what he called 'Fairy stories around campfires.' In reference to the gentle leadership of Uzaleus and Mahreuben, had stormed out of the village with a few of his brutish fellows. Thugs, fighters, closed minds. They left vowing to find Alatar the new leader, and join his force at the stolen royal tower. Here was a creature of purpose and intent, Vaangrad had delighted in bellowing out.

The spirits though, whispered through the leaves of the trees at night here. Skyfawr outwardly portrayed itself as a small, neutral territory in the lands. But here, amongst its truest folk, lay a desire to bring this red eyed one to justice. Or to vanquish him. Yesenia the curator, had known of the power of this creature. She, like Cormac the brave elf, had an earthy relationship with the realms. A grounding. Since Alatar came to prominence, she had prayed the day would come when the ethereal found a chosen one, and indeed they had. Ramona.

The sleeping wizard had been placed atop the spiritual altar within the chapel by James, Jude and a weeping Ruth. Yesenia was not without empathy, but she had to ask Ramona's family and friends to wait within the village where they would be cared for. Theonyra, the stone King had been asked to stand guard outside the main door.

The modest giant, having only just found his great granddaughter, cut a huge forlorn figure, but he would never let a soul down. Oona herself, had bathed Ramona's head and made sure she was warm and then had passed a goblet of something to Yesenia before exiting the chapel. Yesenia and her student Amato were the only two inside now and both approached the altar where Ramona lay. Yesenia carried the goblet and Amato held in his own hands an emerald coloured bowl containing an ointment, made up by Yesenia.

Like the druid Selanius, who Ramona had sent fleeing in shame, Yesenia also was a very good potion maker. The difference being, she used her skills for good and not to drug folk into joining the army of a despot. The two of the chapel, stood one either side of Ramona and Yesenia whispered to Amato "We begin."

The young student bowed his head and awaited Yesenia's instruction. Yesenia began to call out, her voice echoing within the chapel walls..

"Unseen, but all-seeing ethereal spirits. Ours of the realms. You whom we call upon, just as you called upon this girl Ramona to be your chosen one. We ask you now to help awaken her from her fever. She has done and is doing all that she was chosen for.

With all respect, I, Yesenia of Skyfawr chapel and your keen student Amato, ask you to awaken this soul wizard. She is of another reality. She, a baby from that reality, has endured the rapid physical and emotional growth with complete bravery and dignity. Ramona has sent away Alatar's potion maker, she has dispatched many of his army and has galvanised a force of good. Unseen in these realms for lifetimes. I administer this drink of warmth, and with love, to help her awaken.."

Amato, the young student, was aghast, trying to focus, but he had never felt such a force. Listening to the different tone in Yesenia's voice as she conversed with the ether. The chapel began to rumble. Yellow and warm sunlight all of a sudden, flooded through the windows like the brightest sun. The chapel felt alive. Yesenia turned to reassure her loyal yet inexperienced student, smiling..

"They hear us, Amato." She now turned back to Ramona.

"Ramona, young wizard. I give you this drink so that you will awaken. You will be re-energised, stronger than ever. Ready. The spirits thank you deeply for your services to our lands. As do we all. So mote it be."

Yesenia stooped slightly and poured the drink onto Ramona's lips. The young wizard's eyes were darting around under her eyelids the way they would in an animated dream. Then, she licked her lips.

"Thank you Ramona wizard. Do not try to talk or move. Drink some more. You are safe." Yesenia gently poured a little more of the healing drink into the girls mouth. This time she drank it down.

"Amato.. the salve, please.."

The young student passed the bowl of ointment to his teacher.

"Unseen, but all seeing ethereal. We know you care for the good. For we know you 'Are' the good. I now bathe our wizard in a lotion to soothe her mind as she awakens. We thank you respectfully and now, as yours and our chosen one returns, we ask that in turn, she and all who travel with her, are under the protection of the realms as we seek to return our lands to the folk whom love and respect them."

The chapel rumbled and vibrated gently, almost like a humming sound, like a kind whispering voice. Yesenia then rubbed some of the balm onto each of Ramona's temples and a little onto her forehead before gently pouring a small amount more of the drink.

"With the good of the realms and the folk of these lands, this chapel and of Princess Mahreuben, Prince Uzaleus and all those whom worked here before us. Ramona, dear young wizard. I Yesenia, of Skyfawr chapel awaken you. Strong and healthy and ready. Ready to defeat Alatar and the Takers. Never to be alone. I ask the ethereal guardians return you safely afterward, to your own time with your loving family. Thank the ethereal spirits of the realms."

Yesenia turned to Amato.

"It is done."

Suddenly, a bright, fresh faced, open-eyed and very brave young wizard, sat bolt upright. She blinked several times, looked left, right, up and down and said, "Mum?"

Yesenia and Amato beamed.

Outside, behind a stone wall, a snarling red eyed figure cut an angry silhouette. It was all Alatar could do not to use his magic and blow that blasted chapel into dust. But now, he was not as certain as before. He felt as though he was being watched by strong, unseen ghosts. He slunk away to reconsider, but not before sending a flashing red bolt of flame into a copse of trees, causing an instant raging fire. A calling card had been left. A bitter fury burned in Alatar again as once before at the tower.

'Father, why are you so evil?' An unwanted flashback from nowhere. Another stinging memory. The dark one burned down a group of huts in a bid to bat away his own damaged feelings.

"Let us see if your spirits of the realms can reawaken that.."

Domacec, Cormac, Ailbe and several villagers came rushing to the scene. Just as they rounded the corner they saw him. Alatar clasped his hands, bowed his head, and vanished. Red eyes hung in the air for a split second afterward. Staring right at them.

Chapter Forty Six
The Desperate Druid

"Lower the drawbridge!" Came the bellowing cry of Vaangrad, the deputising Captain of the Takers. He looked out beyond the walls of the tower from the high ramparts to see an approaching, bedraggled small group heading towards the gates. Two of the guard wound away at the chained mechanism that brought the bridge slowly down to the ground and the wroght-iron gates were opened with no small amount of effort. Swarming Takers gathered, keen to find out whom Vaangrad was letting in.

Vaangrad had made his way down from his vantage point and was storming across the courtyard, ashen faced, with the two aides assigned as his bodyguards and advisors by the departed leader Alatar.

"Let them cross!" He roared to the guards of the gates. Finally as the bridge settled flatly over the moat, it became evident to the onlooking Takers that it was the druid Selanius, and he was with less of the guard than he had originally stepped out with.

The druid and his two potion makers had been sent with a throng of Takers, led by the conflicted Tanwyn. On the quest to the Paaniz barrens, in search of ingredients to make the now defunct life-force liquid that Alatar had used to control and suppress his legions.

The quest had failed miserably. Alatar had full control of his guard now anyway. They either followed him devoutly or did his bidding out of sheer terror. The liquid was no longer needed. That was not the point. They had failed. Selanius and his two potion makers had been gathering the rare granyaak root, only to be found in the place known as the foreboding barrens of Paaniz.

They would blend it along with other mind altering vegetation and mix it with mysterious powders to create a large new vat of the liquid. Alatar's intention would then be to dispense the drug, especially to the more strong willed prisoners and turn them into Takers, slaves or whatever he decided he wanted them to become. Imprisoned in their own minds.

However, despite having a guard with them, Selanius, his assistants and the Takers were rounded up by Ramona and her new determined army. The leader of the Takers that day, Tanwyn, was nowhere to be seen among this beleaguered looking band of returnees. Tanwyn, just like Domacec before him, had found the liquid wearing off during this assignment and had been filled with pangs of guilt for being part of Alatar's dark plans.

He began to have yearnings for his old life and despite fleeing the Paaniz barrens from Ramona's group during the banishing of Selanius, Tanwyn had gone with hope in his previously drowned heart upon seeing the chosen one, Ramona, taking on Alatar and his army. He had wished he was on her side. Perhaps now, one day, he could be.

Selanius could very easily have been killed that day, and his two potion blenders, and the Takers who accompanied them. Ramona had been pushed to her limits by all of the events and was ready to blast the lot of them into dust. The only other time she had had to use her full magic in this way, was in self defence, a long while back now at the Ivywyrld Inn, to protect her family and Cormac.

It was King Theonyra who had knocked Selanius flying to the ground and then told them to get away, before they changed their minds. The slithering druid had gotten to his feet and scurried across the arid land as fast as his legs would carry him. There was no gratitude in him. He had not tried to help his men or look back to see what had became of Tanwyn.

Selanius knew that Ramona was powerful, but he had been involved a long, long time ago in the altercation that changed Theonyra into stone. He knew Theonyra's heart was good. Soft even, too soft. But it was to Selanius advantage, so why should he care?

Eventually, one of Selanius potion makers had caught up with him and six or seven of the frightened Takers. The druid had said that the best course of action was to return to the tower. He would plead with Alatar for more time to find the ingredients they needed to make the life-force liquid.

The group had thought this may be tantamount to suicide, given the anger and destruction that Alatar was capable of when he had been wronged. There was little other option. At least at the tower, they would be safer among its four heavily guarded walls, than to be wandering around the Paaniz barrens. Starving, thirsty and subject perhaps to being predated by one of the fabled creatures that were said to roam those lands at night. So, walking across the bridge now at the tower, the drained and beaten group came upon Vaangrad.

"Well, well. The druid has returned. You do not look very well Selanius." Hissed Vaangrad sarcastically.

"You are very lucky, you and your group. Alatar has gone to finish the job himself. It is evident to me that you do not have the granyaak root. Where is Tanwyn and your other man?"

Selanius stepped forward. "Vaangrad? You are in charge now?"

"Yes Selanius, I am. You can no longer hide under Alatar's wing, or in the shadow of the top tower. He is very cross, shall we say?"

Selanius could see that Vaangrad was flanked by Alatar's chief aides and so knew that the thug was not lying to him. He tried pleading.

"Vaangrad, as you well know, the Paaniz barrens are a very grim place at the best of times, the granyaak root was scarce, we returned to ask for a greater force and more time.."

"Minus Tanwyn and one of your men and several of the guard, Selanius? I think not. Do you know what I think? I think you came across the girl wizard and her bunch of do-gooders and I think you ran away. Am I correct druid? Do not lie to me. There is a very hungry creature in the moat.."

Selanius instinctively glanced down into the water and felt an involuntary shudder run down his spine.

"Vaangrad, it was not quite like that. The stone King.. He has returned. He was with this Ramona girl. The Prince and Princess too. Also, a strong elven force, the escaped prisoners. We were overpowered. It was.. too much." Selanius was looking at the floor in shame at his flimsy plea.

Vaangrad fixed him with an angry stare.

"Selanius. You, are too much."

Vaangrad turned to the guard.

"You, Takers stood lazing there. Take this coward and his withering party and sling them in the jail. I have seen enough of his face for today. Look sharp, sloths."

With that, the returnees were dragged away unceremoniously and thrown into the cells with the other prisoners. Good prisoners.

Frustrated and angry prisoners.

CHAPTER FORTY SEVEN
LET ME GO

"I don't care Cormac, you should have just woken me. I would have gone after him. I am going after him.."

"Nobody was harmed Ramona. The fires were extinguished. The people are safe, to be sure."

"That's not the point Cormac. He has done it again and that 'is' to be sure. He is getting away with destruction, terrorizing people and murder. If he doesen't do it himself, he condones that bloody worm, Elphinias doing it."

Ramona was having an animated discussion with Cormac from her sick bed. Having slept alone in the chapel for almost two days, she had been transferred to Oona's homely little hut and had eaten a little broth with fresh baked bread, drank lots of water and then slept again. Yesenia had performed many healings and had said there would be a brief awakening and then deep sleep and rest. This is what had happened since the healing ceremony.

During her convalescence, Ramona was left alone, only checked on by Yesenia who kept bathing her forehead and face with the healing balm. King Theonyra had stood watch the whole time. A huge, stony guard whom you would not try anything silly with.

Now, at her bedside, it had been Cormac who had filled Ramona in on all that had happened since she had passed out into fever. Drained, after using her cobalt blue magic to frighten the life out of the sly druid Selanius and the takers guard, led at the time by the now remorseful Tanwyn.

The potion maker, his two aides and the cloaked guard had scattered and fled across the barrens before she had gotten really angry. But Ramona was no killer. It was Alatar she wanted. This little slimy 'soup maker', as she had called him, was just another servant whom needed a good scaring. Having suspended the cowering druid in the air and threatened to blast him away, she had eventually and literally, bought him back down to earth with a bump. She had wanted to do more, perhaps inflict a minor injury or two after the way Selanius had scathingly mocked King Theonyra for having to live his life entrapped as a stone man.

The King though, was tired of the sight of Selanius, so told him to go away before they did harm him. This group of Takers was no real threat to the small army Ramona, Mahreuben and Uzaleus had gathered along the way on their respective travels. Now having all met up and joined as one, they were quite a force. Whether that force was enough to seize back the tower and either kill or imprison the scheming Alatar.. That was another matter. Right now, Ramona, wide awake after much sleep and brain rest, was perched on the end of Oona's comfortable spare bed. Her face was lit up with a fiery annoyance.

Not towards any of her own group and certainly not towards anyone of Skyfawr. They had all played some part in her speedy recovery. It was a brooding anger towards this hateful and nasty creature. Now, he had simply vanished after setting fire to a copse of trees and a group of villagers huts.

"Misused magic to be sure, Ramona." Said Cormac with a look of resignation on his weathered face.

"You were only just finished in a healing ceremony, quite literally. Yesenia and Amato had come to inform us that it was done and that you were asking for your mother. We could not tell you that mere minutes before, that he had been lurking. If we had, you would have tried to do what you are professing you want to do now. You were in a healing Ramona. That does not mean that you 'were' healed."

The caring elf and now, true friend of Ramona and her family was trying his best to reason with her and convince her to rest up, eat a meal and regain her physical strength as well as rest her magic which of course, was raw and new to the young wizard.

"Where was he Cormac, outside? How could nobody see something as gruesome as him. That bloody heartless.. thing. I'll kill him Cormac. With my bare hands. I don't need magic." Blue flames involuntarily crackled at her fingertips in gesture.

"I love you Cormac, but you must move aside. Thank you dear Oona, I am going now. I'm not going to lie around in bed while he goes around burning down sacred villages. I said let me past.."

The feisty, red-faced young wizard was up on her feet and brushing past Cormac and Oona. She got to the door of the little hut, turned with her hands clasped in a praying motion and bowed to the pair of them.

"For the realms." She said, and walked away, closing the door behind her.

Not too far from the little group of huts, sat Ramona's family. They had been constantly looking over or asking Yesenia or Theonyra for updates on her condition. Ruth had been allowed to see Ramona at the chapel when she woke and mother and daughter had hugged and cried happy tears, before Ramona lapsed back into her deep, healing slumber. Now, her brother Jude looked across the marketplace and could not believe his eyes.

"Er.. mum, dad.. Ramona is walking away from the village!"

There she was, striding purposefully past the stalls and huts. Fingertips fizzing with an ocean blue fire. The villagers were gaping, disbelieving as she stormed by. They thought it would be sometime before the wizard had recovered her powers.

"Alatar the dirty coward. Giving people poison, stealing, burning villages. Catapulting people out to drown. I'll kill you. I will kill you with your own weapons. Yes, I'll see how you like drowning with no hope. Vile creature."

Ramona went on and on, ranting, vengeful. Normally smiley and placid, she was cursing under her breath and walking so fast that nobody could stop her.

"Jude, go after her. What on earth is she doing?" Said Ruth. James was already shouting across the marketplace as he ran after her..

"Mona! Mona, what are you doing? Come back. There's nothing you can do. Not like this."

Ramona eventually slowed to a halt.

"Not like this, dad? Where is the bloody action? They say I am a chosen one. That I am to destroy that thing. So I am going to do it, right now. I am very grateful, honestly, I am. But I'm not from the realms. I am meant to be a baby. I want to kill this man, so that these people can live in peace and we can find our way home."

"I know Mona, but.."

"But nothing, dad. Mahreuben came to me in a visitation. When she was trapped at the tower. Alatar was trying to get her to trick me, but she would not do it. She was strong and she warned me. Then she told me she would send us all home when this is all over. So that's what I am doing, dad. I am making it 'all over'. I can't sit around fires and trees anymore, sipping tea, taking part in discussions, planning what to do. There are no plans. Only actions. Please understand me."

James and now Jude, had caught up with Ramona. They listened intently as she spoke with maturity that belied her years. Jude stepped forward and hugged his sister tightly.

"Sis. I love you. You know that right? But do you know how far it is to the tower, on foot.. alone? You've just woken up. Everybody loves you and we know you can do it. We know you can end this thing. Alatar knows it himself. That's why he came here. To try and get to you before your healing ceremony. He failed. He was scared of you and he was scared of the essence of the ethereal, in the chapel. We all felt it outside. Everyone. The whole ground shook and it was like kind voices were whispering throught the trees."

Ramona looked at her pleading sibling. He was reliving a very real experience. She softened her stance a little.

"It was like magic sis. It 'was' magic. Please, I've seen it for myself now Mona. We have to trust them. I know we can't see them and its frustrating, but they are there. I know that now. Yesenia worked with them to wake you up. I'm so proud of you sis, honest. I could burst, but please, come and sit down. Lets sort this out the right way."

Jude gave his sister a heartfelt look. Ramona's furrowed brow relaxed at last. She looked at her brother, he had fought his own battles. Lost in between realities, forgotten. He had come through for her every time on this journey. She dropped her arms to her side and finally smiled.

"Big brothers.. Why did you have to calm me down? Gosh, I'm bloody hungry."

"Come on sis. Lets get you by that fire. Oona's making her soup. We are all going, together. We will get the tower back. Look at Theonyra. He's ready to smash his way through the gates!"

Ramona gazed up at the giant stone King whom had rumbled over to her in concern.

"I am so glad we have you King. I wish we could get you back to your human self."

Theonyra smiled down warmly at the young wizard.

"One thing at a time Ramona my friend. I might as well use this rock body to our advantage. Though I would like to taste hot soup again, as a man."

It was bittersweet. Theonyra, since being turned to stone, had lived for generations. But at a price. Seeing loved ones pass. Losing the need to eat or drink. Simple human pleasures. But his heart never wavered, and how joyful he was upon finding his great granddaughter, Princess Mahreuben. Every cloud, after all. So, Ramona walked with her family back across the marketplace, to sit with a relieved Cormac, while the warm and caring Oona, stirred a huge cauldron of soup.

At the chapel, Yesenia smiled wryly. She admired this girl's courage. She looked up at the ceiling as the sun poured through the stained glass windows.

"Thank you. We need this chosen one. She is good and true."

Yesenia was talking to the realms.

The chapel murmured warmly in agreement.

CHAPTER FORTY EIGHT
THE CONTEMPLATION OF ALATAR

Alatar stung. He had been hurt and surprised by his own inability to breach Skyfawr chapel and interrupt Ramona's healing ceremony. He, the self-proclaimed mighty new leader of the realms, reduced to slithering in and out of copses of trees, eavesdropping behind stone walls. Every time he had made to enter the chapel, he had felt something in his cold bones that he had not felt since he was young and bullied by his father into his barbaric ways.

Alatar had felt blocked by fear. Fear of the power of the ethereal, fear of Ramona's unpredictable magic and fear that he felt fear itself. He may have scared the villagers of Skyfawr when he burned down the copse of trees and when he unleashed his incandescent red magic to set fire to the poor villagers huts, but he had not stopped the healing.

As he had stepped out to enter the chapel and in his mind, simply brush Yesenia and Amato aside. He had wanted to wake Ramona himself and then see the fear in her eyes before killing her and triumphantly making his way back to his tower. That would have crushed her little army, no matter what King Theonyra, Prince Uzaleus and his little Princess Mahreuben had tried from then on. They would have known that they could not beat him if he had gone into the chapel and finished Ramona.

If.

The realms had chosen Ramona for a reason. That had all become clear now. Alatar reasoned that if the ethereal had to choose somebody from outside their own lands, then logic told him that nobody within the realms was strong enough or powerful enough to defeat him. It was just this damned girl, Ramona. A wizard, who had not even known she was a wizard. Dragged away from some family excursion as a newborn baby and accelerated through a rapid growth curve, in body, mind and soul.

Alatar cursed himself for his part in bringing Ramona here. Though he now knew the ethereal meddlers had bought her here anyway. Maybe though, had he not materialised in the road all that time ago, then their vehicle would not have come off the road. They would not have found the Ivywyrld Inn where all the magic began. They would just have gone to their own humdrum little home. Such is twisted fate.

The old inn on the ley line. The gateway between lands. Where Ramona's father had first gone for help and met his realms self, waiting to step into him and become the James he was now. That was strange enough, that the spirits had seemed to guide him there alone, for his transformation. Their plan must have been preordained. James must have already been here.

'No. This is all moot. It is not my fault.' Alatar mused, as though trying to convince himself. Though he kept turning it over, looking for things he should have done.

That scatty mother, always crying, weak minded. She had gone fleeing into the night, abandoning the car and ignoring James instructions to stay there. Carrying baby Ramona in her arms in the cold night. Then met James outside of the inn. Troublemaker, she was. James had not revealed himself to his wife, scared of frightening her while his own merging was taking place. He remained under his hood and took them inside. Ruth had not known it was her husband. She had begged this figure for help.

The baby had then grown in years in a matter of hours and days. She began to talk with intelligence, grew tall and feisty. She found that she had magic in her. As she had instinctively shown when defending the inn from an invasion of Takers.

Ramona. The cursed interfering wizard.

Alatar in torment, pondered some more. He had wandered absent mindedly into a long abandoned village called Emeralfre. It lay somewhere between Skyfawr and the Paaniz barrens. He had drifted away to analyse himself. To be alone. Emeralfre was once, like Old Azmarine, a thriving place of decent people during King Theonyra's rule. In the old battles it had been overwhelmed. Villagers either died in battle or fled. The whole place looked like it was locked in time.

Old homes still stood. Stone circles gathered moss and lichen where once, villagers got together to socialise and offer prayers to the realms for their good health. All of this history was of no interest to Alatar now. It was just a place to stop and think and recuperate for a short while. Even someone as dark and determined as Alatar had to rest sometimes. He wanted nobody around him. Not even his own army. The Takers.

For all he cared at this present moment, they could all crumble inside that tower. He began to think it may be best to return though. He felt it may be time to check on that fool Vaangrad whom he had left in temporary charge. He wondered if the thug was following his instructions. He felt the need to take his anger out on somebody. The prisoners perhaps?

Maybe by inflicting some punishment on those withering souls. It would bring the stupid girl back closer to his forces. His strong and large guard. He knew that Prince Uzaleus, and Mahreuben would have no hesitation in returning to the tower if they felt pain was being inflicted on their own people.

'Yes, draw them in. Bring them to me.'

A plan began to form in the darkest corners of his broken mind. Broken by his father so many years ago. When any goodness was forced out of him. When as a little boy he was told that bad is good. He had eventually been brainwashed by powers of darkness. So much so that he began to crave such powers for himself. He had witnessed how the other red eyed ones dealt with people like King Theonyra and his dreary, predictable folk. He saw how harmony was destroyed. Learned the power of fire, destruction, manipulation, doubt. Total power. Alatar secretly began to learn his craft. He was good. Good at being bad.

Alatar did not care what had happened to his father. He may have had magic in him, albeit dark magic, but he would surely be ageing now. Perhaps one day, he would return to where he had emerged from, which was still unknown to the folk of the realms, even to his own chief aides. He had just appeared here and decided to take over. Perhaps one day he would go back to find his father.

Perhaps he would kill him, for the raging lifetime of torment he had suffered and bottled up deep within his scarred soul. For now, Alatar rested on a bed of leaves. He could feel the residual energy bustling around this empty place, Emeralfre. Battles of yesteryear whispering on the breeze like a ghostly re-enactment. Nothing in the realms was ever as it seemed. Even events of long ago were woven into the fabric of these ever shifting lands.

'I will go back to my tower. I will not have these freeloading imbeciles in charge anymore. I have been mocked enough. I have tolerated idiots too long. I know what I have to do now father.'

His red eyes flickered and closed. Alatar was going to go back. He would cause such a clamour. He would openly let it be seen where he was headed. His thoughts swirled as his body demanded rest.

'Let Uzaleus send scouts for all I care. I will make it so obvious that I am returning to the tower and then, Vaangrad will be gone. I have seen his smug face. He thinks he is next in line. A drunken Skyfawr thug! The deluded moron will be made an example of.'

Alatar was almost laughing. Satisfied with his fresh ideas as sleep enveloped him. His drifting thoughts pleased him.

'First, the oaf shall die in front of my army. That will bring them into line. No more of the like of Elphinias. He was too familiar for my liking. Then our little Ramona and her pretty blue magic will be drawn to my tower. As will the ever empathetic Mahreuben. She will feel the pain most, in her good soft heart. Pathetic. She will feel the hurt, because she is in tune with me whether she likes it or not. My little banshee. Perhaps I will banish her back to those grim, fetid caves where she belongs. Perhaps, I will have her for myself. That would hurt our bonny Prince.

She will have Uzaleus, the elves, Ramona and her family come racing back to try to face me in my own domain, that will be their downfall. I am going to start torturing those prisoners. I do not need them anymore. My guard is big enough and my magic is strong. It is time to start getting rid of these stragglers taking up space in my jail. The punishment will be long and slow for them. That should bring them running.'

Alatar then slept like never before.

Smiling.

CHAPTER FORTY NINE
THE END FOR SOME

The Takers tower. It had become a hive, a busy place, since the red eyed one had taken over and moved his guard in to the huge, sinister looking complex, it was hard to believe it was once a place of peace. Now in the courtyard stood a legion of dark cloaked, drone-like guards. In huge, uniformed rows. Once there had been celebratory banquets, music and joviality when the old kingdom had thrown its gates open to its people.

The beautiful building now cast bleak shadows where birds no longer would fly to or roost. It overlooked the sea from the rear and Alatar, from his personal quarters up on high, often flung his stained glass windows open and gazed out to the ocean while pondering more ways to dominate. It had already seen many changes, much action had already taken place here. More residual energies were being stored by the ethereal. The unseen but all seeing. A sort of energy, rather than a physical presence. The folk of the realms just accepted their invisible guides.

Nobody had ever seen a god-like figure or a master wizard who could have been responsible for all the goings on in the realms. They just.. were. Now the tower was a hub of malevolent intent and within its walls many had come and gone. Elphinias, the cruel-hearted, previous counsellor to Alatar had been more or less executed and dragged to his doom by the creature of the moat.

Prince Uzaleus and many of his men had been imprisoned and later escaped with much help from Jude. Uzaleus had also been used as a bargaining chip by Alatar. Princess Mahreuben, had been cast out to a cave existence by Alatar and labelled a witch and a banshee. He had managed to brainwash many and she was run out to the coast and forced to remain there or face her own doom. Mahreuben had later been dragged back to the tower, a shell of her former self and forced to drink the mind bending liquid.

She was to locate Ramona and gain her trust, draw her to the tower whereupon Alatar had planned to dispose of her. In return for this, Alatar had promised to set Uzaleus free and reunite him with Mahreuben. A promise which of course, he would never have kept. As it was, events had turned out that they had found each other again anyway. The power of true love and of purity.

Selanius, the shadowy druid had worked in secret, making huge amounts of Alatar's mind bending life-force liquid with his two potion blenders. He had now returned with a small band of Takers, minus the remorseful Tanwyn and one of his potion blenders, whom appeared to be suffering with their consciences and rather than return, they had fled in secret support of Ramona.

Now the bedraggled and selfish druid was pleading to be let back into the tower, asking for more time to find the granyaak root to make the drug with. He had been slung into a cell for his trouble by temporary leader Vaangrad, once of Skyfawr. The big thug, estranged husband of Oona had craved this life for years. He was one of the few originally excited by the arrival of Alatar.

Now the tower was running quite smoothly under Vaangrad's no nonsense rule. He was shadowed everywhere though, by two of Alatar's newer chief aides, to which he grudgingly agreed. This was both to advise Vaangrad and to monitor him. It would not matter much longer. The true leader was on his way back from where he had been resting at the deserted, ghostly village of Emeralfre.

Vaangrad, slurping ale in his quarters, would not like what his leader had in mind for him. Alatar had spent a lot of magic, like his nemesis, Ramona. He had planned his next move and then slept deeply and undisturbed for days. He would travel on foot for a while, he liked the solitude.

Nobody was sure of Alatar's ultimate aim. It seemed he did not like nor tolerate a single soul. Did he have secret plans to bring in a queen for himself, to rule with him? Was he capable of falling in love? If so, why would he want to corrupt a bride-to-be? Unless she happened to be of similar make up to himself. It had not seemed that way. There did not appear to be brothers, sisters or friends. Let alone lovers.

It was as though Alatar's soul purpose in life was to rule the realms alone and in a totalitarian fashion. To take. What personal satisfaction this would bring him, only Alatar could say. Where had he come from? Had he ever been good? He was always hooded, glowing eyes scowling under a black shroud. Spindly, skeletal hands. Yet he was tall and strong both physically and magically. Only mentally, did Alatar privately suffer, because of his father.

He never spoke of a mother. He never actually spoke of his father. It was no business of the Takers. They just worked for him. He promised those who joined his guard many things in order to turn their heads and recruit them. He was yet to make good on his promises. Providing only basic living quarters and food, drink and warmth for his mostly drugged and robotic army. He knew that once they had been turned, he would rule by fear. If he wished to make good on any of his promises, he would do so when he damn well felt like it.

It was his father who had left the biggest imprint in the very marrow of Alatar's being. His memories made him feel little, frightened and insignificant. This is why he had tried ever since to be big, powerful and noticeable. The complete polar opposite. Respected and feared by all. Time was spent when young, with his raging father dragging him around huge battling lands and as a youngling he was never settled.

His father, like himself now, had operated with dark armies, chasing power, status and forcing him to watch some gruesome fighting and grim punishments to innocent folk. Alatar had initially loathed himself for what he had become. But it was far too late to go back. He had killed, slain, tortured and drugged. He had completely taken leave of his senses and any pangs of guilt or goodness in him, he quickly fought back down.

He had numbed himself as well as his armies and prisoners, with Selanius liquid. Alatar used it to dull his broken and dark heart. He could not and would not deal with any feelings that he found uncomfortable. They only served to distract and sidetrack him from his goals and that would not do. However, there was no more liquid and so these feelings were surfacing more often within him.

Selanius the druid, was also on his list. Vaangrad had checked over the guard on this particular morning. Unknowing that his master was on his way back. Vaangrad had assumed that Alatar, having gone away alone, would only return when he had executed Ramona, the girl wizard.

He did not think she would be imprisoned. Too risky. The girl had unknown magic. He had made sure that the guard had performed all of their daily routines and tasks and that the prisoners had been fully exercised and then fed and watered as per the new instructions. The prisoners were living in better conditions since Alatar had dispensed of the cruel Elphinias. They ate better food, drank fresh water and hot drinks and were given better bedding to sleep under.

They even fostered some hope now.

This was not really an act of kindness by Alatar, he had merely wanted to nurse them back to strength so that they could be given the liquid and integrated into his guard. This luxurious treatment was also on his list. To be ended.

After the drills had finished and the prisoners had been exercised and led back to the cells, Vaangrad had told his two aides he would be taking to his quarters for a while to rest and study. The mysterious aides simply nodded. Two Takers were positioned outside the door of Vaangrad's quarters as befits a temporary commander. The aides left to drift about their business, working on Alatar's documents and scrolls. Planning.

Vaangrad walked up the winding stone stairways towards his quarters. He was positioned one flight below Alatar's own personal rooms in the top tower. This was to be seen as an honour. This vast room had been previously occupied by the slain Elphinias, the traitor. Feeling he had done his days work, Vaangrad felt that he would sit back and relax for the rest of the afternoon, knowing that the tower was running like a well-oiled machine under his stewardship.

He was now looking forward to hearing of Ramona's demise and awaiting Alatar's return to show him of his good work. Now, Vaangrad would take a long drink of ale and enjoy his balcony overlooking the sea. He nodded to the two guard at his door as he turned the key.

"Stay there until I come out later. I do not want to be disturbed."

Vaangrad let himself into this luxury space for only the best members of the guard. How he had landed on his feet. He grinned to himself and poured ale from a wooden cask into a large pewter goblet, sitting to a large tray of meats and exotic fruits by the stunningly crafted windows, giving an astounding view of the sea.

"Well then, making yourself at home Vaangrad?"

Vaangrad spun around, startled so much that he had jumped and shuddered. Before him was the huge and imposing frame of his leader, Alatar. He had simply materialised in Vaangrad's quarters. His eyes flashed a strange mix and then back to full red. Alatar's rest had bought him back to optimum power.

"Alatar, my leader. I had not heard you come in. You have returned. This is good news. This Ramona?.. Gone?"

Vaangrad was not in control of himself. Despite his earlier bravado. To be up close and personal with his leader in such an unexpected manner had completely thrown him off balance.

"Enjoying the local brew I see Vaangrad? I notice the druid is back and in the cells. What else has gone on in my absence? Or do you not know? Have you been enjoying the view Vaangrad? This room is highly revered. Sought after, even."

"Thank you my lord, yes I am grateful for this honour.. Much has gone on here. Much good work. I will explain."

He was not given time.

"It really is a wonderful view of our resplendent land, is it not Vaangrad?.."

Alatar stared into Vaangrad and how he wished he had stayed in Skyfawr with Oona.

"Dear, oh dear Vaangrad. Resting in the daylight hours. Making merry in my absence. You shall now take a closer look at this outstanding scenery. Goodbye Vaangrad. Say hello to Elphinias when you land.."

Vaangrad began to babble manically, visibly shaking. Alatar then simply blasted him out of the open window with red fire shredding him in the sky, tearing his body to bits as prisoners and guard strained to watch the macabre display from below.

Bits and pieces of what was Vaangrad splashed on landing in the moat. Like Elphinias before him. The huge slimy and snake-like creature of the moat would enjoy this treat. Alatar turned away from the window. An example had been made.

"What a pity Vaangrad. You did not finish your drink."

Chapter Fifty
A Fond Farewell to Skyfawr

It was a new dawn at Skyfawr. Both in terms of the day, turned over like a new leaf and also in the minds of both Ramona and the villagers of Skyfawr. They had felt the presence of the spirits. Witnessed the nursing back to health of their chosen one, Ramona. Now they were preparing to say goodbye to the young wizard and her party as they gathered their things together making ready to push on back to the tower. Yesenia, the wily curator of Skyfawr chapel, stood at the front of the group of villagers with her young student Amato.

Ramona, looking brand new, refreshed and with a natural glow, embraced Yesenia.

"Thank you Yesenia. You have made me well again. I am so very grateful to you. To all the people of Skyfawr. Amato, Oona, all of you for making us welcome and letting us rest and eat good food. I.. I am lost for words.."

Ramona's words tailed off as tears rolled down her face. The feisty, strong young woman persona, slipped for a moment, revealing a poor confused and caring girl. Tears of gratitude, happiness to be alive, and just of release. This brave young soul had borne the weight of expectation on her shoulders for a good while now. Not without help of course. It was not every day that a Prince and Princess, a giant stone King and a throng of elves and escaped prisoners would march behind you.

'You are the nought to sixty miles per hour in a blink-of-an-eye wizard.' Her father, James, had said during her recovery. He was right. Cormac could only imagine how she felt. Being a baby, blissfully unaware of the dangers lurking and the challenges ahead, in your own world, let alone another one. Being doted on by your loving parents.

Then waking the next day to find you are six years old, chatting away, playing. Being a child. The next day you are ten. The next, fourteen. Sixteen, eighteen, twenty. Then, something slams the brakes on. Hard. Ramona had to cope with this as her soul and mind had to catch up with her body. She had done so admirably, but it was not easy for her. During her fever, she had talked in her sleep. Sounding one minute like a baby. Then forming intelligent and articulate sentences. Then crying, shouting. She had been robbed of her childhood. An education at school. Making her own friends in her own reality. In her own time.

Princess Mahreuben had promised the family that she would find a way to get them home. The Princess never made promises she could not keep and had formed a strong bond with Ramona's mother, Ruth. The realms had selected Ramona for their cause. It had initially been seen as quite thoughtless, cruel even. To drag a young family from their own timelines into the realms to try to fix a problem that they apparently could not, or would not. Or were they not allowed to? Nobody knew.

Cormac the elf had explained as best he could of what he knew of the realms.

'The all seeing, but unseen.' He had described them as. Others had skewed from Ramona's world, into this alternate reality. The same fate had been bestowed upon the holidaying couple Luca and Giula. They too had crossed the ley line. The gateway.

To find Alatar waiting.

Luca and Giula were escapees from the jail of the red eyed one, and were now among the founder members of New Azmarine, the hidden coastal village. Rebuilding Old Azmarine. Reinventing their own lives. A phoenix ready to rise from the ashes, among the chaos and uncertainty created by Alatar and the growing army of the Takers. They too, still wanted to go home. To their real home. There were people from Ramona's world, scattered all over the realms. They just did not all know it of each other. All assuming they were the only ones.

Now, Yesenia held Ramona tightly in a warm embrace.

"Ramona, adopted sister of the realms. To be at your healing and to see you now is an honour, a pleasure. A relief! The ethereal ones were with us on that day. Within the walls of the chapel. They spoke to you. The sun came out and the chapel dazzled with their presence. You are magic itself young wizard. They will help you and your family find your way home Ramona. Of that I have no doubt. They whispered through the evening breeze as you slept. Your brother, Jude, heard them. He now knows why he had spent time lost in between realities. It is a short sadness Ramona. Trust me. Brief anger is more than understandable. In the bigger picture, if we step away for a moment, we will see the pieces are beginning to fit together.

Your magic was inside your mother and you were born into it. Born, a soul wizard. This is why you were chosen. When you asked 'Why me?' the answer was 'Why not?' and then you understood. You took all in your stride and are ready for the next chapter. Go with the prayers of the village of Skyfawr. Go with blessings, go with honour. Go in peace."

Yesenia released her grip from her warm embrace and Ramona felt a whoosh of strength go into her very soul. As though she had received some sort of extra boost of power. The curator backed away, bowed to Ramona and winked.

"For the realms. For your family."

Ramona returned the bow.

"For the realms Yesenia. For all of our families."

Prince Uzaleus and Princess Mahreuben and her small army, were saying their own thank you's and goodbyes to the friendly villagers, who had given them warm beds, good food and drink. Skyfawr was of great importance in the bigger scheme of things. Alatar had found that out for himself. Fleeing like a sulking child from his own rising fear.

Skyfawr and its chapel did not tolerate evil. No matter how powerful. Nothing could harm a soul within Skyfawr chapel. Now, Theonyra, the stone King of bygone eras, stood and rose like a granite leviathan.

"It is time for us to go now Skyfawr. We leave with deep respect for this village and most importantly for you, its people. We will not fail. We have Ramona the wizard. We will surround her with our collected strength. We will use our very last breath's if necessary, to deliver her to the tower, to bring down Alatar. Forever."

A huge booming cheer rose up from within Skyfawr. So much so that the ground shook. There was a faint and gentle whisper through the leaves of the trees..

"For the realms. Ramona the wizard. We thank you. We thank you.. Thank you.."

It was them.

CHAPTER FIFTY ONE
SOMETHING STIRRED

"Vaangrad is dead. Elphinias the traitor is dead. Do you all understand this?"

Alatar was pacing up and down in the great courtyard of the Takers tower. Scores of his guard stood silently in huge, dark rows. It was a spectacular if worrying sight. It looked organised, angry. Legions of his followers in a tight, trained garrison. Some willing, some coerced, some threatened. The red eyed one had gathered a vast force compared to when he first arrived in the realms, campaigning with a few orcs and vagrants. All in dark robes, hooded and flashing red eyes. swaying side to side. Waiting silently.

"The wizard Ramona will be on her way to me here. Make no mistake about that. Each and every member of this guard is to be on full alert. There will be no sleeping. You have eaten once today. That is enough. You have had it too easy with my absences. There will be no more coming and going. I am here to stay. There will be no more mistakes. This girl is powerful. We have underestimated her."

Alatar still could not bring himself to say, 'I have underestimated her.'

He had not spoken of his fear of entering Skyfawr chapel. Of how he was scared to enter and finish off Ramona while she lay sleeping through her healing. It was more floating up and down than pacing. Alatar, with his disappearing and reappearing, seemed to be changing into something else. More ghost-like than of flesh and bone. But he would not ever let anyone close enough to him to find out.

"Ramona.." He spat her name.

"The girl wizard possesses a strong cobalt magic, has remarkable powers of healing and she will feel stronger for having overcome her fever. This could make her overconfident. I made my presence known at Skyfawr. If she wishes to destroy me, she will have to come here. She has with her an army. Because of you blundering ingrates, she has a force of escapees. Including the Prince Uzaleus and Cacodem. The pathetic captain has turned on us. He goes by his village name now, Domacec, the dolt. He will must be dIspatched on sight if seen. She has with her also, the stone King Theonyra. He of fable. He of Azmarine the fallen coastal settlement."

Murmuring among the guard. Theonyra had been turned to stone in the battles of old had he not? As though sensing their collective thoughts, Alatar whirled on them.

"No. Theonyra is not dead. It seems that the dark forces of old turned him into a stone giant for an amusing monument in celebration of their little victory. It seems that even the dark forces of old were also blundering ingrates. For stone he certainly is, but very real, strong and angry. Do you understand me? Say so if you do not."

The Takers swayed and hissed again. Nobody was going to say they did not understand.

"We understand Alatar."

"Good. You had better. She has with her also a mixture of elves including their apparent elected leader. Little Cormac is his name. He dotes on this girl and her family. Annihilate him on sight. That should fan the flames of our feisty wizard. The more angry or broken we can make her feel, then the easier it will be for me to eliminate her when she takes leave of her senses.

Her magic is instinctive and destroyed nine of you at the old inn, save for the coward Cacodem, who left your comrades to be shredded into dust. Skulls, spores and rags are all that remain of your colleagues.

She is a killer. Ramona is no angel. Be certain that she will murder in order to protect her family and friends.

To go for her jugular is to target these people as they arrive. Do you understand this clearly? The catapults can be wheeled out if you do not understand and you can join other prisoners and failures. Death at sea. It is a sunny day for it. Again, do you understand this clearly? Say so."

Alatar's eyes scowled a deep red, a wide grin spread across his otherwise hidden face. Red eyes, deadly serious, with what looked like fangs protruding from his mouth.

"We understand clearly Alatar."

"Good, then that is all. You have seen what happens to the likes of Vaangrad. I have no further use for the druid Selanius either now. He has failed. The guard is now vast and strong. You need no more liquid. You are Takers. You are MINE."

Alatar turned to his two aides. The same two that had shadowed Vaangrad during his brief reign before his doom.

"Take the druid Selanius and his potion maker. Also take one hundred prisoners up to the ramparts. Have the catapults readied. I need the space in those jails for fresh captives. Those there now are stealing my food and water. They are weak, they are too puny for this army. Send them to the water. Make a scene. Make it noisy. Make it so it is seen. I want them catapulted out to sea. There is no stone King to scoop them up. He is at Skyfawr and coming here with that interfering girl. He will be too late this time. Go, make it fast and unpleasant."

The aides gave their usual silent bows and summoned a bank of the guard to follow them to the prison.

Selanius was sleeping in a corner of his cell next to his potion blender. He was starting to wish he had not returned at all and taken his chance in the barrens of Paaniz, like Tanwyn. The aides nodded at a huge member of the guard. Kovah was his name, a full convert, pure taker. An orc of some standing. Kovah unlocked several of the cells with the master-keys. Selanius emerged among others. Blinking at the sunlight like a surfaced mole. They were shackled, hands behind their backs. Around a hundred of them as ordered by Alatar.

The two aides, Kovah and the troop of guards pushed and shoved the prisoners into an orderly form. They were led with the red whips cracking at their backs, to the winding staircase that led to the ramparts at the top tower, and the catapults. Selanius felt a horrible rush of adrenaline course through his chilled bloodstream. He tasted rising bile in his throat.

"Where are you taking us, guard?"

Selanius already knew. He also knew that he would get no answer from these drones. Up and up they went. Any screaming or cries of protest were immediately silenced by the hot searing pain of the lashing whips. The prisoners and Selanius knew their fate. They had seen such displays when Elphinias took on the role of punisher. All they could do was pray hard to the realms and ponder how long they thought they could swim or stay afloat. Arriving at the top ramparts, they were ushered like cattle and loaded into the giant catapults that had lain dormant and unused for some time now. The chief aides looked down into the courtyard for Alatar. There was no need. He had materialised alongside them.

"Are they all in and secured?" The aides nodded again, silent.

"Do it."

It was hard to watch even for some of the guard. The huge machines recoiled to their straining maximum. Alatar raised his right arm and then bought it down with a swish. Guards released triggers and the beautiful, pastel blue sky was tainted by one hundred screaming bodies.

There had been an observer from a distance. The observer pondered his thoughts. 'He does well, the red eyed one. He learns quickly now. He no longer tolerates fools nor carries excess. He has improved. He is ruthless, like I trained him to be.'

A grisly figure. Older than Alatar, sat in the dank caverns of the catacombs. Bitter and spindly. Tentacles splayed from arm sockets, stroking the surface of a pool of navy blue. These were the darkest recesses of the huge tower. He had stayed here hidden. His only company had been the creature of the moat, which would surface at the edge of the fetid waters within the midnight shelter of the underground caves. He fired an electrical, red type of magic at the water. Simalar to Alatar's.

An assortment of dead fish and small water creatures floated to the surface.

"Here is your meal Bakkor."

The water stirred and broiled, and the huge undefinable creature broke the surface. Bakkor of the moat. The repugnant looking vermin. It was a terrifying sight. A cross between a lizard, a shark and a giant worm. Like a macabre experiment gone wrong. It growled and groaned as it hungrily devoured the poor, stagnant offerings.

"Ah Bakkor, my creature. Well deserved. Thank you for bringing me to the catacombs. It has been refreshing. But my strength returns. I think it is time to go back to the surface. To get back up to the tower. Alatar has done well. It is time to pay my son a little visit."

It was Elphinias.

CHAPTER FIFTY TWO
THE RIVER RYYGIER

"Well, so far so good." Mused Ramona as the party struck out for Alatar's tower again. The determined group were following a trail suggested to them by the seer, Yesenia, when they bade their farewells at Skyfawr. The huge, crashing river Ryygier. Rocky, deep and fast. A vast forested area thrived on both sides of it, full of sequoias, giant redwood and douglas fir among others. Cormac was quick to start stuffing huge fistfuls of fallen needles into his pouch. Domacec looked at the busy elf, puzzled.

"What are you doing brother? Pine needles won't feed your hungry gulls!" He chuckled.

"Ah, Domacec. Correct my friend. Biggle and Baggle won't go without to be sure. I fed them this morning before they took to the air. No, these are for ourselves. For when we make camp, I will boil them in water over the fire and make us fragrant and cleansing tea. Finola would be proud." He smiled to himself thinking of his lifelong friend.

Domacec grinned at his new companion.

"Your lady friend has you well trained I should say, brother Cormac!"

The elf blushed a little as he fondly thought of FInola. She had stayed with the elven force at their home settlement. She was well respected and kept a keen watch over the young ones. Many elves had followed Cormac's lead in standing with Ramona, but after all, the elven woodland village would not look after itself.

"What do you think sis?" Said Jude as he walked briskly alongside Ramona.

"Well Jude, Yesenia thought it would be a two day march if we throw in a nights sleep, which we all need. We seem to be making good progress. No sign of any Takers. She did say we would be well covered by the Ryygier. I think we just go on along the river as she told us. Make camp in a few hours. Eat, sleep and start again tomorrow. I don't know Jude. Best to see what everybody thinks. I imagine Prince Uzaleus and his men must have been through this part of the realms before Alatar turned up. Maybe he is the man to lead us. I'm flying blind Jude. I am just using my instinct and consulting Cormac with the map Yesenia drafted out for us."

Jude smiled at his sister.

"Well you are doing an amazing job, sis. Lets see what Prince Uzaleus thinks, and I am sure our ageing parents would be glad to put their feet up and drink some of Cormac's pine needle tea!" Jude grinned at Ramona and she giggled as her mother Ruth and dad James strode behind them.

James put his hand to his mouth to feign shock.

"Cheek! He's doing it again Ruth. Hey son, we heard that! Your mother and I have been walking places like this for years. Don't underestimate our.." James paused for comedic effect.. "Fitness and stamina!"

Ruth burst out laughing at her husband. James could never resist a chance to display his self deprecating humour and it had diffused much tension since the journey had begun. He was naturally very witty and funny but his use of humour in such situations was also very intelligent, clever and appreciated by all.

"Keep dreaming dad!" Said Jude laughing at his father's clowning.

"Leave the hard work to us youngsters. You can have a nice cup of tea soon and get your breath back. Right mum?"

Ruth smiled wistfully at her beautiful boy, returned from his own personal twilight zone. Brave young Jude.

"Well, I will be glad of Cormac's tea as well Jude. Stop being cheeky to your poor old dad!"

James looked up at his wife with fake exasperation.

"Don't help him!"

The whole party had smiles on their faces as they pushed on along the river. Looking up, they could see huge rocky tors and cliffs with nesting crows and ravens cackling away. Harriers soared elegantly above, keen eyes scanning for dinner. Paths had to be chosen and woven carefully through the dense forest areas but they were all glad of the cover it offered. The wide river crashed over the rocks but in some parts there were eddys and deep swells, shallow pebbled runs with weed cover and well oxygenated. Two of the escapees, Ailbe and Dayn walked with Cormac now. The elf seemed happy with his pouchful of brew makings.

"Ah my friends. Some large salmon in these waters to be sure. Salmon, char, and trout. Beautiful creatures, good fishing. Very tasty.. when taken sparingly of course." Cormac's eyes misted over at the thought of huge fillets of wood smoked fish with vegetables gathered from the land.

"Oh, for a red salmon dinner. Tender and flaky. Lemon juice and Finola's ground pepper, green vegetables. Ah, waxy, earthy potatoes straight from the ground, a few fine green beans from the woodland allotment.."

"Earth to Cormac, come in Cormac!"

It was Jude, chuckling as he spoke, gently teasing the little elf as he dreamily salivated over his non-existent banquet.

"A beautiful vision to be sure young Jude. Alas I have no fishing equipment to hand and unless you know any friendly grizzly bears to scoop us a few out, then I suppose we had better move on. Get some more miles in before dusk. A red salmon dinner.." Cormac said again, away somewhere else.

So, on they went, negotiating the river Ryygier and its craggy terrain. Ramona looked fresh and reborn following her healing at Skyfawr, especially in the new robes given to her by Yesenia and her people. Her cloak was handmade with a protective hood and pockets.

"Now you look like a true wizard, sis." Chimed Jude.

"Oh, I'm just me Jude. You know that. But I am so grateful to the villagers for all they have done for us. It is a lovely robe though, eh!" Ramona winked at her brother and twirled around laughing.

They had all been wearing the same clothes for so long. Washing them in ponds and streams and drying them over fires. Now they had all washed and bathed at leisure at the hospitality of Skyfawr's people. Dressed in clean, warm clothing. Sacks of food, drinking water and spare blankets. Some of the force had asked Theonyra to swat the huge trees out of their path, given that he was a giant with some strength. Theonyra had refused.

"I am sorry brothers, but I will not break the things of the earth that are hiding us from the red eyed one. A few cuts and scratches are the worst you can expect. I will tread a path ahead to ease the way.." And off Theonyra clomped.

"Easy for him to say, look at the size of him." Muttered Ailbe.

"True brother, but I think Theonyra would rather be back in his human body and down here with us." Replied Dayn.

Ailbe hung his head.

"Aye, it is agreed Dayn. I had not thought."

"Do not give it another one, Ailbe. I am sure Theonyra would not. We are all in this together. Til the end."

"Til the end brother Dayn."

As the hazy daylight faded ever so slowly, the temperature dropped. Only slightly, but enough for Prince Uzaleus to call a halt to the relentless march.

"Good folk of the realms. I believe we should make camp for the evening. We have made a decent fist of it today. This looks a good space to make a fire, cook our dinner and sample some of Cormac's tea. We should try to sleep before tomorrow. Yesenia gave us two days march by her thinking. Then, the tower will be upon us. I do not want us bleary eyed and wandering into any ambush that Alatar may have waiting. We must nullify his Takers. Give Ramona a free run at the swine. Is everybody for staying put for the night?"

Sighs of relief rang out among the throng.

"I will take that as a resounding yes then!" Smiled Uzaleus.

"Sit then, rest and eat. Sleep while you can my fine folk. We will set up a night watch for any of those Takers. I will take first watch. Can I have two men to sit with me?"

"Dayn and I will watch with you, Prince." Called out Ailbe. The poor man still felt bad for his quip about Theonyra. Ailbe had a good heart and was well thought of. He need not worry. But Uzaleus was grateful of his volunteering and of the keen young Dayn, They would make a fine night watch.

"That is settled then. The rest of you can do as you like with this spare time. Eat, talk, sleep. Enjoy this pleasant evening by our guardian, the Ryygier. Do not stray far from the camp though. Keep by the fire."

With that Prince Uzaleus kissed Princess Mahreuben tenderly on the cheek and strode off, huddled in conversation with Dayn and Ailbe. Mahreuben sat with Ruth, glad of the chance to rest and be with her friend. The bond they had formed was growing and they admired each other as the strong women they were. The two had been through so much and had never complained about their lot and their empathetic feelings ran deep.

James, Jude, Ramona and Cormac sat together on the rocks close to the waters edge. The water ran slower here. A pleasant place to stop for the night.

"Looks like you'll have to settle for potatoes and vegetables tonight Cormac, old friend." Smiled James.

"Aye, to be sure James. I am certainly ready for it, and grateful to the people of Skyfawr for our sacks of food. Still, what old Cormac would give for a hot side of smoked salmon.."

Just then, as Cormac stared wistfully at the water, a huge red salmon leapt clear of the surface, taking a fly and then disappearing back gracefully under the water with a defiant swish of its tail.

"Why of all the rotten tricks!" Cried Cormac.

Ramona, Jude and James howled with laughter.

CHAPTER FIFTY THREE
ELPHINIAS RETURNS

Alatar had laid down his strict new regime, to be ready for the expected appearance of Ramona. The Takers guard were on full alert. Ruled by fear. Fear of the catapult. Worried the new self-imposed leader of the realms seemed to be suffering something akin to a mental breakdown. Leaders had to be strict, cruel even. Alatar's temper had become shorter than usual. He was irritable and constantly pacing. At nights he seemed to float around the courtyard muttering to himself about destroying Ramona and summoning the unseen lords of the realms to reveal themselves.

"Cowards.. Gods? I do not think so. Calling on a girl from another timeline to save your precious faerie kingdom. Show yourselves. Let me destroy you, as I will Ramona. Or I shall die trying. I rule these lands now. Not your merry Prince and his pretty little Princess. I shall outcast her again like the wailing banshee she was before. Screeching, broken mess. Crying on cliff sides. Crawling in caves for a swashbuckling clown Prince who ended up in my jail."

On and on he went. The night guard gave sideways glances to each other but dared not question the crazed, red eyed one. Presently, Alatar was in his quarters. Once again pawing over his scrolls and parchments and plans. Plans to extend the tower. He had picked up on something happening at Old Azmarine. Something in his blood told him. He could not place that it was catapult survivors, rebuilding a community in secret and in peace. He could not quite visualise New Azmarine but it would come to him. He knew it would. As sure as a morning mist clears and the sky becomes so crystalline blue, that you could pick out the markings on any seabird. For the moment, it was behind a thinning veil in his brain.

He went to his decanter and grabbed at his pewter goblet with spindly, death-grip fingertips. He still had a little of the life-force liquid in reserve. He used it in tiny amounts to control his busy, spiralling mind.

Then, there was a hissing familiar voice, intruding upon his thoughts.

"She is on her way, you know. She is headed this way, along the Ryygier. Coming for you. Coming to end you. Son."

Alatar whirled around from his desk and for such a strong and evil leader, he quivered briefly and recoiled in shock.

"Elphinias! You?"

"Surprised to see me I notice. My revered leader. Relax, enjoy your drink. You look like you need it. You are losing your touch Alatar. Talking to yourself. Challenging the ghosts of thin air in the dead of night. Even a leader must sleep."

Alatar took a sip from his drink and felt it course through him.

"Elphinias, I.."

"Thought me deceased? Blew me out of the window to a watery death? No, a clever ruse. I am, as you see, very much alive. Son." Elphinias was revelling in watching Alatar squirm.

"But, I saw the creature of the moat, I saw it take you, lifeless, motionless. Surely drowned? Why do you call me son, traitor?" Alatar now felt sick in the gut.

Elphinias paced the room.

"Oh Alatar. My dear boy. So many questions. You always were an inquisitive little scamp. Let me address your queries. The creature of the moat did not drown me. It rescued me. It is called Bakkor. He is like an obedient sort of pet. He helps me, I give him fish. I had a lot of thinking time down there in the catacombs after you tried to murder me. Your own father. Who by blood, bestowed upon you all of these powers you utilise today. Somewhat ungrateful I would say. Boy."

Being called boy, so deliberately, stung Alatar and Elphinias knew it would. Elphinias of course was the tormentor in chief of the poor prisoners. taking great satisfaction at the rising death toll when working as Alatar's chief aide. Alatar crossed the grey, marbled floor and opened the large window and stared out to the emerald sea with his back to Elphinias.

"A miracle recovery it is then, son. Do you not think me to be kind, for not attacking you after you inflicted such a terrible ordeal on your poor, withering father?"

Alatar turned back to face Elphinias.

"I would know. I would recognise you. A simple hood does not allow you to fully hide your face. I would know. You look nothing like my father. I left the dark land to escape that monster."

"Yet, here you are Alatar. A monster yourself. I tell you, you are my son. My flesh and blood. Like it or not. It is fact. And it is only because you are my foolish son that I do not exterminate your wasted life right this second."

"You are.. unrecognisable. How?" Whimpered Alatar, crestfallen.

"Think of it this way, my self-proclaimed leader. You are able to disappear and reappear in different places, are you not? To manifest in one village one moment, and materialise in another in the next. That is part of your skill set. Part of my skill set is to have the ability to change the appearance of my face. I use my various guises to fit in when and where I need to. Call me a chameleon if you like. I change to suit the surrounding people. It has done me no harm as you see.

You are an impetuous fool. Underneath all your cruel bravado, you are the same child who made me ashamed, when we left the dark land to defeat the old royals. Ashamed as you wanted to stay with your mother. Too squeamish for a fight. That is why I had to take tough measures. To train evil into you. To give you this power that has enabled you to overthrow this very tower and make it your own. With all these lands to govern. All these minions to rule.

I gave you that, you did not develop the ability to raze mountains to the ground with a swish of a hand by listening to bedtime tales with your mother. It was I. Me, who gave you all this. Me, who implemented raw hatred and sheer power. Me, who followed you out of the dark land when you left on your headstrong quest. Now it is me, who has returned to supervise your recklessness is tapered. As it is that, which will see this Ramona turn you to dust. I have seen it. I know the realms more than you could ever know, boy.

I stayed in the shadows as your aide, but I could not stand by any longer. That is why I came to this top tower, the day you tried to execute me. While you held Mahreuben in chains. She was in silent communication with Ramona. You idiot. Mahreuben's heart and mind are far stronger than yours boy. More is the pity. By holding her in chains and dosing her with your newfound addiction, you thought you could make her lure the girl wizard into a trap? She went to Ramona in visitation. Mahreuben is not just a Princess you imbecile. Did you not see her stride across the sky to escape you? To escape you as did Uzaleus, Domacec, Ailbe. The boy Jude? So very silly and impetuous. Presumptuous even."

Alatar seethed within now.

"Shut up. Shut your mouth Elphinias you liar. I warn you. You are old, insignificant."

Elphinias smirked.

"Alatar, we are all old. We live for hundreds of years, our kind. You are not the human boy that you wished to be. I am sorry. I come to help you find acceptance, but.. the window is open son. Would you like to try again? Go on, I dare you.."

Alatar raised his right arm above his head.

"So it is, shapeshifter. Father or not. You really wish to die then? You have poisoned my bloodline. So now, goodbye.."

He brought his arm down, pointing at his opposite and his electrical magic, screamed across the room toward Elphinias like killer dragon flame. The crooked Elphinias held both of his hands out, palms raised. Alatar's mouth dropped open. The bolts of magic deflected off an invisible shield and fizzled harmlessly to the floor. Elphinias strode towards his son and grabbed him by the throat.

"Do not do that again. Sit down. For the life of me, I am going to make you a leader. Only I can help you beat Ramona. Sit down. Shut up and listen.. Boy."

Alatar burned with inner torment.

CHAPTER FIFTY FOUR
A PARCHMENT FROM NEW AZMARINE

"Just look at it my love. So beautiful." Said Luca to his wife, stretching his arms out and yawning at the morning sun.

"Not as beautiful as you of course Giula. Nothing comes close to that." Luca drew his wife in close and kissed her tenderly on the lips and they embraced as the salty waves lapped around their bare feet.

"Ah, well rescued Luca! If you weren't my husband and I didn't love you, I would call that a really bad pick-up line. I know you mean it. So I will allow you another kiss."

The stunning Giula, glowed effortlessly, with her emerald green eyes flashing vitality, and olive skin, radiant with health. The sea air was so good for these recovering people.

"Now there is an invitation!" Grinned Luca and moved in close to his wife for another kiss.

Presently, Elysse arrived beside their newly built beach hut. Smiling knowingly. She had become firm friends with the couple from Ramona's timeline and enjoyed their company. Often working with Luca as elected members of the cove council while Giula concentrated on her teaching.

"Ahem.." She giggled.

"Had you better go back into your hut or is it safe to speak with you both?"

Luca and Giula returned the smile and wriggled out of each other's arms.

"Ah, sorry about that Elysse. I was just telling my wife.."

"I can guess what you were telling your wife Luca. Say no more, please!"

Giula cackled at her friend's humour.

"What can we do to help Ellie?" Said Giula as Elysse passed them morning tea, brought from the pot over the nearby campfire. The redheaded realms girl held out a scroll.

"I wrote this last night and wished to see if you could take a look. See if you think it alright or wish to add your own thoughts to it. The gulls are well rested and I am sure they can locate Cormac and the party of Ramona."

Giula rested her arm on Luca's shoulder and they both took grateful sips of tea as they read Elysse's message.

'Dear King Theonyra. We at New Azmarine hope this scroll finds you well. We thank you for your parchment. It was delivered successfully by the black-backed gulls. We are happy to hear from you and hope that Princess Mahreuben is well and reunited with Prince Uzaleus. We are prepared. We have made 'giant' strides, since you departed to aide the quest to remove Alatar from our lands. Please forgive the pun. The children here are being taught a good mixture of the ways of the realms and some useful learning is being administered by Giula of the alternates. The cove you brought us to.. It saved us. It is taking shape as a pleasurable place to dwell.

We work hard. The huts are strong and weather resistant. The fishing is good and the fruit trees and vegetable patches further back are enjoying the sunshine. We exercise every morning. Work, eat, sing and pray at night. In all, we do not want any of you to worry about us here at New Azmarine. What we want to hear King Theonyra, is not so much the destruction of Alatar, we can fend him off, if not defeat him. No. We want to see you returned to your human form and to live out your days as a happy King and the leader we look up to. Which of course, you already are. Every day that passes, we swell with gratitude.

You stood dormant, beneath the waves like a silent guardian, waiting for the right time. You picked us up as our strength faded and we were to drown. Our prayers are also for the ones we lost. The ones who died at the hands of Elphinias. To end him is on a par with the desire to end Alatar.

Our King. I now dispatch the gulls with this parchment in the hope that it finds its intended destination. If you can, please send word back. The gulls enjoy the food and I am sure they won't mind another stay! We know you told us to wait. But the way of the New Azmarine people is built on hope and gratitude. We are fit, renewed, ready to march. Our prayers are sent on the sea breeze of the ethereal. We await only your word. Be safe, all of you. Be strong and well. From the cove of New Azmarine with our love.'

Luca and Giula finished reading the scroll and both looked up at Elysse.

"Wow, Ellie, its perfect." Said an open mouthed Giula.

"I do not want to add to that! It is so well put. I could cry. Your soul really is so gentle."

Elysse smiled and blushed a little.

"What she said!" Uttered Luca. Equally impressed.

"Ellie, you have made our morning. This tea is delicious too. I don't suppose there is any more in the pot?"

"Never mind more tea, you. Lets walk with Ellie and find our winged friends." Giula pushed her husband playfully on the shoulder.

"Oh she's a cruel mistress Ellie. A cruel mistress.."

They all burst out laughing.

"There will be more tea, scamp, and breakfast is almost ready. Giula's right though. If you think the letter acceptable, we should find the gulls. They are never far in the mornings. All sorts of foods wash up for easy pickings."

So, the three of them strolled, up the beach towards the cluster of rocks where the cawing gulls usually took a hearty breakfast of their own. Sure enough, on a large kelp coated rock, the two large gulls stood proudly, casting shadows on to sugary sand. Their feet were holding down a small, poor halibut that had been caught out by the ebbing tide. The gulls did not kill, like birds of prey would.

They were staunch opportunists and fed off the riches that the outgoing tide left behind. One held, the other pecked and vice versa. Clucking in appreciation, they would find ponds or streams later for a freshwater fix to wash down their fish. As Elysse, Giula and Luca approached, both gulls looked up. 'Hop, hop, hop', they called. It sounded like they were talking in recognition of the approaching cove folk.

"Ah, they do understand us!" Smiled Luca, and Biggle and Baggle, gulping down the last remnants of the halibut, hopped over towards the group of three. Elysse crouched.

"Good morning our flying friends. I hope you have enjoyed your breakfast and your stay. I need you to return if you will, to your friend, Cormac, the staunch elf. I have a message for him and Ramona's party. Will you fly for me?"

The gulls yellow eyes flashed in a smiley sort of way at the mention of Cormac. The man they had grown to love and not just for his food pouch! Also, they had watched over Ramona at Oakhampton beach as a little baby. Before her growth acceleration, instigated by the realms. Of course they would fly for Elysse. She and the cove folk had shown great kindness and they had enjoyed a well deserved and extended rest period. For they too, were in the fight against Alatar. As guides from the air and now as vital delivery birds!

Elysse crouched gently beside the two loveable birds and gently attached the rolled-up piece of parchment to the leg of the reliable Baggle.

'Clack, clack, clack.' She squawked and looked Elysse in the eye.

"Clever, beautiful friends are you. We will not forget you. There is a place here always at New Azmarine for you both."

Biggle and Baggle, parchment attached took a small run across the damp sand, flapped a little, and then soared into the beautiful morning sky. With the sun shining yellow and bathing all in warmth as cotton wool clouds sailed lazily across the pastel blue backdrop.

Luca smiled at Elysse's kind manner.

"Wonderful sight Ellie. Truly wonderful. And such a beautifully written scroll. You mentioned more of this hot tea though and er.. something about breakfast?"

Elysse rolled her eyes skyward in mock exasperation, but they were smiling eyes and gave her humour away. Giula simply laughed at her husband and said..

"Men! All they think about is food!".

CHAPTER FIFTY FIVE
THE ADVANCE

"I have it in my locker Jude. In my heart. It's just there, you know? Please, don't worry. Its just what I need to do."

Ramona sat with her brother from between dimensions, next to what would probably be the final campfire before the march to the tower. Jude sipped his tea.

"Don't worry? Sis, Its what big brothers do. Even though we are nearly the same size now, what with your growth. I'm so proud of you Mona. But I'm angry. Can't you see why? You have been denied an entire childhood and you are putting your very life at risk to save these invisible spirit folk that did it to you. Whatever they are. I can feel them around, but why the secrecy when we are helping them? I am sorry for them. But why not reveal themselves to us? Its time to be selfish Mona. Cash out, cut and run. Get our lives back.

Why don't we just go? We've done all we can. Our new friends are strong now and they have proved they can find places to live undisturbed, like New Azmarine. I want my sister back. I want to know what its like to hold you as a baby. To take you to the park. I want to look after you. Stay out late messing about. I want my mum and dad to tell me why they didn't know who the hell I was when I walked from god knows where to end up here. Clueless, with a mum and dad struggling to remember me

It will be something to do with these bloody realms, timelines shifting and all of this.. stuff. That's why. It clouded everybody's memories. I woke up in an empty deserted house. I was slung out by a nasty, bad tempered bloody estate agent. In our own home sis. Calling me a squatter and directing me to a soup kitchen. I wanted to smash his face in Mona, but no, Jude is never bothered, Jude's always calm. None of the neighbours knew who I was. I was looked at as a tramp or a thief. Its nuts sis, bloody nuts. I don't care if they are listening. Its unfair."

Ramona sat up close to Jude and put a supportive arm around his shoulder, she could see he was wound up tightly and though coming from a caring place, he was also full of confusion, rage and resentment was really building. He needed to vent and be heard.

"Look at me Jude. Look at me, in the eyes. I am fine. I know what to do. You are fine. We are all going to be fine. I know the answers to all of our questions are going to come to light. Let us deal with Alatar. Yes? Lets get this maniac gone. Lets mess him up. We have an army. We have strength, magic. muscle. Heart and soul. Jude, bro, we have what he will never ever have. We have each other. We have love."

Jude went silent. Thinking. Taking in his sisters ever maturing words. Gosh where had that little baby gone? He sipped more of his tea and gazed at the yellowing moon as the fire crackled and flames danced. He hugged her back.

"I love you Mona. I believe you. I know you know what to do. But my question now is this. How, do you know? What has changed? We all saw how you dealt with Selanius that rat druid. But we also all saw what it did to you. You were pale white, sis. Comatose. It took all your magic. Sapped all your strength. It made you feverish, you were babbling. None of us want to lose you. Why you Mona?"

Ramona, pulled down her hood and let her face warm by the fireside. She directed her best sisterly smile at Jude.

"Why not me? Is my answer brother. I love you Jude. You know, things have changed inside me. They have been doing since the day dad's car came off the road. Since the day I woke up next to mum at the Ivywyrld Inn. A toddler from a newborn in one night. We know the rest. Every day was a crazy day. A confusing, emotional day. A struggle. For me. You. It still is, agreed?"

Jude nodded his strong agreement.

"It was especially hard for mum and dad. Mum has been our glue. Dad has been our laughter, our guardian, and the friends we have made are true. They are not out for their own ends brother. They love us. And we them. I know you know it too. We are both headstrong. It must be in our blood. We have adrenaline rushes. Mum is an empath, dad a protector. They gave us such gifts Jude. Look at mum. Look at what she has taken on and dealt with. She has had to accept that dad was two people! Now there's a 'bloody' for you!."

A half smile played about Jude's handsome face. She was making him calm down and see the bigger picture. His respect and love for her grew even more. It was time to let his little sister have the floor. Ramona continued..

"Dad, not even knowing who he was anymore. Going for help to find his realms-self sat waiting. I'm getting bigger by the day. You arrive and god knows I love you Jude. But from where? And when? All we really know is what you have told us of waking at the house in Gardelwyn. The house I cannot remember, as I was just a gurgling newborn in my short time there. You were sleeping rough, Jude, in a blended dimension, between that of the realms and that of our own time.

Please don't smash anyones face in bro. I'll banish him to our jails, when we get back to Gardelwyn. Anyway, do you not think I am a wee bit angry too? And mum, dad? Theonyra? Turned to stone. Mahreuben malnourished, chased away from her home. Written off as a wailing banshee. Cormac, with us all every step of the way. Giving up his time, his home. His friends, his own kin. Finola, his soulmate? Left behind with the elvlings, not knowing what the hell is going on.

Perhaps Uzaleus has something to say? Locked in those cells at the tower. Whipped to near death and torn from his Princess. I know you get the picture Jude. I love you and I agree. I want to go home. Like this, or as a baby. I don't care. I am braced for whatever. I know I will be fine with my family. In the end."

Jude winced slightly at his mention of getting selfish and leaving.

"Wow, I am sorry Mona. I sounded really thoughtless, uncaring. Its just frustration. I love you too. All of you. I was just so angry with it all. Good god, I wouldn't mind that holiday with you, mum and dad!"

"Just not Oakhampton bro. Never Oakhampton. Listen, when I was in the chapel during the healing with Yesenia and Amato. I was out of it. But I learned as I recovered. I learned in my sleep. You remember what you said to me? I'll tell you.

'We heard them while you slept. We felt them, the realms, they do exist sis. They saved you. They'll save us all.'

You said that to me brother and that's when I was having my doubts. So now I must help you with yours. Because..?"

"That's what sister's do?" Said Jude, half smiling now.

"That's what sister's do. Nailed it, bro. And at that beautiful chapel at Skyfawr, with King Theonyra stood guard and Yesenia and Amato watching over me as you all made camp and worried for me. I learned. They were not dreams. They were not visions or prophecies. They were not jumbled thoughts.

They were lessons.

They were teaching me Jude. How to harness my magic. How to use it without risking mine, or any of these people's lives. Now all of us can march with our many talents. Our strength, put in unity, in friendship and love. I am no chosen one Jude but if they wish me to spearhead a campaign against these Takers, these damn drones. Then spearhead it I bloody well will."

Then, she winked at her brother and grinned.

"So no more outbursts you. I've got plenty of tricks up my sleeve, more than him. He's a little coward. Lighting fires and burning huts, like a naughty boy with a box of matches. He hadn't the guts to enter the chapel. He won't have the guts to destroy us. I am ready. So come here and give your little sister a hug. She needs it!"

With that, the two reunited siblings warmly embraced. They had neeeded that time alone, to talk and to be brother and sister. A short distance back, sat the others. Letting them be.

"They've been ages." Said Ruth to James. "I wonder what they are finding to talk about?"

James looked adoringly at his wife. So beautiful inside and out.

"Life Ruthie. I believe they are talking about life."

In the dusky sky, King Theonyra was pondering at a cliff edge as he chanced a look up. A broad smile spread across his granite but human-like face.

"Cormac! Your birds are here!"

Sweeping down out of the evening blue, came the great black backed gulls. With a delivery, from New Azmarine.

CHAPTER FIFTY SIX
SIFREYA LEAVES THE DARK LAND

It used to be called Tuteaas. There was a nice inlet from the local bay called Eanyys Grove. All orange and lemon trees, lapping tide and cool sand in a secluded arc. It was a fair but brisk walk from the busy inland territory. Here sat Sifreya. Her hair was almost silver, her face careworn, weary. There had been and still was beauty in her. It had to be ignited by passion though. Today, although her passion was still there, it had become dormant and buried under sad and reluctant acceptance. Only when she smiled and her deep brown eyes flashed warmly, would you see the true nature of her grace.

Now, she rarely smiled.

Sifreya sipped a squeezed fruit and water drink from a small gourd as she sat on a rounded rock at Eanyys Grove. Her rock. The one she came to every morning to think. To breathe in solitude. To be away from the centre of Tuteaas. She had not been able to bring herself to leave. But this large and diverse town of man, elf and animal had changed. Tuteaas was where they had ran to. The elders. Elders now, at least, or long since dead. Sifreya had to preside over this beautiful setting and watch it change. Watch it become a training ground for bad. A breeding ground for unwanted soldiers. She had to watch it have its name changed. Changed to be known as Tuteaas the dark land. Sifreya was the suffering wife of Sylam, the alias of the creature Elphinias.

She was also Alatar's mother. Her doleful yet stunning eyes, gazed wistfully as the sea, clear as glass, hissed and foamed gently and the yellow sun rose further into the morning sky, announcing another day. Within Tuteaas or now, the dark land, Sifreya was liked. Well liked indeed. But this industrious town now worked for Sylam, for Elphinias. She would always call her home Tuteaas. Much to her bitter husband's annoyance. It felt to her as though he had departed to search for Alatar and his tower long ago now.

Changing again along the way to become the chief aide Elphinias to his sons relentless crusade, rather than announce himself as Sylam, his father and tutor of evil. He had left Tuteaas under his mark. Fearful of relaxing. Elphinias the ageless. Some sort of shapeshifter. Capable of the grotesque. A magician? No, they were just clever tricksters. Elphinias was a wizard, but a student of evil. A seeker of power. Driven and mysterious. Of malevolent intent. Just like when Alatar had appeared in the realms and had then begun to convert villages, settlements and townships. To build his army of Takers.

So too had his father before him, sought to find a home to rule. After the supposed silencing of King Theonyra generations back, few had survived. Save for the now risen stone King. Theonyra. Wrongly thought to be a huge lifeless statue swallowed by the sea. Then there had been the snivelling, spindly druid Selanius. He had renewed his bitter rivalry with Theonyra at the barrens when ambushed by Ramona and friends. Now decades on, he was suspected drowned, having fled back to the tower after his confrontation with Ramona had gone wrong. It had also drained Ramona. Hence her party's diversion to Skyfawr chapel.

Selanius gibbering return had yielded no granyaak root. No ingredients. So no more mind numbing liquid could be made. A passenger then. Useless, and a drain on food and water. The cowardly druid would be slung out to sea by Alatar, via the catapult for his failings at the barrens. A few soldiers on either side had scattered across the lands in search of nothing but safety from war.

Then there was Elphinias. The twisted changeling. Attracted to bad. He had come to Tuteaas in guise as Sylam, a warrior from battle, seeking refuge and was taken in and fed and given charity and kindness by the townsfolk. As his strength returned, he would preach of returning the kindness he had been shown by the people of Tuteaas and so would work every day in helping build more new huts to house families. By doing this he had begun to gain their trust. Not only that. He had taken a shine to the beautiful Sifreya. A slender woman, young and very becoming.

How he would gaze at her effortless grace as she seemingly floated around the town on her duties delivering food to the homes of the Tuteaas people. An earthy, sunlit and connected young woman, vibrant and bewitching. He wanted her. To carry a son. One time, after a hard day of building, Sylam had seen Sifreya making her way over to the small inn for refreshment at the end of her deliveries. His eyes lit up. Then they subtly flashed red, then quickly back to the dark blue of his guise. The brave soldier, now hard worker and brother of the township of Tuteaas.

Sylam. Accepted. Liked. Later to be revealed in his true light as Elphinias. He had slipped away from his master after being told the working day was over and on seeing Sifreya, he had slunk over to her side. Smiling. False but convincing.

"Good evening to you Sifreya. I..I should like to get you this drink. If you would permit me?" He feigned a nervy stutter.

"I actually should like to get to know you a little, if I am to be honest."

Elphinias perfected a shy glance down and even managed to blush. Sifreya had been enchanted by him. He seemed mysterious, strong and attractive. All she had known of Sylam really was what everybody else had thought that they knew. That here was a good soldier seeking refuge and wanting to start a new life. He appeared to show gratitude and worked hard.

He would initially, always smile, wave hello, but rarely would he engage in full conversations. Often after a days work you would see him striding through the town with the makings of an evening meal and stoop straight into his hut. Today he was here. At the small Tuteaas

Inn. With Sifreya. His wife-to-be. She was taken by his apparent shyness and had accepted the drink and then another one. That evening they would dance together among the other people of the village. Men and elves alike.

Horses whinnied and cantered in the warm dewy grass. The sun went down behind the bathed hillsides giving way to a shimmering cool white moon. Sifreya forgot herself and unbeknown to herself, fell for the changeling. All happy, building a bright future for Tuteaas. For themselves and future generations. Sifreya would later mourn taking that drink and that first dance. She hurt from falling in love with evil itself. Sifreya got up from her rock. A kept woman she had unwittingly become.

'No need to work any longer, my love.' Sylam had announced.

'You, will look after our child. I will build this town. We, will rule it. The end.'

She had seen his eyes glow. Sinister. Faintly red and his face briefly contort. Adrenaline rushed through the young woman. A short blast of fear. But in a split second, he was the handsome and blue eyed Sylam again. She chastised herself for imagining things. Sifreya wanted to work though. She was not ready for motherhood. She was young. She worked hard and was a giver. Not, a Taker. Elphinias though, had gently manipulated her, swayed her. Eventually she had lied to herself.

'No harm in having a child now, I suppose. At least Sylam can give us a good home for the baby. What with all his work. His plans.'

A home he had given them. A prison, for the heavily pregnant Sifreya. She was only allowed to leave her home now with the ever more strange Sylam. He made her feel insecure. Full of self doubt and so feeling she owed this man a child for the security he gave her. Poor, frail grateful Sifreya. Sylam displayed narcissistic tendencies that she could not spot.

Mumblings begain among the people of Tuteaas. Concern for the usually bubbly and friendly Sifreya. Such mutterings hushed up whenever Sylam strode by. Seeming to be bigger and more muscular. He had taken over as master of building and now he drew plans. His manipulation spread to the townsfolk. Here was a truly great builder. A hardworker. He got results.

Tuteaas expanded in size. People shrank away when Sylam marched through the town in the evenings with a growing and rowdy entourage. Then, Sifreya had given birth to a baby boy. She loved him instantly. Elphinias snatched the newborn from his mother's arms and she whimpered. Tired and weak from giving birth.

'Let me look at you. Boy.'

The baby looked with wide eyes at his father.

From her bed, Sifreya called to Sylam..

'I should like it if we called him Leandro..'

Forgetting his guise, Elphinias eyes briefly flickered red as he held his baby son aloft like a prize. Completely ignoring his wife. Her duty was done.

'Welcome to my world.. Alatar.'

The daily memory recall was too much for the lonely and now older Sifreya. She wiped away the tears she could only cry here. At Eanyys Grove. She still had to live while her maniac husband searched for their runaway son. Off she trudged, back into Tuteaas. The dark land of Sylam, the fake. Elphinias, father of Alatar. The two red eyed ones.

Sifreya prayed for her son as she walked.

"I will pack up and leave. This is not Tuteaas anymore. They are not my people. I will find my Leandro and take him back from that monster and we will flee."

Poor Sifreya. She had not known what had gone on at the tower. She had not known it was too late to save Alatar. From his father.

And from himself.

CHAPTER FIFTY SEVEN
AN ETHEREAL VIEWPOINT

They had finally decided to talk. Not to intervene. Just talk. The all seeing but unseen. The ethereal spirits of the realms. They were neither human, elf, animal nor ghost. They just.. were. While all of these things were happening, unfolding within their lands, it was time to review. They consisted of few, the ethereal. They themselves knew not why they had been selected. Nor who by. Realms folk would think of them as transcendental beings, watchful and caring.

There was no real head of the table as such, at these extremely rare comings together. The meetings were open and transparent. It would seem however, that in the end, no being was divine. Whether god-like or of monumental intelligence, and this had been the case here with these beings of the realms.

The ones who the like of Yesenia of Skyfawr and Princess Mahreuben, Cormac the elf and now Ramona and her family, had come to believe in. To feel connected to. They had not been invented and put upon a pedestal for folk to herald and worship, in the hope that we all go to a better place. They were real.

Ethereal.

Still, they had souls. Some things were just not right. It was the disturbed equilibrium of one such soul, a younger entity, named Lesidyn, that had finally bought them to counsel.

"At last we are here. It is time to discuss this before it goes much further. How long can we preside over what is becoming some sort of macabre experiment? You must all admit that you could not have foreseen this. We have intervened before. Why not now?"

The passion radiated from Lesidyn's spirit.

"Your points are well made Lesidyn. Your compassion and empathy are evident and are to be commended. Unfortunately, we seem to be playing the role of guides.. If you will. Guardians, watchers. We have certain capabilities Lesidyn, yes. In that we were able to steer things from our vantage point. To enlist help. To select young Ramona. Who or what, gave us this right? This power? I do not know Lesidyn. Do you?"

This older voice came from a being known as Topia to her fellow counsel members.

"No, Topia. I do not know. All I know is that we are so close to all of them. The good, the bad. You and I. All of you know they can feel us. Hear us on the breeze. Making the chapel shake to scare off this madman Alatar. We intervened then. Helped direct Yesenia in Ramona's healing. I ask again. Why not now?"

A more authoritative voice hushed the exchange between the animated Lesidyn and the reasoning Topia.

"The two of you must be silent. If only for a moment. Let me explain of what I know. I am no preacher, but I was asked to play a part in bringing Ramona from her reality into ours. I hear the concerns among you. I believe they are well founded and caring. Else we may not find ourselves in this lofty position. Being of the all seeing unseen can be difficult. It can force us to make uncomfortable and difficult choices. I know this, as it was I who was asked to make the final decision on bringing Ramona here to the realms. Now, I do not know if I did right."

There seemed to be a heaviness in his voice. It was the voice of a spirit, named Ualdin.

"You see. We are here, beings it would seem, connected to three. The earth, the sky and the ether. The concerns are valid, the points are well made and there is no need to lower your vibration, should I pass by you. The cruel plucking of a baby and her family from a place of relaxation within their own timeline. I hear this. The growth acceleration. The mysterious merging of the father, James. Ethereal interfering."

The counsel listened in silence now.

"I heard the burning tears of Ruth, a loving mother. I experienced synaesthesia. I saw the music of pain. Tasted the disbelief in her mind. Heard the redness of heartbreak. I know this. You felt the hurt also. It manifested within us all. The selectors, if that is what you wish to think us. Ramona was born and then came within our land. To us, this baby gave off signals. It is the only way, I for one, can describe it. From my own point of view. You must make up your own minds in the end when all becomes clear."

Ualdin's weary tone had now lifted and became more passionate. Nobody in the realms really knew who or what these folk were. Magical or spiritual. Flesh and bone or something else? Or all of these things. Some would dismiss them as mythical, the stuff of legend. The more sceptical would call them fireside tales. Real they were however. In a way we of the now, could not process."

Ualdin continued, though he could feel the others waiting for a chance to express their view.

"Let me finish and then the meeting will be open to discussion. You have to think of Ramona as a homing beacon. She gave off these signals when she was born to her mother Ruth. Ramona is a born wizard. She was birthed into magic. Magic so strong that the signal from her timeline became too strong to ignore. Yes, she is a chosen one. Special. That is all we knew. Born into strong and good magic.

When her family were at the place they know as Oakhampton, the coastal town on the ley line. That is when we were pressed into making a decision. They had come into our timeline despite the accident of their vehicle crashing. We were only just becoming aware of the dangers of Alatar. The red eyed one. We thought he could be dealt with humanely.

This could ultimately and sadly, not be done by us. He is life also, like or loathe it. Alatar had also crossed the ley line. He had intervened well before we had. He had obviously picked up on the beacon within Ramona and sensed a threat to his plan. Evil he may be. Perhaps not fully at the start, but driven and dangerous. He was tuned in when Ramona was born. So Alatar appeared to them, causing their vehicle to veer fully into the realms. To skew here. Beyond the ley line and crash. We had to act. Do you see? There was no choice. They would have died. Shock, cold. Fear."

This time the murmurings from the counsel were empathetic and understanding.

"James had another self. Some do. Some do not. Sometimes some exist between parallel worlds unknowing of the other. This is why the realms James, of the Ivywyrld Inn was waiting. To merge, become one full self. To see that his family were safe. His power was the love he had for his wife and children."

Ualdin trailed off and the ether was quiet. Then, the feisty Lesidyn spoke.

"Thank you Ualdin. For your honest words. I for one, am sorry, should any ill will or doubt from any of us, have been felt by yourself. We all want our lands to return to the way they were before Alatar. I was headstrong. I just did not like to see drownings, these good people from the alternates, suddenly stumbling into foreign lands. Not just Ramona. Many others. Giula and Luca, for example. It is like sitting here watching a kingdom fall. Like watching an adventure be spoiled from behind a force field. I am beginning to understand though Ualdin. I see Ramona is unique."

If an ethereal spirit could have smiled and nodded, then that is what Ualdin did toward Lesidyn. Topia came forward again.

"Perhaps this needed to happen. Look at Ramona. She has galvanised her own traumatised family, when it is she who bares fantastic trauma of her own. She has bought together man and elf. Standing now as one. We have seen the reunification of our Prince and Princess. The resurrection from the water of King Theonyra, who felt able to tell his great granddaughter finally of his existence and his yearning love for her. Takers have come good again. Look at Tanwyn, Domacec. Selanius, the dark maker of mind bending liquid, he is now finished.

Father and son fighting. Takers squabbling within their own ranks. Ramona has bought this to us. The hope now rising over New Azmarine, Skyfawr. Even some are returning to Emeralfre. Tuteaas also, must now harbour some hope, of being rid of the dark land tag. Sylam the charlatan we now know to be Elphinias, gone to the tower. Perhaps their minds will be their own again. Perhaps the fair Sifreya can find her peace. With or without her distorted son. And without any intervention. Guidance perhaps, when necessary. I also understand more now Ualdin. Thank you."

Spirits warmly murmurated and agreed.

Ualdin felt better.

"So mote it be. Ramona has proved her love, honesty, empathy and compassion at great cost to herself. It is this that I firmly believe will overthrow Alatar. Despite the reappearance of his puppet master father. She is our chosen one. She will prevail and give the realms back to its people. Of this I feel certain."

Lesidyn chimed in..

"Then we can intervene? Send her home, with her family?"

"Then we can intervene Lesidyn. Yes, and send her home, with her family. Are there anymore questions today before we dissipate?"

Topia projected a warm vibration, but did not speak. The ethereal were in full agreement.

"So it is. We have other matters to attend to. Be well. May your spirits be still and settled. So mote it be."

Then, the ether fell silent. There was a glorious vacuum of stars dancing.

Calmness descended.

CHAPTER FIFTY EIGHT
AN UNEXPECTED PAUSE

Theonyra rose from his slumber. If you could call it that. Since he had been turned to stone in the ancient battles at Old Azmarine, he tended to just close those wise old eyes and enter a dormant state. Always though, with an underlying alert system, within his mighty frame. He was still a living being, however you looked at it and he had bowed to the need for rest.

The night had passed without any incident. Save for the two gulls arriving back safely with the message from Elysse at New Azmarine. Cormac had been delighted to see his flying friends and they had all eventually curled up by the crackling fire, before the morning march to the tower. To find Alatar and exterminate him for good, by any means possible. Might or magic. Time would tell. Ramona and her spirited party though, for all their planning, had not known of all the goings on at the tower. Nor of the apparent resurrection of Elphinias and his astonishing reappearance and revelation to his bewildered son. Theonyra had rested by the high tor, where Ramona and Jude had talked long into the night, bonding even more as brother and sister with so much to discuss, to find out.

He had eventually nudged them back to camp, urging them to sleep, or at least rest until the morning. After that, Theonyra had laid himself down. A sleeping watcher of the lands. King of generations gone. The Ryygier had rolled on toward the sea, through the dark and lulled him into calm. It was quite beautiful a moment to him. Now though, the earth rumbled slightly as he rose.

"Today then, friends. It is here. I shall take a walk round the circumference and see that all is as we hope it will be."

The camp was roused. Cormac yawned and automatically reached for his pouch. The gulls had been standing silently beside him for the last hour!

"Good morning, my friends of the sky." Said Cormac, stretching.

"It is good to have you both back with us to be sure, with welcome news from our friends at the cove. Better than we had hoped for. That is certain."

He tossed some mixed berries and a little dried crabmeat to Biggle and Baggle. They hopped over to the offerings and looked quizzically at Cormac, heads cocked to the side.

"Oh I see. A light breakfast not good enough is it my friends? Looking at those full bellies I see the fishing was plentiful at New Azmarine, to be sure. Can old Cormac at least get some tea from the pot before he tries to upgrade your pitiful meals?"

"Hop, hop." The gulls retorted.

Ramona waked over to the elf, shawl about her shoulders, sweeping wisps of hair from her sleepy face but smiling at her friend.

"Oh dear Cormac!" Said the young wizard grinning from ear to ear.

"Berries and dried crabmeat? Looks like our friends have been spoiled by Elysse and the cove people! Perhaps you had better scurry down to the water to see if you can scoop out a tasty salmon for them to share!"

Cormac allowed a quick smile and harrumphed in jest at Ramona.

"Scurry and scoop? Scurry and scoop I will not, young Ramona. If our friends have developed a taste for the high life, then welcome to it they are. Find it themselves they can. Turning their beaks up at a hearty nutritious start to the day. Scurry I will not. Now, tea. Alright for some, and no mistake.. sea bass, crab, shrimp, now salmon. A daily banquet then, for our choosy gulls, to be sure. Hmph, scurry indeed."

Cormac plodded off muttering, towards the fire with his mug for his tea. Bemoaning his lot and babbling about rotten fruit.

"You and your tea Cormac. Grumpy little elf!" Cackled Ramona as he trudged for his wake up drink.

"I heard that, scamp! I will speak, after the said tea, Ramona wizard. Oh how the youngsters are having such fun at old Cormac's expense. Of all the rotten cheek.."

Ramona sat howling with laughter at her friend's comedic display. She had grown to love Cormac and knew he was playing up for the audience, so as to start the day with a smile. Uzaleus and Mahreuben had joined the circle by the fire. Cormac explainedd to them about a lack of gratitude from seagulls, being mocked by leaping salmon and suffering Ramona's infectious laugh ringing around the camp.

"And all before your morning tea. Poor Cormac. Poor, poor Cormac." Mahreuben bent and kissed the elf on the forehead. Cormac blushed and bowed humbly.

"Why, all of a sudden, old Cormac feels a wee bit better. More tea anybody?" More laughter resounded.

Uzaleus had slept beside his men, but had gone to be with his Princess as dawn had broken. Now the small army imbibed their tea, water and whatever food was available as they began chattering about the day ahead. The small assortment of weapons they had gathered were being sharpened on stone, and spears had been crafted from strong, healthy wood. Makeshift it may be. But driven by love, unification and magic, they were.

There was good natured banter and determined voices rose from the ranks. Domacec, the Taker turned good again, was meditating. He had been changed by Alatar's life-force liquid when he was taken against his will a long while ago now. Dragged from his village, separated from his wife and made captain of the Takers. Drugged by the potion made by the hand of the conniving druid, Selanius. Domacec had been given the lazy moniker, Cacodem, and was conned into believing that he was to benefit from Alatar's manifesto. Having fled the Ivywyrld Inn where he had led a group of nine other Takers.

All destroyed by Ramona's first display of self defence, Domacec had, like so many others, been thrown into the cells for his failings.

In this time, the now defunct potion had worn off and Domacec had gone through an agonising sickness. Eventually, he had come back to himself, gone through nightmarish visions, and sought forgiveness from Prince Uzaleus. He had said there was no need and welcomed the help of Domacec when they were freed by the daring Jude.

Domacec and Ramona had both felt inner torment about that day and had talked it out in a long heart to heart. There was no malice now, and much empathy. In between eating berries and fruits, Dayn, Ailbe and some of the other escapees were making an inventory in readiness for the march. If you had squinted, you would see the spire of the stolen tower glinting over the landscape. Once a gleaming sanctuary, shimmering on the beautiful coastal trail.

Jude was with his mum and dad, speaking of his eagerness for another crack at Alatar. Remembering how he had gone back to the start and found the deserted family car. He had ploughed across the open land and smashed through the gates at the Takers tower in a real act of courage. He recalled plunging the dagger to the heart of Alatar and of his despair when he disappeared before impact. Nevertheless, Jude had freed many from the overpopulated jail. He now wanted another try. In the distance was the giant outline of Theonyra. Returning from his morning scouting.

"Look, Cormac. Theonyra is coming back. I hope everything is alright and we can get going. I am done with waiting now." Called Ramona excitedly.

Cormac walked briskly to the edge of the high tor next to Ramona, and scoured with his keen eyes.

"He is not alone young one. He carries a woman. Ramona, get water, food, blankets. She may be hurt or dehydrated."

Ramona's face turned purposeful and she ran to the camp. Theonyra's giant strides bought him quickly back to his comrades. Ramona and a throng of folk came to Theonyra.

"She is alright. Tired and in need of water. We have talked. She has come a long way. She makes for the tower like ourselves."

The giant, laid the striking looking woman onto a blanket and covered her up with another one.

"You just found this lady walking alone, Theonyra?" Spoke Uzaleus.

"I did Prince. That is why my scouting took a little longer than I had thought. She is looking for peace. Like all of us. Also, she is looking for our blessing. That we let her go to the tower alone, before we descend. I was not sure but she explained. She begged for us to hold off for one more day. She asked me for a chance to go ahead. Then, she fainted."

Ramona came forward and knelt beside the stricken lady.

"So pretty. Frightened though. She looks exhausted, Theonyra."

"She has travelled Ramona. From the old dark land. She came on a whim and a rush of blood. No thought for herself."

"The dark land. The place of the evil. The captured village of Tuteaas. The old battles?" Replied the bright wizard.

"That is correct, young one. She could stay no longer. Her heart is broken. It is not her home anymore. So she fled."

Ramona stroked the woman's face tenderly.

"We must help her. She should not be left to wander alone again."

Ramona recalled her experience at the barrens which had led to her healing at Skyfawr chapel. She did not want to watch this lady go to her doom. Theonyra looked down at Ramona. A troubled look etched upon his stony face.

"She begged me young one. And I said I would make good in my word to her. When she awakens and is fed and watered, I will escort her as close as I can to the tower and then withdraw. She must have her day Ramona. We stay a day behind."

Ramona stood. Feisty.

"I cannot believe what I am hearing Theonyra. Even as our king. I can't stand by and watch this woman go to her death at the hands of Alatar. No. I vehemently disagree."

"Disagree you may Ramona. But I have given my word. You are entitled to your opinion, especially after all you have done. This woman though, will go to the tower first to do what she thinks she can do."

Ramona's face screwed up angrily and she flushed red as frustration set in.

"Ha! And what does she think she can do, Theonyra?"

Theonyra knelt. Still dwarfing the confused gathering.

"She thinks she can save her son, Ramona. From his controller."

"By going to Alatar and his drones?"

"Ramona.. This, is Sifreya of Tuteaas. Alatar's mother."

The young wizard's mouth fell open in shock.

Chapter Fifty Nine
Sifreya and Ramona

Sifreya had awoken. Following leaving her home at Tuteaas and then wandering the realms in search of Alatar. Her only son. Son of Elphinias, her husband and tormentor. The man whom had called himself Sylam. He had twisted Alatar and now had gone to twist him even more. Now, having had King Theonyra carry her into camp while passed out, she had slept long and had eaten, drank and bathed.

She had been, and still was, very weak, in the opinion of her new companions. They advised her to at least stay with them, before their own march to the tower. The final leg of their quest to bring down the crazed red eyed one. They had known nothing of Sifreya and also very little of the shadowy Elphinias. Just like Alatar himself, they had thought Elphinias to be the Takers cruel chief aide and not a shape-shifting, malevolent father. Cruel and violently strong. A puppet master, or so it seemed. Now it appeared that Sifreya wanted to help Alatar. Theonyra looked troubled.

"She is his mother, Ramona. Think about your own mother, Ruth. Right or wrong, your parent would fight for you. Die for you. Sifreya wishes to save Alatar as her son, her once little boy, who Elphinias trained into what he is today. She will not go there to let him wreak more havoc."

Theonyra had reasoned with the young wizard. Still, Ramona was not happy.

"Son? That thing is no son, Theonyra. Sifreya, I am sorry, so truly sorry and I wish you no harm. I am trying to find my empathy. Do you know though, what Alatar has done? Is continuing to do? I am not of these realms Sifreya. I was a baby of another timeline. An 'alternate', as you say here. My timeline, my home. The home of my own mother, father and now my own lost brother, Jude. He has, through love and determination, found his way to us. Stuck between both of these worlds."

Sifreya looked from Ramona to Theonyra, trying to understand.

"Sifreya, your son caused my father's vehicle to crash and very nearly killed us and took away my entire childhood. I know you did not know of this. It is not your fault, but we want to go home Sifreya. My friends want their homeland back too. So, I have to destroy your.. son. I was chosen, it seems. The realms have given me a task. I do not want blood on my hands, Sifreya. To look at you, I see a beautiful woman with a good and honest heart. A wronged woman. I have no doubt Sylam.. or Elphinias, was as cruel to you as he was to the now dead prisoners at the Takers tower when he sent them to drown slowly. The stolen tower that your son took for himself."

Ramona was trying to use her psychology, not magic, to try to make Sifreya see the dearth of the chaos Alatar had caused. Regular mentions of son, to reiterate what Alatar had done. To make it real to her that he was no longer her baby, Leandro. Though Ramona had not been at the Tuteaas dark land and only knew tales of the old battles from Theonyra. She did not know the backstory of Alatar. Of Elphinas cruelty to mother and child, or whatever creature it was that Sifreya had borne. At this moment in time though, she did not care. Maybe she could show more understanding when he was dead. She went on..

"To outcast Princess Mahreuben and imprison Prince Uzaleus in cells with no justification? So that he may present himself as the leader of a sick and drugged new order and rule by fear? Comply or die, is the message he sends out, Sifreya. Would you have him as leader of this beautiful land? Alatar does not have blood in his veins. He runs on evil. It is not personal Sifreya. He has got to be stopped. He would eliminate myself or any of us, if it halted his progress. Will you try to eliminate me Sifreya, now that I have told my own truth? Will you as Alatar's mother, try to stop me? He is a maniac, Sifreya. I wish you did not have to come and see what he is."

Ramona's face was animated and bright red. It had taken a lot out of her to speak as bluntly and as factually to this poor woman who had roamed miles to find Alatar. She was not without feeling, this mature wizard. It felt cruel to Ramona. She told herself she was being cruel to be kind though, by presenting these facts to the mother of the red eyed one. Sifreya had tears welling in her eyes and all the while had listened intently and not tried to interject, defend or excuse her son. She wiped her eyes, drew breath and spoke.

"I am thankful King Theonyra, and to all of you. I do not underestimate your journey. I do not know where to begin. but I must try. We are all on journeys it seems. Hard lessons are coming at us. The realms are changing, although beautiful lands, Ramona, they can test any heart. Dear wizard, I am full of sorrow at your tale. I had felt the murmuring in the realms from Tuteaas. I had to come. Now, I have to leave again. My estranged husband, the liar Sylam, is Elphinias. He is pure evil. I know this. He came to my home at Tuteaas from the battles of old that you have spoken of around the fire. He portrayed himself as a tired warrior, fighting for the realms.

He lied.

He asked to stay at my village. He worked hard in return for his meals and warmth. He took over Tuteaas. It was he who renamed it the dark land. He said it would ward off threat. None of the people of Tuteaas knew that this being was a shapeshifter, a student of bad magic. A corrupt magician. I was.."

Sifreya stifled a sob. Realisation was setting in at the magnitude of this horrible chain of events.

"I thought.. I was ready to find love and to bare a child. I allowed Sylam to seduce me with his promises. He made the village of Tuteaas secure and well protected from evil. He wanted to keep Leand.. Alatar and myself like pets. He bullied us. We did not know the evil was within our walls and I did not know that the evil was Elphinias. So I married him. I gave him a son. Leandro. My.. boy. He snatched my baby from me, Ramona. I was weak and feverish from labour. He named him Alatar without consulting myself. His own loving wife.."

Sifreya was almost wailing now and Ramona, beginning to feel guilt ridden, went to her and held her tightly. Ramona wept herself now. The empathy she had spoken of earlier was pouring out of her now. She had imagined what it may have been like for her own mother, Ruth. If she had had to see such cruelty as this. Ruth had already seen enough. Watching her baby become a young woman within such a short, unnatural space of time. Growth acceleration, high expectation, kidnap. There were many similarities. The raven haired wizard looked at her opposite with new eyes.

"Sifreya. I understand. Do not let my earlier words trouble you. I was.. I am.. tired of this evil. Tired of these.. Takers." She gritted her teeth.

"We have all been hurt. Dragged around relentlessly. Even your.. son. But your plan is to go to the tower alone and rescue Alatar? From Elphinias and from himself? To expect him to remember you and believe you and for Elphinias to let you do this with open arms? Elphinias is destroyed instead and parity is restored and we all live happily ever after?"

The maturity in Ramona's words stood out as did a disbelief at all that had happened.

"I will need much convincing Sifreya and I want to believe that you can do something. Anything, to make him stop for good. With no blood spilled. Not even.. of your son."

It stung Ramona. But from naive, enthusiastic talented girl, to strong young woman. She was truly feeling for Sifeya. Though still not for the red eyed one. That was asking far too much with scant evidence he was ever good. Sifreya clasped Ramona's hands in her own.

"Good hearted child. What a true daughter you are. What a mother, is your Ruth. I ask for one day. Keep me in sight.. If it pleases. Let me go to my son. Let me reason with Elphinias. Let me try."

Sifreya glanced around the camp at the assembly in pleading hope and then at King Theonyra. Then she silently met Ramona's eyes once more. The wizard of instinct gave a heavy sigh.

"A day then, Sifreya. You are a mother. You must do as you see fit for him. One day. We keep you in sight the whole time. I still think this is suicide, Sifreya."

The mother of the red eyed one gave a look of steely resignation.

"So be it, Ramona."

CHAPTER SIXTY
A TOXIC ARMY AWAITS

"I will not address a leech such as you, as my father."

Alatar leered at the changeling Elphinias, as they held counsel in his top tower quarters.

"You did however prove useful as aide. Albeit a treacherous one. Looking out for its own ends. So lecture me not, on what is to happen. You have lost the element of surprise Elphinias. I have listened though, to what you have had to say, ancient one. It may be useful and with your magic and my own, perhaps we can call some sort of truce between us, in order to rid the realms of this sickly sweet wizard girl."

Elphinias size was immense and he almost dwarfed the usually imposing looking Alatar.

"A truce, boy? A pact? I have told you that I would make you leader of the realms! Does this not excite you? Your parlour tricks have failed. Oh dear, you silly little lad. You really do dwell on the past far too much. You have run out of the life-force liquid, your officers have failed you. You could not enter the chapel at Skyfawr through quivering fear. Father tried to kill you. There is always something with you, child."

Alatar had been sat at his new work table, staring at his plans, rather than look Elphinias in the eye. Now, he grimly stared straight at the changeling.

"Silence, father."

The red eyed one glared with contempt at his unwanted parent, and while staring, Elphinias clutched his chest and groaned in agony. Alatar smirked. Then, his feet lifted off the floor and he hung in the air, flailing and wincing in pain. Alatar swished his hand at this hated father figure. Elphinias flew backwards and slammed into the slate grey wall. He slid down and collapsed on the marbled floor, sucking in oxygen as though his life depended on it. Now it was Alatar circling the heap on the cold concrete.

"Try not to over exert yourself papa. Your heart is not what it was."

The leader of the Takers sneered at this traitor who had attempted to ruin his life as a baby at Tuteaas with his mother, Sifreya. Who, whilst serving in disguise as chief aide, had tried to seize the tower from him and attempted to kill him, before Alatar had blasted him out of the window.

Elphinias though, prised himself off the floor.

"Fair is fair then Alatar. You have had your fun. Say what you will. You have obviously listened and studied your art. With my bloodline already in place within you, you are ready to kill the girl. Are you finished with your demonstration?"

Alatar leered at Elphinias in disgust. As Elphinias rose, there were slippery tentacles receding into the arms of his robe, morphing back in to hands.

"That is a taste of things to come, slug. You are nothing but repugnant, mutating slime. Sit down before you keel over. Did you think I had not thought this through when I fled Tuteaas? Did you think I was a little boy lost without his Father? You sicken me Elphinias. You destroyed my childhood. You stole the heart of my mother. It is you who made me evil. Made me like this."

The recovering Elphinias put a wet, slimy hand on the shoulder of Alatar who shuddered and recoiled from his sinister parent.

"It is a good feeling is it not though, Alatar? Tell me. When alone, do you relive events of your childhood? When you kill or injure or imprison, is a tiny part of your damaged soul screaming at you not to do it? Do tears roll down your face when you take rest? Can you rest at all, knowing what you have done to these innocents?"

"I rest as I need to, slug. Do not lecture me."

"It is pointless wrestling with what you are, son. It is advisable to embrace your power, rather than cripple your heart further, with what might have been. I instilled root evil into the marrow of your being. I am afraid that a good cry will not change you back. It is done. Your mother grows older now, and presides over a minuscule village of tradesmen and drunken dwarves, bartering for fish and ale. Is that the legacy you want to create for yourself? Come to the window and look at what you have already acheived, son."

The two twisted magicians, walked to the large open window. The same one Princess Mahreuben had escaped from, on her daring sky walk. To the right was the emerald sea. Still and serene. It had sometimes stirred feelings in Alatar of yearning and compassion. They were fought down and quelled with liquid. To the left and way down below was the huge courtyard. The Takers were preparing.

Kovah, the bulky key holder of the jail, was a prominent figure amongst the veiled crowds. Striding up and down, uttering instructions to the growing guard. Hidden in dark robes and drone-like, they stood in impressive, regimented rows. Polished weapons gleamed, as the sun glinted off them. A totalitarian and unquestioning army. Bought, drugged or willing. The army was now well drilled and strong, waiting like a coiled spring or a cocked gun. Ready to go off on command.

"Look at what you have created son. From leaving Tuteaas as a young angry boy in search of his true self. Petty recruitment drives and pit stops in villages, performing to idiots to try and form a small following. You knew you were no threat to Uzaleus and Mahreuben's kingdom then. But you persisted Alatar my boy. You razed settlements to the ground you destroyed townships and rebuilt them in an instant with your powerful and bitter magic."

Alatar grudgingly resisted the urge to say anything. Perhaps the slug could help him. Elphinias gestured to the courtyard.

"They listen son. Now they all listen. It is too late for them. Walking dead, and rightly so. For doubting you, mocking you. The life-force liquid was no more than a placebo. You did not need that imbecile Selanius and his soup. It dulled them, I will say. Made them comply in your early days. Now they are all yours. Completely devoted to the way of the Takers. The new order of the realms. Built by you. Alatar the red eyed one. My son. All you have to do now is harness this complete power to destroy Ramona."

Alatar turned from the vast balcony at a knock at his door. Opening it, his two high guard stood, trembling almost.

"What is it guard?"

The taller one, Foryonn, not that his name mattered to the leader, inched forward.

"Alatar. We have taken in a woman. She wishes only to speak with you. She is very insistent. She is alone and made no attempt at violence."

The eyes flared like broiling lava. Foryonn though, pre-empted his leader.

"No. It is not Ramona my leader. It is Sifreya of Tuteaas. She claims to be.. Your mother."

CHAPTER SIXTY ONE
THE PLEA

A breathless Cormac scurried back from his hilltop vantage point to the awaiting camp on the outskirts of the coast. After getting as close as he could to the Takers domain without being detected, he gave watch duty to Dayn and Ailbe, the escapees. Cormac was no stranger to the tower, having reported back to the family at the Ivywyrld Inn, way back at the start of Ramona's unwitting journey. He knew the lands and so had now volunteered to track Sifreya on her seemingly crazed mission of mercy.

The Elf took deep breaths.

"Sifreya is inside. Unharmed it would seem. Though my eyesight is not what it was. She was immediately flanked by the Takers as she drew closer to the drawbridge. They are obviously on watch from the ramparts. I am surprised she was not simply slain on the spot. Maybe Alatar was not aware of her approach."

Prince Uzaleus gave a sigh of resignation..

"Swarming, like the drones they are. It is the best we could have hoped for then, that she was not killed on sight. Who knows what is going on at that dark place. It is a sinister den now, Cormac. Well done, for your report. It would be nice for the realms to claim that place back and get it cleaned out of the vermin. He has done a good job building an army, that I will say. They have rendered many villages into places of fear now. Existing to serve only, or they are seized and given that damned potion."

Princess Mahreuben squeezed her Prince's hand tightly. She had recovered from the attempted drugging by Alatar and had forewarned Ramona of his intent. It was nearly time. Mahreuben could feel the whispers of the unseen. Soft voices on the gentle breeze.

'Trust.. You must trust..'

She glanced at a pensive looking Ramona, pacing and biting at her nails. A tense look was etched on her striking features and a furrowed brow made her scrunch up her fiery eyes. Mahreuben tried to offer some hope and comfort to the young woman.

"Sifreya of Tuteaas has done well, young wizard. Whatever we think of her idea. We must now give Alatar's mother the time we agreed. It is the way of the realms."

Ramona stood still and sipped water from her flask.

"I still do not like it Mahreuben. Letting her go alone into that vipers nest. If our scouts report anything that looks like danger, I am going in there myself and to hell with the time we agreed."

Mahreuben bowed her head and said no more. She could not imagine the pain of this family and felt deep sadness that Ramona had been fast-tracked through her formative years. Ramona had been pumped with knowledge, vocabulary, keen eyes, physical prowess, magic, observational skills and taken it all on board, into her growing frame. It was like being wired to a super computer in her own timeline. Though she only knew of those from her mother and father. She was an adopted realms girl with a metaphorical memory card inserted into her being. Ramona had never complained throughout. She had accepted her lot with good grace and practised her art and been a loving friend to the people of these new lands, as well as protective sister and loving daughter into the bargain.

Cormac looked concerned.

"Ramona, our beautiful, brave wizard. The realms are indebted to you. This I feel. As I believe, does Princess Mahreuben. Theonyra too, all of us. All will be revealed. All will be well. To be sure. Or my name is not Cormac of the elven wood."

Ramona smiled warmly at her friend and thought of all he had left behind. All they had sacrificed. They had all been hurt or robbed in some way by this despot and his growing force. The elf continued whilst taking a drink after his hiltop walking..

"Sifreya had come all the way from Tuteaas. Her home. Renamed by Sylam, her husband, or whatever he is. Now the dark land. A thief of settlements, is Elphinias. A trickster, and as we now know thanks to Sifreya, a shapeshifter. We have to remember that she knows this dark one better than anybody in this camp. She is a mother too my friend. Just like your mother."

Cormac nodded sideways in gesture to the silently observing family. Ramona's parents, Ruth and James gazed lovingly at their daughter. Jude, her forgotten brother, so strong, the loving sibling she had needed during this bizarre time. The holiday baby. Now carrying the hopes of another world upon her young shoulders.

The elf continued again..

"Despite what the red eyed one has done, it appears he was heavily influenced by who we now know to be his father. From his own birth he was duped and polluted by him. The changeling Elphinias."

The fire burned in Ramona's eyes once more.

"So that makes Alatar exempt does it Cormac? None of this is his fault? All those poor drowned folk. Prisoners, whipped with his electric ropes. What is this Cormac? All is forgiven? Poor little Alatar was bullied, let us ask him to him stay then, shall we? Master of his stolen domain. Perhaps if we pacify him, he won't hurt us. What will Sifreya do, Cormac, my friend? Gone alone to a fortress of trained murderers, just waiting for the order. What will good Sifreya do to stop him, bake him his favourite cake? Give Elphinias a good talking to?

No. They are murderers, the end. Both of them. Like father, like son. We need brute force to get into that damn tower and distract those guards, so that I can confront these demons and bring them to task. Alatar? I will leave his wretched fate to your ethereal angels, if you feel he has been a conduit for Elphinias. I tell you, that changeling though, is walking dead. You just bloody watch me."

She kicked out at a fallen branch, turned her back to the assembled force and gazed at the sky, as though she wanted answers from the guardians. She, and all of them certainly deserved something, having kept their faith in an unknown force all of this time. Cormac felt for Ramona. For all of her family.

'They should be together in their own timeline. Be with their own friends and by now, probably hysterical families. They should be eating, drinking. Living their own lives. Loving one another and seeing their own world.'

These thoughts raced in Cormac's mind as he too visualised his own village. Halved in numbers by those who had joined this quest. Finola, he missed her most. His soul friend. He had been with Ramona all along though. He would not run off home now.

"Your frustration is understandable Ramona, to be sure. And your fiery heart burns with good. I know that you are itching to get at him, but the ethereal would look favourably on giving the mother her chance. Let us see what she can do. Look, Dayn and Ailbe have replaced me on watch and they are keen-eyed. They will not sit idle if there are any developments."

The wizard wiped long locks from her face and nonchalantly swished her hand at a cluster of boulders. Her face was one of anger now. Anger on all of their behalves. There was a crackling sound. Cobalt fire, flew from her fingertips at her target and the rocks disintegrated into a gritty shower.

"That is what I plan to do to Alatar. To Elphinias. To all of them. They are an infestation. I am sorry Cormac. I grow tired of waiting." She looked at the smashed up rocks and felt a pang of guilt.

Grey soot and gravel blew around and settled on the empty space where the boulders had lain. King Theonyra had been listening in silence. He now rose from his own boulder, which had doubled up as a seat for his awesome granite frame.

"Ramona, save your magic please. We need that power. I implore you."

"A few rocks Theonyra? I have learned much since Skyfawr. My magic is limitless now."

The King knelt, but was still towering over the girl from another timeline. An 'alternate', trying to save them.

"My friend. These may be just rocks and yes, your power has grown strong. Strong enough to win. I truly believe that. We all do, but your impulsiveness is what they will try to exploit. Such as drawing attention to us with your display."

Ramona flushed red, defensive.

"Then get the ethereal to do it, my King. What do they want from my family and I? It was never our fight. They are game players, your precious gods. I am an unnatural experiment Theonyra. My family has been torn apart. I do not care if it has drawn attention. Bring them to me, filthy orcs and potion addled replicants. Anyone who wants to leave can go their own way, with my love and deep thanks for helping my family on our path home. The end."

She folded her arms peevishly and turned away again. Theonyra looked forlornly at the pacing wizard.

"Nobody is leaving Ramona. We all love you and your family. We are all one family with the same goal. To finish this. Let us, as Cormac and Mahreuben have said, give Sifreya her chance."

Ramona picked up her cloak from her resting spot.

"Very well Theonyra. I do not have to agree. I do not have to like it. And I do not like it."

She began to stroll off from the camp. Jude looked alarmed..

"Sis, where are you going now?"

She turned to her brother.

"Not far Jude. To sit with Ailbe and Dayn. To see what I can see. We move soon. All be ready. If I am the chosen one as I am repeatedly told, and with all respect for you as my companions, then I have to make my own decisions. Just be ready."

With that, she took off up the hill.

CHAPTER SIXTY TWO
A MOTHER'S LOVE

"Well, this should prove interesting. Thank you guard. You may leave."

Elphinias wore a look of mock amusement. Alatar looked stunned.

"Here she is my boy. Your beautiful mother. Though you may not remember much, nor recognise her. Given her haggard appearance."

Sifreya stood in Alatar's vast quarters before the two male figures who had featured so prominently in her life.

"Sylam. You." Sifreya spat at Elphinias.

"I come to speak with Leandro. Not you, shapeshifter."

Elphinias barked a sneering laugh at the gaunt, but still stunning woman of Tuteaas.

"Ha, Leandro is it then? I knew you would come, my darling wife. I am sorry, I quite enjoyed playing the part of Sylam, the brave and true warrior. This calls for a drink then does it not? Alatar, fetch the gourd and pour your mother her favourite. The drink we took on the night of our first dance."

Alatar ignored Elphinias and gazed at Sifreya in a mixture of curiosity, and sadness..

"Mother?"

"Son, Leandro.. My boy. What has he done to you? Yes, it is me. How I have missed you. My first and only child. I have come to offer you a way out of this mess. To show you the beauty you were robbed of. I bring love, hope and the chance of a peaceful future, within the realms. Ramona knows your soul was poisoned. She will not attack you. You have my word. That of your mother."

Alatar's unreadable expression turned contemptuous at the mention of the wizard's name.

"She.. is with you?"

Quickly, Sifreya responded..

"No, Leandro, she is not. She has allowed me to come alone. There are no tricks. She knows of your story now. She knows of this vermin, who separated us.."

Elphinias clutching a pewter goblet of mead, cackled again and his callous, deep tones seemed to vibrate and bounce off the walls.

"Well, Sifreya my love, I will say this.. You have come a long way. Now our little family is reunited." He sneered, amused at his own sarcasm.

"Nice isn't it, Alatar my boy, that Ramona gave your mother permission to attend. Will you seek Ramona's approval also, son?"

There was only silence.

"No? Then I propose a toast. To the gruesome destruction of Ramona of Gardelwyn. To the demise of her interfering brother and meddling parents. It is James who caused all of this Alatar. He was two people. Two halves looking to become one. The James of the realms melded with the idiot father of Ramona. This is his fault. He needs to be broken. You seek only to unify this land my boy. To the claiming of the realms then. To be governed evermore, in the name of Alatar. The offspring of your tender loins Sifreya, my good lady wife."

Elphinias, dripping sarcasm, did not move from his spot near the huge open stained glass window. Instead, a huge and long tentacle extended from his robe towards Sifreya, procuring a goblet of wine in three slimy appendages that used to be fingers. Sifreya slapped the goblet out of the grasp of Elphinas and it dropped to the floor. She recoiled in disgust.

"I do not want your drink. Filthy changeling. I want you to surrender my.."

Sifreya choked the next words out. "Our.. Son.."

Elphinias looked at the goblet on the floor.

"A real vintage Sifreya my love. What a waste. Funny though.. do you not think the claret to be the same colour as blood? The blood which will soon be spilled all over the courtyard when your new friends try to intervene."

Sifreya gave no ground and stared hard into the crimson eyes of the pulsing figure stood in front of her.

"Let me speak with Leandro. You are nothing Elphinias, Sylam.. evil, repugnant filth."

Alatar, stunned, looked from his mother's pleading face to the snarling, hateful countenance of his cruel father. Within the drenched recess of what was once his heart, he felt something. Alatar felt like the weeping boy he was when his father had forced him to watch the torture of innocent realms folk.

The scared child, who was force fed bad magic. He began to feel sadness. He began to understand how Ramona, must have felt when she too, was robbed of her own childhood. Despite reasons of extreme contrast, was this empathy he now felt? Could it be that it was not too late? His mother felt so warm and genuine, despite Elphinias poisonous words against her. He saw the huge risk she was taking by being at the tower.

"Mother, is.. my name Leandro? Am I not Alatar? Can I escape from the red eyed one I have become?"

The self-proclaimed leader advanced tentatively towards Sifreya, a remorseful whisper in his tones. Elphinias made no move. He gulped down his wine and poured more into his goblet. Watching perversely.

"Go on boy. To your mothers bosom. Hide in her arms as did the sickly child I was so pitifully ashamed of before. Let her fill your head full of her sweet fairy tales. Of perhaps escaping to her little sanctuary at Eanyys Grove, where you can eke out your days with cantering horses and cooked fish by the fire.."

The shapeshifter drew up close to mother and son.

"Yes, talk of peace and of coming understanding from Uzaleus and Mahreuben. Be with those other pathetic dreamers at Tuteaas, fools. I am Elphinias, shapeshifter. The true power of these lands. The man behind the boy. It is my armies who turned that fawning king into crippled stone. It is I who exterminated his island paradise and left him anchored to the ocean floor, to be perennially reminded of his inept failure. Left alive inside, to feel true self loathing for letting his people die at my hand. A walking souvenir.

It is I who seeded this gormless woman of the realms. Sifreya, delivery girl, pauper, child carrier, vehicle. Used for my pleasure, to enable my power and my bloodline to live on. In you, Alatar. It is I, who will now oversee you take your rightful position as leader. The red eyed one. Master of the army of the Takers and of the reborn and new realms."

Elphinias shrugged and sipped his drink casually.

"So be it. Speak then Sifreya. Have your moment."

Sifreya moved gently and with grace towards Alatar. Completely ignoring Elphinias cruel bragging, so as to not give him any satisfaction. She felt no fear. Leandro.. Alatar, what did it matter? She had seen the conflict in the eyes of her son. She was sure they had flickered their original blue, albeit briefly.

"My young son. No, you are not Alatar the red eyed one. Not by birth. Leandro was your given name when you were delivered at Tuteaas. He had agreed to this. Before he revealed himself as this slug before you. You were so good my little one. I do not believe he can have truly taken that all from you. He kept me locked in the home he had built for us. Built by good,unknowing men of Tuteaas. He had worked for them in guise, as Sylam, and with his strength, manipulation and prowess. He took over our settlement.

Subtly at first. Then he ruled by fear. He changed the name of our home. Stirred up unnecessary conflicts. Leandro.. my name is Sifreya. I am your mother. I was seduced by the lies of this malevolent reptile. He cares not for you.. nor I. He never did. He will push you before this girl, Ramona, to die, due to his own self-doubt at his power.

He does not think he can destroy Ramona and so will test the water. Using you Leandro. Like he used me to bare you. If you clear the way for him, I have no doubt he will cast you aside. You left Tuteaas to escape him. I understand. He has broken our hearts my baby son. Please, come with me. Do not let him break us again. Come to Eanyys Grove with me Leandro."

She took another step toward Alatar and he to her.

"Mother.."

Tears rolled down Sifreya's cheeks and she threw her arms around the apparition that she called her son. She held him so tight she could feel his heart beating fast against her chest. She felt Alatar's own tears, wetting her face as she clung to him.

"Mother. I am sorry.. But it is too late.."

There was a puncturing of skin.

Then, Sifreya felt the breath leave her body and felt as though she had been punched in the gut. Alatar had pierced her stomach. His right hand had become a sharp, elongated blade. Pointed and deadly. Changeling blood now coursed through him. Neural conflict. The confused leader retracted the hand and it slid out of Sifreya's innards. He stepped back.

"It is easier for you this way. You should not have come."

Sifreya, in shock, held her chest as her robe turned a damp, claret red.

"My son.. Do not.. let him.. Do not let .."

She stumbled backwards now crashing into the table. Her breathing rattled, shallow. Elphinias stroked his chin and looked on, unmoved, smirking. Alatar picked his mother up and carried her to the open window overlooking the moat.

"Why, Leandro?"

Sifreya spluttered, not afraid, but broken inside.

Alatar hissed..

"Now, father.. Let there be no doubt as to who is the leader of these lands." He bent to look at Sifreya revealing his red eyes. Fangs hung in his mouth. He kissed her forehead gently.

"You are of no further use.. Mother."

The last thing Sifreya saw was her son's glowing eyes, evil. Lost to her forever. Then, her broken heart finally stopped. Alatar shrugged casually, then threw her lifeless body out of the window to the cold stone of the courtyard.

The wizard felt a chilling shiver run through the centre of her soul.

"Ramona! What is it?" Dayn cried out, as the stricken young wizard tore off back down the hill to the camp.

"Ailbe, come on. After her.."

The two watchmen sped behind the young wizard, but she had left them trailing in her wake. Now, Ramona stopped and stood standing before the gathered camp. All looking at her. Startled. Silent. Concerned.

Theonyra, the stone King, got to his mighty feet. He knew this was not good news.

"Ramona wizard, what have you seen?"

The raven-haired young woman slumped against a large oak tree. She let out a heartbroken howl. It was blood-curdling. She wailed and cried and kicked and thrashed until she lolled motionless. Her family raced to her and held her close. Jude ran for water. Ramona buried her head in Ruth's shoulder. Sobbing uncontrollably. James stroked her hair, whispering..

"Its alright Mona, its alright, mum and dad are here."

Their brave daughter was distraught. Ramona looked into the eyes of her mother. Ruth welled up herself.

"She is dead mum. She is dead."

The wizard turned now to Theonyra.

"Now do you believe me? He has killed his own mother. Sifreya is dead."

Theonyra winced. His stone face screwed up in sorrow.

"What did you see Ramona? Are you sure of this?"

Ramona wheeled on the king.

"I saw nothing. I felt it. I knew. You let her go. All of you realms folk let her go. Where are your ethereal now? Where are your damned saviours? Remember this conversation. You just remember it. Sifreya is dead and we let it happen. I just wanted you to know that."

Nobody could answer.

Ramona curled up in her mothers arms like the child she had never truly been, and wept.

CHAPTER SIXTY THREE
OF SKYFAWR AND YESENIA

Oona, wife of the deceased thug, Vaangrad, carried on her work within the grounds of Skyfawr chapel. With other willing helpers, she pruned the rhododendrons and cultivated interest from butterflies in the stunning array of buddleia outside the chapel.

The news of her husband's death bought no tears. No tears at least, for his passing. He had brought trouble to Skyfawr and to her personally. No, she wept a little only at the realisation that for her it was probably too late to bare a child. 'Better no child than one borne of Vaangrad.' This thought comforted her and she took solace in the beautiful garden she helped create and maintain.

Inside the chapel itself, Amato the young apprentice of Yesenia, was replacing candles along the walls and humming cheerily to himself.

"Happy, today, my young friend?" Asked Yesenia.

Time had passed now since the settlement of Skyfawr had become something of a hub of activity. What with the healing ceremony for Ramona and the visitation of Alatar himself. The boy turned to the curator and smiled..

"I am as happy as can be, given the circumstances Yesenia. Alatar may have burned our huts and trees, perhaps scared us, but he showed weakness. He could not or would not enter the chapel. I think he can be beaten. Yes teacher, today I am happy."

Yesenia gave a warm smile.

"Then that is a good thing Amato. Come, I wish to show you something interesting. I feel you are ready.."

The young student looked puzzled, but put down the woven bag of candles.

"Interesting, teacher?"

"Yes. Close the doors my boy. Oona will know."

Amato shrugged and made his way to the huge doors of the chapel and pushed them both shut. It took an effort. Solid oak, thick and heavyset. The boy puffed his cheeks out.

"Good for the lungs Amato, a little exercise." Yesenia giggled a little at the lad's efforts.

"Secure, my teacher. I will say that much!"

Amato drew a large gulp of herbal tea. With the doors closed now, Yesenia strode toward the altar of the chapel and Amato followed without question. At the front now, Yesenia kneeled on a small cushion that she used for solitary prayer. She motioned at Amato to do the same, nodding towards another cushion by his side.

Amato took it and knelt himself..

"Yesenia, What are we..?"

The boy's question trailed off into a gasp. A mist appeared before them. Silently swirling powdery blue, circular, gently growing.

"Ualdin of the ethereal. I ask you, spirit of the realms, to appear to I, Yesenia of Skyfawr chapel. I have only my student with me. He is named Amato."

Yesenia was looking directly at the mysterious, cloudy form before them. She glanced sideways at Amato.

"You felt the whispers of the realms at Ramona's healing my boy. Now, you will see them.."

Amato's eyes were wild and wide. Then, as Yesenia bowed, the student instinctively mirrored her actions. A face began to form or at least, a representation of a face. Ever so faintly at first. Feeling privileged and somewhat awestruck, all Amato could do was whisper..

"They are here."

With the face fully formed now, within the mist, a deep but gentle voice spoke.

"Ah, Yesenia of Skyfawr chapel. A delight it is for me to manifest in such a place of sanctuary."

It was Ualdin, the ethereal being.

"Ualdin. We are deeply honoured that you felt able to present to us. I call you to show my pupil today, why we believe so much in our unseen. I also, for my curiosity, have some questions. Can you answer them, Ualdin?"

Within the mist, the face of Ualdin smiled.

"It is my pleasure Yesenia. I will certainly try to help you. Amato, the young student. We are aware of your progress. A great future awaits you son. If you tread the right path."

Amato's face was agog.

"Yes..Yes.. thank you, Ualdin. The honour is mine. I will study hard with my teacher and honour the ways of the realms to the best of my ability."

Ualdin replied reassuringly.

"We know you will son. You have the best teacher in Yesenia. We too have students here in the ether. Keen just as you are. Topia and Lesidyn are with me today. Now to your teacher's questions young one. Yesenia, we are listening."

Amato's face flushed red in both excitement and humility. Yesenia smiled. It was not often she would ask the spirits to manifest. It could expend energy and, as a respectful curator and a woman connected very well to the earth, she never spoke of such occasions outside of the chapel.

"Ualdin, my love and the love of Skyfawr, Amato here included, goes to all of our ethereal brothers and sisters of the realms. I ask you today for guidance. Life here has settled again since we sent our brave young wizard and her selfless warriors on their way."

Warmth exuded from the spirit as Yesenia went on.

"The huts that the dark one burned down in petulance are now restored. No Takers have attempted to invade our village and our folk are now calm again. My question is this. Ualdin, can you tell us if the realms will ever fully return to us? To you in the ether? Our faith is unshakeable."

Ualdin interjected.

"I sense a 'but', my dear lady?"

A wry smile from the curator.

"You sense correctly, Ualdin. But.. the folk of Skyfawr and, I would say many other settlements within the realms, are living in fear. A constent sense of unease prevails. Folk are trying to go about their daily tasks as normal, that is for sure. But after the visitation of the red eyed one.."

Ualdin sighed audibly at the mention of Alatar and the windows shook.

"Alatar again and his residual menace. I can tell you this Yesenia and I think it will only confirm what deep within, you already know. We, the ethereal have been in conference. We cannot intervene nor interfere. Only observe and guide. Ramona the young wizard is our chosen one and just like everybody else in the realms, our hopes rest on her young shoulders. We possess certain magic powers, yes. But.. and here is my 'but'.."

Yesenia gave a sigh. Ualdin continued.

"We are not allowed to kill. So my answer is this. Yes, go about your business as you have been, all of you. Skyfawr and its chapel are ancient and as such, protected. Save for petty outbursts from petulant upstarts like Alatar."

Amato sniggered.

"It is true my boy. No, what we can do, is throw our collective will, might and prayer, that Ramona can put this despot where he belongs. In a burial ground, forgotten. But the ethereal do promise you this.. Skyfawr is vital to this quest. My ability to manifest grows weak now Yesenia, but we will be watching, make no mistake. We will be watching.."

With that, it was over, Ualdin gone as though never there. As Yesenia and Amato rose, the young apprentice said " What do we do now teacher?"

Yesenia smiled at her keen pupil.

"We go out there and make those gardens more beautiful than ever. To celebrate a wizard named Ramona."

CHAPTER SIXTY FOUR
THE GIRL HAS GONE

"Get up, all of you. No time for eating. Grab what you can. We leave now."

The thunderous footsteps of the roused King Theonyra, jolted the hillside camp awake.

"We gave Sifreya the chance she wanted. Ramona was correct. We failed her and should have restrained her, to save her from herself."

As the morning mist rose from dewy grass, waking bodies stretched and drank water as Theonyra's words snapped them alert. Jude went to Theonyra's side and rested his head forlornly against the giant Kings thigh.

"Its sad, King, too sad, she was one of us. I'm ready to get in there, avenge her. Where is Ramona? Have you spoken to her this morning?"

The stone King looked down wistfully at Jude, the returned son.

"I am afraid she is like you my son. Tired of discussions. The girl has gone my friend. We need to follow. The group are readying themselves."

As Theonyra's words left his stone lips, Jude was already halfway down the hill running across the scrub, towards the tiny looking tower on the backdrop of the morning landscape. Theonyra shrugged. He did the same as a young King before he was turned to granite in the ancient battle. He would have done the same if he were Jude.

Cormac was now at his side.

"We are ready, to be sure, my King. Ruth is distraught though. Even James can't calm her."

"My Mahreuben will shadow her, Cormac. Good, strong elf. Send the gulls forward will you? We need their eyes."

"It is done, my King."

Cormac called the gulls from their rock-face camp and scattered dried fish and berries as he outlined he would need them to fly ahead. Check on Ramona, and now Jude. They gratefully ate up and clucked their understanding. Dayn, Ailbe, Domacec and the warriors stood ready. Weapons slung over their backs as they ingested some fruit and water.

Princess Mahreuben had formed a sisterly bond with Ramona's mother and embraced her fellow brave woman. Stoic, adaptable and uncomplaining all along. How James loved Ruth. Yet now, he felt so helpless. Prince Uzaleus put an arm round James shoulder.

"Without your family brother, we would all be dead. Make no mistake about each of your own unique and vital contributions to this cause. Ale afterwards brother. Then lets see if we can get our ethereal to help you home."

James raised a smile at the Prince's caring efforts.

"First though my friend, I smell bad wizard. Fancy the hunt before breakfast?"

The wry smile of a battle ready warrior, lit up Uzaleus handsome face.

"Lets go and find my daughter, Prince. Then, ale for everyone!" Rallied James.

About a mile ahead, striding through the tall, wet grass, Ramona's face was all business-like. She had on, a woven robe given to her by Oona, whom took her in for bed rest at Skyfawr. She had two apples, a flask of water and an elven dagger. She was dubious about using the dagger but it afforded a little extra protection. In some yellow gorse bushes to the left and out of the corner of her eye, she spotted two dark wraith-like shapes, skulking. Fearlessly she strode over to the bush and stood hands on hips.

"You two. Out."

Two Takers tried to rush Ramona. She stood firm as a tree, and they bounced off her to the floor as though an invisible shield had repelled them. She stooped over the downed Takers.

"Get those bloody hoods off. Lets see you for what you are."

She pulled the hoods away from pale, bony faces. Looking at one, an orc-like, snarling creature, not human, or it had not been for a long time. "You are pure Taker, a devotee." It was a statement, not a question.

"I'm going to spare you your misery."

The scowling creature faced Ramona head on. "We serve Alatar. We shall kill Ramona, the witch." It hissed in defiance.

She snapped his neck. He knew no more.

"You took part in horrific cruelties in full support of his methods, orc. Goodbye. Now you rest."

The second recoiled in terror.

"You? You are not pure Taker. Recruited. I see your eyes. Given the liquid?"

"Yes lady. I am Claudiu of Emeralfre. I was an opposer. Until he threatened to kill my wife and boy. I took the liquid and obeyed, so that they might live." Claudiu knelt before Ramona, expecting death.

Ramona's expression changed from ruthless to sad.

"I believe you. Here, drink this water. Not all of it. I Intend on living. Take this apple. Walk south. Take that bloody robe off. Tell them Ramona sent you. Ask for Uzaleus. If you see anymore Takers, play your role, but walk on. Go in peace Claudiu."

The Taker looked moved to tears.

"Ramona wizard. You truly will save our lands. Go in peace, good lady." He bowed and scurried off southerly.

Ramona shouted after him and he turned..

"Claudiu! You are no longer a Taker! Find your wife and boy."

He bowed again and shouted back..

"We thank you Ramona wizard. Go and win."

Then he was gone. Ramona looked back down at the deceased, nameless Taker.

"Your sort have no souls. God bless your poor family."

She knelt, closed its eyes and strode off purposefully. She stopped by a brook that fed the estuary that eventually became the sea. The water was clean. She drank, ate the remaining apple, refilled her flask and sat on a lichen covered rock. A red kite soared above majestically. She felt nature would prevail again, in time.

Across the brook now though, five more of them. Murmuring, hissing and cooking fish over an open fire. They looked accross the water, startled, then wary, then aggressive. Ramona was on them. Fierce and sharp.

"Morning boys! Start the day on a fish I always say. Jolly nice day for a campfire. My brother has a guitar, he'll be along soon. We could have a little sing song, eh chaps?"

Ramona's confidence was playful, but never was she cocky. She remained alert. Hand on dagger. A strange grin crossed her determined face.

"You are the girl wizard.. You must die." Snarled the ringleader. They stood and began to glide towards her.

"Oh no boys. I'll come to you. Don't let the fish burn. They look tasty!"

And she waded across the brook.

"Foolish girl.."

They circled her.

"If any of you are not pure Taker, say now. Or die.."

"I am Gislaas. Pure Taker. All of us, pure Taker. No liquid. Now, pretty witch.. Talk is over."

They drew swords. Gislaas snarled.

"Wow, what a nice blade my friend, so shiny. New, is it? Don't stand on ceremony boys. Come and chop me up then, with your magnificent weapons."

Puzzled at this apparent sarcasm, the ensemble advanced closer.

"Just close enough that fellas. Perfect. I don't do swords. I do this.."

Ramona rose effortlessly into the air and performed a series of brutal, knockout roundhouse kicks on all five Takers. They dropped face down into the brook like deadweight. She knelt again.

"Oh and Gislaas my boy. Don't call me pretty. I'm more.. gorgeous. You look thirsty, take a drink." She slammed his shocked face into the stream. His eyes rolled into his head under the water. He was dead. The others, concussed. She looked at them. She wanted to make a statement not go on a killing spree.

"Fish smells lovely boys. I'm taking them for my bonny wee seagulls. Give my regards to Alatar." Ramona shrugged with nonchalance.

"So long then fellas, and thanks for all the fish."

Her confidence was sky high, self belief ignited, but she remained humble, wary and grounded. She splashed her face with water and washed her hands in the brook.

"Dirty, smelly little things.."

Off she went again, as though she had negotiated a minor invonvenience. Not far behind now, Jude, running hard, came across Claudiu. He was ready to go for him, until the dazed survivor cried out..

"Ramona.. She sent me. She said to ask for Uzaleus. She saved me from life as a Taker. Set me free."

Jude relaxed a little. Though he kept his dagger close. "I am Jude, Claudiu. Ramona's brother. Keep going, you will find our guard. Tell them what you just told me. They will know. Drink this.."

Claudiu drank gratefully, he was dehydrated from the drug. Having no real food or water had sapped his strength. "Jude, it is my lucky day. Ramona also gave me water. I thank you humbly."

"You can't survive on liquid drugs my friend. Where is Ramona now?"

"Perhaps a mile north, and moving quickly, Jude."

"Thankyou Claudiu. Blessings to your family. Uzaleus will look after you now. Cormac will give you food, to get your strength up."

"I am humbled once more. I am sorry to have been a Taker. I could not let him harm my family. Good luck friend Jude. Spirits of the realms be with you."

A mutual bow was exchanged. Jude stared ahead with intent.

"Now lets see what carnage you've caused sis, you little diamond."

His faith in her was unshakeable.

CHAPTER SIXTY FIVE
A BURIAL

Just as dawn had broken over Ramona's high tor camp a few miles inland, so too it was now at the Takers tower, looking out to sea. With a fired up and dangerous Ramona now close and Jude and the realms army not far behind. Things were hanging in the air. An impending, crackling atmosphere. Destiny.

Ethereal beings whispered on the sea breeze. Ualdin, Topia, Lesidyn. Watching from the wings, hoping. The as yet undetected New Azmarinian's, were rebuilding under Alatar's nose. They were makiing rafts, to bring them to fight for the realms they had been catapulted away from, by himself and his murderous father. The venomous shapeshifter.

The Takers night guard were yawning their way towards the end of their watch. Damp misty dew gave way to the first rays of dappled sunlight over the once resplendent courtyard. Now, it was a bustling training ground for the drones. The rest of the Takers gratefully slept, grabbing respite from their chosen regime. A forced regime, if they had been given the liquid and saw it from the point of view of those drugged.

A sleepless Alatar had made his way down from his quarters whilst his twisted father Elphinias, slumbered in the palatial rooms below. He was carrying a body. That of his lifeless, beautiful, but now slain mother, Sifreya. Retrieved stiff from the courtyard. Extinguished by the hand of the son she loved unconditionally and had selflessly tried to save against all sane hope.

Leandro.

He did not want to be escorted by guards, and he walked past the jail ignoring the gawpings of early rising prisoners. He simply strode by, head bowed. Down rarely used winding steps he carried Sifreya and out onto the little shingle cove that his window overlooked. A view he had numbly grown used to and taken for granted as the teachings of evil and the imbibing of the mind bending life-force liquid took effect.

Now, truly turned, Leandro, son of Sifreya of Tuteaas, had become Alatar, son of Elphinias of the dark land. But even now, as his mother's congealed blood seeped through her gown and onto his skeletal hands, he hated himself. For his drowning heart was still trying to swim.

Better as his shapeshifter father had said, to accept root evil and embrace it, than to try and rewind time and rescue the heart of an impressionable young boy. He hurt. The dark and heartless world wrecker. He really hurt. Still these pangs of something called love, manifested in Alatar's fading conscience, as physical and mental pain. He strode across the wet, stony beach towards a small cave, always looking down at Sifreya, draped in his robed arms. The peaceful sound of the waves would romance any normal soul. Not Alatar. Not today.

'Mother. Why did you have to come? This was the only way I could spare you.'

His thoughts raced as he entered the small cave mouth. No Takers ever came this way. It was ruled out of bounds and rarely used, even by the higher ranked. This was Alatar's place of contemplation. As the tide slowly came in, he rested the body of Sifreya on a large, raised block of stone and covered her with a silk blanket. Stolen luxury goods from the industrious village of Skyfawr.

'Do as I say, or you will die.' He had told the tradesfolk in his early campaign, after fleeing his father's wrath at Tuteaas. He had wanted the best furnishings for his tower. Now, he bathed the blood away with saltwater from his mothers midriff, and gently placed the silk blanket back over Sifreya's peacefully rearranged features.

Now there was more saltwater, from the eyes of the son. They dropped onto her still, porcelain face. Once the vibrant delivery girl of Tuteaas. Her infectious smile and laughter lifting the spirits of the industrious fishing port. Until seduced by Elphinias. All of that energy, blossoming life. Taken. Alatar bent and kissed her cheek and unknowing to himself, his eyes flashed their innocent boyhood blue. He took one last look.

"Your favourite place of solitude was Eanyys Grove. May the tide carry you home. I love you. Mother of Leandro."

He turned, finished, and left as emerald water swelled around the cave, surrounding Sifreya. Then, he grimly headed back to the courtyard at pace. He wiped away his tears and arranged his face into business mode. On his return, sat at the counsel table, still damaged from Jude's crashing the family car, Elphinias sat, sipping liquid. Sneering as Alatar approached.

"Did your little funeral ceremony ease your conscience, boy?"

"You shut your mouth, dirty changeling. I cannot listen to any more of your bile."

"Temper, temper. No time for tears son. Your enemy is near. I feel it. The time is upon us my boy. Dry your eyes and ready your magic and wake your lazy soldiers. My wife is at peace now. You having murdered her and relieved her of a broken heart."

Alatar grabbed Elphinias by the throat..

"You never speak of my mother again. You killed her. I took away her pain. You made me into this walking dead. This is not success, you octopus. You are manic, derranged, sewage. It will undo you. This over confidence. You should have stayed under the moat with your disgusting pet slug. Speak again and I will salt that damned Bakkor. I will deal with Ramona. Do not worry about that. You.. You stay the hell away from me."

He banged his fist on the table and walked away. The tears welled up again. Elphinias shrugged and sipped his liquid.

Over the courtyard, two scouting black-backed gulls circled briefly then flew away.

At the cove, Sifreya slipped beneath the waves and began to drift. Where her spirit was met by Ualdin. The Ethereal watcher.

CHAPTER SIXTY SIX
THE READYING OF NEW AZMARINE

Fizzing waves washed soothingly over the shingle at the edge of the beach at the cove settlement of New Azmarine. The rest of the sand was untouched, like having sugar in between your toes. The once fallen coastal dwelling, had begun to rise like the proverbial phoenix. So much so, that Theonyra had felt able to leave with Princess Mahreuben, some time ago now, to lend his vast presence to Ramona's adopted task. Mahreuben would never have asked him to leave, had she not had complete faith in the abilities of the new cove people.

Also, given that the Takers had thought Old Azmarine long destroyed and disappeared into myth like status. The rebuilding project was taking place in what appeared to be relatively safe circumstances. Back in the woodland areas, where it was cooler, they had now built a small and thriving little village. Strong family huts, campfire areas for social gatherings and meetings, a larger wooden building for schooling, food and fresh water stores. They had all worked extremely hard.

A minor miracle for the realms, when considered that these people were ex-prisoners in the jails at the Takers tower. Catapulted out to sea to drown, asphyxiate. Some had met harrowing fates. It still mentally haunted many of the recovered villagers. The King, who many had thought to have been a giant, decorative statue. Put together by the people of the dark land in mocking celebration of victory in the ancient battle. To show that they had turned the mighty Theonyra into a standing stone, receding into the ocean like the rest of Old Azmarine.

Unfortunately for Elphinias, the druid Selanius and the old armies, their spell had not fully worked. Turned Theonyra to stone they had, but blood ran within his rock veins and he had all the time in the world to consider a plan. Not of retribution or revenge, but a plan to take back and rebuild what belonged to the decent people of Azmarine.

Nothing had happened for eons and so the stone King, enveloped by the sea, pacified himself by learning to converse with fish, dolphins, diving seabirds. Then, the bodies fell from the sky. From the gargantuan catapults at the Takers tower. Sanctioned by Alatar and mercilessly carried out by the gleefully grim Elphinias.

Today however, was different. Most of those flailing bodies, swallowing seawater, suffering panic attacks, had been scooped up and carried back to shore by the woken King Theonyra. They had clung to his legs, his arms, midriff, shoulders. Any part of his anatomy that would allow them to continue gulping oxygen.

When you are about to die in your mind and you are sure of it, every breath is worth more than the purest gold. For the first time in decades, those giant strong legs powered ashore to carry these poor, cruelly treated and malnourished folk of the realms to the cool, welcoming sand and continuing life.

Three such grateful folk, who had put all their effort into this project, had been the married couple, Luca and Giula. Of the same timeline as Ramona and her family, and befallen of the same fate. Another prominent figure had been the fiery young Elysse. A pretty, red-headed realms girl, separated from her own babies during the invasion. Coldly thrown in the cells and later, grown skeletal and weak, deemed useless and flung out to tread water in blind, terrified hope.

Today, Elysse had become a respected counsellor and confidante to the other survivors. An empathetic soundboard, despite her own inner heartbreak at her still missing children. She had become firm friends with Luca and Giula and often worked alongside Luca in such counselling sessions or meetings about the rebuild.

Giula had been a school teacher in her own timeline. This skill was now employed and gratefully received here at New Azmarine and the growing crop of children loved her teachings. With all of this said, none of the new people were lazy, having learned the true meaning of gratitude for life itself, they dug in as a unified group and built and nurtured and became healthy, bronzed and strong.

In fact on this day, the rafts they had been building for future use, were nearing completion. A small but sturdy fleet of strong wooden skiffs, capable of transporting good sized groups, were proudly lined up a few hundred yards back from the green waters.

Biggle and Baggle of course, the black-backed gulls, had not only been Cormac's eyes in the sky. They were now employed as a flying postal service! The birds had taken word from Elysse' beautifully worded scroll, back to Theonyra, assuring him of their health and safety and continuing gratitude. This after Ramona's party had sent their own parchment at the King's request, checking in hope of their continued health and survival.

"Do not come to our aid. We are grateful but need you to build your strength.."

This had been the tone of the King's message to the New Azmarinian's. Now, they had politely ignored his request. They were never hungry or thirsty now. The small but well drilled guard kept a keen eyed and vigilant watch for any sign of being discovered by rogue Takers, and the children were protected at all costs.

The counsel of New Azmarine had now decided it was time to set sail. To head north and back inland. To fearlessly join the fight to overthrow Alatar and his totalitarian regime and seize back the tower that had for an eternity, belonged to the good people of the realms. The last word they had heard was that Ramona and company were heading that way to do this very thing. They knew she was the chosen one of the ethereal. They knew she was a heralded and humble adopted realms girl and they knew her organic magic was becoming honed and strong.

But their desire to aid the cause and express their gratitude for their newly extended lives and also out of love for this family from another timeline, willing them to be free to go to their own home. This empathetic desire persuaded them to politely ignore the advice of the King's considerate and kindly worded parchment. Elysse looked out to sea to the tiny speck across the waves that was the Takers tower. With a fiery glint in those sharp eyes, she turned to Luca and Giula as the golden sun beat down on the cove and whispered..

"Let us set sail then. Let us help Ramona and the King. Let us find our wives, husbands and children. Let us exterminate this vermin once and for all."

The three friends stood on the beach, hugging and crying, tears of feisty determination. Luca then also spoke.

"Agreed. Let us go to our wizard, under the guidance of the ethereal. And kill it."

CHAPTER SIXTY SEVEN
AN INEVITABLE COLLISION

"Good Morning Leandro my boy. I hope your rest period was not too coloured by all of your recent trauma." Whispered Elphinias almost cheerily, and laced with sarcasm. Alatar had appeared in the courtyard at the table of the counsel, sipping hot liquid from his pewter goblet.

"Thank you father. I am deeply honoured and shall now bathe in the cool morning darkness of your embittered, repulsive shadow, you grotesque walking squid." Replied Alatar, his own response, loaded with hateful barbs.

"Very nice boy. Very nice indeed. So now that your hatred, masqueraded as sarcasm, has been vented. Have you anything constructive to say? Ramona shall be here very shortly. Are your blundering drones ready, son? Only, my vision was very clear and vivid as I took my dawn brew at your precious counsel table. Wrecked by the boy, Jude, was it?

Travelling in his father's crude transport, which is still here. A strange mode of travel. Fascinating. Yet another lazy monument of your inept leadership. He did well that day Alatar my lad. I saw from the tower, where I was so close to having Princess Mahreuben work for us. So close she was, to slipping into the seduction of the life-force liquid, so very close. Her eyes were closing. Then my lad, you performed your disappearing trick on the child Jude and went hiding in the tower. Scared of the boy were you?"

"Be quiet, changeling. I will not respond to your baiting."

"You be quiet Alatar, dolt. Can you now see that your act of cowardice, fear of the boy, not only helped Mahreuben to escape, but that by leaving the courtyard, you enabled Uzaleus and the prisoners to break out of the jail? As the guard raced to rally to you, in your traumatic battle against this human boy, odds so obviously stacked against my poor, overwhelmed son. Your drug-addled orcs did not leave any of their swollen number to maintain a presence at your rusting cells.

The result? A mass breakout led by a malnourished Prince. A befuddled ex-captain and a smattering of flea ridden, faerie followers! You are a cretin Alatar. So, you flee the boy, free everybody else, and try to exterminate the only being capable of getting you out of your self created chaos. Me. You are a mess, Alatar. A mummy's boy. Baby Leandro, the murderer. Throwing your mother out of the window the way you did. I liked it though. Ramona of the realms however Leandro, well, I must say, travelling alone, she has done admirably on her way here..

I saw it you see, Leandro. As you slept. Hiding again. Here she was in my vision, son. Striding with purpose. Turning your drones back in to people. Giving them food and water and the benefit of the doubt. That is what Ramona offered your men. It appears she is killing the pure Taker though I am afraid. She left many in her wake. I like her, Alatar. What a shame she too, now has to be killed. Twice, to make sure.

You are the type of creature Alatar, who rounds up a million foes, puts them into jail cells and saunters off to celebrate his feats, having left keys in the locks. Enjoy your drink though boy, and warm through that cold heart I gave to you. My son has a fight on his hands, and I have a front-row seat. It shall be nice to see what you are made of when faced with a real danger. More tea then?"

Pure sarcasm and scorn poured from the slit-mouth of Elphinias, as Alatar stared at him from the other end of the table, sipping hot liquid.

"Are you finished with your tirade, slug? You like the sound of your own voice don't you? Changeling." Alatar was prickled. But now, used to the scorn of his blood father, he maintained a modicum of calm control.

"I have questions for you, slug, and if you wish to be a father to me, for the first time, perhaps you will listen. Now that you have driven my mother to an early grave, you have me all to yourself. If, you can tear yourself away from your freak pet Bakkor for long enough? Why, you have gone soft father. What is it? Has that putrid slime not had its fish this morning and come to the surface for a loving pat on the head? Shall we fetch the last of the prisoners as well, so that you may satisfy your sick bloodlust?

The catapults have lain dormant for a while. Is it a sadness at your favourite toys going unused? Damn you father for all my repulsion at your shapeshifting, you will listen to me. Or I will salt that swimming slime in the moat to a burning, agonising end. You must let me face Ramona. Your catapults no longer interest me. Nor the drowning of the weak or wretched. I do however want you with my guard, Kovah, on the tower ramparts. You are good at watching. There is a name for that my voyeuristic, reptilian ancestor. So, to my plans. Boiling vats would be a start. Supervise the guard, station them at every entrance. Scare them, father.

Sharpen their swords. Glistening daggers and optimum strength I need. To get rid of her jolly band of chaperones. That will give me Ramona. The ethereal girl in waiting. She can then join my mother. I no longer care where her spirit goes. I want her off this map. Her family, I want dead or gone, and then that praying hub at Skyfawr, reduced to rubble. Then there will be no wizards, no consecrated ground to ordain to.

Just us. Then the ethereal can float away and whisper on the wind as they please. Their chosen one amongst them. Another heartbroken onlooker from another timeline. Stuck in the ether with harmless watery folklore, as this land is governed by the red eyed. Shredded at the hand of the Takers. Ruled by Alatar. ME. Leandro is dead. Will you help me, father?"

Elphinias writhed in his chair, grinning ecstatically.

"Backbone they call that my son. You have made an old changeling very proud. I will help you bury them, with pleasure. All you had to do was ask."

Then for the first time since boyhood, Elphinias and Alatar sat together.

Smiling, grimly.

CHAPTER SIXTY EIGHT
THE BREACHING OF THE TOWER

Despite everything that had happened on Ramona's epic journey. From babe in arms, to this strong, young woman now hunting down the foes of the realms, it was only Jude who had come face to face with Alatar. Prior to that, and much earlier, James had swerved the car off the road. The family had inadvertently crossed a ley line and gone through the gateway to this new timeline.

That was when Alatar had appeared on the country lanes, flashing those red eyes. Warning the family to leave. The accident had changed everybodys fate. How Alatar had cursed his interference, causing the ethereal to meddle in affairs. Ramona's intense growth acceleration in body, soul and mindfulness, had presented him with an unwanted, yet worthy opponent. He would have to fight now for his self-bestowed title as new leader of the realms.

Now, the ragtag army of the realms, raced to catch up to Jude. Led by the giant stone King. He of the blood that ran through granite. Jude, speedy and of huge heart was aching to catch up to his sister. Closing the gap now after running into Claudiu, the manufactured Taker. Released from his liquid induced torment by Ramona. Ramona, with a trail of dispatched Takers in her wake, save for the recovering Claudiu, headed across the scrub and closer to the tower. Closer to Alatar, to going home. So near, that now she could smell the salty, sea-weedy air of the coast.

That which she had not smelled since a baby at Oakhampton with her doting parents. It invigorated her and she moved on. She wanted her family and new friends with her. But she was not scared. This Ramona was in battle mode and of singular mind. The land began to open up before the young woman. Subconsciously, she drew in a huge gulp of oxygen and puffed her chest out. She patted the inside pockets of her robe and made a fist with her right hand. She smacked it into the palm of her left and checked in all directions.

Nothing.

"Wish me luck, if you can hear me.."

She whispered up to the clouds. She walked on at a quicker pace. Now she could hear the cries of seabirds. Curlews, oystercatchers, choughs, skuas and all manner of gulls. She had come to the coastal path. Not too far from the cave that Alatar had banished Mahreuben to, and nastily labelled her a banshee. A trickster, a witch. The realms folk had doubted his word but did not dare to intervene. They had seen this demon raze hills to the ground, burn down and reseed forests, with swishes of those gnarly hands.

In the distance, Ramona could now make out the ocean. Sunshine bounced off the emerald sea, so that it looked like dancing stars on the surface. She wondered how far across those waves it would be to New Azmarine, the rebuilding cove settlement. Despite Theonyra's protective warnings to stay away, would they come to her aid? To the aid of their kinfolk? Something told Ramona they were already on the way. Her intuitive skills were growing stronger. With another surveying glance, she traced across hilltops, a stretch of what looked like barren land. Then, as though carefully looking at a painting, she came to some tall standing stones that stood like silent, knowing monoliths. More to the right now..

There it finally was. The Takers tower. Drawing closer with every stride. Coming into focus more. Sharper outlines. Turrets, ramparts, ancient windows. Giant, death shaped catapults. For the first time in a long while, Ramona felt a rush of Adrenaline, it tightened her chest unpleasantly and she shuddered.

'My god.' She thought. 'I am just a human. A girl. I should be a baby. Can I do this? I bloody well have to do this!'

Just like any human being, wizard or not, Ramona was experiencing a fight-or-flight response. Just like any human being, a million thoughts swirled in that one brain all at once. Being born, mummy and daddy, something they travelled in with wheels. Funny bird calls, laughter, intimacy, whooshing waves. A skidding sensation, a crash.. red eyes, hanging in the air. She spoke aloud to nobody, save the voices of self-doubt in her mind.

"Shut up! I can do this. I will do this."

She took a moment to drink some water and check her tiny amount of belongings. Small elven dagger, some berries, the water and the orcs fish, saved for the gulls. Suddenly there was somebody or something behind her, given away by rustling leaves. She drew the dagger and spun around with electric speed.. there, stood her brother at last.

"Sis? My god it is you, wait! Just bloody stay where you are You dare run off again and I'm telling mum!"

Her brother from between timelines. Jude, was puffing and slowed to a halt. Ramona exhaled and put the dagger back into her cloak. Jude grabbed his sister's arms and pulled her close in a very tight hug.

"Jude you mug, I could have stabbed you. Creeping about like that!" Said Ramona more in relief than annoyance.

"I am never letting you out of my sight again. Even if it means not sleeping!" Replied her brother. Jude's tracking and the help from the freed Claudiu had paid off. He was back with his sister for the final stretch.

"You are NOT doing this alone.."

Ramona made to speak but was instantly shut down by her brother who raised his voice now.

"You are NOT doing this alone. The end."

Ramona's questioning frown melted away and she grinned at her brother. They were so similar despite their separate and disjointed journeys.

"Well then Jude, it looks like it was meant to be! Its just you and me brother."

"Well, I wouldn't go that far sis!" Jude replied glancing up and to his left.

"Eh?" Was all Ramona could utter.

"Look behind you, on the coastal path.."

"My sweet lord!" She gasped, drawing in a sharp intake of breath. It was the people of New Azmarine. Coming down the sand dunes, onto a rocky path towards her. Smiling, backslapping camaraderie. Full of renewed hope. They were dragging rafts, small skiffs, weapons and food sacks, behind them in groups. The New Azmarinian's stood still now, not far away from Jude and Ramona, two of their people came forward.

"Ramona, sister of the realms. My name is Luca. This is my wife Giula. We came through the gateway just as your family did. We had no clue either. We were captured immediately before we even knew where we were. Behind me is Elysse of the realms. She is keen. She has family missing. Young ones. There are many stories in our party. We wish to help in any way we can. We are strong and healthy now and New Azmarine, although small, is a hidden and growing inlet.

Our scouts and watchers have seen very little of the Takers, save the odd coastal path scout party. We have been left alone it seems. All we can think is that the area of Old Azmarine, to Alatar, is of no more importance and thought as long gone under the sea. We are a mixed group of survivors Ramona, from the tower jail. Catapulted out to sea to die by Alatar and Elphinas. Rescued by the stone King Theonyra. We think it is what you might call.. payback time.."

Ramona stood silently, listening intently. Anchored to the floor, as though frozen. Then she sighed a deep breath of relief, sadness, empathy, anger.. and then, she dropped to her knees, clasping her hands in a grateful prayer motion. Tears began to stream down her face. Tears of relief, happiness.. of hope.

"I knew. I felt in my blood, you would come. Bless your beautiful hearts. The King wanted you to stay safe. You have been through enough.."

"And lived Ramona, and lived. Now where is that disgusting vermin. I want my children back." This was the red-headed Elysse, eyes on fire with passion, simmering rage and of happiness also, at meeting a kindred spirit with one goal in mind. That of peace.

"He is over there. Waiting, I feel. His army has grown, his drones are unthinking. It will not be easy. Some, perhaps many of us, will die." Said Ramona, looking sideways and upwardly nodding towards the slate grey and imposing looking tower. Once flowery and beautiful. Once of kings and queens, banquets and revelry.

Then after, a fading relic, used as a food, grain, plant and water store by the rebuilding realms folk after the ancient battles that saw Theonyra turned to stone. The giant who was now on his way with Cormac, Uzaleus, Mahreuben and Domacec among many others. They had followed the trails left by Ramona and then Jude and also had with them now, Claudiu the reformed Taker.

"Then I will gladly die." Said Elysse with feisty conviction.

"After I have seen my babies safe and when that maniac's severed head is on top of my spear. Extra sharp, just for the red eyed one and his bloody filthy drones."

Giula stepped forward and wrapped comforting arms around her newfound best friend. Ramona could only look at Elysse with sad acceptance. He really had spread his net of destruction across all of the realms.

"I am called Jude. I am the brother of Ramona, though our story is complicated, long and sad. Though not now. We will not cry over lost time nor advanced growth. We will do everything we can to find your children, brothers, sisters.. parents.."

Jude choked out the last part, thinking of the first time he saw his mother. Opening the door at the old Ivywyrld Inn. The gateway.

"My sister has matured in a way I cannot fathom. She grew fast and had to fill a bigger shape in order to carry out what had been ordained as her destiny by the ethereal. I was not sure of these guardians. Then, with my sister possibly near death at Skyfawr chapel.." He looked proudly toward Ramona and went on..

I felt them. I knew they were there. Whispers. The ground vibrating. The swirling skies. Then I knew Ramona was the chosen one. I had no doubt in her. She is my sister. I love her. I will die fighting for her stolen chidhood. I will die to save my mother and father and I will die for you all. I am with Elysse here. Lets go. Together, as one. Its time to kill this thing and go home.."

The New Azmarine folk cried out in a huge roar. People were in tears. Chanting mantras. Barking out 'Death to Alatar. Death to him now.'

Jude turned to his sister..

"What do you think Mona? Nice little speech or what?'

Ramona wiped her eyes from all the emotions crackling like live electricty.

"It was very.. ethereal, brother. Very eloquent. I am proud of you. I love you too. With all my heart."

Then Elysse, for a small, fiery young woman herself, gave an almighty shout..

"For our children. Forward!!"

CHAPTER SIXTY NINE
THE CONJURING OF THE GATEWAY

"You are sure you can do this Ualdin? I mean, really sure?" Topia of the ethereal was sensing her elder statesman formulating something he had not done for many long lifetimes.

"It is achievable Topia, yes, I believe so. I also hear the prayers of Princess, Mahreuben. Do you not also feel them resonate within the ether Lesidyn, Sifreya?"

The other three gathered watchers, went silent at Ualdin's words. Alatar's mother was newly arrived to the ether and still trying to find acceptance that she no longer possessed bodily form. Mahreuben's voice came through now, whispering, pleading. Her words were not being spoken in this moment but were more like recordings of past prayers, that Ualdin was somehow playing back to the other spirits in the ethereal domain.

"I will send you home Ramona. I will make sure you and your beautiful family come to no harm.. I will send you home Ramona.. When this is over.. Please, hear me. I know you can. Help me make good on my promise. I have to. I cannot fail."

Mahreuben seemed close to tears in these wispy messages. The spirits listened intently as she went on.

"This gentle soul, a baby taken. Her mother, father and brother, have given our cause their whole lives. I cannot fail. Please, help me send Ramona home.. Hear me ethereal of the realms as you hear Yesenia of Skyfawr chapel.. I pray you can help me fulfil my promise.."

So Princess Mahreuben's residual tones hung in the air, repeating after short pauses.

"She has made a promise. Yet had no way of fulfilling it herself. The only way she could, is by her own death." Rumbled Ualdin to the gathering.

Lesidyn, the keen young spirit spoke now.. "How can our Princess promise things such as this? We are not supposed to intervene, I was of that impression at least?"

Topia drifted to the fore.. "We are not supposed to kill, Lesidyn. I believe we are still permitted to guide.. Ualdin?"

Ualdin chuckled grimly. "Topia is correct my fellow beings. Perhaps on this occasion, my own elders may turn a blind eye, metaphorically speaking, to shall I say.. a 'bending' of the rules!"

Warm laughter resounded around the translucent arena of the ether. Ualdin continued..

"Princess Mahreuben is destined to become one of us. A member of the ethereal. Just as our beloved Sifreya of Tuteaas has now arrived, thankfully with her kind soul intact. Our lady Mahreuben must feel this destiny, and so is willing to die in battle. Even sacrifice herself deliberately, so that she can take her place beside us and try to conjure a gateway for Ramona and her family. Or at least try to manipulate one of us to try.. She may be destined for the ether, but their are two things she will feel in the coming days.

The first being that now, is not her time to die. She has been through her own ordeal. She is young and reunited with Prince Uzaleus. They have realms bound duties to attend to and also, happiness to enjoy.. For some time before she is up here, prodding, enthusiastically albeit! We already have one such amongst us, do we not Lesidyn?"

There was more soft laughter. If the keen Lesidyn could have blushed, he would have.

"So Mahreuben is to remain then?" Added Sifreya, beginning to feel her spirit self take form now.

"Yes Sifreya. Mahreuben is to remain." Ualdin answered.

"I will not let her die of martyrdom to fulfil her promise. She is bound for other things. But I will help her make good on it.. If I can."

"So you are to open the gateway, when? May I ask, Ualdin?" Questioned Topia, tentatively.

"The gateway, providing I can conjure it, shall be opened the moment that Alatar is known to be clinically dead. This was the arrangement when baby Ramona was chosen. This was the assignment that I was given by my own spiritual elders. Elphinias was not in the conversation. I fear he is powerful and has slipped through the net many times, as we are now seeing below."

Sifreya seemed to whimper at the mention of her so called husband.

"I understand Sifreya. Your boy Leandro has become entrapped in the monster Alatar. Perhaps, and only perhaps.. He too may be freed after the death of Alatar. But he will not be permitted to the ether. Your son, in whatever guise, has killed many innocents, Sifreya. Whether influenced, guided, drugged or poisoned by his changeling father..

None of this is attributable to you. You are and were a good mother, wife, worker and person. It is well known and you are cherished, loved and missed. He though, is still answerable for his unforgivable crimes. The only small, saving grace he has in his own mind, is that he somehow thinks he spared you. By killing you Sifreya. You, his mother.

His logic is warped but we did see flashes of the once good boy Leandro, as he set your bodily form drifting towards Eanyys Grove. But it is far too late for him to redeem himself, at least here, in the ether. In the eyes of the elders, Sifreya. I can only offer prayer for his delivery from evil and hope that as your spirit-self grows, you will gain some acceptance around this awful matter."

"I.. understand, Ualdin. I really do. My boy is lost. I tried, but Alatar had taken over. Now in death, I pray his own end is swift at the hands of Ramona. So that he may be poisoned no more by that.. thing.. that I married. I believe my boy is filled with painful remorse, Ualdin. Under too many layers. I know of his and his father's atrocities. I had seen enough of it back at Tuteaas when I.. When I was.. Alive.."

The whimpering again.

Ualdin came back.

"Speculation over Alatar is wasteful to us and to the folk whom march with Ramona. It is now those very people to whom we must turn our attention, give our full permitted guidance to all souls involved, and then.."

"And then, what? Ualdin?" Whispered a calmer Lesidyn.

Ualdin seemed to ponder.

"And then it is down to Ramona, our chosen one, to complete this unfortunate task that was bestowed on her by my own self. It was with a heavy heart, but after many rounds of discussion and much protestation from myself.. We felt it was preordained that she and her family appeared on the ley line, despite Alatar's meddling. We feel she would have come. Her parents were unfortunately brought over as we began the growth acceleration, for protection of the baby Ramona and so as not to be separated from her even in such a traumatic scenario.

Now, I must work.

I have a gateway to open and a way home for the people of the alternates. This gathering must now come to a close, my friends of the ether. There can be no more questions today. It is time."

"What will the rest of us do now, Ualdin?" Asked Topia, the female spirit.

"The rest of you will pray, Topia. The rest of you will pray."

CHAPTER SEVENTY
THE DEATH OF AN ARMY OF GOOD

Ramona, Jude and the people of New Azmarine, finally struck out on the last leg to the tower. It was so near now, they could see the outlines of hooded figures, gliding about the ramparts at the very top. Below, the drawbridge was raised up and wrought-iron gates were shut tightly. The moat was wide and very deep and unpleasant creatures had replaced the graceful, placid fish of the old royals. It was just another functioning part of the towers defence mechanisms.

"It is locked down Ramona, that much is obvious." Said Luca, as they trekked across the open land.

"I am surprised they have not sent some of their number to try to repel us. That would be the normal approach. It is as though.. as though he is inviting us to invade. What say you, Ramona?" Asked Elysse, the flame-haired realms girl. Her face was scrunched up in a quizzical expression.

Ramona turned to her new friends, gathered behind her and Jude, and answered..

"I think he is Ellie, he wants us at those gates. Getting this far has not been an easy ride for any of us, coming from all corners of these lands. But he will not come out of his hole. He thinks he has the upper hand. To a point, he has. Why would he come out? Even surrounded by hundreds of his Takers, he does not know how many we are. He does not know of our numbers. He does not seem to know of any threat from New Azmarine, or else I believe he would have attempted to stop your rebuilding a long time ago.

He knows that any final conflict has to come from us. He is content now Ellie. Sitting there, heavily guarded, he no longer has to step out and conquer settlements and villages. He has already taken what he needs. No, he is happy to see the rest of us scurrying about like confused ants. I think he knows that we know this and he will wait for us."

"You have a plan to get around this, sister?" Ventured Ellie.

"I do Ellie. He will not have to wait any longer. Small numbers of his forces are nothing to me anymore. I say this with no over confidence. Just assurance. I will not waste further magic on fours and fives of his scouts. They are easy pickings and to extinguish their lives would be murder. He keeps his strong guard within. Elysse, Giula, Luca, this is what I need from the New Azmarine people. As I said, there will be unpreventable deaths.

My own life is no more important to this cause than that of any of you, of our gulls and of those whom have stayed back to look after the young in those very settlements and villages. All you brave people of New Azmarine. When we arrive at the tower. I want you to be ready. It is then he may try sending guards out. Whether it is that or whether we force an entry, I need you to target these guards and keep them off me. As I say, I am just another being. But I think if I can get to him, that I can take this piece of filth down for good.

If not, I will die trying. I understand I was chosen to do this and that your arrival here at this exact time is preordained also. Keep them off me. Kill them. There will be no time to look who is a pure Taker and who is not. They are too far gone, it is sad. But clinical decisive moves are needed. We will all mourn and grieve later. We have our families and homes to go to. Let us now move on. Keep the unit tight. have any weapons close to hand. Straight ahead and brisk everybody. For the realms.."

"For the realms!" Came a collective cry from the gathering.

Then, suddenly the ground began to rumble, ever so slightly under the feet of the entourage. It was a warm and familiar sound now. Ramona felt the vibrations within her being. Then, Jude, who had been looking out across the land, whooped with delight.

"Theonyra! It is King Theonyra, and Cormac! Uzaleus, Mahreuben, the elves. Sis, look!"

Jude punched the air in recognition as the huge granite outline of Theonyra, the stone King of Old Azmarine, strode purposefully across the plains with the rest of the army they had gathered over their long travels. He drew up close with his giant strides.

"Ha-ha! Our Ramona, bless you my lady, and Jude lad. It is good to see you both intact!" Boomed the kind warrior.

"Ah, well, well. My New Azmarine builders are here. En masse, eh! Why does this not surprise me, I knew you would dismiss my parchment. How this warms the blood in my heart. Brothers and sisters, together in peace, together in battle. Remember this day of courage. It will be the last time we go to fight. It will be my final war. This, I have known since I stood dormant under those waves for generations. I knew they would come. Just as I now know that we will wash them from existence. Onward then, friends."

Theonyra's eyes were glinting, a wry but determined smile spread across his marbled human-like features. After all, human he was, underneath all that stone exterior.

Elysse called up to the King..

"It is because of your brave and kind heart Theonyra, that we lived on and did not drown under those waves. You saved every person here from certain death at the hands of Alatar and that vulgar Elphinias, and their damned catapults. We walk with you our King, so that you may reclaim your rightful home, as King of the royal tower of the realms.

Now that we have our lady Ramona, we stand with her, so that she and her family may return home, and so that Luca and Giula, my friends, may cross with them also. This unexpected lease of life is to be spent as warriors, ridding the realms of his poison. Not one of these Azmarine folk had to be forced to be here my King."

Elysse bowed and offered a curtsy to the King smiling down at her.

"You would make an old man blush young Ellie, if I could of course. You are not to serve me, you are to be the individual equals that I love you as. Equality and peace is our mission. Ramona Wizard, eh. You are ready, sister of the realms. Though we go as one." He glanced mischievously at the young wizard..

"We go as one." Smiled Ramona.

"Equality and peace, King Theonyra. Onward, by your leave of course, my friend?" She winked and grinned at the King. Full of adrenaline, hope and zest for life, the fear had subsided and she was ready, with Jude her brother and personal guard by her side.

"I'm watching you sis.." Jude smiled at Ramona..

"Ah, your not so bad yourself brother.."

She laughed out loud and it was beautiful and infectious and the party at full strength and bolstered by the New Azmarine survivors, struck on. Cormac looked skyward at Biggle and Baggle..

"This is it my friends, you have led the way for us from the very start. There is the finest smoked bass waiting for you, that is to be sure my companions!" A tear welled in the eye of the kind elf, as he watched the birds soar above. They would no longer be needed as guides but nor would they desert their friends after their own personal epic journey.

"Hop, hop, hop!" They cawed in unison and swooped onward.

"Now come on Cormac, no time for sentiment you silly old fool." The humble, selfless elf, steeled himself one last time and he ran with the party, one eye on the sky.

From the ramparts of the tower, both Alatar and Elphinias stood sneering. Flanked by heavyset shrouded guards.

"They are here father. She has come, look on.." Alatar made a sweeping gesture with his now ghostly looking hands.

Elphinias stroked his pointed chin. "I see her my son. I presume you still want me to leave the stupid girl for you to deal with alone?"

"You presume correctly, changeling. You may do as you wish with the other pawns. I have my own mother's blood on my hands. I want it washed away, with hers." Alatar pointed at the approaching Ramona, visible now to the naked eye.

"So it shall be, boy. I will amuse myself by finally finishing off this walking stone monument, Theonyra. The concrete King of nothing. I will end his torment and do the job properly. He only lived due to those bungling idiots, poor spellcasting of generations gone. Now, he will die a true death and he will never come back again. Come then King Theonyra. Come and die before your superior.. Elphinias, the shapeshifter. It will be slow.. and painful. So mote it be."

Elphinias turned and walked away leaving Alatar alone watching Ramona draw up to the moat.

"Alatar! Alatar the red eyed one.." Came a bellowing solitary cry from a young woman named Ramona. She stood before the moat. Her loyal army looking on. Fiery, her wispy raven hair, blowing in the breeze and grim determination etched upon her striking features.

"I Ramona, soul wizard, call you out, Alatar the corrupt. You are now far beyond reasoning with. Open these gates, filth, and let us see you for what you are. A coward and a killer.. Hiding!"

Ramona screamed the words up to the leader of the Takers, who looked down scornfully at the wizard. Barely moved by Ramona's bold words, or if he was he did not show it. His expression was one of sheer hatred and he bared his teeth, sharp as daggers and his eyes were like a glowing hellfire now as he paced back and forth atop the ramparts.

"Call me out will you, girl? Call me out! You have some guts, I will grant you that Ramona, the self-proclaimed wizard.. But you are a very stupid, overgrown baby dwelling inside a sick experiment. How amusing to know that the beloved ethereal, have stolen some eighteen, twenty, of your years?"

He barked out a derisory snort.

"Yet you child, not even of this world.. and all of your gormless farmers, fishermen and elven jesters, unwanted prisoners and these absolute fools of Azmarine.."

Luca, Giula, Elysse and the Azmarine party looked startled..

"Yes.. Idiots, I knew of your rebuild. I wanted to let you finish your little project before I claimed it for the Takers. A useful addition to my lands I would say. What say you, stone man? You seem ever so quiet. Nothing to say, statue?" He leered at the old King.

Theonyra glowered bitterly, right into the eyes of Alatar and known only to himself, the stone King saw a flicker of fear in those red eyes. He knew it.

"Open those gates Alatar. I have business with your father."

"The gates I will NOT open, monument man.

Why should I? This is my kingdom and is not open to peasants and waifs and strays, silly delusional girls. Nor to oversized walking gravestones. You are in no position to make demands old King. This is my palace, not a hostel for a travelling circus. As you have seen.. Ramona, stone man, all of you loyalist followers. They are imprisoned, and then recruited to my army.. or mercilessly killed."

With his black robe billowing behind him and surrounded by faceless Takers, Alatar was not going to be making deals or be taken by surprise it seemed. Ramona turned around to her gathered army. Jude by her side like a magnet. Then to Uzaleus, Princess Mahreuben, Cormac and the elves. Domacec, Ailbe, Dayn and the escapees.

"People will die. Run, if You feel the need. there will never, never be judgement from us. We are one."

Nobody ran.

Then there was Theonyra. The stone King. Waiting silently as he did beneath the waves for generations, waiting for his time, his chance. Ramona looked up again at the foe who had stolen her childhood, caused her father's car crash and his merging, and sent her mother sick, with worry.

"Alatar the leader. Ha! You call ME self-proclaimed? I was born this way, you are the sick one, little goblin child. You were made. Made by a changeling that poisoned you and lives in you. You are a street magician Alatar. Part shapeshifter. Turned by that thing, Elphinias. Killer of your own mother. Sifreya. Good, kind Sifreya, Sifreya.."

Ramona kept repeating the name of the mother of Alatar to see if she could stir a reaction. She winked ruefully at the army behind her, silently communicating to them to be ready for anything. It was going to be a guessing game, but they expected the worst.

"Alatar the red eyed one.. Do you hear me? Mother killer? Murderer of the good Sifreya of Tuteaas, patron of Eannys Grove. Loved by all.. Everybody in these realms knows what you have done. Everyone. There is no place to run Alatar. All you have is this tower that belongs to the old royals, and well you know it. Your guard.. Inept followers, brainwashed at your street rallies, they do not care for your cause, they seek only food and water and shelter and hope not to die at your cruel hand.

I will bet that wielding those impressive weapons does not seem such a proposition now. I will bet they would give anything to return to the bosom of the old royals.. and of the new. Prince Uzaleus and Mahreuben here.. You did not kill them Alatar. You did not defeat them. You will not defeat us."

This was enough now for Alatar.

"Enough talk now child. You like the sound of your own words too much. Now you will learn what is like to have the blood of your own on your hands. This guilt you will now carry for your eternity, whether as young wizard or withering old crone, like your Princess. This is your doing. Little, insignificant Ramona. You brought them here. Remember."

With this, Alatar performed his readying process. Arms raised above his head, spindly fingers pointing to the sky. No praying here. Only dark concentration.

"You had better start running. Ramona of the realms."

His bellowing tones shook the ground with unmistakable menace. The sky fell dark. A clap of thunder resounded. It began to rain. Alatar's arms came down, eyes hung in the air, and he began to circle and swish in all directions in an unpredictable and erratic manner. His magic was of electrical red. Deadly.

Ramona's small army began to scatter but the bolts had already begun to scythe down some. Ailbe and Dayn, the escaped prisoners now scouts, would not be lucky a second time. The last Ramona saw of Dayn's face was a terrified ashen white expression before he crumbled to dust. Ailbe's arms stretched in desparation for a hand, but it was his last action. He fell and burned away from sight leaving only scorched earth. James, Ramona's doting father, pushed Ruth out of the way behind the nearest boulder he could see. But for James he would not reach the flimsy hiding place. The bolts caught his legs as he tried to dive for cover with his wife and he let out an agonising scream.

"Ruthie!" He looked into his wife's eyes one last time. Blood spurted from his calves in a harrowing display of pain. Ramona turned and looked back at her writhing father in mute horror. Alatar, grinning calmly, identified James and zoned in on him again.

"You see Ramona wizard.. I am as good as my word. You brought them here did you not? Now you shall witness the death of your own father. There will be no happy return to your time. For any of you.."

More volleys of the scything bolts shot mercilessly at James. This time he was caught in the chest and he fell in the open on to his front. His eyes were white as he glanced at his daughter. He managed to shake his head.

"No, Mona. Stay away. Look after your mother. You can do it. I love you.." James winced in final agony.

"DAD!"

Ramona went to sprint to her fathers side but was held back by the strong, muscular arm of her brother. Tears spilled from the eyes of Jude, but he held on to his sister's hand despite her wrestling and cursing.

"No, sis. You heard dad. Stay here. Remember, it is you who was chosen. He is scared, Alatar. Remember your own words. We will grieve after. Stay focused. I love you Sis. Do as dad says."

With this, Jude sprinted away in a zig-zag motion. His speed and agility got him to the boulder behind which his mother lay screaming hysterically. He held Ruth in an iron grip to stop her rushing to help a cause that was now bitterly futile. They crouched hard against the rock. But this cover would not last, Jude knew.

James, heartbreakingly fighting to live, dragged himself along the ground in blind hope. He rolled onto his back and looked at Alatar on his ramparts and screamed..

"You have no idea about me Alatar. You have no clue who I am. You are just bile. You will never find out what magic is really capable of. You will die.."

A guttural laugh rang out across the courtyard as Alatar bellowed down at the stricken James..

"I think it is you, who will go first James. I know all too well who you are, merger, fellow changeling. You are as as repulsive as Elphinias. Enough!"

Alatar's final act against James was to cut him in two with a pristine, razor sharp shot through James middle. The unforgettable screaming from James was soon over. His body fell apart into two. Just as this happened, he began to disappear from sight. Sky blue light poured out of his middle and into the air. Like tiny neon stars. Particles, millions. Glinting as they did at the Ivywyrld Inn where he merged. A scintillating white followed. A blanket of brilliant mist. Then a whisper..

"You have no idea about magic. No idea who I am.."

Then, James was gone.

Jude pulled Ruth in close as the fire took to the scattered trees. She buried her head, sobbing, into the broad chest of her returned son.

"I'll never leave you mum. Never."

Ramona, up front and alone, wailed and made a screeching, harrowing sound, almost inhuman.

"DAD!"

Ramona

CHAPTER SEVENTY ONE
WALLS COME TUMBLING DOWN

It was a grim scene now as the rain lashed down on the plains and Ramona and her army, reeled from Alatar's devastating onslaught. She could barely see as the tears stung her eyes. She could not bare to look at the remains of her friends, her father, now strewn about, lifeless and silenced forever. The soil was scorched acrid and blood red.

James broken body lay still and in two bloodied pieces. She could not stand it. She prayed that his soul had departed before Alatar's final blows had been cruelly delivered. A short distance away, behind the boulder, Jude held his quivering mother Ruth and tried to survey the area.

"Mum, we have to move. We have to! We can't help dad like this, come on.."

Jude could see that Ramona was physically alright, or at least, not dead. He had to trust in his sister and in the guidance of the ethereal. It was hard for him not to bowl into the fray. Jude dragged Ruth to her feet and she saw her husband out ahead. Dead.

"James! No. James!"

Ruth began to bawl in final realisation and tried to wriggle free from her son. To go to her husband. In sickness and in health. Jude was strong and held her waist and dragged her in the opposite direction. They retreated away from the frontline. Jude had to keep his mother safe. He wanted to fight but this was his part for now.

"Mum. I am not losing you or my sister. Stop fighting me. Drink this, you must stand up, for dad."

He pulled out some water and Ruth gulped it and slumped down against a giant fir tree, sobbing forlornly, drained again, as she had been at the start. How much more could one woman take? Jude could see the damage Alatar had caused to the army. Elves, humans, warriors, peaceful souls, lay stricken or trying grimly to crawl away from the fires. It was gut-wrenching for anyone to witness.

But Ramona was still alive, still there. Up at the front. Theonyra resolutely behind her. Jude had stopped her running to their father, he had bitterly accepted that his parent was going to pass and that James would not want Ramona to die in vain. What were the shimmering blue particles though? What had happened to James? The white light that surrounded him at the point of his death, it had to mean something..

Didn't it?

The family all knew of James merging at the Ivywyrld Inn. Jude could only say prayers in his head. Now, he had to shake his mother into action or they too would undoubtedly perish. Cormac showed now, with several elves and some of the New Azmarine people. They held their ground and stayed about the rocks. Jude sighed. He had just found his father and now he had watched him die. Once again, the earth began to shake. It was King Theonyra. The stone giant strode closer to Ramona's side through the flaming trees and over clusters of boulders, such was his size. There was no point in him hiding and he would not anyway. Not from these sorts.

Ramona turned around to see him and momentarily stopped weeping.

"It is over before it started King. It is all my fault. The red eyed one is right. I have all this blood on my hands. Just as he does, his own mother's, now I have my father's and that of our dead friends."

Theonyra stooped to speak to the stricken wizard.

"Nothing is ever over Ramona. You are a precious soul. We all knew there would be losses. Your father will watch over you now. This was preordained. The realms will take good care of him, of this I have no doubt."

Ramona looked into King Theonyra's kind eyes. Human. Under all of that stone. What he had been through for generations. Here he was. Carrying the fight. She had to put her own grief to one side or die herself. It was that cold and clinical.

"Then what now, my King?" She whispered..

"Now you leave this part to me. Trust in yourself. Trust in this group of friends and family and trust in the ethereal. Stay at a distance. I am going to pave the way. Our good lady Ramona, do not fret. We have only come this far because of you. You are the leader, not I. Leaders do not have to shout and scream and look down on their own. Not only are you a wizard Ramona.. but an example, of hope. Listen to what you brother said.. stay focused. Listen to your own words.. we grieve afterwards. Now. I am going to smash those bastard creatures into nothing. You are our chosen one young lady. Remember this."

With this, King Theonyra of the old royals, stood to his full height and ploughed towards the tower's moat.

Alatar was still watching on from the top of the ramparts as Theonyra stepped into the moat and although it partially submerged him, it did not swallow him. His size and weight caused the water to splash upward like giant raindrops.

Alatar turned to the stocky guard Kovah..

"Get down there. Rally the guard. This granite gravestone intends to make a fight of it. Go, we shall throw ropes around him. Fire is no good here."

Kovah turned and fled towards the giant winding staircase. It seemed he was just as glad to be away from his master as he was to be out of any firing line of Ramona's army. King Theonyra had negotiated his way across the moat now and although the drawbridge was up, it made no odds to him.

Hefty boulders and vats of boiling oil were thrown over the side by Alatar's desperate Takers, in a futile hope of stopping the advances of the courageous giant.

"Fools. I told you to get down away from the ramparts. You waste resources. Go to Kovah and the aides." Roared Alatar and the remaining guards abandoned their efforts and followed the example of Kovah and scurried away.

Suddenly, Elphinias materialised beside Alatar.

"I said go away.." His words tailed off.

"Father. It seems you get your chance. The stone man is upon us."

At that moment, Theonyra rose up out of the water, bellowing battle chants and tore down the drawbridge with his massive rock hands and placed it roughly across the moat.

"Scum. Elphinias, you are the changeling of the past. Today you meet your fate. I have waited for you. Now it is time. Do not think our army to be weak. You are wrong. Come Ramona, come army of the realms! Cross into our tower. Reclaim what is ours.. Now coward, I shall deal with you.."

King Theonyra ripped out the huge, hulking gates, the last line of defence of this old regal tower. It now exposed the open courtyards. Seeing this, Prince Uzaleus and his men advanced with swords drawn. The elves and the folk of New Azmarine followed.

"The King has shown us the way!" Cried Uzaleus.

"Let us slay these vermin and shield our wizard. For the realms!!"

Seeing a pathway cleared into the grounds of the Takers tower, the realms army charged into battle. As the remaining warriors moved into the field, Elphinias materialised in the centre of the courtyard. Right by the counsel table.

James' car, still there, untouched after Jude had crashed it into the table. Another monument. The stone King had seen the shapeshifter appear and in two strides, he was towering over Elphinias. The shapeshifter sneered at his old nemesis.

"Theonyra, the old King, and so it is.."

"So it is, filth.." A repulsed expression spread across the slate grey face of Theonyra.

"Your vile insurrection here has come to a close. Your son has had his day now. We are here to destroy you, just as you are us. Your old armies failed to kill me. Change me they did, but I refused to die in this stone body. I knew I would be called upon. The ether spoke to me in a way the likes of you can only dream of Elphinias. You see, your boy and yourself... You crave instant power. You have no connection to our ethereal. It cannot be bought or stolen nor conjured or invoked. This tower belongs to the old royals."

The two ancient rivals circled each other, a King and a sorcerer, locked in mutual hate.

"Now they have passed at the hands of your predecessors, we are here to take it back Elphinias, to restore it to the folk of the realms. It is to be a place of joy again, overseen by Princess Mahreuben and the Prince Uzaleus. You, lizard.. will now finally die.."

On the ground beneath, Elphinias stood simmering, alone. He was approached by a throng of Takers.

"Go away drones. You cannot help.."

Led by Kovah, the Takers stepped back a little.

"Elphinias, Alatar sent us to assist you. What chance have we against this giant?"

Elphinias turned around to face Kovah and the trembling guards.

"I said.. Go away!.."

Now those strange hands of Elphinias began to change and extend into the slimy, grasping tentacles of a shapeshifter. They grew longer and longer and wrapped around Kovah and the screaming guards.

"What are you doing Elphinias? In the name of the realms!" Kovah screamed, gagged and then choked and his head lolled to the side in the tight grasp of the repugnant changeling. Another guard suffered the same fate in the other apendage of the twisted creature.

"Bakkor!" Screamed Elphinias, and he slung the two dead Takers into the moat. Kovah and the fallen guard splashed into the water like bait and the creature of the catacombs rose from the depths of the murk.

Theonya stared in disgust as the massive mottled and slug-like Bakkor broke the surface. It opened its gaping mouth and razor sharp rows of teeth came crunching down on the head of Kovah the big, stocky guard. It was so violent an attack that Alatar from the ramparts above heard the fracas and turned away from his post, to witness his father's pet dragging the two Takers under the surface and then the moat became still once more.

Alatar fumed. He had no emotional attachment to any of his guard, but the likes of Kovah and the stronger of his drones would be needed. His father was down there revelling in his moment. The guard were being squashed or swatted away now by Theonyra's granite hands and feet. Crushed like insects or batted away to drown in the moat. Any empathetic feelings Theonyra, or any of Ramona's army may have had for the Takers, had either gone or been completely forsaken in the moments of this chaotic confrontation that was now spilling all over the grounds of Alatar's domain.

Uzaleus and his well drilled men scythed heads and limbs off with well sharpened swords. Elven daggers found their mark as the Takers began to fall themselves. It was not all going as easily as Alatar had foreseen now that King Theonyra had breached the drawbridge. Alatar went to the stairway and began to walk briskly away from the ramparts, saving his full magic for later.

"That vile changeling is not my father. He is killing my own. He is letting them swarm over us. That sickened imbecile."

He was flanked, fore and aft by dark cloaked, obedient Takers as he cursed his way down the winding, endless stone stairway.

King Theonyra finally had seen all he wished to see.

"Enough! Elphinias, creature of the dark land. I cannot now say Tuteaas, for it is no more that land. Poisoned by your kin now and the blood of Sifreya is upon it. I cannot kill anymore of these playthings of Alatar. It is no challenge. I will not take advantage of my size and strength. I have given our army a fair chance. Now, it is you, only you. You crawl through life sucking blood, draining love from any soul you can find. Leech. You sapped the soul of Tuteaas and its most beautiful people. You have changed this boy, Leandro.. Into a demon.

Now, I shall tread on you like the freak of nature that you are. Hybrid scum from the devils world, it is now your time to depart!"

The giant right thigh of Theonyra flexed its pulsing stone muscle and a huge leg rose upward. Elphinias squinted, as a giant shadow of the King's foot came down above him. He would be flattened like the other Takers. With this, Elphinias disappeared, just as Theonyra's foot slammed own onto the bloodstained courtyard. Stone cracked and fractured, such was the force.

Then in the ensuing stillness, a singular noise. Clapping. It was Elphinias. He had vanished at the last second and rematerialised a few yards from Theonyra's giant feet. He was still alive. Elphinas stood as billowing clouds of grey dust cleared around him. More sarcastic applause.

"A grand display of force from a true warrior. Not enough though I fear, stone man. Swat Alatar's puppets aside all you want. I do not care for them. Yes, you are correct, my ancestors and I could not kill you completely as you dwelled beneath the waves of Azmarine. I am afraid though, your long generations of planned revenge were wasted, old man. Now, once and for all, you truly shall become frozen in time."

The waving tentacles of the maniacal Elphinias snaked out towards Theonyra and wrapped tightly around his legs. Sucker pads stuck, leech-like to all parts of his frame.

"Alatar and his ropes, ha! Witness this my son. This is how you rid yourself of tiresome enemies."

Alatar had arrived in the courtyard and looked on, eyes flaming at the macabre spectacle unfolding before him. Elphinas, now unrecognisable as the chiselled warrior he had portrayed to dupe Sifreya, had morphed into something resembling a monster octopus. He had a leathery death grip on the legs and torso of the struggling King.

"Do not prolong your suffering Theonyra. It is pitiful to see. Let me cool you down."

Slowly, from his feet and upwards, a coating of a shimmering white frosty substance, spread up the legs and body of Theonyra, like a rash of ice. Theonyra made to walk forward to try to stamp on Elphinias again, but as he tried to lift his leg, it simply separated at the knee and his lower limb was left frozen and no longer attached to his body.

For the first time, terror showed on the freezing, whitened face of the king. He was tottering on his one remaining leg, but that too, was now rock ice. Fragile and ready to shatter.

"Perhaps I do not have the decorative red fire of my son, old man, but as you now see, my magic is equally, if not more effective. And more deadly."

Theonyra's face glazed over. Frozen in time. In horror. Elphinias tentacles began to retract from the stiffened body of King Theonyra.

"So mote it be. Man of stone to man of ice. It is done."

The petrified huge frame of the stone King Theonyra, guardian of Azmarine, toppled forward and smashed into a million crystalline, ashen-white pieces.

CHAPTER SEVENTY TWO
A TOWER OF CONFRONTATION

Screams rang out from the realms army.

"The King has fallen. The King is dead!"

It was Cormac. The little elf was beside himself shouting, wide-eyed in despair as more of the Takers began to swarm into the courtyard like angry wasps. Princess Mahreuben had been fighting her way past the black cloaked figures, to try to get to her great grandfather but it was too late.

Theonyra was now no more. After all of the massive journey he had undertaken, he was now broken. All Mahreuben and Cormac could see through the chaos was shattered stone. Cormac reached up to the lithe figure of the Princess and pulled her away and they ran down a side wall, underneath ivy covered, stained glass windows and buried themselves against it. Takers were now everywhere. The fighting had seemed to even out after King Theonyra had smashed the way in for the realms folk. He had given them the chance he promised he would.

"We cannot stand still here my Princess, to be sure. We must keep moving and scythe down as many of these things as we can. Stay with me Princess. We will get you back to Uzaleus. We cannot help the fallen. Our job is to clear these things out of the path of Ramona. They will find us here soon enough to be sure. Let us live to fight them."

Mahreuben turned to the elf, stricken with pain in her heart, and then hatred manifested in her doleful eyes.

"He froze my grandfather's blood. He froze him until he could no longer stand, Cormac. Now him, this Alatar, is up there, watching it all like a guest at a performance. They are destroying our world Cormac. I will not hide behind a wall and I will not wait for my Prince to rescue me. Look at all of these bodies. Bodies of our kinfolk. Bless you my brave Cormac of the woodland. Your heart is true and stoic. I shall see you at the end."

Mahreuben, effortlessly beautiful even in the midst of the mud and rain of battle, bent down and kissed Cormac on his forehead.

"I love you gentle Cormac. Go to your men."

The Princess was gone, sprinting towards the swollen outline of the disfigured and delirium ridden Elphinias. Cormac knew there was no point trying to dissuade the Princess. It was the same everywhere. Jude could not stop Ramona. All they could do would be to stand and fight with them. Or like Theonyra, fight for them.

It was becoming every man and woman for themselves as these factions and groups split and and spread into messy sub-battles.

Fights within fights spilled over the courtyard and up the many winding stairs. The remaining prisoners roared and banged on the gates of their cells in a mixture of support and final clinging hope of rescue. There was no plan. No well executed drill. You could not guess what was going to happen. There was only one briefing. Kill the Takers or die trying.

Ramona had seen enough now to know that Alatar was still up there somewhere in the tower. She had crossed the makeshift bridge, tucked into the middle of a throng of New Azmarine fighters and once in the courtyard, she had seen Theonyra fall. She had made no attempt to go to his aid. She had listened to him and remained focused. She was still fraught with internal agony at her father's grisly death. Not wanting to drain her own magic, Ramona used stealth instead of power. Ducking and weaving her way through the madness until she found herself at the foot of one of the many convoluted staircases.

"You are up there Alatar. I feel it. I know it.."

She whispered this to nobody. Perhaps the ethereal spirits would direct her. She knew though, that they could not intervene. As she stepped out to move up the stairs, three of the hooded guard were coming down the last few steps. They spotted her at the last second. It was too late.

Ramona had honed her fitness and her physical prowess during her transformation. She had been a sponge. Soaking up languages, information, sights, smells, sounds. Knowledge. Pumped full of data. Some stored, like a memory bank, to be used instinctively when needed. Her brain had not developed in a natural human manner. Hence her instinctive actions, her fast understandings. Like instant downloads.

Here, she would need the physical. The first guard was met by a dagger to the heart. A swift, precise and measured thrust. Stabbed into the chest. A thump. His eyes went from red to dull grey as he hit the ground. Like a dying torchlight. The other two guard stood before her, hissing.

"The witch is here, the witch must die. In Alatar's domain you trespass."

"Do not try to stop me. Do not take another step closer to me. I will kill you both. Pure Takers get no second warning from me. You saw your friend. He is dead, do not advance."

They did not listen. So far gone were they, programmed to obey Alatar, they tried to barge into Ramona. To bowl her over and try to slice at her with scythe shaped weapons. Mindless hacking. She had spotted their move before they even started it and as they slid past and tried to regroup, the dagger found they eye socket of one guard, he yelped and dropped to his knees, groping at his gauged eye.

The guard let out a scream and dissipated into black fragments before imploding in a low boom. Dark powder sprinkled like ashen snow. The spores. Ramona spun to meet the other in a seamless move. Pointing her own dagger directly at the remaining Taker, who was trembling in realisation.

"I told you." She whispered sharply.

The dagger drew across the throat of the final guard in a chilling slice and his head sagged to the side, he whispered something nearly inaudible.. Nearly..

"You will die.. Bitch." And it sneered at her. Ramona punched its head clean off and black liquid spurted from its neck.

"Pure Taker are you. Filthy bastard."

She kicked the head and it smashed against grey stone. Its tongue hung out, eyes fixed in a death stare. Ramona disappeared off up the stairwell in a flash.

In the courtyard, Mahreuben had located her own target. Elphinias. His tentacles were now recoiling and winding back into his body as he stood looking at the mass of rubble that had been the stone King Theonyra.

"It is finished. So mote it be."

He scowled at the mess he had made of his old foe of generations gone. Behind Elphinias, there came another new voice..

"Admiring your handiwork Elphinias? That is my great grandfather lain there, you sick worm."

Elphinias turned, glaring as the sluicing rain started to slow and before him, alone, stood the sodden, seething Princess Mahreuben.

"Ah, the tortured Princess is here. The banshee woman. An extra surprise for me this is, to see the generations all together again. I am afraid you are far too late to save your heroic old King. He has had a good run. You next then,is it? The escaped witch."

Mahreuben faced him down, unflinching. Elphinias paced back and forth.

"I saw your sky walk, amazing feat of magick, witch. As I waited in the catacombs. My idiotic son could not run an inn at that time. I returned, just as you have now, witch. Just so you know, your grandpapa, King Theonyra, will have been in searing agony as the freezing first stopped his blood flow and then his heart. Beautiful, slow pain. There was a lot going on in the old man, underneath all that rock exterior. Complexities. A fascinating character.

His death would have been a choking, chilling asphyxiation. His organs shutting down, deep within his granite exterior casing. Tricky he was, very tricky. Quick to the eye his extermination may have looked. An eternity to him. Mind you, he was used to long waits was he not? Now, as you see, haridan.. He is quite dead."

Elphinias kicked casually at a pile of rubble.

Princess Mahreuben though, was looking beyond Elphinias now. To the moat. The revolting shark-slug, the Bakkor, had returned to the surface, gulping in oxygen after its previous meal.

"You have thought of everything between father and son haven't you? I cannot argue Elphinias. I cannot win. We.. cannot win."

Mahreuben's shoulders drooped and she walked listlessly up to Elphinias as though defeated, but then past him, to the moat where the Bakkor was circling below.

"He will enjoy the taste of the flesh of a Princess, a real delicacy."

Elphinias walked purposefully to the edge of the water, somewhat puzzled by Mahreuben's actions, or lack of them. Drawing up to her side. He looked her right in the eyes, his own, glowing, mocking.

"What now, sweet little Princess?"

Then, she jumped in the moat. Elphinias stepped back and drew breath, startled.

"Suicide? I had thought her braver.."

A dorsal fin cut through the moat as the Bakkor sensed both food and duty. Elphinias observed a dull outline of Mahreuben, diving further below the surface until he could see her no more. Under the water, Princess Mahreuben turned and saw the Bakkor, gaping mouth open, displaying its rows of razors in its wide throat.

A look of terror was etched on the watery gaze of the Princess, but she held as it came closer. Her elongated dagger in her hand. What could this puny weapon do against this huge, scaly scum? It came to her.

'Mine is the power of the ocean!' She thought, in mute realisation at her own forgetfulness.

She was able to manifest mermaid qualities. So she did, with great haste. The Bakkor was upon Mahreuben in a swish of its tail and it widened its mouth and groaned in anticipation of another crunching death grip. At this, Mahreuben used her own mermaid tail now and powered upward above the creature as its bite met nothingness.

The Bakkor was confused. Its target had disappeared and it could feel its master, Elphinias, willing it on to kill. Its brain was dull. It survived on sight and smell. It could smell its quarry still, but the woman was not there. There was a crunching sensation. This time not made by the Bakkor's teeth.

Princess Mahreuben had floated above its broad, mutated head. Her sharp dagger plunged into slimy flesh. The shark-slug felt a sick adrenaline course through its nerve endings as it began to swim in a rapid, erratic fashion. Mahreuben held on tight to fins, gills, scales, anything she could grip.

She drove the dagger deeper into the skull of the mutation with all of her might belying her slender frame. It found the brain of the pitiful Bakkor. She was posessed now, was Mahreuben. Jamming the weapon harder, further into the neural system of the Bakkor.

It choked and gagged. It no longer wanted to hunt. It was in shock. Nothing worked. It swam manically and thrust up to the surface.

Princess Mahreuben let her grip go and kicked away from the demented creature. She swam away. Quickly.

At the side of the moat, Elphinias approached the edge. He was receiving confusing signals from below. He wanted confirmation of the death of the Princess. Having seen off the King, he was ready to leave the realms and go back to the dark land having addressed his own demons of the past. He did not care what happened to Alatar now, his Takers, his tower or the god forsaken girl.

"Where are you creature? Do not defy me, or I will see you dead myself."

Elphinias gaped into the murk for signs. He got one. The crazed Bakkor propelled upwards like a giant rocket and came clean out of the water. A mass of slime and teeth and screaming bloody agony. It came down hard on Elphinias and bit down mechanically on his skull. Its last functional thought was revenge. Elphinias, arms and legs kicking and waving automatically, was dragged underwater by the brain dead and fading Bakkor.

It was too late for the shapeshifter, tentacles, claws, horns, spines all began to break through his skin as he sank in mouth of the beast. Many faces and guises manifested in a macabre, brief flurry permeated by his final death throes. His changeling days were over. This second, grotesque reunion would be the pairs last.

Cormac had been watching, he would not abandon the Princess. His eyes squinted, scanning the now still moat. Then, just below the makeshift bridge, a spluttering, exhausted Mahreuben was clambering to the bank.

CHAPTER SEVENTY THREE
THE HEART OF ALATAR

The ethereal observed in silence. Ualdin pondered. When shall he conjour the gate? He had located the home town of Ruth and her fallen husband James. Gardelwyn, another world, a different life.

"Ramona is to confront the red eyed one. She approaches his quarters. When this is done, she must gather her family and pass back to her own timeline."

Lesidyn asked his elder "If she can beat the red eyed one that is, Ualdin?"

"It is written. Whichever way this confrontation shall go, we shall have no more involvement in the aftermath. We chose our girl. Now, she aims to deliver. Then, I must make good on the promise of Mahreuben and the stone King.. and send her home."

"As the young woman we see before us.. or as the baby whom was identified by the ethereal at Oakhampton?" Ventured Topia.

"Over this, I do not know. A ley line will be conjured. She and her family shall cross.

After that, I cannot control the whims of the overseers of Ramona's own timeline. Her world is unlike the realms, Topia."

"Not without more trials for our girl then, Ualdin. Though I understand." Topia mused.

Sifreya, the mother of Alatar, now ethereal spirit, saw to comment also now..

"All of this is the fault of mine. I gave birth to this being. I created him. Now the lives of many are extinguished by him and his forces.

I.. I do not want this ethereal spirit I have become. I feel I am cheating, I died, Ualdin. Like so many poor folk down there. Why this for us and not all? No, I wish to be erased, to not preside eternally over mindless bloodshed in the form of transparency. I need to affect things or to not be alive in any form. Release me Ualdin. I can see no more, hovering above like this.."

Sifreya's spirit went silent.

"You are the mother of the baby Leandro, Sifreya. The carer of the young boy with whom you would play in the fields of Tuteaas. Tell glorious tales of magnificent animals and creatures of lore. To show him the splendid boats that passed Eannys Grove, where you took respite from Elphinias.

It is the deceased shapeshifter whom duped you Sifreya, and it is he whom created the red electric magic and cold blood that made Leandro become Alatar. You, in your own words 'affected' Leandro, in only a positive and loving manner. I cannot send you back nor extinguish your spirit Sifreya. You are now ethereal and so it is. I also am ethereal, I, fortunately, passed of old age. You died bravely, but in pain, Sifreya.

Who knows why we few are selected? Why was Ramona selected? Why me who had to action her transition? I do not either wish for the burdens sometimes thrust upon us. You will find acceptance Sifreya, this I am sure of. Or you would not have been elevated to us."

Sifreya went silent, pondering this acceptance, and now observed with her kindred spirits.

Below, the battle continued. Cormac had escorted Princess Mahreuben to a throng of New Azmarine folk whom fought off swarming Takers in the courtyard. Numbers on both sides were thinning and those that remained were tiring.

Prince Uzaleus and a scattering of men had gained the jails and hacked through the locks with any weaponry they could bring to hand. The prisoners gratefully embraced their rescuers and were directed to the shingle cove behind the tower, where they mostly collapsed in exhaustion and gratitude for oxygen, onto the cool sand.

Alatar had lost control of the battle. He had watched Elphinias demise from the huge window. This viewpoint had seen so much since his occupancy at the tower began.

The death of his father registered nothing with Alatar. He felt nothing except a tiny sense of justice for his mother Sifreya, who he murdered to spare her further agony from the changeling that was once her husband.

It had been a twisted plan but was the only way Alatar could comfort himself at what he had done, or in his puddled mind.. been forced to do. Now he paced around his quarters. All that he had presided over. All of his parchments and plans to build from the tower outwards and across the realms. Still in its infancy was his vision and now his throngs swarmed around down below, being hacked and hewed by this ragtag army boasting only love and hope as their weapons.

He had used his own magic to swathe through elves and men. He had cut down Ramona's father with slicing bolts. He had burnt many of their force into petrified dust. Still they fought on. He knew Ramona was outside. He knew the head guards would be dead at her feet,

"She has learned to kill without thought." He said aloud, only to himself.

Ramona had to kill without thought. Or all of her family, friends and the warriors would die. They all had to kill without thought.

"I have killed without thought. Except for my mother. I can never be Leandro. I am Alatar the red eyed one of the dark land. Son of nobody. Leader of the realms."

Presently, the hinges of the huge oak door creaked and groaned and the door swung open. Alatar spun around and directed his gaze to the floor. As expected, his two head guard lay dead. Here now in the doorway to this huge room, this centre of operations, stood Ramona, the wizard who had not known she was a wizard.

Until now.

"So it is, Ramona, daughter of James. You have reached your destination point, chosen one. You are here to destroy me, I take it?" Hissed Alatar.

Ramona pulled back her hood and swept long raven hair from her muddied face. She fixed Alatar with a hawk-like gaze as she regarded him up close for the very first time.

"You take it correctly Alatar. I am here to eliminate you, so that the people of the realms can be set free and go back to their own families and live as before. I also, will be taking own family to my own home. When you are dead at my feet."

Ramona took a few steps toward the towering sorcerer. A sickly grin creased the face of Alatar, eyes now burning their strongest red. Fire and hurt were in those deep, large eyes. Glowing with defiance and menace.

"Dead at your feet shall I be, Ramona wizard? Like your parent, poor James was at mine? Not only is your father dead, I have also brought about the eternal misery of your empathetic mother Ruth. I will however spare her afterward, as I did my own mother. I shall kill her like James and then onto your brother. The gallant Jude, whom I have already had the pleasure of meeting.

First Ramona wizard, you must die. Then as you lie fighting for breath, know this.. I will be slaying all of those squabbling fools outside for invading my domain and I will be ridding the realms of these insects forever."

Ramona took another step closer.

"You will be left with nothing Alatar. Even if you get your wish, then what? You will pace back and forth in this room, gaze out of this window over a beautiful but empty world.

Nothing left to destroy or conquer. Your army, drones addled with potion or blind loyalty. When these parchments here, are become real, then what? Eat, sleep, kill a few rebels? Round up some stragglers from remote outposts? Hardly the stuff of dreams Alatar.

It is never too late to surrender. To see sense. You will meet justice but perhaps salvage something of Leandro when you are passed.

Maybe your spirit will find that of your mother Sifreya. Lay down your arms Alatar, red eyed one. Die in peace. My magic is strong now. There will be no agony. Unlike your kind, I seek only justice, not cruelty. Lay down your arms.."

Alatar never took his hateful gaze off Ramona while she spoke. Soon they were face to face in the middle of this grand old chamber. All pillars, windows and gothics.

"Sweet, foolish girl. What a pretty speech. You expect me to have a sudden realisation? A pang for what might have been? You are not of these lands Ramona. The ethereal are cowards, not I. I sought only change. A new order. I offered much to my followers and you paint me as selfish.

Discipline was called for in this failing world. The like of Uzaleus and his banshee are blind. Skipping through daisies, throwing open banquets. There is danger out there, girl. I made them aware, I opened their eyes. If you saw as I do, you would join me."

He studied his foe, scrutinising Ramona's features for any sign of weakness.

"Oh Alatar. You gave the people nothing. You swept in from the dark land and decided you would take. You had a few followers, the mindless ones, looking for trouble, bereft of natural stimulation. Already dead behind the eyes. You drugged the rest or kidnapped and beat them into submission.

They follow in fear. There are no incentives. Only for you. Taking. Look at those bodies out there, scattered on the floor. Lifeless.

Your own men. Innocents. My father. What had he done to deserve the death you brought upon him? You think I Could ever join you? Murderer."

Ramona's eyes welled at the thought of her father, prostrate and cut in half. Alatar saw this and grinned, showing fang-like teeth.

"As I said, girl, progress. The weak minded were dispersed with as neceessary. I would say it is nothing personal. But with you, it is.

I enjoyed seeing you cower behind stones with your hot-head brother. The reaction of your mother. Distraught, heartbreak personified. It gave me much personal pleasure, albeit briefly. To the matter at hand now, Ramona. Adopted hope of the realms. Red electric then, to bind you to the pillars.."

With his right hand, Alatar aimed his long fingers and red flame began to manifest at the tips. Ramona saw this and stepped back.

"You intend to keep me here then twisted one?"

"For a short spell, to watch you wither away would be amusing. Imagine, Ramona of the realms, saviour. The chosen one. Bound for eternity to the pillars of the tower of Alatar.

Until your fragile skeleton is sagging from shackles and chains. A beautiful reminder of my glorious and inevitable day of reckoning. Imprisonment then, wretched girl.."

He bought down his hand in his familiar swish and the red bolts that had seen off many, flew into Ramona's midriff. She was knocked back and onto the floor. Ramona gasped for air and held her stomach, badly winded. Alatar circled around her like a cat toying with a cornered mouse. He bought forth more crackling red rope from his closed fist, a whip, which he twirled about in amusement before bringing it down across the back of the young wizard.

Ramona screeched in blinding agony as Alatar lashed her further, tearing through her cloak and garments leaving stinging long rakes across her flesh.

"You see Ramona, I cannot let you go on. I know you possess a strong magic. But it is in its infancy. You are too new to these realms. You have not harnessed your power. You have said you will not join me. I see that these ethereal meddlers have tried to pump you full of growth. Spells, languages, intelligence, vocabulary, physicality, magic itself. But you are a baby. It is you who is drugged not I.

I gave your father the opportunity to turn his vehicle back a long time ago as you have come to learn. But here you are. Dying on the floor of my personal quarters. A fitting end to your futile story. A story that will blow away like the black spores of dead Takers. Forgotten. Your bones will be displayed in time, as a warning to the folk who believe in the unseen of the realms, the ether and any other factions who dare to try to stop me. It is finished. The realms are mine and so, the chosen one is beaten with ease."

Ramona lay on the cold stone, wincing at her injuries and with tears in her eyes once more.

All manner of things began to flash through her mind in milliseconds. The gulls, Cormac, Jude, mum and dad. The beach. Now her grandparents, standing over her cot smiling down. Her own home.

Things she had experienced all too quickly before she had been whisked away and had nearly two decades of life pumped through her in a mind-boggling short space of time. Things she had yet to experience. Implanted future memories of what might yet be. Her brain was overloaded. The natural growth process of body and mind had not happened to Ramona. She was an experiment, and it was beginning to show.

She let out an unearthly scream as Alatar stooped and grabbed her up by the scruff of the neck.

"Look at me, girl. Look into my soul. I rule this world that is not for you. I will dispense with this cruelty presently and end you. Do you see now? I have been called a monster, a despot, manic, of broken mind.

NO!

I am saving you more unnatural agony. You are overloaded by ethereal games, experiments gone awry, like that putrid Bakkor. You are unnatural. You are too dangerous to be freed, even if you went home as a baby. I cannot allow it.

My vision was clear, and now the seeds that I had sewn are blossoming. My parents matter not to me now. They are dead, and good.

Do you see now that these ethereal folk have presided over a macabre experiment in a manipulative way? It is they, whom are power hungry and insecure, else they would not have performed this cruel trick visited upon you. I said look at me!"

Alatar jolted Ramona's sagging head up and she stared into his red, baleful eyes.

"Now you see the heart of Alatar. Your time is at an end Ramona. You will be well displayed. Goodbye.."

Alatar dropped Ramona back to the floor and she began to flicker out of consciousness. He raised his hands skyward, clasped and called on the red magic once more. His incantations began.

At this, Ramona glanced up to see his exposed chest. She was failing badly and could not call any defensive magic, a whimpering blue flicker at her fingertips only made Alatar bark with derision. Now he stood towering as flame crackled and the tower began to groan and shake disagreeably. Even the ethereal spirits were fearful now. Alatar's cackling echoed and bounced off the walls.

"You could have been my Queen, Ramona. Now you die."

As he brought down his hands to direct his final death swipe, Ramona willed herself like never before on her journey. She called on every molecule of her being whilst praying desperately in her mind. As Alatar's hands came down, she rolled to her left and screaming in pain, manged to push her body up and onto her feet.

She drew the elven dagger and plunged it into the heart of Alatar as his hands came down. His arms dropped to his side as misplaced red flame and electrical bolts hit the floor and began to ricochet all around the room. The dagger found its mark and Alatar fixed Ramona with a blank stare of shock and disbelief. It gave her much needed seconds. She plunged in the weapon a second time and twisted the handle. Cutting a hole.

Now it was Alatar's turn to scream as he let out a horrible gut-wrenching wail. A dark, thick blood spurted from the deep chest wound inflicted by Ramona and he fell against her. Ramona was slammed back to the floor under the mighty dead weight of the fallen Alatar.

She felt as though she was being crushed and struggled for oxygen as her lungs complained bitterly. Alatars breath was on her face. Fetid, rasping and shallow. Ramona, on the brink of losing consciousness, thrust her right hand deep into Alatar's chest and ripped out a bloody slowing heart.

He stared finally into Ramona's own fading eyes and whispered..
"My equal. My Queen."

The red eyes flickered and went a mottled grey. A final death sigh.
Ramona writhed from underneath the huge frame and rolled on her
side. Then, she too saw nothing.

Chapter Seventy Four
The Fleeing of the Takers

Alatar lay face down on the cold stone floor of his quarters. There was no doubt he was dead. His huge frame was motionless and a dark congealed liquid seeped from the gaping wound where his neglected heart had been exposed. Something strange was happening to the red eyed one now. Like James, Ramona's father, Alatar's form began to dissipate and shatter into tiny black and red particles.

There were thousands, perhaps millions of them. It was as though this huge mass of energy was alive. The form of the fallen leader became unrecognisable as his remains became swirling, living ashes. Once again the tower began to rumble. This time it was not at the cackling of Alatar. It was the murmuring of the ethereal. The gathering of Alatar's soul was happening and it was whisked out of his huge viewing window and flew away into the clearing sky like a malevolent tornado coming to its end. It flew higher unto who knew when and where, as his fragmented cells and particles did not arrive in the ether.

Nobody had witnessed the spectacle. Finally, this maelstrom that had come and wreaked havoc on the peaceful lands of the realms was vanquished into its own mysterious vacuum. Ramona had moments earlier lain only a few feet from him, the heart of the red eyed one, clasped in in her hand like a death grip. She remained unconscious. Apart from the two dead aides outside Alatar's door, there was no activity on this top tier of the old tower. If any of his guard of Takers knew anything of what had happened to their leader, they did not rush to intervene.

For some, the life force liquid that had been administered to them early on in Alatar's reign, was wearing off.

The same things that Domacec had felt when he had lay in the jail, serving punishment for his failure as captain Cacodem, were now happening to them. The liquid of Selanius the druid had long run out. Alatar of course had his devout followers such as Vaangrad, whom he had slaughtered, and many of his ilk. They had needed none or little of the potion. They wanted only to fight, to kill, to ruin.

The members of the Takers however, who had been recruited by kidnap, brute force and imprisonment and trained and drugged into obeying. They were the ones experiencing the same awakenings as Domacec. Alatar was not there to stop them now. The larger and more domineering of his guard were otherwise occupied fighting the realms army. Sensing opportunities, they began to flee. The realms army had been instructed to kill and not to think. Some of the changing Takers were struck down by unknowing realms folk before their transition back to sanity could take effect. It was Luca and Giula of New Azmarine whom noticed the strange turning of the Takers.

Only the staunch, pure Takers remained in combat, the hissing, orc-like fighters with nothing to lose, those who had no respect for the old royals and craved the regime of Alatar.

"Look Giula! They are not coming at us, they turn tail and run for the bridge. Most of them flee. What has happened?"

"I don't care Luca, they're bloody running away and that's good enough for me!" Replied Luca's wife.

Now the remainder of Ramona's army saw each other across the courtyard as more bodies fell from both sides. The fragmented groups of realms folk and New Azmarinian's gradually came together in a large defensive circle in the middle of the great courtyard. Prince Uzaleus and his men were prevailing now and cut through a horde of Takers with new energy and vigour. It was as though Alatar's death had given them some sort of new vibrancy even though they had yet to find out of Ramona's completion of her task. They somehow felt lighter. More and more of the drones were cut down.

Jude had stayed by his mother's side for the duration of the battle but had not shied from the fighting. Ruth too, she was in a state of shock at the passing of her husband but together as mother and son, they fought with aggression and anger and found their way to the circle. Princess Mahreuben and Cormac had spotted the small group of survivors now and raced across the courtyard to the safety of numbers.

"Uzaleus?" Shouted Mahreuben, still bloodied and drenched from her own epic battle with the Bakkor. Her Prince, still conducting and issuing instructions to his brave warriors, spotted his love and strode at pace to her side.

"My Princess. How I love you more than life itself! You are safe."

Uzaleus and Mahreuben embraced tightly. They wanted that moment of gratitude and relief to last for the rest of their days but they still had to fight. Breaking from their coming together, Uzaleus turned to Cormac..

"And to you Cormac! The bravest of elves. I thank you for overseeing the safe return of my love. To you my friend, I am forever indebted."

Cormac, though in pain with his own cuts and bruises, smiled at the Prince.

"You owe me nothing Prince Uzaleus. I will let your good lady tell you of her escapades!"

Princess Mahreuben, though glowing with happiness and relief, turned to the army surrounding her.

"Now, let us find Ramona of the realms. She will be alone. We must find her. I made a promise to send her home. Fight now warriors, one last effort to find our girl. To Alatar's tower!"

The army of the realms, battered, bruised and having lost many loved ones and allies, stormed as one to the winding staircase like a ball of fury and ploughed through the now half hearted hackings of the tiring Takers. Domacec was fleet footed and swift. He was first to the top and saw the dead guardsmen at his feet. The door was still open and he gazed about the vast quarters.

Spotting a shape curled in a foetal ball on the floor, there she was. Domacec gasped and cried out..

"Ramona!"

CHAPTER SEVENTY FIVE
THE OLD CAR

Domacec had knelt down beside the motionless figure of Ramona, still curled up on the floor clutching the cold heart of Alatar. She had a pained, blank expression and her face was cut and bruised. Upon seeing her like this, Domacec drew in another sharp intake of breath and glanced quickly around the quarters of the red eyed one. Scanning for the leader. He was gone.

There were tell-tale signs. The black dust and spores from his dissipation formed a bleak outline of his departed body. Shredded rags of his gown lay strewn like a grim confetto all around the room. She was breathing. Shallow, rasping and quiet. But she was breathing.

"Ramona." Domacec gently nudged her and prodded her arm in an attempt to stir the stricken young wizard.

"Ramona of the realms, what has happened lady? Do you hear me? It is Domacec. By the ethereal spirits, you are alive!"

Then, there was a groan and the opening of eyes. A sharp wince as Ramona came to and felt the burning of cuts and tender bruising to her slender frame.

"Domacec?"

"Yes lady. Be still a moment."

She tried to move but it was clear she was hurt.

"Where are the others? Where are my family?"

She made to sit bolt upright but was taken by dizziness and so Domacec helped her up and sat her gently against one of the tall stone pillars.

"The others are safe young one. Ruth and Jude are back in the circle. The Takers are fleeing! They just.. stopped fighting us. It is as though they are waking from a nightmare. When they charged, we though it was to rush our army. They ran right past us. We stopped killing them, the ones running. There are some of Alatar's men beyond redemption though. They continued to come. Our people cut them down. They seem to just.. dissolve. I drank of that potion lady. That liquid that he drugged them with. Only the druids know what goes into it. But they die like wraiths. We cannot rest until they are gone."

The redeemed Domacec shuddered in flashback to his days as Captain of the Takers. He went to the huge window and surveyed below. Most of those in the dark shrouds drifted away from the battle. Painfully trying to remember something of their former selves. He could see some of the elves and men of the realms dragging fallen bodies from their company and laying them together against the walls. Keeping them together even in the sadness of their deaths.

"Friends of the realms." Domacec sighed heavily and looked further out to the sea.

Activity on the shingle beach. New Azmarinian's still scudding away on their sleek canoe-like vessels. Taking the rescued to safety. The scuffling of the pure Takers, still trying to stop them in the name of Alatar.

The tide was lapping away at the little cave where he had left his mother Sifreya before her departure to the ether. Domacec turned away, his mind overloaded and offered Ramona water from his pouch. She drank gratefully.

"Pure Takers still pursue our friends Domacec? I came across those when I travelled across the plains. We cannot let them escape."

Ramona held up the huge, bloodied heart of Alatar in her right hand.

"And this, is why."

Domacec nodded in strong agreement.

"Prince Uzaleus and his men will see to that, have no fear lady. I am in awe Ramona. Alatar, dead! We knew you could do it. You have fulfilled your role as a chosen one. They will find a way now to send you home. To your place of origin."

"As a baby, Domacec, or as the young woman I am now?" Ramona whispered soberly.

"Of that, I cannot say my lady. For myself, I have grown to know you as you are here today. For you, I can only empathise, truly.

You missed your formative years and although you are now wise, compassionate and knowledgeable, they have been quick and harsh lessons. You have been accelerated in an unnatural manner and your memory and your brain were filled with information and instruction and back story. It is a great shame that you have no life experiences to call precious.

It is also a great shame that the ethereal saw no other way. I know you are not bitter and for that I bow to your beautiful and kind spirit.

With this said Ramona, you have been through so much to become whom you are today, here and now, what a shame it would be to wake as a baby. I.. No, I cannot say either way my lady.."

Domacec looked to the sky and said a silent prayer for the girl who saved him from a life as a drone under Alatar. Domacec gulped a little and cleared his throat and saw to change the subject.

"But where is the red eyed swine now, young one?"

"I cannot answer that Domacec. It happened so fast. His magic was powerful like a lightning bolt, and physically he was immense. I could not summon my own flame. He used all his might to batter at me. All I can recall is that he exposed his heart to me while he was finishing me off. I was struggling to see or stay upright, Domacec. As things faded, I stuck this elven dagger into him, twice."

She motioned towards the sharp blade, blood stained on the marbled floor. Then, her head fell and she sobbed..

"I met his mother, Domacec. I met Sifreya. She died at the hands of Alatar, her son. All this killing. I am not bitter no, but I did not sign up to make myself a killer."

Domacec put a hand on Ramona's shoulder.

"This is the work of Elphinias, the puppet master of his son and the bully of his wife. Any killing from our side has been in self defence Ramona. You issued warnings to the Takers. They laughed and attacked us.

They are at peace now. If I had not recovered in the jail, then I would rather die at your hand as Domacec of the realms than live as the hallucinating Cacodem the drone. Your hand was forced. You watched him die then, lady?"

"No, Domacec. Though I prayed my last action would kill him. I ripped out his heart. He suffered. He called me his equal and his.. Queen. I felt his breathing slow. Then he gasped and then, I saw nothing. Now, a son is dead.."

Domacec, seeing her empathetic tears for even this madman, Alatar, and for everything that had happened since the Ivywyrld Inn, wrapped his own cloak about Ramona's shoulders and checked over her for injury.

"He is dead because he was bad. He was corrupted and poisoned by Elphinias. Do not feel sorrow Ramona. Nothing broken my lady. That is one saving grace. Let us get you down this forsaken staircase and return you to your family. Enough is enough. It is time. Hear me ethereal! Send our wizard home! Make good for Mahreuben. For all of us."

His words echoed and bounced off the walls of Alatar's chamber. Domacec slung his arm about her waist and together, they made for the stairs with Ramona still clutching the heart of Alatar. The room shook a little and a yellow light shone through the great window.

"Whispers. They hear us Ramona. Come on, to the courtyard my lady."

In the ether, Ualdin spoke once more

"It is done. The red eyed one has taken his last breath. Ramona is the true chosen one. Now, we make good on our promises and that of Princess Mahreuben."

"The conjuring?" Whispered Lesidyn of the ether.

"The conjuring, my dear Lesidyn.."

The spirits drew together in a circle. Ualdin, he of great responsibility to the ethereal and to the realms and now to the out of time family. Topia, the wise female spirit. Lesidyn, the keen student. Many spirits were in attendance, in their own inimitable way.

Last of all, the newest of this high ethereal circle, came Sifreya's soul. Mother of Alatar.

"Once upon a time, he was Leandro. My baby boy. Now he is gone and can harm no more folk of the realms.. Nor himself."

Sifreya seemed to want to say something else, but went silent and drifted back to the circle. Ualdin had been concentrating hard and was in a deep meditative state. He was chanting about gateways and journeys and all was an ice blue channel.

"An incantation Ualdin?" Ventured Lesidyn.

"The gate is conjured at the cove on the shingle beach behind the royal tower. This is where Ruth, Jude and Ramona of the realms must now go. Ramona's magic is blue. She will know. They will go back over the timeline and into the land named Oakhampton. From there, they must find their own way home to Gardelwyn, but there will be no more meddling. I have sealed the ley lines so that this may not happen again.

"But will she find it?" Spoke Topia.

"She will know." Replied Ualdin.

"Luca and Giula too, they are of Ramona's timeline. What of the husband and wife?"

"They have chosen to stay with Elysse and continue the rebuilding of New Azmarine, Topia. It is done. Those ley lines were a freak of the shifting of the realms. We cannot have people coming and going between the two timelines. It would cause disturbance in the ether. So mote it be. The gateway is open."

Elysse of New Azmarine came running from behind the tower with several of the cove people and into the open courtyard, her face was flushed with excitement, a little boy and girl at her side.

"The ethereal! A gate has been conjured. Oh for Ramona! With the realms as my witness.. Where is Ramona of the realms? A gate has been conjured!" Elysse eyes darted all around in uncontrollable excitement.

From behind the royal tower came a shimmering light of azure blue. It sparkled and flickered like a new constellation and soon, the whole sky lit up like a beacon, calling the family toward it. Elysse stooped to embrace the two wide-eyed youngsters at her side. They were smiling. Rescued from the chaos. She had her babies back.

Jude was stood by the counsel table that he had rammed the family car into in his confrontation with Alatar. The vehicle was a mess, but it was still there. He looked at his mother and hugged her tightly.

"Mum, I love you. Get in."

Ruth simply obeyed her son. Her brain was filled with imagery now after James had died in front of her eyes. She clambered into the battered vehicle.

"Jude, where are we going my love?"

"To get sis."

Jude answered with a look of steely determination. At the foot of the spiralling staircase and out in the open now, stood Ramona and Domacec. Blinking at the brightness of this all encompassing light from the ethereal world. Cormac, stood with Princess Mahreuben, was the first to shout.

"Our girl! There she is! Domacec has come good. He truly is a good man. Look Princess, it is our Mona. A welcome sight to be sure."

Domacec supported the hobbling young wizard and she gazed across the courtyard at the scene. It was a broken battleground. Jude looked at his mother to see she had secured herself in the backseat of the family car.

"Mum, are you alright?"

Ruth looked out of the window, spotting her daughter. Her baby girl. Her Mona.

"I am now Jude. Start the engine."

Seventy Six
A Journey Through the Blue

"You are alright lady, in this strange method of transport?" Whispered Domacec as he sat a shaken Ramona in the backseat of the battered family car, giving her water from his flask.

"Domacec my friend, this strange method of transport has never failed us before. Luca and Giula will teach you of them I am sure."

"Interesting. I shall stick to my sailing vessel or my feet, but I would like to see New Azmarine and hear Giula's teachings of your timeline. Not in one of these mechanical chariots though lady. Things with wheels are for transporting food."

Ramona's shattered face lit up with a grin.

"Thank you for finding me Domacec of the Realms, you are a good man."

"Thank you, for allowing me to redeem myself, Ramona of Gardelwyn."

Domacec looked sad. Sad at what he had briefly become under the spell of Alatar's liquid. Ramona spotted this in his face.

"There was nothing to redeem my friend. You gave me understanding. When I first destroyed those Takers, I was just a girl defending my family from an attack."

Domacec's furrow smoothed.

"You broke the spell and released them Ramona. Now, you can be free also. To the light of the cave then, it shows you the gateway home.

The Takers are being put into the jail cells. We will have to see what happens, what we can do with them. No more cold blood. Perhaps they can find a way back as I did, with your help."

"Agreed friend. No more cold blood. You are the example to follow Domacec." Smiled the young wizard.

Jude revved the car engine as Ruth too, got strapped into the old vehicle. They slammed the doors shut.

"Lets go, family." Jude grinned.

Ramona thought, as the car started, how despite everything, she had grown up in the realms, albeit at a ridiculous rate. She remembered little to nothing of Gardelwyn, but it was her blood home and she knew Jude would be with her now to support Ruth. Jude too, having been in between worlds, was unsure of what they were going back to. But it was theirs. Their origin. James would be so very proud of them all. Ramona prodded her mother in the front seat playfully on the shoulder.

"Hello mum. Are you alright love? We going home then?"

Ramona giggled and Jude cackled at his sister's playful banter. There had been no time lately for the family to laugh together. Ruth grinned for the first time since James had passed in battle. She believed he was with them. He was of magic. It comforted Ruth now.

"I love you Mona, my beautiful, funny baby."

Tears rolled down Ruth's face. Wherever it was they were going, her husband would be with them. He had departed in a spectacular fashion. They lived in hope that it meant something.

'You don't know who I am. You have no idea.' James dying words had to have meant something. Didn't they?

Domacec shouted through the window now.

"Look at that light, friends. Shimmering blue, icy white. It is them. Follow it down the side of the tower. To the shingle cove. If in any doubt, look to the sky."

Biggle and Baggle soared above the courtyard, the sun had come out. The eternal eyes in the sky. Faithful friends all the way, cawing in unison. Calling goodbye. Then another face appeared at the window, stricken looking, making them all jump. It was Cormac, looking fraught that he may miss them.

"Your father told me the expression is, 'Any chance of a lift me old mate?' Well, is there?"

The whole family screamed laughing, even Ruth. During the whole journey James and Cormac had always seized the chance to lift everybody's spirits. Jude still sniggering, said to the amiable elf..

"Jump in the back then dude."

"Cheers dudes." Replied the elf completely deadpan.

"I am to guide you to the shingle cove of the beach where more friends will be wanting to see you off, to be sure."

They shouted goodbye to Domacec. The new captain-to-be of the rebuilding realms defence alliance. A sucessful turnaround for a good village man. Jude then drove them away from the broken down staircases and the smashed bridge over the moat. Earlier it had all looked so hopeless. It wasn't all high spirits as they remembered nothing and everything all at once in a group sharing of relief and of sadness at the costs. Takers lay scattered like skittles, nothing more than cloth rags on drones, that may once have been good husbands, wives, children.

The mottled giant body of the shark-slug the Bakkor, hung half out of the water. Dead and mindless, with the rank evil Elphinias crushed skull, still in its slackened, grinning jaws. The shapeshifter was finally beaten by his own pet. Tentacles, arms, legs and fins all protuded from his body. His face had contorted into many different guises fighting to escape. Now, rigor mortis had frozen him into a grotesque ornament. He had never really known what he was.

They shivered in the car at this chilling scene. The lights behind the tower began to flicker in the sky like lightening now. Cormac spoke up.

"They have conjured your way back, but it flickers. It won't hold too long, to be sure. The ethereal can influence worlds when it is the right thing, but they will not interfere indefinitely. No sad goodbye, my friends. Make haste and know that this elf loves you all, as do all of us for what you have done. I would beg them bring your father back if I could but.."

Jude slowed the car and pulled round the side of the back tower. That once of Alatar. He slowed for a moment and shook the hand of the caring elf.

"I know you would Cormac, and we love you too, always, brother." Cormac swelled with emotion.

Jude looked ahead now. "Sis, mum, come on, look there. The cave! My god. Back at Skyfawr sis, when we prayed over your healing. Well, I felt them, the ethereal.. I really did, and I believed from then on, that we could get back."

He thought of the wise Yesenia at Skyfawr chapel, with Amato, her pupil and the part they had played in saving Ramona from Alatar's onslaught. They gazed in awe now, at the mouth of the cave of Sifreya's strange funeral. Now a glittering gateway. Waiting for them. Conjured by Ualdin and the ethereal spirits in thanks and sadness that they had to choose Ramona and her family. But it was preordained, as things are in the realms.

"I shall get out of the mechanical chariot transport vehicle now my friends." Said Cormac in a complicated assessment of the family car. It had seen better days but still functioned and that was all they needed

"Whitsomin lake awaits and my gulls need their fish! Thanks to you, we live, and my Finola waits."

"Finola's woodland tea and your salmon dinner at last eh Cormac!" Smiled Ramona. He blushed a little, thinking of his best friend back in the woods. The misty eyed elf reached around the car grabbing Ruth, Jude and finally his lovely friend Ramona. Not just a wizard to him. Squeezing them all tightly. As he jumped out of the car he called..

"Do not worry about the waves. Drive straight forward. Know that those of us here are all willing you home safe, to be sure. So now my wonderful companions, goodbye.."

Cormac got out and closed the door. A tear in his eye, would he see them ever again? It was doubtful. Along the beach there were many familiar faces. Also many bodies sadly lost to the manic plans of the derranged shapeshifter and his power crazed son. There was Elysse, waving and smiling with her rescued children, all mouthing.. "We love you Ramona."

Luca and Giula holding hands, they had decided to stay in the realms, teaching and building at their New Azmarine home.

Tanwyn, a Takers lead guard, but now in deep remorse, was being led away in shackles and he glanced dolefully at Ramona for his part in all of it. Ramona nodded in recognition to him through the car window. She knew he would reform. Above the still emerald sea and the glowing cave entrance, a circle of white shapes drifted and the whole beach vibrated in a low hum. Deep, whispery, magical voices. It was the ethereal. Presiding in a perfect sky to show the family the way.

"Jude?" Said Ramona, still sniffling from sad goodbyes.

"Yes sis?" Replied her loyal brother.

"Will we come out in Gardelwyn, at home? Or Oakhampton? Will we, you know, go on as normal? Except, well.. I'm now a woman not a baby." She had no idea what was to come and wanted reassurance from her big brother.

Jude sighed "I just don't know sis. I love you whatever happens to us. We can overcome anything. Lets get home. You want to do it? You too mum, ready?"

Ramona and Jude both replied in harmony..

"Drive."

Jude floored the vehicle across the smooth damp sand and into the lapping waves towards the cave. Suddenly, Ramona shreiked..

"Good god!.. His heart!"

Ramona pulled Alatar's still black heart out of her robe. Jude looked in the rear mirror.

"Bloody hell.. Its him! Throw it out of the window sis.. NOW!"

Ruth screamed at the sight of it. Alatar's heart, held in her daughters palm. Ramona pitched it hard out of the window.

"This is the end Alatar. Your reign is over."

Ramona had thrown the bloodied organ into the sea just as the car sped into the cave. A noise like a sonic boom followed. Inside the cave, it was dark. As though they had entered a void in space. Ramona shouted to Jude..

"Did we do it? Did we get home? Are we through Jude?"

"I dunno. I think so. Good lord, that was some Sunday drive Mona. I hope we are through sis, its so damned dark. Mum, are you alright?" Jude had done his job. Ruth groaned in relief.

"I'm alright kids, I'm alright. Where are we?"

"Its time to find out mum. Stop the engine Jude. Lets see if this adventure is finally over."

Ramona steeled herself once more and stepped out of the car. It was indeed damp, dark and hard to see. They trusted Ualdin and so would look for the way out. Ramona was now a true wizard. A hero and a brave daughter.

"I am Ramona of the realms." Her eyes sparkled and azure blue flame flashed at her fingertips. A fiery, determined smile crossed her lips..

"I am ready for anything."

Back on the shingle beach behind the reclaimed tower, the lightshow and the glittering magical force had stopped suddenly. The wispy ethereal circle disappeared, floating back up to their unseen station. Their promise on finding the way home for the family had been delivered. Ualdin had done it. He had carried some bad feeling from being the decision maker on bringing Ramona to the realms. Now, he felt lighter.

Smiling and cheering, the realms folk checked the cave. No car. No Ramona, Jude or Ruth were within, and all the lights that glittered had gone. Save for the emerald glow from the tide now filling it.

"It is done! Our beloved friends are away in safety." Cried Prince Uzaleus hugging his beloved Princess Mahreuben, both weeping in disbelief and delight. The new defence alliance of the realms, led by Domacec, made their back to the tower with their heroic dead being carried back respectfully and the steely-eyed surving throng who fought til the end. Fought to get their lands back. There in the corner of the battlefield, as folk filtered back through the entrances, lay the huge rubble heap of granite that had been the mighty stone King, Theonyra. Frozen and smashed to pieces by Elphinias cruel, tormenting assault. But now, a human being resembling him, clambered out of the mess.

Coughing and spluttering and brushing white ash from his ancient robe. Theonyra it indeed was. He stretched and stepped into the courtyard as Ramona's army gazed in shock. Mahreuben wept. Uzaleus shouted in excitement.

"By the grace of the ethereal! Our king has returned. King Theonyra has risen again."

The King surveyed the scene..

"Ha, those stupid, blundering fools. I tell you, dark land sorcerers are halfwits. Could never do a proper job. It was worth the wait. Our friends made it home. I saw the lights, the ethereal spirits. She did it, by the heart of Azmarine. Ramona did it."

King Theonyra's laughter, infectious and joyous, bellowed around the courtyard. The reunification of a loving realms family of generations had begun. With Ramona and her family heroically departed, the sun set over the scene of the hard earned victory of their safe departure. The gulls happily chattered, stamped their feet and went to roost. Their jobs done.

Slithering along the beach though now, like a sidewinding snake, out of the hissing foam of the waves, a dark heart found a tiny beat.. and then a stronger beat. The dark heart crawled and struggled away from the glassy saltwater and shuffled to deeper wet sand and buried itself like a grotesque, burrowing insect. It was a pathetic sight. But the dark heart had made it. It beat with a hateful purpose, and lay dormant.

To hibernate.

And recover.

Way up above, flashing, angry red eyes hung in the midnight blue sky.

Waiting, for a body to inhabit.

THE END

About the Author

Debut author Andrew Evans is a father of one and enjoys film, sport, nature, music and travel. In this, his breakthrough year, he has several short fiction pieces awaiting publication in magazines as well as concentrating on writing his second full-length fantasy novel. Andrew has enjoyed studying at his local college and is always looking at new courses to aid his learning. Writing since a very young age has been an education and an escape and to become an author of books is a boyhood dream fulfilled.

Andrew cites literary heroes as Arthur C. Clarke, Alan Garner, J.K. Rowling and Ben Bova.

NOTE FROM ANDREW EVANS

Word-of-mouth is crucial for any author to succeed. If you enjoyed *Ramona in the Realms*, please leave a review online—anywhere you are able. Even if it's just a sentence or two. It would make all the difference and would be very much appreciated.

Thanks!
Andrew Evans

We hope you enjoyed reading this title from:

www.blackrosewriting.com

Subscribe to our mailing list – *The Rosevine* – and receive **FREE** books, daily
deals, and stay current with news about upcoming
releases and our hottest authors.
Scan the QR code below to sign up.

Already a subscriber? Please accept a sincere thank you for being a fan of
Black Rose Writing authors.

View other Black Rose Writing titles at
www.blackrosewriting.com/books and use promo code
PRINT to receive a **20% discount** when purchasing.

Printed in Great Britain
by Amazon

36070890R00223